what comes after

blair leigh

This book is dedicated to ... me. Every version of myself, at every age, would be so damn proud that this is finally happening.

... not falling in love with him was simply impossible.

Eliza Davis' new home is everything she wanted—community, a sense of belonging, a fresh start. An added bonus was living with her best friend, Simone, and befriending the jilted groom whose wedding day disaster she was witness to. But Jack Peters was not someone to be pitied. Sarcastic, caring, and, most importantly, crazy about her daughter, Jack helps take Eliza's mind off the pain of her past and allows her to just have fun.

But small towns are known for meddling, and everyone assumes there's more to Eliza and Jack than the two can see. Eliza is adamant that they're just friends. Even if he makes her daughter laugh again. Even if he comes over to chase ghosts out of the attic without a second thought. Even if he makes her heart squeeze in ways she forgot.

Just. Friends.

Content Warning: Depictions of anxiety and grief after losing a loved one.

*T*he ceremony began ten minutes ago, but I'm still sitting in front of the bride, holding concealer, mascara, and a bag of cotton pads I am using to continuously dab her tears so her cheeks won't stain. This is definitely not what I signed up for. When I first moved to town and opened my salon, this beautiful redhead with excited eyes and roots in need of a touch-up asked if I was available to do hair and makeup for a bridal party in six months. *Hell* yes. Bridal parties meant two days of regular clients at my salon. Start at eight in the morning, out by five in the evening, and free snacks and gossip? It's the dream.

You know what's not the dream? Talking the bride out of pulling a Julia Roberts. It all started when one of the already-drunk bridesmaids peeked her head in to alert the bride they would be lining up in ten minutes. Once the door closed, Gwen's breathing became shallow and her eyes suddenly glassy.

"Hey, hey," I said to her with a soft laugh. "No messing up the face before you walk down the aisle."

"Eliza, I can't go out there." Her shaky reply was coupled with a trembling chin. "I can't do this." And then began the uncontrollable, un-ending waterworks while I —the most incompetent human being in the consoling department—stared at her, helplessly.

And it hasn't stopped. She has said nothing in the past fifteen minutes to indicate why she can't marry this man —just that she can't. It was two minutes past her cue by the time the planner came in. I told her she needed to warn the guests of a slight delay, and she has poked her head through the door several times since. My patience is growing thin. Let this woman have a moment, Janet.

The bride's cries are finally slowing, and I'm dabbing under her eyes, making sure the mascara hasn't smudged, because forget waterproof mascara—she needed luscious lashes. There was no reasoning with her when I first arrived. No orange-tinted blush, no sparkles in the bronzer, no red lipstick, and she would absolutely *not* use waterproof mascara. I wanted to laugh at how naive she was. No waterproof? In this November air? At a wedding? But, alas, she *is* the bride.

"There," I whisper, smiling as she begins to calm down. "Just nerves, yeah? Jack seems like a sweet guy. You seem so happy." I have no idea if they are. I've never even seen the groom. At this point, I just need to get my money and get out.

She gives me a weak smile, and her bottom lip quivers. *I swear to God if she starts crying again ...*

"I can't do it." She takes a deep breath, attempting to stop the next batch of tears threatening to spill over her bottom lid.

"You can." I pick up the concealer and try to fix this dreadful red puffiness she's caused.

"You don't understand," she begins, choking on her last word.

Well, fuck me.

My shoulders fall, and I sigh but keep a patient smile painted on my face before grabbing those ever-useful cotton pads again. Just as I start to wipe away her tears once more, a light knock on the door pulls my attention, and a handsome—*really* handsome—bearded man steps through with a bow tie and a cautious smile. "Gwen? Are you okay?"

"Oh, Jack," she hiccups. Then the floodgates really open, and I scurry to catch the falling tears while simultaneously stepping out of her line of vision so she can speak to her groom. Pure talent. "I'm so sorry."

She's a blubbering mess at this point. I should probably throw my hands up and say, "Screw it," but that feels a bit selfish.

He comes in, and the door closes with a soft thud. Walking over and nodding to me, he speaks carefully. "Could you give us a moment?"

Gladly. "Absolutely," I say with a sympathetic smile and step away from Gwen, but her hand flies up and catches my wrist to stop me from moving.

"No, I need you here." I'm suddenly nervous. *Is this guy abusive? Is he going to hurt her?* I narrow my eyes at him and nod, remaining next to her. *Not today, bucko.* She sucks in a shaky breath. "I can't do this. I thought I could, but I can't. Oh, man." She stops and puts her fingers over her mouth. "Oh, God. I'm so sorry, Jack."

"Hey, it's really okay." He gently reaches forward to take the hand that isn't grasping mine. *This is cozy.* "I understand nerves, trust me."

"It's not that." She's snotting and pulling away from

him to wipe at her face. The perfectionist in me is seething, but my compassion is overriding it for the moment.

"Okay." The word is a slow drawl as he glances up at me, surely wondering why the hell I'm still there. *Me too, pal.* "Well, tell me what's going on."

There's a brief pause before her shoulders violently shake to accompany the sobs that spill out with her word vomit. "I slept with someone."

Plot.

Twist.

This is probably *the* most uncomfortable moment I have ever been in, and I am crawling out of my skin. Unfortunately, Gwen keeps a tight grip on my wrist. So, I do what any sane beautician would do. I reach forward and gently dab her cheeks as her groom (ex-groom?) stands in shock in front of us. He glances at my hand then at me then back at Gwen. Repeat.

"Wh-what?" It comes out like the air has been knocked out of him.

"I slept with someone, and I can't do this without you knowing. Jack, please. I'm so sorry. Please, can you please forgive me for this?" She's in complete hysterics.

How the hell did I get here?

"Who?" He manages to utter.

She looks baffled, staring at him with a furrowed brow. "What? No."

"*Who*, Gwen? Don't you think you owe me that?"

Yikes. His tone is so sharp, I feel as though *I* have personally betrayed him.

"I—" She nods and looks away from him—still gripping my arm, mind you—before muttering a barely audible, "Steven."

"Steven? My Steven?" He's almost choking on his words, and the poor bastard can't hide the shock written all over his pretty face even if he tried. I sure hope Steven isn't at this wedding.

She doesn't verbally reply, but nods and leans down, placing her face in her hands and ruining the hour I spent contouring her perfect features.

Now free from her grasp, I take a step back. Jack stands in silence, staring at the wall. His hand runs over his mouth, smoothing his short beard.

This is my chance to bolt.

He chuckles without mirth, shaking his head. "You cheated on me. With Steven. And you tell me now? At our wedding?"

"I didn't know what else to do." Her tone is muffled by her hands as she hasn't yet looked back up at him.

What. Am. I. Still. Doing. Here.

I'm slowly backing toward the dressing room door, cursing to myself that I haven't been paid yet, but seriously, getting out of this *The Young and the Restless* moment before it escalates even further is priceless to me. I should probably find Steven and warn him of what's to come, but it sounds like the bastard has it coming.

Neither notice when I open the door and slip through, gently closing it behind me.

Passing Janet—or whatever her name is—in the hallway, I give her a firm shake of my head to let her know the bridal suite is off-limits for the time being. As if she automatically knows it's bad, her eyes widen in panic.

I'm out. I did my job. I'm done here.

I'm closing for the evening, pulling my hair up into an elastic band to get it out of my way while I sweep up piles of shed hair around my gray salon chairs. The doorbell chimes, and I look up, immediately recognizing my new patron. Standing up straighter, I push a stray strand of hair behind my ear. "Hi. Can I help you?"

"Hi, yeah. I'm Jack," he begins with a tight smile, stopping to stand in front of me. "I'm uh—" He pauses with a shake of his head. "I'm—"

"I know who you are," I cut in with a nod, trying my best to give him a reassuring smile.

It's only been ten days, dude. It's not like that happens to me regularly.

A humorless chuckle escapes his lips, and he runs a hand through his unkempt hair. "Right." He smiles slightly, the gesture not reaching his eyes. "Guess it's hard to forget the face of the guy you saw get dumped on his wedding day."

"No. I mean—" I shrug, leaning my broom up against the station to my right. "It's still fairly fresh, is all. I'll probably forget you in a few months."

"Comforting."

I cringe at the way that sounded and press a hand to my forehead. "Ah, that's not what I meant."

"Yeah. Well, anyway." He pulls his wallet out of his back pocket and plucks a check from the opening. "I needed to pay you for your services. You ran off too quickly for anyone to compensate you—not that I blame you. I wanted to run out of that room, too."

I take the check from him, honestly surprised. I wasn't going to push for payment under these circumstances. I fold it without looking at the amount and drop it in the pocket of my apron. "That's very nice of you." I want to add a *you didn't have to*, but I'm honestly not that charitable. "How are you doing?"

"You don't have to do that." He's quick in his reply, his tight expression softening ever so slightly. "I know this is uncomfortable. *I'm* uncomfortable. So, let's leave it at this."

I'm five and getting scolded for talking through naptime. I'm tragically awkward. I will never know how to navigate truly tense situations. My eyes drift back to his hair. I want so badly to cut it but insulting his appearance would probably be the final straw. I don't know him. He could snap. I nod, remembering I haven't responded. "Well, haircut on the house anytime."

He nods back, smiling slightly as he does. "Yeah." He self-consciously touches the side of his head. "Thanks. I, uh ... have a guy."

Right. I mean, I'm probably a big, fat reminder of his wedding day, anyway.

"For sure." I don't even know what that means.

Say words. Nod. Smile. Get this interaction over with.

"All right, well, good seeing you again." The phrase stumbles out of his mouth with a light laugh at the generic farewell he probably gives familiar faces at the grocery store. "Or, I guess, under better circumstances."

"Yeah, sure." I nod enthusiastically. "Great to see you. Have a good one!" I call out as he turns and quickly exits my salon like he's on fire. I exhale a deep breath I didn't know I was holding and grab my broom again.

"Stop!" Simone's shoulders are shaking, and one hand is pressed to her chest as she laughs, leaning back on our couch with the stem of her wine glass in between the fingers of her other hand. "That's so awkward."

That's an understatement.

"Uh." I chuckle as well, coating my second toe with a shade of maroon—my favorite nail color. "Just a little bit."

"I mean, at least you got paid, E." She finishes off her glass of white. "You didn't think you would after that disaster."

I look up at her and nod, dipping the tiny paintbrush back in its bottle. "And what a nice guy to actually track me down and pay me. I mean, he went out of his way to pay for his unfaithful bride's stylist."

"Maybe he thought you were hot and is looking for rebound sex."

I bark out a laugh as she rises from her seat with her glass in hand—going for a refill, no doubt. "He was so uncomfortable. If that was his attempt at spitting game, he could use a lot of work."

"Or maybe," I hear her call from the kitchen, "they worked it out and are back together, but he's still embarrassed."

Oh. That is a possibility I didn't consider.

Simone comes back in and tucks her satin robe closer to her as she plops back on the couch with a fresh glass in hand. "I'm still going with the rebound-sex option. Is he hot?"

It doesn't take much to conjure up the image of him standing in my salon. Tall—so tall he towers over those around him. And large. You can tell he takes care of his body, but it doesn't look gym-made. Years of hard labor have created his broad chest and rocky shoulders. His hair is reddish-blonde and wavy—so is his beard. His beard that is a little unruly today, unlike the clean groom that highlighted his cut jaw on the day of his wedding. And yes, I also noticed his eyes were a dark sea-green and serious. He looks like the type that would have freckles scattered across his shoulders. I very much appreciate that thought.

I clear my throat to shake out of my daydream and smile to Simone with a dramatic exhale. "Yeah, I'm not going to try and play it off. That man is beautiful."

"Why didn't you lead with that?" Simone shrieks, nudging me with her foot as I carefully try to apply my second coat.

"Hey, hey," I complain, glaring up at her before dabbing the paint that dripped on my skin. "Because it was a weird scenario to notice how attractive he was. 'Hey, Simone. This weird thing happened at the wedding. A really hot groom got dumped right before the ceremony'?"

"I don't see a problem with that," Simone replies, shrugging her shoulders. "So, anyway, are you going to see him again?"

I laugh at her question, rolling my eyes before looking back at her. "He came to pay me. Honestly, that's it. I probably won't ever see him again."

"What a shame."

I lean down and blow on the wet paint smoothed over my toenails, ignoring her comment. She means well. I know that, but ever since I moved in with her, she's been so focused on getting me back into the dating scene that her own love life is non-existent.

Simone and I have been standing in each other's doorways, bags in hand, since we were six years old. We sat next to each other on the first day of first grade and instantly connected over our identical *Rugrats* lunch boxes. At first, it was small duffel bags holding stuffed animals and VHS tapes for sleepovers. Over the years, the luggage became larger and the overnights became longer.

When we were sixteen, Simone lost her mom, and her dad asked if she could stay with my family while he tried to find a job closer to home. I spent the first few nights with her head in my lap and *Legally Blonde* on repeat to soothe her broken heart.

At age eighteen, I realized going out of state for college was probably an impulsive, angry-at-my-mother decision. So, I came home after the first semester and crashed on Simone's couch until we got an apartment together at the University of Tennessee. That's where I met Aaron.

Age twenty-three, Simone showed up at my door in hysterics because her recent boyfriend, Marcus, had been cheating on her. She lived with Aaron and me for two weeks before moving to Connecticut for medical school.

Twenty-five is when Aaron and I adopted Nova. Simone flew home to meet her goddaughter and brought enough luggage to stay a week because she knew I'd need her.

The next few years were back-and-forth flights for weekend visits until year thirty-one. She was at my door ten hours after I called her, holding me on my front steps as I fell apart in her arms. Aaron was sick, we had a six-year-old, and the doctors told me to *make him comfortable*. Simone was my rock—sacrificing her life in Connecticut for the last two weeks of Aaron's life. And then staying another for Nova because I was a shell of a human being.

I moved in late May, nine months after my husband died. The town we lived in was small—which is the type I love. But the compact size made for awkward, pitying encounters, and memories of my family that was now one person short. I coped with the overwhelming sadness the only way I knew how: not coping at all. Instead, my daughter and I used the map in our library and chose a new place to live.

Well, I chose. She was dead-set on living *in* Disney World. She was seven then, okay? With much grunting and many arguments from my sassy sidekick, we set off on our new adventure.

I wish I could say it was as random as me throwing a dart to the map and seeing where it landed, but it wasn't. We sold almost everything that didn't hold sentimental value, and took off. The trip to Connecticut took two days because there was no way I could drive twelve hours straight.

I thought Simone was crazy to welcome a widow, her handful of a daughter, and their large golden retriever into her life in such an intrusive way. But she was adamant. When I called her with the idea to move closer to her, she took it a step further. The next couple of months were spent planning. I used Aaron's life insurance money wisely: I put the majority of it away for Nova's future, bought a building in Chester for my salon, and split the down payment with Simone.

Aaron's parents were understanding. They wanted me to find happiness again and do what was best for their granddaughter.

My mom had an absolute fit, topped with a literal pity party she tried to disguise as a going-away party.

So, at thirty-two, I knocked on the door of my new home—unsure, scared, and worried I was uprooting Nova's life far too soon after her world had been completely altered. As soon as Simone swung open the door and flung her arms around me, I felt at peace.

We were going to be okay.

I hear a beep from the kitchen and wince, hoping it didn't wake my daughter, who's already fast asleep. Simone sets her glass down, hopping over me to get to it. "Pizza rolls are ready," she sings, skipping to the oven. When she returns, a bowl of snacks in hand, she plops down on the couch with a happy sigh. "Seriously, Eliza. I need you to promise me you're going to have fun for yourself when Nova visits your parents after Christmas."

"And do what?" I raise an eyebrow as I steal one of the rolls.

"Oh, come on, I'm sure your young employees know all the good hangouts in town. What're their names? Claire?"

I nod in response, chewing the hot pocket of cheese and grease. After I swallow, I look up at her, wiping the corners of my mouth. "Katrina and Claire."

"Okay, cool. Katrina and Claire. I'm sure they can show you a fun night." Simone winks, taking a generous gulp of her wine. "Promise me you'll try?"

"You'll have to come with me," I reply, momentarily giving in.

"We'll see." Her grin is not promising.

2

*W*hat was I thinking? Sure, I'm thirty-two—I'm not old by any means. But am I a twenty-five-year-old with no kid and a high tolerance? Not even close. I should have never listened to Simone. Listening to Simone has landed me in a string of foggy night clubs until we finally settled at a casual bar—which I have declared my last stop. This is not how I wanted to start the new year, and yet, five days into January, this is my life. I'm trying to keep up with Claire, Katrina, and their young, tight-bodied friends, but this was an awful idea. A few drinks ago, I could form proper sentences and keep my eyes from drifting close. An unidentified number of shots later, and I can barely stand in these awful heels. Heels! *Eliza, you idiot.*

Nova is with my mom, Simone is on-call, delivering babies, and I was stuck with nothing to do on a Saturday night. My employees have been begging me to "go out" with them for months. Simone talked me into taking them up on their offer.

I regret everything.

The girls are still going strong, dancing against each other with the magic of looking not even the slightest bit tipsy.

"Another shot! Eliza!" Katrina calls, shoving a tiny glass in my hand. They all throw one back, and I sigh, heavily, before doing the same. Another mistake.

Oh man, the floor is moving. It's a carousel. I squeeze my eyes shut and shake my head before nudging Claire and nodding to the bar. I need to sit. She acknowledges my attempted telepathy, and I walk toward one of the stools. I swear it's glowing with rays beaming straight from the heavens. A chair. A seat. My poor feet need it.

When I finally pull myself to the top of the stool and steady against the bar, I feel like I've climbed Everest. I let out an amused huff—how ridiculous I must look.

"Water?" I hear and look up to see a kind smile from a gruff man behind the bar.

I smile in return, my laughter not subsiding. "Is it that obvious?" I ask through my sloppy giggles. "Yes, water. Please."

When did the room become so dark?

I close my eyes again, briefly, before glancing at the person beside me. His profile looks so familiar. *Where have I seen it? A client?* I shut one eye to get a better look and lean forward, almost slipping off the stool in the process.

That catches his attention. He turns to look at me, and I almost gasp in excitement.

"Oh my gosh, I know you!" I can't help but giggle at the absurdity of this night. "You're the jilted groom."

That was not the right thing to say, but it tumbles out of my mouth faster than I can control it. He closes his eyes, and his mouth is a thin line before he looks back to the bottle clutched in his hands. "Yep," he exhales, chuckling slightly. "That's me. I should put that on my dating profile."

My giggles continue, but his face is serious, so I quickly change my demeanor and shake my head with wide eyes. "Oh God, no. No ... don't do that."

"Obviously." He brings his beer to his lips and takes a generous gulp. I watch his Adam's apple dip and feel a pinch in my stomach. *Yep, I'm definitely cut off.*

"Oh, good. You were—" I pause, forgetting the rest of that sentence. The room. So dark. "Joking." *There's the word.* I take a deep breath and press my hand to my forehead, the always faithful bubble of nausea rolling in my stomach and causing a thickness in my throat. Shots. *Really, Eliza?*

I hear the vibration of his voice next to me, but I can't focus on the words he's saying. Shit, that shot had a late kick. I grasp at the water that appears next to me and take three large gulps. My mind is telling me it's helping my buzz, but the fullness is most definitely not helping my nausea.

"Hey," I hear, and I look up at his furrowed brow. "Are you all right?"

I nod and look around the bar. *How much time has passed?* I can't find the girls. I fumble for the phone in my clutch and see missed calls from Claire and Katrina. The last text came in five minutes ago, giving me a heads-up that they were moving on to the next bar in this seemingly unending bar crawl. They left me. *Cool.* I mumble something that *I* can't even comprehend.

"Your friends left you?" The groom asks, making sure he heard me correctly.

Yeah, that's probably what I said. I feel myself nod, and then my cheek is against a cold surface.

"Hey," he says again, louder this time, but I can't open my eyes, because I'll vomit. "Can you get home? Can you call your friends?"

I hear more muffled voices. And a, *"Hey, what's your code?"* I lift my head to speak, but feel sick from the dizziness. Everything becomes blurry, even words.

Jilted groom offers to take me home.

I accept.

I am so irresponsible.

I'm a mother, dammit.

I wake up on guard. I remember leaving the bar with— dammit, what is his name? Oh God, am I that Carrie Underwood song? In my morning stupor, I check my left hand. Nope.

I am, however, in a bed that isn't mine. But I do have a vague memory of getting here, and I'm still in my clothes from last night. I search for my phone around me and can't find it. The sun is barely shining through the curtains in this massive bedroom. I try not to freak out. I feel fine. I remember most of the night. I am going to have a serious talk with Katrina and Claire about buddy systems and responsibility.

Responsibility. *Ha.* Look at me.

My head feels heavy when I sit up and throw my legs over the edge of the bed. There's a bottle of water next to Tylenol on the nightstand beside me. Despite the fact that I spent the night in this stranger's bed, I don't trust him enough to take pills he supplied me with.

I get up and run my hand through my tangled nest of hair-sprayed curls. I'm quiet when I open the door, seeing a long hallway behind it that opens into what looks like a living room. I tiptoe down the wooden floors and pass pictures of ski trips and fishing ventures on the walls.

When I reach the living room, I hear a light snore. I'm close enough to peek over the couch to confirm my version of last night's events.

His left arm is thrown over his eyes, the other hanging off the couch that he's too big for. One leg is resting on the armrest while the other is limp and mostly on the floor. Even the blanket is too small to cover his large frame. His shoulders are broad, his jaw is strong, his hands are huge, and he's quite a lovely-looking specimen.

A sudden jingle of a collar coming from behind me makes me jump, fall slightly on the slick floors, and stumble into the barstool behind me. I catch myself on the bar, but am not as successful with the stool, and it clamors to the ground with a loud thud.

My host jerks awake and sits up, alert and on guard. His breathing is deep and heavy, his cheek imprinted with lines from the decorative pillow he was pressed against.

"I'm sorry. I'm so sorry." I'm quiet, as if another person is asleep somewhere. *Hell, there could be.* I look down to see a beautiful brown-and-white mane and two light green eyes staring up at me. A bushy tail is wagging, and a pink nose wiggling to sniff me out.

The perfectly disheveled man shakes his head and clears his throat, pushing the blanket off before standing up without giving himself time to wake. "No, it's fine. Are you okay? Did you sleep well? I put Tylenol by the bed."

"I saw." I don't bother to mention I didn't take it. "Thank you so much. And thank you for bringing me here. I am not usually this irresponsible." I lean down and offer a hand to the curious pup.

The man with no name shrugs, waving off my thanks as he walks past me to the kitchen. "You got drunk. It's not a crime. Your friends are the irresponsible ones for just leaving you."

"I should have been more careful with my intake," I argue, watching him pour himself a glass of water and chug it without a breath. "But, again, thank you."

"Don't mention it." He shakes his head and watches me pet his dog—I can feel his eyes on me. "Her name is CeCe," he says, introducing me to her. *Great, I know his dog's name before remembering his.*

I move my hand to scratch behind her ears, earning a contented sigh as she leans the weight of her head into my palm. Oh man, I'm in love. "Hi, CeCe," I whisper.

He clears his throat and looks down into the empty water glass. "I, uh ... I answered your phone. I'm sorry. It was your mom, and it rang, like, four times in a row at six this morning. I thought it may be an emergency."

"You talked to my mom?" *Fuck.* I stand up quickly, on the defensive. No, no, no ... not my mom. She'll ask so many embarrassing questions. CeCe uses this opportunity to leave my side and head toward her food bowl. Traitor.

"I told her I was a friend and you were asleep. She said to call her back when you were awake and that everything was fine with your daughter."

"You talked to my mom," I repeat, more of a statement this time. *Oh boy.* Is she going to give me the third degree, or what?

"I'm sorry. I just thought ..." He trails off, his face pinched into concern.

I shake my head and hold my hand up, knowing I'd do the same if the roles were reversed. "No, it's okay. Thank you. I'll call her when I leave."

We stand in silence for a moment—the longest moment.

"My name is Jack, by the way." He's looking at me with the first genuine smile I've seen from him. It's one of those smiles I did my damnedest to avoid in high school.

Charming, but could ruin you.

"You called me groom all night."

I press my hand over my face and groan, catching a whiff of my awful morning/hungover breath. "Oh no, I am so sorry."

"We apologize quite a bit." His chuckle is warm as he shrugs his shoulder. "It's okay. I only know your name because of a signed check."

My laugh is awkward, and I look down at my feet, feeling self-conscious in this outfit now that it's not in the nightlife. Low-cut silk top with a leather skirt and black pantyhose—*who am I?* I pull my hair up and throw it into a ponytail as we stand in silence again. "I should probably get going. Mind if I use your restroom?"

"Of course not." He gestures to the first door in the hallway. "Do you need a ride home?"

I shake my head with another awkward laugh. "No, no," I say, walking backwards toward the bathroom before I pee down my leg. "No. That's enough favors from you, I think."

He smiles again and nods, turning from me to open his refrigerator, which I am *so* grateful for. For some reason, him watching me walk into his bathroom is a different kind of discomfort I don't need.

I've never done awkward morning goodbyes with a complete stranger, but I think I nailed it. If you ignore the part where I literally bounced out of the bathroom and cheerfully said, "Well, thank you again, sir. I bid you adieu," before bowing like the last eight hours had been a production.

I can't blame him for the mildly weirded out expression that briefly crossed his features before telling me goodbye. I did just bid the man *adieu*.

Once I'm in the *Lyft*, I send a group text to my two employees: *We need to talk Tuesday. Hope you're safe and had a good night.* I hate feeling like the mother to two mid-twenty-year-olds, but someone should teach them what they should already know.

With that out of the way, I hit the contact *Mom* in my call log.

One ring.

"So, there's a Jack?"

Well, she cuts right to the chase.

"Hi, Mom. How are you? How's my girl?"

"She's eating cereal on the couch. She's fine. I'll get her in a minute. Where are you? Who is Jack?"

I don't want to tell my mom about what happened last night. She will scold me for getting basically blackout drunk and going home with a rando. "He is just a friend. A friend of a friend, really. A *boyfriend* of a friend. The friend I stayed with last night."

This lie is growing.

"Oh." I'm unsure of whether she bought that. "Well, he was very polite."

I smile a little at her comment and nod, running a

hand down my exhausted face. "Yeah." I take a moment to reflect on last night's events. "He's a good guy. So, back to you and Nova. How is it going?"

"Perfect, as always. I don't want to bring her back to you." I hear her pout over the phone, like she always does when the subject of an end to a visit is broached.

"Too bad. She's mine," I tease, and suddenly, I miss her even more. "Your flight is in the morning at nine, right? School starts back on Wednesday." Of course, I know this, but I need her confirmation. Confirmation eases the gnawing feeling in my stomach.

She sighs heavily. "Yes."

The *Lyft* pulls into the driveway of my house, and I push my purse strap back onto my shoulder, unbuckling my seatbelt in anticipation of hopping out. "How long are you staying when you get here?"

"Until Thursday." Her voice is laced with sadness. She wants me to tell her to stay longer. I love my mother, but not a chance.

I pull my phone from my ear and thank the driver before slipping out and walking to the front door. "Well, good. Dad probably doesn't want you gone too long."

"Ugh, that old grump couldn't care less." She huffs, and we both know that isn't true. My dad is a lost puppy without my mom's loud personality bossing him around. "Do you want to talk to Nova?"

"Please." I smile at the thought, unlocking the door and stepping inside. I flip the foyer light on and put my purse on the side table. Nails click against the brick floor before Chief appears at the doorway. "Hi, boy." Leaning down, I kiss his face and scratch his ears. "Is Aunt Simone still sleeping?"

"Oh, honey," Mom cuts in after a few seconds of

silence. "She's fallen back asleep on the couch. Do you want me to wake her?"

"No, no." I shake my head, swapping the phone to my other ear. "Let her sleep, and get her to call me when she's awake, please."

"Of course. You go rest, and let me know when you're ready to stop lying about who Jack is." I almost drop my phone at the mention of his name again.

Groaning, I stand upright to head down the hall towards my bedroom. "Mom, I'm telling the truth."

"Sure. Love you!" She releases two audible kisses into the phone.

"Love you," I reply, walking into my bedroom and falling face-first into the mattress.

3

*O*ne thing I hate about moving is trying to find new physicians for the family. I'm extremely picky. Primary care physicians, pediatricians, grief counselors I'll blow off for as long as I can before Simone jumps down my throat—you know, the necessities. Including a new veterinarian for Chief. This town is incredibly small, but there is a surprising number of vet clinics in the area. Katrina recommended Dr. Peters—the, in her words: "hot vet on Cherry Ridge."

Hot vet, it is.

What a glowing recommendation.

"Chief Davis." The vet tech's voice echoes in the small but cozy waiting room. Chief's leash is in my hand, and his head is hiding behind my legs.

"Come on, big boy," I coax, standing up and tugging the leash gently to get him to follow. Which he does, reluctantly. We walk down a hallway covered in painted portraits of different animals, all by the same artist. It makes for a calming aesthetic. I usher Chief into the exam room, and he tries to hide under me when I sit on the bench against the wall. "Stop it," I hiss, scratching his ear to try to ease his anxiety.

The door opens, and I look up, my stomach flipping in surprise. When the veterinarian's eyes fall on me and recognition crosses his features, he exhales an easy laugh. "Hi, I'm Dr. Peters."

"This town is fucking small," I blurt, in disbelief. Jack Peters? *Are you kidding me?* I shake my head and let out a laugh much different from his, looking down at Chief to break this awkward encounter. "I promise I'm not following you." Though, honestly, it would appear that way.

"I don't know if I believe you." *Is he teasing me?* The flash of white teeth as he kneels down beside the exam table confirms that. Oh, okay. Teasing Jack is kind of adorable. "Hey, buddy." He tilts his head to catch the eyes of my hiding companion. He clicks his tongue a few times to call Chief over, with no luck. He smiles up at me and takes a treat out of his pocket, holding it out to bribe him.

"Come on," he urges, but with a treat, it doesn't take long for Chief to come out from behind me and slink over to him. "Attaboy." Jack rubs his ears before standing and nodding to me. "We'll be back. I'm going to do some tests on him before we give him his shots."

"No problem." I watch them as they leave, shoving my hands into my pockets. This is unbelievable. I've seen more of this random man in the past couple of months than I have my regular clients. And, *of course,* he's the hot veterinarian. I pull out my phone and shoot a quick text to Simone as I wait on him and Chief to return.

I text: *Jilted groom = hot veterinarian*

Not even a second passes before my phone lights up.

Simone: *Mystery Jack? I am starting to believe he's a figment of your imagination.*

I laugh out loud at her reply and send an eye-roll emoji before shoving my phone back into my purse.

When Jack comes back in and helps Chief on the exam table, he's quiet. He starts his inspection—ears, eyes, teeth, reflexes. I'm oddly uncomfortable in the silence and find myself watching the muscles in his arm twitch with every small movement.

Cool, Eliza, you're sexualizing your dog's doctor. I snap out of my daze when another man walks in and places a clipboard on the counter behind Jack, who stands up and looks over his shoulder at it. He nods before looking back at Chief. I try to think of something to say to him—make him talk to me. We need a better impression of each other than the few we've had already.

"I donate to ASPCA," I exclaim, almost too loudly. Am I trying to start a conversation or impress him? Both?

He smiles—damn, that's a pretty smile—but his eyes stay trained on Chief as he presses a stethoscope to his abdomen. "Hey, that's great." He sounds charmed. I've charmed him.

He doesn't need to know those donations only occur when I'm intoxicated. Drunk-spending is a thing. Though it usually happens on bras or sex toys. Not me. Nope. I wake up to: *Thank you for your generous donation! Because of your contribution, blah blah blah.* Drunk me is such a humanitarian.

Jack looks up at me as his hands move to stroke Chief's head, attempting to soothe him since his whole body is a scared, trembling ball of fur. He keeps turning his head to me, giving me the most pathetic pleading eyes he can muster. It guts me. "How long have you had Chief?"

"Oh, probably six years now?" I guess, trying to conjure up the memory of me sobbing at the shelter as I pressed my nose against his through the gate. Instant soulmates. "He's seven years old, though."

"Well, he's in great shape. He's heartworm negative, his blood work seems fine, and he'll just need his yearly vaccinations, and you're good to go. I saw on his chart that he's been using the shot for his heartworm vaccination. Are you still okay with that?" Jack stands up, running his hand over Chief's nose and stopping on top of his head, repeating the action several times.

I watch as Chief leans forward with sleepy eyes, pressing his face to Jack's stomach as he continues to shower him with affection. I can't help but smile, because he has been successfully calmed. Dog whisperer.

"Yes, please. It's much easier for me that way." I take Chief's leash from Jack once he's done and help him off the examination table. We're alone in the room now that Jack has slipped out, so Chief is in a much better mood.

He's wagging his tail, excited for the treat he knows comes right after he gets poked and prodded. Like the master beggar he is, he sits in front of me, deep golden-brown eyes locked with mine, ears perked, body swaying with the vigorous tail wag. I snort as I dig in my purse and pull out a dog biscuit. When I toss it to him, he catches it midair. Greedy sucker. He has no idea he's about to get at least five more pokes before we leave.

"I'm going to take him back for his vaccines. You're welcome to come back there. It'll take all of five minutes." Jack's words sound practiced.

I'm a horrible dog-mom. "No, thank you. Needles wig

me out. He should be fine." My face turns a shade of pink at how awful I must sound to him.

But he shows no sign of distaste and nods with a shrug of his shoulders. "I don't blame you. We'll be back."

I'm fidgeting while they're gone, unable to keep still. I check my emails, scroll through social media—honestly, anything to keep busy. The door opens, and Chief runs over to me, his tail tucked as he hides behind my legs once more. He's panting, probably from working himself into a tizzy.

"I think it's safe to say he shares your fear of needles," Jack comments with a chuckle as he jots down a few notes on the clipboard in his hands. "All right, we'll send you a notice in six months for his heartworm preventative and for another round of vaccinations this time next year. Hopefully, I won't be seeing you until then."

I'm taken aback by his words, my face flushing. *Jeez*, he doesn't like seeing me around. "Oh, uh." I'm flustered as I stand up and grab Chief's leash. "Look, I really didn't search you out. It's a small town, and you were recommended to me. I can find another vet for Chief, though."

"What?" He shakes his head, his brow furrowed before realization flashes over his features. "No, no, no. Eliza, that's not what I meant." His words are hurried with a lighthearted grin. "I just meant, hopefully, Chief won't need to see me until then. As in, I don't want him to get sick."

Duh, Eliza. I close my eyes and hang my head with an amused huff. "Yeah, of course that's what you meant." I force a laugh. How ridiculous do I sound? I look back up at him and take a deep breath. "I feel like we need to start over."

"From?"

"The day we met?"

He laughs, his hand running over his mouth before crossing his arms over his chest and leaning against the counter. "I don't think that can easily be erased."

"Well, you're Chief's vet, so how do we get past it?"

Jack tilts his head to the side as if he's confused by my request. "You think I don't like you because of how we met? How could I possibly blame you for that?"

I shrug my shoulders, exhaling as I do. "I feel like we're always tiptoeing around each other in an awkward way. We should establish some sort of acquaintanceship. That way, when I come in, we can exchange pleasantries, and it won't be like *this*. I'll ask how CeCe is, you shoot the shit about whatever it is you're interested in, and we maintain a healthy back and forth until we die or one of us moves."

"No argument here."

"Perfect. So, in six months, I'll come back here and we won't have this weirdness between us."

He finds this amusing—his smirk and raised eyebrow are betraying him. With a brief nod, he stands straight and extends his hand for me to shake. "Deal."

I narrow my eyes, convinced he's patronizing me. My hand slips into his bear claws, and we shake on it, never breaking eye contact. "See you later, Dr. Peters."

"Call me Jack," he requests, removing his hand from mine as he does. "We are going to be acquaintances, after all."

"Jack." I nod. "Okay. See you later, Jack."

"You too, Eliza." He looks down at Chief and grins, giving him a quick scratch on his head. "Bye, Chief."

———————

I lift Simone's face up, angling her toward the light above the mirror in my bathroom. "Your hair is going to need another trim soon," I mumble as I carefully paint eyeliner on her bottom lid. "Unless you're wanting it to grow."

"No, I like it like this," she says, not moving her head as her eyes stay trained on the ceiling. "Thank you for doing this."

I roll my eyes and focus my attention on her other lid. "Please, you know this is barely considered a favor. So, what is this event you're going to?"

She sighs, trying her best not to blink, but backs her head away from me to do so without smudging. "It's a charity banquet."

She fans her face so her eyes won't water.

"Got a hot date?" I guess, resuming my task when she's done. I pull out the mascara from the bag between my legs and set it on the table to use when I'm done gluing her false lashes on.

Simone laughs, shrugging her shoulders at my question. "Going with a surgeon from the hospital. It's nothing romantic. We've been friends for a while, so we just decided to go together."

"Sounds hot," I deadpan.

She laughs again, turning her head to dodge my hands that are closing in on her with the lash glue. "I don't have time to build a connection, okay? Unlike you, with all the attractive clients you get."

My cheeks burn, a ball of discomfort lodged in my stomach, slowly creeping up to create a lump in my throat. I laugh, but it comes out in an uncomfortable snort. "Yeah, I guess I get a few."

I didn't mean to make her give me the look. But she's

giving it to me, and I hate it. She checks herself and gives me another grin instead. "So, I haven't seen you much since the run-in with veterinarian-groom a few days ago." She wiggles her eyebrows, making me chuckle.

Leaning in close, I apply the glue to her eyelids and use tweezers to strategically place the thick lashes. Press and hold. Blow. "I swear, that man is everywhere."

"Fate."

"Small town."

"I haven't met him, yet."

"How do you know you haven't run into him at the store or something?" I'm working on her other eye now, trying to keep her head steady. She's the perfect model, letting me move her in whatever way I need to get the job done.

She stays still, but raises an eyebrow at the question, the right corner of her mouth tugging upward. "A tall, bear-like man with a broad chest, sharp green eyes, and strawberry-blonde hair?" she asks, repeating my former description of him. "Sounds impossible to unknowingly run into."

She makes a fair point. I blow on her eye to dry the glue, and hear a soft padding of feet close in on the bathroom.

I hear Nova behind me. "How much longer until we can wash out my conditioner?"

I look at my phone next to Simone's elbow and turn to my daughter with a smile. "Sorry, Supernova, you've got seven more minutes."

"My scalp itches," she whines, pointing to a spot on her head and dancing in place at the discomfort.

Gently removing the no-longer-warm towel from her head, I lift the shower cap and scratch the area she's pointing to. She sighs in contentment. "There we go. Now, seven more minutes, and I want you back in here so we can wash it out."

"How are you doing her hair?" Simone asks after Nova bounces back into the living room.

I shake my head a little before grabbing the mascara on the counter. "I'm going to give her hair a break for one more week, and then I'll braid. Maybe box braids since she's been begging for them."

She smiles and touches the bun atop her head. "I think that's what I want to do next, too."

"I can do them if you want," I say, before instructing her to blink every time I smooth the mascara over her lashes. "We'll make a day out of it."

As the palest white woman you've ever seen, I am forever grateful to Simone for teaching me how to care for Nova's hair since the day her beautiful curls started to grow. I've become fairly good at maintaining Nova's natural hair and, in turn, can style Simone's for her, free of charge. What I didn't pick up from her, I learned in cosmetology school.

"Oh yes, I'll make sure I'm not on-call." She blinks a few times to adjust to the lashes.

I stand up and turn her around so she can look in the mirror. She grins, looking at me through my reflection. "I pity the people who don't have a live-in beautician. You're amazing."

"No, that mauve lipstick with your complexion is amazing." I smirk, turning her back toward me. "Let me set you, and then you're good to go."

"So going back to our earlier conversation," Simone pipes up before pausing to close her mouth and eyes for my spritz. "What do you think about going on a date?"

I freeze for a moment before deeply inhaling and shrugging my shoulders. "I don't know. I don't know if I'm ready for that, yet."

"Completely understandable. I just wanted to ask. I have a friend at the hospital who saw you when you brought me my wallet last week. He asked about you."

I nod, a little too aggressively. "Sure, yeah. That's sweet. I just ..." I trail off and give her a weak smile. "Soon, okay?"

Simone takes a hold of my shoulders and locks eyes with me. "I am not rushing you. Take your time." I exhale, at ease, until she adds, "But you've made a counseling appointment, haven't you?"

"Haven't found one to take my insurance, yet," I lie, almost too effortlessly. *Dammit, Simone. I hate these conversations.*

"I have a list," she counters, eyebrow raised. "Please, Eliza. Promise me you'll at least go to one session."

She's right. I know she is. After Aaron passed away, I shut down first, and then when I was no longer a zombie, I went into protective mode. I made sure Nova was okay— two different child psychologists said she was handling everything in a healthy way. I planned for our next steps; I set up accounts for Nova's future; I made a will. I did everything right, but only where everyone else was concerned. I didn't have time to talk about me or how *I* was feeling. And then too much time had passed. "I promise." And I do. Promise. For now. I'll try.

"Momma, I think it's been seven minutes!" I hear down the hall.

"Duty calls." I smile and give Simone a pat on the ass to shoo her out of the bathroom.

———————

"So, I kicked him out, and I don't regret it," Lonnie finishes before taking a deep breath as if telling me of her recent drama has exhausted her. Lonnie Finn is one of my new clients. She's extremely chatty, which I love, because the more she talks, the less she expects me to.

I give her a sympathetic smile as I twist my wrist to put waves in her freshly colored hair with my straightener. "Well, you don't have to. You do what you think is best for you."

"Thank you!" she exclaims, throwing her hands up to emphasize her frustration. "My mom told me I was too harsh with him. I'm just not a doormat like she is."

I don't know her mom, but she could be a client, so I only nod my head and comb through the waves I've created. "No one is in your shoes but you. You do what makes you happy."

She's content with that answer, giving me a smile in the mirror. I finish dragging my comb through her shoulder-length locks and use my nails to give it texture up top. The door sounds beside me, and I look over to see none other than Jack Peters walking through, his eyes on me. I am utterly confused. And pleasantly surprised.

"Hi," he says with a polite nod. "Do you take walk-ins?"

I raise an eyebrow. "I do."

"I need a haircut if that's possible." He walks a little closer to me but maintains enough distance from my workspace. Much appreciated.

Don't question it, Eliza. Oh, who am I kidding? "Don't you have 'a guy'?"

The smile forming on his face is enough to make any

woman in the room fall to their knees in front of him. "I did, and now I don't. So, can you fit me in?"

My eyes shamelessly sweep over his body. *Probably.* I clear my throat at the inappropriate thought and shrug my shoulders with a polite smile. "Sure. Let me finish up with this client, and I'll get you when I'm done."

Lonnie stays silent in her chair, but when my attention falls back on her, she has both eyebrows raised. "You have a thing going with hot Dr. Peters?"

My laugh comes out too loud, my cheeks burning. How could she have possibly come to that conclusion from that brief interaction? "No, no, no," I practically snort, smiling as I apply a light coat of hairspray. "He's my dog's vet, that's all."

"Oh." She's nodding thoughtfully—she does not believe a word I am saying. "Well, you should work on your poker face, then."

I furrow my brow as I unclip her cape and use my foot to lower the chair back down. I take personal offense, knowing good and damn well my face is a brick wall. I am *known* for keeping my reactions in check. People compliment me at PTA meetings. *Don't argue with the client.* I playfully roll my eyes and give her a friendly laugh. "You're reading too much into it. Go set your next appointment at the desk. I'll see you soon. And take care of yourself."

"Thanks, Eliza." Lonnie smiles before giving me a sultry wink. "Have fun."

I honestly don't know how to respond to that. Awkward laughter is my go-to, paired with a friendly wave.

I quickly sweep chunks of blonde hair into a dustpan before guiding Jack to my station. He settles in, looking up at me with a sheepish smile. "I feel like a giant in this chair."

It eases the unnecessary tension, and I laugh as I spread a black cape over him and clip it in the back. "I can raise it." My foot is already under the pedal to do so.

"Much better." He chuckles, a smooth growl from his throat, looking at me in the mirror for a brief moment before moving his eyes back down to his lap.

"So," I begin, moving from behind him to get my clippers ready. "You wanting anything different or just normal upkeep?" I try to picture the way his hair looked when we first met and, again, when I woke up at his house and scurried out as fast as I could.

"Normal," he confirms. "I don't like a close shave on the sides."

"I know." I change the guard on my clippers. When I turn back to him, a small smile is on his lips, and I think about what I've said. "I only mean I have seen you a couple of times, and I *am* a hairdresser, so I pay attention to that sort of thing."

He gives me a short nod and shifts in the chair. "Well." He gestures to his head. "Work your magic."

His hair is wavy, more strawberry than blonde, and soft under my fingertips. I turn on my clippers and watch them slide through the mess of curls. We sit in silence as I work. I glance up in the mirror every once in a while, but never find him looking at me, which is a relief. I'm an awkward person when I catch someone in a stare. I'd probably give this weird wink and then hate myself for the next week. I change from clippers to a comb and scissors and wet his hair before I start snipping. While I run my comb through the waves, his voice catches my attention.

"Is that your daughter?"

When I glance up, I notice his eyes on the picture framed by my mirror. I smile when I follow his gaze, and nod, a section of his hair between my fingers. The picture is from a four-day getaway last summer with Nova and Simone. Simone and I are on either side of Nova, our full plates in front of us, the beach behind us. We asked the waitress to snap a quick photo because we had neglected to take a single one the entire trip. One of my arms is around Nova's back, and my other is placed on top of my floppy beach hat, keeping it from blowing away. A strand of my highlighted hair is blowing in my face, and my freckles are prominent from a day's worth of sun. Simone is laughing at something Nova said right before the moment was captured, her eyes brighter from the one cocktail she had had. But Nova's grin is my favorite part of the whole picture. Carefree, youthful, and not an ounce of sadness for the first time in several months. "Yeah." I snip his ends. "That's Nova."

"And your wife?" He looks up at me before holding his hands up. "Or girlfriend?"

I shake my head with a warm smile. It's not the first time we've been asked that question, and it probably won't be the last. With Nova's skin only a shade darker than Simone's, people have mistaken her to be Simone's daughter for years. Ashamedly, I used to get jealous if I was somewhere with Nova in my arms and Simone standing beside me as some bystander would look point-edly at Simone and tell her how beautiful her daughter was. *No,* I wanted to snap, *Nova is my world.* That was within the first few years of Nova's birth—I've chilled since then. People are naturally curious individuals. And Simone was always quick to correct them with a kind smile. She loves Nova, but I don't think it's possible for anyone to love her more than I do. "No, that's my best friend and roommate."

"Oh, I didn't mean to assume," he begins, locking eyes with me in the mirror. I hope he doesn't think it offended me.

I comb through his hair and smile, placing my hand on his shoulder. "It's okay, really. People assume that all of the time. I could be so lucky to have someone like Simone."

He grins at that and runs his hands up and down his legs. "I'm sure she'd say the same about you." He ducks his head down after that, clearing his throat and quickly changing the subject. I note it. "So, when did you move to town?"

"Oh gosh." I tousle his damp hair and inspect it for any uncut strands. "I moved here from Tennessee last May. Simone has been here for a few years, though."

"Why'd you decide to move here? For Simone?" His curiosity doesn't rub me the wrong way. It's not like the prying gossips who cannot fathom why I'd move several states away to live with my female best friend. He just sounds like someone trying to get to know another.

I move to his right side and work on the uneven pieces there, combing them down as I do, to avoid creating cowlicks. "Oh, well," I begin, brushing away the snipped strands of hair. I take a deep breath, the next sentence coming out as if I have rehearsed it. "My husband passed away about a year and a half ago. My daughter and I both needed a change of pace, and honestly, Simone has always been a safe place for me to land."

Jack's face falls, and he shakes his head—luckily, I wasn't mid-snip. Customers can be so careless. "I'm so sorry, Eliza. I feel like an ass for asking."

"No." I catch his eyes in our reflection. "Please, don't apologize."

He nods, but stays silent, his face furrowed, as if concentrating. I go back to my task, but the silence filling the space between us brings the onslaught of emotions I was trying to escape in Tennessee—pity, sympathy, self-doubt from someone asking me a simple question for fear that I'd snap.

"Have you lived here long?" I change the subject for two reasons. One, I don't want him to think he's made me uncomfortable; and two, he seems uncomfortable himself.

"My whole life minus when I went to college and vet school." He's got an easy expression paired with a deep exhale. There's a pause before he speaks again. "You came to the right place, in my opinion. It's small, but I think it's got healing qualities."

Healing qualities. I like that. I give him a grateful smile and finish up his cut. After blow-drying and styling the boyish waves that complement his bone structure so perfectly, I work on manicuring his beard.

Once I'm done, I step back and appreciate my work. *Hot damn.* My look of pure appreciation gives me away because he raises an eyebrow and looks around me to see his reflection. I want to bite off his hand when he runs it through his hair and ruins my style, but it is *his* hair after all. When he smooths a hand over his beard, he looks up to me, his laugh lines showing. "I like it." I release him from the cape over his shoulders. "Can we do every four weeks?"

He unfolds himself from my chair, looking down at me from where he stands. I take a step back so I can look at his face without craning my neck. "So I have your approval?"

His laugh is warm and familiar. It's like feeling the sun on your skin as you swing in a hammock. He wipes the shed hair from his neck and nods, checking his arms for any he may have missed. "Sure." Jack smiles. "Pay at the counter up front, right?"

"Right." I step away from him, folding his cape over my arm. "See you soon, I'm sure," I tease, which earns me another laugh from him.

"Oh, I'm sure." He nods to me before stepping away to check out with our receptionist.

4

Though there are many upsides to chaperoning field trips—spending the day with Nova, free lunch, a day off work—there are still downsides. For instance, riding a bus down bumpy roads with over forty loud second graders singing Kidz Bop this morning? Not my cup of tea. Luckily, I don't usually get carsick, or it could have been ten times worse. Nova is excited, though, and that makes everything else worth it.

She's been talking about this trip ever since the permission slip and volunteer information sheet came home in her backpack. I signed up to be the field trip volunteer at the beginning of the year, mainly so I wouldn't be responsible for any of the snack days. The other mothers put me to shame with their carefully crafted cupcakes and themed cookies. It's much safer to stick me with the job of corralling the rugrats.

I had forgotten all about my duty as chaperone until Nova slid the papers in front of me at dinner. *Walking tour at Reginald Farms with demonstrations on caring for the farm animals by **Dr. Peters***. Of course.

The large brick Victorian house stands sturdy on rolling hills, and the barn to the right of it is almost as big as my home in Tennessee. Despite the less than ideal ride over, the actual farm is magnificent, and to top it off, the weather is amazing. The snow receded over a week ago, and the sun eases the slight wind chill.

I pull my jacket closer to my body and walk with my rambunctious group to our next activity. We're rotating in groups of twelve, and we've just finished the Christmas tree farm tutorial. The only glimpse I've ever gotten of a real Christmas tree farm is from Hallmark movies. Learning the process and dedication of tending to it, was a little boring, but also impressive.

We haven't been here *too* long, but I've already grown immune to the kids' loud chatter. It dies down when we step into the barn where Dr. Peters is—get this—bottle-feeding a baby calf. It's like he's always wearing a sign that says: *I piss excellence.*

When he looks up from the calf, his eyes immediately find mine, and he breaks out into a grin, shaking his head slightly before giving his attention to the wide-eyed students in front of me. "Hi, guys." His voice is low and gentle. "Be very quiet so we don't startle Delilah. But you can come closer. Just walk slowly."

Surprisingly, the noisy kids I've had to shepherd all day are now saints as they move cautiously towards Jack and Delilah. I sit down with the other chaperones on the nearest bale of hay and listen as Jack describes the daily routines of caring for the animals on the farm. Nova keeps looking back at me with an enthusiastic grin on her face. She's oddly always wanted a pet cow. The answer is still no, dear.

Hands fly up with questions once Jack is done with his

overview, and he takes his time, answering each one. I glance at my watch toward the end of our session and stand up to get the kids ready for their lunch break.

The walk back to the picnic tables near the horses is filled with an excited buzz, and we distribute the packed meals for the kids before taking our seats. Most of the chaperones are eating together, so I sit at a table near them that isn't as crowded. My head is turned, chiming in on their discussion, and when I go to take a bite of my sandwich, Jack is sliding in on the bench across from me.

"Hi, acquaintance." He smirks, peeking into my cooler to see what I brought to eat before looking back at me. "Couldn't wait two more weeks to see me?"

I habitually glance up at his hair and shake my head at the fast-growing curls. "I swear you shampoo with *Miracle Grow*."

"You avoided the question."

"I thought it was rhetorical. I'm obviously here with my daughter." I take a long swig from my water bottle before continuing. "The question is, why are *you* here? Don't you have patients?"

Jack laughs at my question with a nod of his head, leaning back from the table to situate his long legs underneath. "I do this every year. *Reginald Farms* is my family's. My dad inherited it from my grandfather, who inherited it from his father. The Christmas tree farm business wasn't started until my dads took over when I was a kid, though."

"You're David and Matthew's son?" I can't help but smile, having met the two earlier in the day. *Of course* he is. Not only has he not presented me with a flaw, but his parents are two wealthy, philanthropic gay men? Go away, Jack.

"I am." He wipes his hands on his pants before folding

his arms in front of him on the table and leaning forward. "How did you like the tour? Pop can get a little long-winded when he gets going about the trees."

Oh, he definitely did. I suppress a laugh at his comment and nod, swallowing the mouthful of water I had consumed as he spoke. "It was cute. And very informative. You grew up learning all of that?"

"I can tend a crop of trees in my sleep," he teases, but he's wearing a proud grin as he does.

"Mom," I hear from my left, and I see Nova making her way toward us, giving her signature shy smile to Jack as she comes to stand at my side.

I put my hand on her back when she gets to me and look up at her. "Hey, girly, you okay?"

She nods, placing her arm around my shoulders and leaning down to my ear to whisper, "Can I have an Oreo packet now? I'm done with my lunch."

"Of course." I unzip the pouch on my lunch box to pull out a packet of Oreos. "Dr. Peters, this is my daughter, Nova. Nova, Dr. Peters and I are friends. He's one of my clients and also Chief's doctor."

"Really?" Nova asks, excitedly, looking back at Jack. Speaking to children on a field trip and bottle-feeding calves puts you high on the list of celebrities in a seven-year-old's eyes.

Jack returns her smile because it's contagious, and nods in agreement. "It's true. Nice to meet you, Nova."

"Nice to meet you, too." Her voice is firm, and she puts her hand out for him to shake. Oh boy, I can see the influence my father has had on her. I'm sure the grip is as tight as her little hand can make it, too. I can hear him. *Handshakes are the most important first impression.* She looks back at me then and nods to the friends she left. "Can I go back?"

"Sure." I laugh, watching her jog back to her table. She sits down and immediately starts talking, and then six pairs of eyes look at our table. Hanging with the field trip celebrity ... I'm a cool mom. "You're famous." I look pointedly to Jack, nodding toward them.

He looks over and gives them all a small wave, causing them to immediately avert their eyes. When turns back to me, he's chuckling at the scene. "I'll take it," he shrugs before adding, "I'll also take you calling me your *friend*. We've graduated into friendship. Man, this is moving fast."

I almost choke on my water, laughing at his comment, and roll my eyes. "Don't get ahead of yourself. I wanted to look cool in front of my daughter. She's obsessed with cows right now, and you're the magician feeding one with a bottle."

"Oh, yeah? She likes cows?" His grin is boylike and causes my heart to swell at his genuine interest.

"Loves them," I correct him, holding my hand up. "So, the kids in her class have to choose an animal to do this end-of-year presentation on for her science class. She chose cows."

His expression is one of pure amusement. It's kind of adorable. "What kind of presentation? What does she have to do?"

"She has to write an essay and then give an oral presentation with visual aids." I repeat Nova's words. "She wanted to do something like an inside look of the everyday life of a cow."

Jack smiles, but shakes his head a little. "Difficult task

when she's learning from library books. She needs to learn from the real thing. You should get her one."

"Wait. Buy my daughter a cow? For a project?"

His face is serious, not a trace of teasing can be found. He glances around before leaning forward again. "Nothing prepared me for adulthood and responsibility better than *this* farm. Taking care of an animal? That's a life lesson in itself."

He has to be joking. Where would I even put a cow? I'd have to fence in our land, and that sounds like it would cost a pretty penny. I shake my head in disbelief, an incredulous laugh escaping my lips. "She doesn't even remember to feed Chief half of the time, Jack. How would I prepare her for owning a *cow*?"

Jack leans back on the bench, crossing his arms over his chest with a thoughtful face. He tilts his head from left to right as if he's pondering something before looking back to me. "All right, so maybe up and buying your kid daughter a calf isn't the best idea."

"You think?" I snort.

"But," he adds, all but cutting me off. "I still think her presentation would be more developed with hands-on experience."

"Sure." This seems more and more like a joke. "With the fake cow I have at my disposal?"

He rolls his eyes with a good-natured smile. "No. With Delilah." He nods towards the barn. "Look, no one knows more about taking care of barnyard animals than Dad and me. We've done it our whole life. Delilah is two weeks old, and she's a good learning tool."

I tilt my head to the side, my eyebrow raised. "So, what are you proposing?"

"Oh no, I'm not proposing anything," Jack responds, throwing his hands up. "I'm just offering a suggestion. Any time you and Nova have a free day, you are welcome to come to the farm, and we can teach her everything we know about cows. She can learn by taking care of Delilah."

I glance over in Nova's direction—she's standing at the fence, with one of her teachers and David. He's showing her how to feed the horse from her hand, and she has a nervous grin on her face. When I look back to Jack, I narrow my eyes. "All right," I concede. "I'll ask Nova if she would like that."

"Sure, and just let me know." He holds his hand out to me. "Guess this is a good time to give you my phone number."

"Wow." I slip my phone from my back pocket to place it into his palm. "That was an elaborate way to get my number. Do you always try that hard?"

Jack chuckles as he shakes his head, taking my phone from my hands. "Believe it or not, I don't usually have to ask." He raises his eyebrow with a smirk, and it's dangerous.

"Uh-huh," I hum with a smile, watching as he keys his number into my cell.

He shrugs when he hands it back to me, drumming his hands on the table quickly. "So, yeah, text me if you decide to come out here."

"Yeah." I nod, looking up at him as he stands from the picnic table. "I will. Thank you."

"Not a problem. I need to go check on one of the pregnant horses while I'm here. Have a good rest of the field trip."

"Thanks." I laugh, watching as he turns to walk away, before adding, "Good to see you again."

"You too, *friend*." He smirks over his shoulder.

————————————

David is obsessed with craft beer. That's one of the many things I've learned about him since I started bringing Nova to the farm on the weekends. I'm not complaining—he has a different brand for me to try every time I show up. Today's is an "earthy citrus" flavor from a brewery in Louisiana, and despite my distaste for canned beer, it's pretty good.

Nova has been excited about today's visit for a while. After six weeks, Delilah is finally able to be in the same pen as her mother and some of the other cows. Apparently, she had to stay in a separate one for two months because calves can easily develop infectious diseases.

Yes. I've become a cow encyclopedia.

"You're staying for dinner, right?" I hear from beside me and turn to see Matthew approach with a glass of red in his hand—he's not as fond of beer as his husband. "I made enough lasagna to feed the town."

The second time Nova and I came to the farm, Matthew insisted we stayed for his famous meatloaf. It has since become somewhat of a Sunday-night tradition. If we count four Sundays in a row as "tradition."

One of those Sundays, Simone joined us and immediately hit it off with Matthew—both avid fans of *Downton Abbey*. On another Sunday, I met Jack's aunt, Penny. She's David's sister and an absolute gem. Penny is a traveling artist with an insatiable longing to see everything with nothing holding her back. I love her.

Once I met her, I took notice of the art inside the Peters' home. Most of it was done by her, and the style was familiar. Jack later told me she painted all of the animal portraits in his clinic as well. Her talent is incredible.

"Of course." I take another swig of my beer as I watch Nova run a brush over Delilah's side in a careful manner. David is filling the trough with fresh water, and Jack is on his knees, checking the calf's hooves. My eyes linger on him a little longer. From where I'm standing, I can barely make out his features, but I've been blessed with 20/20 vision, so it's not impossible. His face is pink—probably a combination of being wind chapped and a bit flushed from manual labor. His jawline is sharp—which is a fact usually covered by his beard, but he shaved recently, leaving a five o'clock shadow and a jaw that could cut glass. Staring at Jack has become a bit of a Sunday pastime. He's pretty, okay? No one could ever dispute that.

"Looks like you're getting Miss Nova a cow soon." Matthew chuckles, breaking me out of my stare.

I laugh as well because that's a long way from becoming reality. "Don't you dare put that in her head."

I finish my beer just in time. Jack helps Nova guide Delilah into the large pen with the rest of her family before they make their way back towards the house. I push myself off the large white oak that serves as the halfway mark between the house and the barn.

"What do you think, kid?" I stand with my hands on my hips, waiting on them to catch up. "Got enough material for your presentation on Friday?"

"Yes!" she replies, a little breathless. "Can you print those pictures we took on your phone?"

"Yep." I hold out my hand for her to latch onto once they make it to me. Nova has made me take several pictures over the past few weeks so her *visual aid wouldn't be lacking*. Those were her words.

As we approach the house, CeCe's head pops up, causing Nova to excitedly take off running to the porch steps to play with her. I keep a leisurely pace, watching to make sure she doesn't fall.

"Nova invited me and Dad to her presentation Friday. Is that a thing?"

Well, that's new news. Nova is not necessarily shy, but she's also not an open book. "Is what a thing?"

"People attending the presentation," Jack replies with a laugh, like that was obvious. "I don't want to disappoint her and not show up."

"Uh, well. Yeah, I think." I glance over at him. "I'll be there, and I think Simone will, too. It's not a huge deal, but the teacher did tell me they would present in the cafeteria since it's the whole second-grade class. I know other parents are going."

He nods, looking down at his feet as we walk, his hands shoved into the pockets of his jacket. "Well, then, I'll try to make it. If that's okay with you."

"Of course it is, but you know you don't have to."

He smiles up at me, rolling his eyes at my comment. "I know that. I just want to see what she's learned these past few weeks. She hasn't given me any insight."

"You too?" I practically exclaim, the words falling out with laughter. "She's been so secretive with me. I was sure she had told you or David *something* about her presentation."

"Not a word." He chuckles, glancing over his shoulder and back towards the barn. I look as well and see his dad locking the door before heading our way.

"Hey." My eyes fall back on him as we approach the porch steps. "I can't thank you enough for taking the time to help her with this."

Jack waves me off, his easy smile never leaving his face. "Come on. I offered in the first place. I enjoyed it. You don't have to keep thanking me." He pauses for a moment, looking down at his work boots again before raising his gaze to meet mine. "I'm kind of going to miss you guys being out here."

Warmth radiates into my soul at his unexpected admission. I smile, tilting my head to the side, with my foot on the first step, ready to go up. "Jack, don't you know we're destined to continuously run into each other in this town?"

"Until one of us dies or moves away," Jack replies, mimicking my words from the day I took Chief to the vet. I laugh and nod in agreement, continuing up the steps to Nova and CeCe.

———————

I have this impulse to get to events early. I think the possibility of getting the time wrong or missing an important announcement brings me anxiety. Honestly, I have anxiety about a lot of things lately that I didn't have before Aaron passed away.

I shake my head to rid myself of that train of thought and weave through the crowd of parents to get a good seat. Nova's school seriously makes the biggest deal out of *everything*. It's an oral presentation on animals, and you're labeled *that parent* if you don't show up to support your child. I usually steer clear of the expectations of overzealous parents, but I also never want Nova to feel left out.

I find a row of empty seats in the cafeteria and spread my things out to save them. The chairs from the lunch tables are lined up to make an audience for the kids—like I said, *big* deal. I don't see Nova, or any kids, for that matter. I glance up at the clock before looking towards the entrance. I can't stop the wide grin on my face when I see Jack and David walk inside. It's not that I didn't believe him when he said he wanted to come; I just didn't actually expect him to show up. And David, too? My heart is aflutter.

Simone slides into the seat next to me five minutes before the kids start their presentations. We sit through a good forty-five minutes of different animals before I watch Nova set up her visual aid—an adorably decorated collapsible poster-board with several pictures of Delilah, her mother, and a few candids I took of Nova taking care of the calves.

A knot forms in my stomach when I notice she's twirling her braid around her finger—her nervous habit. As soon as her eyes find mine, she smiles, her face relaxing. I resist the urge to give her a double thumbs-up. She's at the age where you never know if she will find that cool or embarrassing. Is there an age where double thumbs-up is cool? Probably not.

"Hi, my name is Nova Davis, and my presentation is called Six Weeks with Delilah." There's a slight tremor in her voice that tugs at my heart. I don't ease my grin, because I want to make sure she sees a smile every time she looks my way.

"She's nervous," Simone notes from beside me in a silent, almost inaudible whisper.

I nod in agreement, but don't take my eyes off of her. I'm not the kind of parent who takes photos at events. My mother scolds me for it, and she's partly justified. I'll want them one day. But I also want to enjoy the moment without an electronic device shoved in my face. I don't need fifteen pictures of her opening her birthday presents or riding a horse for the first time. I can take one good picture before or after the moment and tuck it away for her to see later.

"During the daytime, it was okay for Delilah and her mother to be in the same pen. However, at night, Delilah needed to be separated. But she still needed to be in a pen that was right beside her mom's," she carefully instructs, pointing at a couple of pictures on her poster as she does.

I glance over at Jack briefly, and find him leaning forward, with his elbows on his knees, his hands clasped into a fist and resting under his chin. He's intently listening, and my God, it's endearing. I look back at Nova, and we lock eyes as she describes the feeding schedule of the calf. I'm not a sappy person, but I can feel a lump forming in my throat. When did she get so grown up? When did she get so smart? I must be showing my hand because Simone reaches over and places hers on mine.

"I'm being a sap," I whisper, laughing at how ridiculous I'm acting.

Simone shrugs and nudges me with her shoulder. "You're being a mom."

Once her speech is complete, our row goes a little overboard in the applause. We sit through another few kids' presentations and wait on the crowd to clear once it's over. It doesn't take long—parents and grandparents ushering people out of the way to get to their kid. Nova is giggling with her friends, so it earns us a few minutes. My mother's "*ladies don't rush*" resounds in my head. She's a gnat that won't go away, I swear.

When I finally get to Nova, I pull her in for a hug, leaning down slightly to envelop her without it being awkward. "You did so well! You gained that confidence from your dad," I assure her with a laugh. "I always had a pretty bad case of stage fright."

"You?" she questions with a surprised glint in her brown eyes. "I don't believe it."

"Oh, she did. She was a trainwreck." Simone is behind me, moving in front of me to get her own hug. "You, on the other hand, were a rockstar, kiddo. I wish I could stay a little longer, but I need to get to the clinic."

Nova nods, removing herself from her arms before her eyes drift behind me, and an excited grin breaks out. "Jack and David came?"

Well, screw Simone and me, then, am I right?

"They did." I smile and give a small wave to Simone as she turns to leave the room. I hit the jackpot with her, and I will continue to say so. "Let's go say hi."

Nova immediately leaves my line of vision and takes off in an awkward half-run to get to the wall where Jack and David are leaning, facing each other in easy conversation. I watch as she approaches them, wasting no time before diving at Jack's legs for a bear hug. I'm a few strides behind, but I can see the crinkle of his eyes when he smiles down at her. The noise of the cafeteria muffles what he's saying, but his lips are moving and she's still grinning.

When I reach them, Nova's hug has transferred to David.

"... I think I even learned a few things from you." David chuckles, leaning down to be eye level with her.

She's bashful, shaking her head with a giggle at his words. I look down at her and then glance up to see Jack looking at me. We share a small smile before both of us focus our attention back on Nova.

"What do you say to them?" I place my hands on her shoulders and give an affectionate squeeze. I don't know the exact day I started using what I refer to as *Mom Language*, but it's, like, my default now. Gross.

Nova looks up at me before shifting her gaze back to the guys. "Thank you for coming and for teaching me about cows. Can I still come visit Delilah every now and then?"

"Don't mention it." David's reply is accompanied by a warm grin. "You are welcome at our farm any time you'd like. Your mom, on the other hand ..." He trails off, teasing me. David has picked up this habit, and I would be lying if I said I didn't immensely enjoy it. He's a quiet man, so a lighthearted pestering is a sign of him liking you.

"Watch it." I laugh, giving him a playful glare.

"I would be personally offended if you never came to visit again." Jack looks pointedly to Nova. Honestly, he and David look so much alike. He also has a few resemblances to Matthew—which is entirely impossible, I know that. But I don't know. I see Aaron sometimes when I'm looking at Nova. Little things like expressions or her laugh. She may not be biologically ours, but she acts just like us. Well, more like Aaron than me.

I hear a loud call from the front of the room and turn to see Nova's teacher corralling her kids so they can go back to class. I look down at Nova and kneel to be eye level. In a couple of years, she's going to surpass me. She's already tall for her age. "All right, Supernova," I begin, kissing her cheek. "Go kick your math test's butt, and I'll see you this afternoon, okay?"

"Okay." She's pouting. I know she wants me to check her out for the day, but it's not going to happen when she has a test in one of her classes. She's cute, but she's not *that* cute. Okay, kidding, she's literally the most adorable human I have ever been around. Nova turns her attention to the guys and gives them a brief goodbye before following her classmates to line up by the door.

"Eliza, you have one hell of a kid," David remarks, lifting his cowboy hat to run a hand through his reddish hair that's slightly graying. "Thanks for letting us be a part of this today."

"I do. Do you guys want to go get lunch? I don't have a client scheduled for another couple of hours."

David ponders for a moment before looking at his watch. "Oh man, I wish I could, but I need to get back to the farm." He stops and moves his gaze to his son, placing a large hand on his shoulder. "Jack doesn't have plans, though. He can go."

"Only if you want to," I blurt to Jack. "Don't feel pressured."

"I don't feel pressured." Jack laughs but gives his dad a look at the subtle push. I notice it, and it makes me even more uncomfortable. "I could do food. What did you have in mind?"

I was right before. I will never *not* feel awkward around him. "Oh." I shrug, giving him a tight-lipped smile. "Whatever you are in the mood for. I'm usually not very picky."

"Tacos?" he offers, and I am appreciative of his decisive nature.

I nod while pushing my purse back onto my shoulder. "Tacos sound perfect."

Jack oozes charm. Seriously. It's effortless for him. The young woman behind the counter was putty in his hands when he ordered his tacos and engaged in lighthearted banter. When I ordered after him, her demeanor wasn't exactly the same. She was nice enough, but she certainly wasn't giggling at my every word.

She's come by our table several times, easily giving us more attention than any other table. I watch her walk away before glancing back to Jack with a raised eyebrow. He's smirking only a little as he looks down at his plate and scoops up his half-eaten shell to take another bite.

"Are you oblivious to it, or ...?" I trail off, smiling as I go in for another bite of mine as well. It's a heavenly flavor of steak, cilantro, and some sort of avocado-lime sauce that I want to bathe in.

"Not at all." His answer is quick before his bite. He's suppressing a grin as he chews, and I roll my eyes, successfully swallowing my bite before washing it down with a swig of my water.

"I'm sure that makes it easy for you to find dates," I muse aloud then immediately regret it. It's been a few months since his wedding, but is it still fresh? Should I have kept my mouth shut?

He shrugs his shoulders in reply before looking up at me with a good-natured smile. "Probably." At least he's honest. "But that's not really a priority for me right now. Seeing as my last relationship didn't end so well, I am looking to stay away from that type of drama for a while."

"It doesn't always have to be full of drama," I reason, though I don't know why. I have no skin in this game.

"Yeah? Have you been dating since you moved to town?"

I laugh at that question because it still feels weird to

me when someone wonders if I am dating. *Of course I'm not dating; I'm married.* Oh. One day, that question won't leave me with a knot in my stomach. I shake my head and use my fork to gather the pieces of steak that fell from my shell. "Not at all. I've just been focusing on Nova and my business. Simone keeps trying to set me up, but ..." I shrug, stopping myself with a shake of my head. He doesn't need the heaviness of this situation on him at a friendly lunch.

"But what?" he asks, anyway, starting in on his third taco. He grabs the napkin next to him and wipes his hands before reaching for his water bottle.

"I'm not ready," I say after a second's hesitation. "Which probably seems pathetic because it's been over a year and a half since my husband passed awa—"

"It's not pathetic," he all but cuts in, shaking his head forcefully. "Don't let anyone make you think that way. You're ready when you're ready."

I look up at him, surprised at the finality of his tone. I give him a grateful smile and move the guacamole around on my plate with my fork. "Thanks." I'm unsure if that's the right response.

He waves it off and glances back down at his plate. "Speaking of your business," he starts, and the fact that he changes the subject so quickly tells me we're going to have a great friendship. "What made you want to go in that field?"

It's weird, but no one has ever asked me that. My clients, though inquisitive about the rest of my life, never care about why I chose to spend my life painting faces and styling hair. "Well, I've always been really good at—and really experimental with—hair," I say with a laugh. "But I honestly never thought about making a career out of it. When I was in high school, I'd do hair and makeup for my classmates for dances and stuff. But I always saw it as a hobby."

"What changed?" Jack's attention is fully on me. It's intimidating.

"I went to college and couldn't find the right path for me. I changed my major, like, five times before I ended up graduating with a general studies degree. I felt a little lost and started working for my dad, but I was miserable. So, I began doing hair again for events, and then one day, it just clicked. *This* is what I need to do. I went to cosmetology school, worked for a fantastic salon for a few years, and then made the steps to open my own. Then my husband got sick again, so I put those plans on hold. Opening my own salon was a request he had before he passed. It's been really scary, branching out on my own, but I've been more successful than I expected to be here."

The way Jack looks at me when I speak is refreshing. He cares. He grins at me and finishes his last taco before using his napkin to wipe his beard. "You've built quite the reputation here."

"I'm taking that as a compliment."

"As you should." He laughs.

I know I've said it before, but his laugh is downright marvelous. I bite my lip to stop the enormous grin threatening to break my face. "What about you? I mean, it's obvious you're a huge animal lover. Is there some cool story about how you decided to become a veterinarian?"

"I wish I were that cool." He leans back in his chair. "Honestly, it was as simple as me loving animals and growing up on a farm. I was also always really good at biology. I loved learning about different species, and it seemed like the right fit for me. Nothing else made sense."

I'm envious of how simple it was for him. But he doesn't give off the vibe of having anything handed to him. It's more of a confidence about himself and his hard work. He knows what he excels in, so he pursues that. Easy as pie.

I glance down at my watch as his phone rings next to his empty plate. His eyes drop to the screen before giving me an apologetic smile. "It's the clinic." He holds his hand up before answering it.

I'm not worried. I need to get going, anyway. I have a client in forty minutes. I'm checking my texts and barely listening to his conversation. When I look back up at him, he's hanging up and placing his phone beside his plate. "Need to get going?"

"Yes, I'm sorry. I really enjoyed lunch." He sighs and honestly looks conflicted.

"Jack, it's fine." I can't help but laugh. "I have a client coming soon. I enjoyed lunch, too. Maybe we can do it again?"

Jack's eyes light up, matching the grin on his face. He nods as he takes out his wallet to drop a few bills on the table. "I'd like that. I'll hear from you soon?"

"Sure," I reply, also setting a couple of dollars down on the table to add to his tip. "I'm pretty sure Matthew and David would hound me if I didn't continue coming by the farm every now and then."

"You know it." Jack laughs, and we both get up to leave. He's standing there, awkwardly, facing me with his back to the door. I'm unsure of what we're supposed to do here, so I give a tight smile and open my arms slightly. A hug is normal, right? Whether it is, doesn't matter, because he steps forward and accepts it, wrapping his large arms around me to give me a brief squeeze. "See you around."

Well, damn. He gives *really* good hugs. I step back after our brief embrace and smile, nodding to him. "See you, Peters."

We walk out together and go our separate ways, but when I glance back over my shoulder to see if I can still spot him, he's doing the same. *Abort, abort.* I snap my head back around and turn the corner, no longer in his line of sight. I can't stop smiling, though.

5

"*Y*ou're a lifesaver!" I call from the porch once Jack steps out of his truck with a grin on his face. He waves me off and walks to the back of the Bronco, opening the tailgate to pull out his pressure washer. "I promise to get it back to you tomorrow."

"Eliza, I can pressure wash your porch for you. It's no big deal." He carries it at his side as he walks up the steps to meet me. "You sounded frantic on the phone about running out of time to do things. I can handle this."

I shake my head, holding my arms out for him to hand it over to me. Is it heavy? He makes it look so effortless. "Not a chance. I asked to borrow it, not for you to do the labor."

"I already planned on it," Jack replies with a shrug, his grin amused. "However, I do find it interesting that pressure washing your porch for an eight-year-old's birthday party is this important to you."

I gesture at my house, which, yes, is beautiful. But it's also a little old and kind of creeps me out. "The house is already haunted," I begin. "I don't need it to *look* haunted as well."

"Haunted?" Jack raises his eyebrows as he drops the washer at his feet. At that same moment, I hear the door open behind me and turn to see Simone walking out, rolling her eyes.

"Again?" She groans, her coffee mug in hand and her white coat already on over her scrubs. She looks from me to Jack and then shakes her head. "Hi, Jack. Thanks for the pressure washer, and our house is not haunted."

"You don't hear the noises!" I argue, knowing I probably sound irrational. It's true, though. The house makes noises. And not the normal creaks of an aging home, but deliberate noises. "I'm telling you, Jack. It's haunted. It didn't start until we were living here for at least six months, but every now and then, I hear long scratches in the ceiling, followed by loud stomps."

"And you never bothered to get this checked out?" Jack's previous grin is still painted on his features. "Go up in the attic and look around?" He's amused by this instead of being horrified. Those are the first ones to go in horror movies. *You are not an ally, sir.*

"Hell, no," I respond, crossing my arms over my chest. "You are more than welcome to, but I've watched way too many scary movies to entertain that idea."

I can tell he doesn't mean to laugh, but he chuckles anyway as he stretches out the power cord to the washer. "All right, fair enough." He looks up at me, his previous chuckle threatening to break into full-blown laughter. "I'll wash the porch and then go see what's up your ghost's ass."

"I'm glad you think this is a joke," I remark, defensively.

Simone is infected by Jack's contagious laughter, and she joins in, glancing down at her watch as she does. "I better get going. I'll be back this evening to help with the treehouse," she assures me, leaning forward to press a kiss to my cheek. "Jack, you're forever a saint for putting up with us."

"Oh, whatever!" I call as she leaves my side, insulted by the insinuation that I'm anything less than a delight.

"Anytime." He smirks, his laughter finally subsiding. He plugs the long cord into the outlet next to our front door, and looks up at me when Simone is already back in the house. "When do you have to be at the salon?"

"Not for another few hours." I look out to see the sun rise over the hills, peeking through the trees that block my house from the immediate morning rays. "What time do you need to be at the clinic?"

"At nine," Jack replies, nodding to me as he does. "You may want to go inside while I do this."

"Right." I hold my hands up as I turn to go back into the house as well. I check the clock on the oven as I walk past it to head to Nova's room. When I push the door open, she's wrapped up in her comforter like it's a cocoon. I can only see the top of her head emerging—her mermaid sleeping bonnet snug over her curls.

She's constantly changing, and yet, when she's asleep, I still see the round baby face she's only recently grown out of. I quietly walk over to her bed and sit on the edge of it, nudging her gently. School is out for the summer, but she begged me to sign her up for the two-week-long art camp at the cultural center downtown. We're ending the first week, and she loves it, but I think she's ready for the sleeping-in phase of summer to begin.

"Supernova." I use a sing-song voice, watching her

grunt and squirm from beneath her orange comforter. "One more day until your birthday party. Up, up, up!"

"Mom," Nova groans, ducking her head beneath the waves of fabric.

Ugh. That usually works. I grasp at the comforter and pull it down, ridding her of the shield. She opens one eye and makes sure her eyebrows are furrowed in a sleepy glare. I smile and dance in place to make her laugh. "Birthday par-tay, birthday par-tay," I chant as I shrug my shoulders and shake my hips. It works. She breaks out into a smile, giggling as she shoves her face down into her silk pillowcase. "You've got ten minutes to be out of bed," I inform her, laughing as well.

I get another unsatisfied harrumph slicing through her laughter. Her face is still shoved into her pillow, so I flip on the light on my way out with a smirk.

"Mom!" she shrieks, her tone slightly whiny.

"Up, up!" I cheerily repeat, grinning as I leave her door wide open to let Chief do his thing. His thing being that he follows after me and jumps up to lie beside Nova until she rolls out of bed. As if it's rehearsed, he trots past me, tail wagging, and I hear her bed squeak as he piles in on her.

I walk down the hall and run my hands down my clean face. Clean face. *Shit.* Look, I'm not the type of person who thinks I *need* makeup. However, I am the type of person who has a general distaste about people seeing me without any coverage. Mascara, blush, even a little lip gloss would suffice. But, no. I forgot Jack was going to be here at the asscrack of dawn, and therefore, I forgot to apply anything at all. Which is unfortunate for me because I like to look put together. Without putting on a little war paint, my eyelashes barely look like they're there, my freckles are prominent and in your face, and my lips are the palest of whites, blending into my pasty skin.

I get it. I am a huge advocate for loving yourself. But I am allowed to have my insecurities. As shallow as it seems, mine is being seen like *this*—especially by beautiful men with sexy beards and bedroom eyes.

I make a quick dash to my bathroom, paint my eyelashes black, and rub on a muted-pink lip gloss.

Better than nothing.

When I walk back out to the kitchen, Nova has risen and is making herself a bowl of cereal in her morning zombie-like way with Chief at her heels, begging for her to drop anything at all. I glance out the window, and my eyes decide to stay put. Jack holds the hose with one hand while the other pulls the bottom of his shirt up to wipe sweat from his face. I catch the smallest glimpse of his abdomen and feel my throat tighten and my skin grow hot.

I quickly turn away and smile when Nova faces me, her eyes swollen from a good night's rest. "Good morning, kiddo," I chirp, distracting myself from the man out my window.

"Jack's here?" she mumbles, taking a bite of her cereal.

So much for that.

I nod and grab the nearest rag to keep busy by wiping down counters that are possibly already too spotless. "Yep. He's cleaning off the porch for your birthday party. Isn't that nice?"

She turns over her shoulder and sees him through the window, as the noise of the pressure washer against the porch causes a loud vibration inside. "Yeah, it is."

"All right, I'm going to go grab your camp shirt from the dryer. Eat up, then brush your teeth, and I'll fix your hair." Our itinerary is rehearsed, but I still smile while I say it before walking to the laundry room. My heart is a wild thump in my rib cage. It's evident I've been single for a while, because the mere presence of a man is turning my insides into knots.

I'm still taming the edges at Nova's temple when a Tahoe pulls into my driveway. I glance outside and see Jack packing his washer back into his vehicle as Bonnie Tucker gets out of her car and greets him.

I roll my eyes. Every other time Nova has carpooled with Bonnie and her kids, Bonnie has stayed in the car and patiently waited on me to walk Nova to her.

You're transparent, Bon.

"Your ride is here." I set down the toothbrush I use to smooth the sculpting wax over her baby hairs. I run my thumb over each side one more time and smile down at her. "All done."

"Thanks, Mom!" She dives in for a quick hug, almost knocking me over with her unexpected force. "See you tomorrow!"

"Don't forget your overnight bag!" I call back to her, pointing to the duffel bag that sits in the middle of the dining table. Bonnie may annoy me with her obvious flirtation, but Nova loves her and her daughter. And you know Bonnie loves her, too. So, I shouldn't be so catty. Besides, she's doing me a favor by keeping Nova tonight so I can set up her treehouse reading nook all afternoon.

I follow Nova out the door. She stops and says hi to Jack, giving him a high five before throwing her bag in the back seat and climbing in. I can't quite hear the conversation between Jack and Bonnie, but I'm not trying to. I swear. I walk down the steps and over to them, smiling when Jack looks up at me with a relieved expression.

"Bonnie, thank you so much for keeping Nova tonight." I grin and cross my arms over my chest. "I have so much to get done for her party, and I want some of it to be a surprise. I can come pick her up any time in the morning, though."

"No rush!" Bonnie chirps, always enthusiastic and always way too peppy for early mornings. "Her party starts at two, right?"

"Yes," I reply with a nod, glancing past her to watch as Nova buckles her seatbelt.

"Then, I can keep her until around one and bring her over. That way, I can get here early and help with anything."

"Sure." I know my grin is genuine because it's practiced. But that idea sounds kind of miserable. Everyone knows Bonnie is a bit controlling—especially if it's any kind of event or party. "But don't feel like you need to."

"Don't be silly!" She looks at Jack with a sweet smile, placing her hand on his arm. "So nice of you to help out, Dr. Peters. I guess I'll be seeing you tomorrow as well?"

"Maybe," he says with a polite nod, his eyes kind and welcoming. "Good to see you again."

When she finally tears herself away from his presence and gets in her car, I look at Jack with a raised eyebrow. "What is it with you and the women of this town?"

"I'm single, and I like animals. That's usually enough to seal the deal." He didn't miss a beat. "So, let's take a look at that ghost, shall we?"

I'm standing at the bottom of the ladder that ascends into the attic. Jack's halfway inside of the opening in our ceiling, shining a flashlight as he looks around before going all the way up. I'm trying not to stare up at him, because in all honesty, there's nowhere else to look but at his ass. Which is being hugged quite nicely by his light washed jeans, might I ass—err—add.

"Well?" He's awfully quiet. I mean, he's only been there for a solid two minutes, but I'm growing increasingly anxious.

He remains silent.

I'm getting antsier, switching from one foot to the other as he takes another step upwards, into the attic.

"Shit!" he curses, his legs slightly bending as if he was startled by something.

The movement, coupled with his swear, makes me jump, a surprised shriek coming out unintentionally. "What?" I yelp, backing away from the ladder. "What is it?"

"It's fine. It's fine." Jack's laughing as he cranes his neck to look down at me under the arm he's using to brace himself on either side of the opening. "I just saw claw marks on the wall right here."

"Claw marks?" I practically scream, backing up even farther. I knew it. This house is haunted. Someone died in the attic or something, and they want to kill me. "What the fuck kind of claw marks?"

"Animal claws, Eliza," Jack answers, still laughing. He disappears into the attic, and I wait, impatiently, at the bottom. It's eerily silent except for the gentle thuds of his shoes. His steps are deliberate as I hear him approach the opening again. He doesn't say a word when he steps down the ladder and gently closes it so as not to make any noise.

"Uh, okay." I furrow my brow at him. "Did it curse you into silence? What was it?"

"You have raccoons." His reply is simple, and he clicks the flashlight off, turning to me with a shrug. "I can get them out without hurting them, but they are definitely there."

"Raccoons? More than one?" I wish it were a ghost. Nova would be ecstatic, my little lover of all creatures. I, however, stick to regular, domesticated animals. Or ones that *I* think should be domesticated. The rest terrify me.

Jack grins at me, folding his arms across his chest. "I need to go see two patients today, and then the rest, my partner can handle. I'll come back to take care of our friends. Deal?"

I glance up at the attic, shuddering at the thought of them scurrying around while I sleep. "Okay, deal." I exhale dramatically. "Thank you so much."

"Now, if I remove them and you hear those noises again ..." he trails off, holding his hands up, "we need to call a priest."

"Go away." I laugh, pushing him as he turns to walk away from me.

———

I was awake most of the night with Simone, trying to finish the birthday prep after spending all day building the reading nook for Nova in the backyard. And I've been up since an ungodly hour, making cupcakes. Oh, I didn't mention I've received a call that the inflatable water slide I ordered was double booked, so it had to be canceled. And to top it off, I still have animals living in my attic. Jack said it would take time to get them out because it's a mother and her young.

He set an unusual odor loose to disturb the momma and get her to retreat. He also looked through the attic to see where possible entrances were. Once he shut them all off, except one for them to leave through, he closed the attic door and told me to wait.

And even after spending most of the day helping me with my damn household chores, he stayed to help Simone and me build the roof to Nova's treehouse. Which, by the way, turned out amazing—I just need to put in the pillows and add the rug to complete it before she gets home.

Despite my feeling like I've used the guy for the past twenty-four hours, I still text him to ask for recommendations on any other bounce house companies to order a water slide from. He graciously says he'll call around. I shouldn't let him, but I'm too tired to argue.

I drag the rolled-up rug outside and climb the ladder, spreading it out on the floor before going back in for pillows. Simone meets me at the door, with the cushions already in hand, showered, and ready for the party while I'm still in my pajamas.

"Any luck on water slides?" she asks, handing over two large pillows before walking outside with me, two in her arms as well.

I sigh as we walk, shaking my head before climbing the ladder. "No, but Jack said he'd call around for me. He'll call me if he finds anything."

"I'm sorry, is Jack a superhero?" Simone laughs, handing the cushions up to me as I reach down for them. I laugh as well because it honestly seems like it. And he does it all without expecting anything in return. Like I said before—he pisses excellence.

Organizing the pillows takes me all of ten seconds, and I grin when I see the outcome of the adorable little private area for Nova. I climb back down the ladder and dust my hands and pants off. "Yeah, he's pretty damn perfect. I need to remember to do something for him as a thank you for all his help. Including all the cow-raising lessons for Nova."

Simone wiggles her eyebrows, bumping her hip to mine as we walk. "I'm sure I can think of the perfect thank you," she teases, her tone suggestive. What a horn dog, I swear.

"Okay, no." I laugh, shaking my head. "He's been a really good friend to us. That's it. Friend. You are so dead-set on me screwing him."

"Eliza." Simone groans, dragging my name out with every syllable. "Have you seen that man? He is sex on a stick."

"Then, you screw him!" I suggest, but then immediately want to take it back. *No.* Please, no. Bringing sex into this would ruin the friendship I'm building.

She's shaking her head anyway, crossing her arms over her chest. "See, that's the thing. He's absolutely beautiful, but I don't get a vibe when I'm around him. My lady bits don't get excited. They do, however, get excited when I see him get all flirty with you."

"Well, that's something we should probably discuss," I tease, ignoring her comment about his flirtation. People flirt. It's healthy and fun, but it doesn't mean you should mate, for crying out loud.

An annoyed groan escapes her lips. I give her a look, and she reluctantly drops it, admiring the yard set up with tables, chairs, and teal balloons everywhere. "Why don't you go shower and get dressed? I'll be on phone duty to see if Jack calls," she says, instead, changing the subject, much to my satisfaction.

She's also right. I need a shower. I nod and hand my phone over to her before walking inside and heading toward my bathroom.

I pull my still-partially-damp hair into a messy ponytail and apply a light coat of makeup before throwing on the clothes I laid out the night before. When I walk through the kitchen to go back outside, I see Simone and Jack through the window, spreading a rather large tarp where the waterslide was supposed to go.

I walk down the porch steps, looking at the stacked boxes of slip n' slides and water hose attachments that produce sprinklers for the kids to jump through. "What's all this?" I ask with a smile.

"Well," Jack begins, walking over to me after the tarp is stretched tightly and staked to the ground. "Unfortunately, it was too last-minute to get a replacement slide. But I bought two slip n' slides and brought this big-ass tarp and a shit ton of soap to make it extra slippery. Don't worry, I made sure to get soap that won't irritate the eyes."

My gaze goes to Simone, who's giving me a look that can only be explained as: *just friends, my ass*. I quickly direct my attention back to him, ignoring the triumphant look on my friend's face.

Though, I honestly cannot believe he did all of this for Nova.

I shake my head with a smile and look around before

picking up a box to help set up. "I have some cash inside to pay you back. You're a genius."

"I used to play for hours with a tarp, a water hose, and soap. They'll have just as much fun," he unnecessarily defends, ignoring my offer as he pulls bottles from a plastic bag.

"For sure," I agree, grinning while I unfold the slide from the box I set on the ground. "This is so great. Thank you so much, Jack. Seriously, you really have been the biggest help."

Jack brushes me off, setting everything up for when the kids start arriving. "Don't mention it. I checked out the treehouse when I got here. It looks great. She's going to be so excited."

"I think she would have liked a cow more."

He laughs at that and shrugs his shoulders, glancing over at the tree before looking back at me. "Nah, she'll be so excited about it that she won't even think about cows."

We both know that's a lie, but I appreciate it anyway.

Birthday. Parties. Are. Exhausting.

Even after all the kids have grabbed their goodie bags and jumped in their parents' car, you still have the worst job of all—cleaning up the tornado they left behind.

Aaron's parents, Gail and Henry, who never miss an event, are currently cleaning up the kitchen, insisting I take a break.

I love them.

Not only have they treated me as their own since day one, but they bring another piece of Aaron back to me every time they come around.

Despite their wishes, I'm folding up the tarp in the front yard with Jack as Simone clears off the trash and leftovers on the tables where kids devoured cupcakes and ice cream. I walk my side of the tarp to him, and we meet in the middle. He's quietly concentrating, his eyes on the corners as he aligns them perfectly and takes it out of my hands. We briefly lock gazes, and I smile at him before turning to pick up the rest of the materials.

The slides were a brilliant idea—literally three hours of pure entertainment for everyone at the party. And, bonus for me, no injuries! I mean, there was one scraped knee, but I still count that as a win. The kid didn't even flinch. She stood back up and ran to the top of the slight hill to slide again.

I carefully fold the slip n' slide back into its original packaging, which is damn near impossible, and glance up to see Jack already loading the tarp back into his truck. When he turns to walk back toward me, his shirt is damp and clinging to his abdomen.

My tongue feels too big for my mouth.

Simone got in my head.

I quickly pack the soap into a box to carry inside. I can feel the heat from my face, so I can only imagine the shade of red on display.

Gail is in the kitchen, over the sink with a dish in one hand and a soapy sponge in the other. I set the box down on the counter and slide over to her, glancing around for Henry as I do.

"You know you don't have to wash dishes, right?" I attempt, knowing it's fruitless.

She glances up at me with twinkling eyes but shakes her head as she rinses off the plate. "You know I like to keep busy."

"I know," I respond with a grin, putting the dried dishes away to help her. It's quiet in the house for now, which isn't common with three loud females and a vocal dog. I knew Nova wouldn't hang around once her party was over. When the last guest left, she couldn't contain herself any longer. She got dressed, grabbed a book, and headed to her new treehouse.

Success.

She didn't even mention a cow.

Gail turns the water faucet off and faces me, leaning back against the counter as she does. She smiles and dries her hands on the towel beside her. "Jack seems very nice. Henry enjoyed his company today, and he's great with Nova."

I narrow my eyes slightly and nod slowly, turning to put away the glass pitcher in my hand. "Yeah, we like having him around." I'm careful with my words. I feel like I'm stepping over landmines.

"Well, he's a keeper," she replies, her voice warm.

If I jump on the defensive, she'll think there is something between us. If I don't acknowledge that she's implying we're an item, she will continue to think so. I'm stuck here. I decide to simply nod at her statement, smiling back at her. "Yeah. Friends like him are hard to come by." *Friends*, Gail.

Gail hesitates, a knowing smirk on her lips as she turns away from me again. "Mhm," she hums, turning the water back on to finish scrubbing the silverware.

Cool, so I'm not safe outside, because of Mr. Wet-T-shirt-Contest, and I'm not safe inside, because my mother-in-law is trying to participate in girl-talk about said man. Maybe I should go to the nook with Nova.

"Eliza, can I get your help?" I hear from the back

porch and smile, relieved to hear Simone's voice cut through the golf game on the television in our living room.

Ever the savior, she is.

I'm finally able to crawl into bed around eleven. As soon as I melt into my sheets, I hear my raccoon ghosts. I look up at the ceiling and sigh, slamming my head back into my pillow in annoyance. They better be scurrying around up there because they're looking for a way out.

This is probably a bad idea, but I pick up my phone anyway. I let my fingers hover over the keyboard once I open up a new text to send to Jack: *How long did you say it would be until these squatters gtfo?*

It's only after I send the text that I feel a little odd about it. Does texting after a certain time mean you're looking for a booty call? Are those the rules? I seriously don't know.

My screen lights up.

Jack: *It'll be a few days. Lol. I'm sorry. And I'm leaving the day after tomorrow for a camping trip. So I'll check in when I get back.*

A camping trip? What if that smell he released is supposed to kill them? What do I do with dead animals? I panic and quickly type a reply: *Wait. You're going to be gone? What do I do when they die?*

Jack: *Hahaha. They're not going to die. The smell is going to make them retreat. They'll be gone by the time I get back, I promise.*

That eases some of my anxiety, but I still don't want to go two more days with live animals known for carrying rabies, running above me every night. Before I can even reply to his texts, I get another one.

Jack: *Hey, why don't you, Simone, and Nova come along? A few of my friends are joining me. Dad and Pop are watching CeCe. They can watch Chief, too.*

I feel my heart beat faster at his question, and I honestly don't know what the cause is. I haven't gone camping in years, so that could have something to do with it. But, also, Simone is going to be at a conference in New York, and Nova is leaving for the week as well. It would be just ... Jack and me.

I wait a moment before responding: *That sounds so fun! Thank you for inviting us. Unfortunately, Simone will be out of town, and Nova, too. She's spending a week with her grandparents.*

Jack: *That's too bad. But you could still come. If you wanted.*

There goes that unpredictable heart, beating wildly against my chest. I stare at the phone a moment longer when another text comes through.

Jack: *But, of course, don't feel pressured. It would be fun, though.*

He's right. It *does* sound fun. I would have to find a sitter for Chief because I feel too guilty throwing him off on Matthew and David. But this would be good for me. I can move around my appointments and take a much-needed break. In nature.

With Jack.

Without thinking about it more, I send: *Okay. I'm in. Let me get some stuff in order. Thanks :)*

I watch my phone, awaiting his reply. I sure hope he wasn't just being friendly with extending this invitation.

Jack: *Yes! All right, cool. I'm excited. Let's talk more tomorrow.*

God, that's one thing I really like about Jack. He doesn't hide what he's feeling and isn't afraid it makes him look desperate or eager. He simply says it. I send him a quick message before putting my phone up and rolling over to sleep. *Sounds great. Night!*

6

It's a four-hour drive to the campsite, so I'm not exactly sure why Jack wants us to leave at four-thirty in the morning, but we do. On the ride over, I learn exactly four essential facts about Jack.

One, he is very much a morning person. Not only can he easily wake up at any hour without complaint, but he also *enjoys* it. He's chipper and chatty in the wee hours of the day, and I am most definitely *not*.

Two, he makes quite possibly the best coffee I have ever had. I don't know what he uses, or how many scoops he puts in one pot, but the second that elixir of life touched my tongue, I was a changed woman. It was also extremely thoughtful of him to bring a thermos for me.

Three, he *loves* nineties hits. I'm not complaining, because I am also a huge fan of them. It just surprised me. You have this gruff farmboy, who drives a Bronco and jams out to Counting Crows.

Four, Jack doesn't talk much about himself—always asking me about my life and my thoughts, but rarely giving his own. I guess that's why I try to hoard away all the little tidbits I learn about him.

When we arrive, I'm focused on my phone. I didn't receive a text from Simone, letting me know she got safely to her hotel. I try not to let it bother me, and keep the intrusive thoughts pushed to the back of my mind.

Is she safe?

Did the plane land?

Did she get in the right Lyft?

I have to swallow the bubble of irrational panic and force myself to not text her again.

Once we've secured the tents and set our campsite up, we decide to fish for a few hours. It was then that I got the apologetic message from Simone, assuring me she was in her room. I could relax.

Jack and I haven't talked much, sitting on the bank with our lines cast. This is the only day we will spend just the two of us before a couple of his friends join us for the next two, and it's comfortable—especially since I've calmed my internal worries.

I'm relieved to have phone service out here. It helps me keep up with how my girls are. I know Nova is safely with her grandparents after checking in, but I get nervous when she's away for too long.

I feel a jerk on my line, and I perk up, clutching onto the pole to secure it. "Oh!" I squeal, excitedly, standing up to sturdy myself. "I have a really big bite."

"Okay." Jack pops up as well, standing to the side in case I need him. I appreciate the fact that he isn't trying to take over. I love my dad, but that's something he would do. "Carefully reel him in. Don't jerk, but reel fast."

"Lot of rules, Peters," I mutter, frantically, adrenaline

pumping through my veins. The fish is so strong that it's possible I am reeling in a fucking alligator. "Fast or careful, pick one."

Jack chuckles but stays where he is. "You can do both, just don't jerk until you get closer to the bank, okay?"

His gentle coaching is sweet, but I'm breaking an unnecessary sweat over this fish. It better be huge. "Okay, I need your help." I grunt a little, feeling like the pole is going to slip from my hands.

Jack is behind me in a matter of seconds, his arms coming around and grabbing the pole as well, pulling it back as I reel. "Shit, it is heavy," he says, his mouth next to my temple as he helps me.

I am not too focused on this catch to notice the warmth of his body against my back. He's worked up a sweat since we got here, and smells like a mix between fresh-cut grass and a quick, soapless shower after a workout. It's distracting.

We get the fish closer to the bank, and he does a swift count before jerking it up. The momentum causes me to stumble backwards slightly, falling against his solid chest. He doesn't even budge. He's a brick wall.

A warmth spreads through my stomach. My pulse is rapid like heavy raindrops.

He laughs, a light chuckle, and wraps one arm around my waist, making sure I don't fall to the ground, but his other is still secure on the pole. His muscles are twitching as he tries to control it with little help from me, as I'm currently losing my balance and all. I struggle to stand up as we lower the pole to the ground, and Jack works on unhooking the large trout from the line.

Are my legs weak?

"Damn, Liza," Jack exclaims with a grin, glancing up at me. *Liza.* I like the sound of that coming from his lips. Surprisingly, I don't know if anyone has ever called me that. Lizzie was a nickname from Aaron, and I was so adamant about being Eliza to everyone else that no one ever shortened it. Simone calls me E sometimes, but never Liza. And it came so effortlessly to him—like he's been calling me that his entire life.

What are you doing to my senses?

I walk over to him to get a look at the catch. It is quite large. I'm pretty damn proud of myself—even if I needed Jack's assistance bringing it in. "Wow, that is a big fish."

"Hell yeah, it is." He laughs, picking it up to take it to the ice chest we brought. "It's a Rainbow Trout. It's got to be at least ten pounds."

"I caught a big fish!" I'm overly excited and unable to help it. "I mean—*we* caught a big fish."

Jack shakes his head in disagreement, closing the ice chest's lid before walking back over to check his pole. "No way. You did that. I just helped you reel it in. That's nothing."

"Okay, well, now I have to catch *all the fish*." I pick up my pole to bait it again. It's become a sport to me. I cast my line back into the lake and smile over at Jack, reaching beside me to take a swig of my water.

He laughs, re-casting his line as well but to a different spot. "It's a little addicting once you catch your first fish of the day."

"Do you fish a lot?" I ask him, holding the pole in my lap as I look out at the horizon. It's beautiful out here, and the weather is perfect. There's a slight overcast, which makes it bearable, but it's warm, and there's still sunlight glistening against the waves of the lake.

"I used to fish more than I do now. I miss it," he replies, glancing over to me as he does. "I'll probably start coming more. We went a lot when I was a kid. Family camping trips were bi-annual for years."

I feel a small jerk on my pole and start to reel, lifting slightly to see that whatever it was, took the bait and ran. I bring it in to re-bait it. "What happened to that?"

"Life," he answers, simply, and I immediately get it. "When I went to college, it became a rarity, and then in Vet school, it was damn near impossible for our schedules to align. Then we fell into a habit of wanting to schedule time for it, but never doing it."

"Camping with Matthew and David sounds like it would be a blast." I throw my line out a little farther to the right. "Why didn't they come?"

Jack's smile is warm at my comment, and he nods in agreement, taking a sip of his water bottle. "They're the best, for sure. But Pop is worrying about the tree crop right now, for some reason. So, he said they'll come next time. He wants to keep an eye on it."

"Oh." I'm unsure how to follow that up with questions. I know nothing about gardening. Not a damn thing. Simone keeps wanting a garden, and I know I will inevitably kill whatever we plant. "Are you worried?"

"No," he answers, simply, chuckling. "Pop can be a bit irrational about his crops. He sees one little peculiarity and thinks the entire crop will be ruined. Dad and I learned not to fight him on it. I'm sure it will be okay."

Jack's plastic buoy sinks into the water, and the end of his pole dips down, signaling a fish on the hook. He stands up to reel it in and effortlessly brings it to land. Not to be a braggart or anything, but my fish was bigger. He takes it off the hook and tosses it in the ice chest.

Once he slides another worm onto the hook, he tosses the line out and smiles over at me. "Not a ten-pounder, that's for sure."

"Don't be so hard on yourself. You'll work your way up to it." I grin, teasing him as I look back at my line.

His laugh echoes at my comment, and a blush rises to my cheeks. Why do I get so much pleasure in making him laugh? He's not a stoic man, but he's known to be quiet around strangers. I've seen him in social outings, smiling at genuinely funny things, but barely breaking into a chuckle. It's almost a challenge to get a full-body laugh out of him. But I do it so easily. I take odd pride in that.

"Eliza, I think you have something." He breaks me out of my trance.

I jump up, getting ready to reel in another big one. But this one is a little easier, coming in without much force. It's smaller when I pull it out of the water, and I glance over at Jack, a satisfied smile on my face.

"Two to one," I state, walking over to put the fish in the ice chest, with the others. When I look back at him, his eyebrow is raised, a smirk on his lips.

Oh, man. That smirk is dangerous. How many women have undressed themselves at the mere sight of it?

"You've done it now. I love a challenge." His voice is a little husky. Okay, cool. That didn't make my stomach pinch in the best way or anything.

I quickly bait my line again and join him to catch a third.

"So, Penny is your biological mother?"

"Yeah. It was hard for my dads to adopt in the eighties,

you know? Aunt Penny never wanted kids of her own, and still doesn't to this day. She loves me, but she knows I'm her nephew—not her son. She did the artificial-insemination thing. Pop is my biological father."

"That's why you look so much like Matthew *and* David." I'm excited to finally crack the code. With Penny being David's sister, and Matthew being Jack's biological father, the resemblance makes so much more sense.

He laughs at my enthusiasm and nods, baiting his hook to throw it back into the lake. We've had no problem with awkward silences. Both of us know how to fill a void. I ask way too many questions, and he answers them at length.

"If you didn't know your biological mom, do you think you'd want to find her?" It's a deeper question than the ones he's already been fielding, but there's a reason for it. A selfish one, admittedly.

He hesitates for a moment, looking out onto the water with an easy expression. When he looks back at me, he shrugs with a smile. "You know, I don't know. My instinct is to say yes. I would wonder about her, but it wouldn't be because I didn't love my dads. Some people are different, of course. I just have a curious mind."

"So does Nova. I'm always worried I'm not doing enough. She's asked about her biological parents one time, but she never said she wanted to meet them. Of course, I'll keep the door open for her. I just don't know if I should be doing more. Should I encourage her to seek them out?"

He looks over at me, making sure our eyes meet. "Look, my situation is different, but I say don't push her. She knows she's adopted, and if you've been open with her before, she knows she can come to you if she wants to meet them. Make it clear to her that it's her choice. That's all any kid can ask for—a parent that lets them have a say."

"I appreciate that," I begin, breaking our gaze to stare out at the glistening water in front of us. My shoulders fall in a sigh. "I don't know if I'll ever feel like I do the parenting thing well. When we adopted Nova, Aaron and I had a plan. We were going to tackle the hard stuff together and pick up each other's slack where we needed to. Now, for the most part, I'm doing it alone."

The warmth in Jack's voice catches me off guard but soothes me in an unexpected way. "She's a great kid, Eliza. I think you've got the parenting thing on lock."

"I don't know." I hear the catch in my voice and pause, swallowing down the bubble of emotion that appeared. "Nova is so innocent, and I have to teach her about all the unfair hardships she is going to have as a woman in our society. And as if that isn't hard enough, there are things she has to face that I never had to face because she's Black. I have to teach her about a level of protection she needs that I never needed." The familiar feeling of breathlessness takes over, and I close my eyes. "I can't lie. I would be lost without Simone—for more than one reason. I am *so* thankful for the things Nova and I *both* learn from her."

Jack is silent next to me for a beat before speaking. "What makes you a great mother is that you know what Nova needs. You know that there are things you can't relate to and things you have to learn. You know she *needs* Simone in her life. That's big. Not many white people can recognize they can't *be* everything. And a little girl raised by you and Simone? What an unstoppable force."

That uneasiness in my stomach is hard to settle, despite his encouraging words.

Our eyes meet, and my grateful smile is met with a knowing nod. "I do think she's pretty kick-ass," I say, thoughts of Nova always weighing heavily on my mind. If I think it brings *me* pain, I can't imagine what Simone and Nova have to face. I never will.

He turns back toward the view with a soft smile and casts his line again. "That, she is."

A silence falls between us, and it's comforting. It's not awkward or tense but, instead, *knowing*. He understands.

A tug on my line disappears before I can reel it in. I glance over at Jack's concentrated features. "I can't even imagine living on your farm my whole childhood. In that incredible home? How did you ever leave?"

His grin brightens his face, and he shrugs a shoulder. "I didn't appreciate it until I left, to be honest. My own house is fine. It's enough, but it's nothing like what I grew up in. Which is why I've been drafting plans to build."

"Build your own house? As enormous as your dads'?" My voice has reached an unrecognizable octave in my excitement.

"God, no. Not as big as that one, but pretty big. I can show you the plans later. I have pictures on my phone. I inherited some land, and I'm hoping to break ground in the fall and, you know, maybe be in come spring."

"I didn't realize you were doing all of that. That's amazing." I watch him for a moment. Why is there something so hot about a man with his shit together? He gives me a barely visible smile before taking another long sip of his drink.

The fish count is twelve to nine—I'm kicking his ass. We've been at this for five hours, but the overcast we had before is turning into actual dark clouds. I glance up when a low rumble erupts in the sky, and then look over to Jack.

He turns his head to me and winces, picking up his phone that has been lying face down by his feet. "It wasn't supposed to rain until we were already asleep," he mumbles.

A cool drop falls on my forehead, dripping down my nose before I swipe at it. "Well, it looks like it's coming a little early."

"Come on." He stands up and gathers our gear.

The rain is falling at a quicker pace, and I'm scurrying to get to my tent while Jack is going at a much more leisurely pace—the rain not bothering him.

I crawl inside the tent and look down at my damp clothes, shivering at the wind blowing against the unzipped entry. I close it up and dig through my bag for something dry, the air cooling my wet skin. Jack's finally nearing; I hear him unzip his tent and shuffle inside.

"You must be soaked!" I call over to him, stripping off my tank top that's sticking to my skin. I change into a cotton sports bra and throw a loose long-sleeve shirt over my head before pulling dry gym shorts over my legs.

He doesn't respond, but then I hear him mutter a string of curse words that eloquently flow together. A pause. Then, "I'm sorry, Eliza. It looks like it's going to be like this for a couple of hours."

His sincerity tugs at the corners of my mouth. "Don't apologize. You didn't bring the rain in."

I hear a heavy sigh across from me, and I lean back against the pillows I stacked in the corner of my tent. With all the confidence I can muster, I blurt, "So, which one of us is going to brave the rain to join the other? I will say, I have a deck of cards over here."

"That's very hard to turn down." I hear the smile in his voice.

"My tent is also just a little bit bigger than yours."

He chuckles, and I hear him exit his tent. I crawl over to let him in, unzipping it all the way down, but holding it up until I see his shadow. He quickly jumps in, shaking off the rain that dampened his hair, making his tousled curls stick to his forehead.

I wince at the droplets that fling across my cheek and wipe them away with a smirk. His movements are quick as he shuts the flap and turns to me, hunched over. He's carefully taking off his shoes, squatting down to a sitting position—which, in all honesty, is the only way to move around in a tent.

Once we're both settled, legs crossed in front of us, knees almost touching, I pull out the deck and wave it in my hand.

"Speed?" I ask him, referencing an old card game I'd play with my dad to pass the time on dreary days.

His eyes light up, and he grins. "I haven't played that in years."

"Let's do this, then." I'm so dramatic. I take the cards out and shuffle them, taking my time and trying to look professional as I do it. I only have so many skills, and I rarely get to showcase them.

The game starts off slow, both of us getting the hang of it again. Before too long, our hands are flying and loudly slapping against the stacks. I try to throw him off, asking him random personal questions to see if he will slip up. But he's good. He answers, without missing a beat. He shoots one back at me, and I'm not as coordinated.

Jack's eyes never leave the war zone between us. "Childhood movie you watched way too much."

No hesitation. "*It Takes Two*."

"Never heard of it." It's a quick comment that, I guess, I'm supposed to ignore. But that's not going to happen. Never *heard* of it? Blasphemy.

"Pause." I demand it, and he stops, his eyes lifting to mine. "You've never heard of *It Takes Two*?"

His concentrated features soften, his lip twitching, fighting to stay neutral. "The name doesn't ring a bell. I may have seen it and just not remember it."

"Well, that's impossible." An annoyed huff escapes my lips without permission. "Mary-Kate and Ashley, Kirstie Alley, the guy from *Three Men and a Baby*?" I'm trying to pull the memory from his brain, but his brow is still furrowed.

"Tom Selleck?"

I scoff. "No. God. Uh, *Police Academy*."

He briefly nods, his face mimicking amusement at my aggravation. "Steve Guttenberg."

"Yes! Guttenberg! So, do you remember the movie now?" I'm enthusiastically hopeful, which only makes his amusement grow, producing a low chuckle that sends a current through my body.

"No. I have no idea what this movie is."

That movie was watched so many times in my house that I ruined the VHS tape. It's decided. He has to see it. "Well, we need to fix that. Movie night at my house, no objections. Nova loves it, so she'll be pleased to introduce it to you."

Jack leans back, adjusting the position he's been in for the last fifteen minutes at least. "Okay, okay, wait. What do I get out of this arrangement?"

"Men are so entitled. You get an evening with me and Nova. Is that not enough for you?"

He flashes a grin and rolls his eyes at my comment, nodding at the game between us. "That is not what I'm saying," he begins, getting back into it. I hastily catch up, eyeing the cards in my hand and placing them in their rightful stack. "I'm saying, I'm sure there are some movies from my childhood you and Nova haven't seen. I'm offering a double feature."

Four cards at once! Score. I pull from the spare deck and shrug a shoulder at his offer. Honestly, I love the idea. But I need to bluff—make it look like this deal is a tough one to make. "What movie?"

"*Mighty Ducks*."

"Seen it."

"*The Little Giants*."

"Puh-*lease*." I make sure my eye roll is pronounced when we lock gazes before going back to the task at hand.

His laughter turns into a groan when he sees I'm running out of cards faster than he is. "Uh." He's distracted by the game. "*Camp Nowhere*."

I stay silent, our showdown intense, racing to be the last one to drop the final card down. I let the title sit in my brain for a brief second, realizing it doesn't sound familiar at all. After dropping my last card with a triumphant *whoop!*, I take a relaxing breath, letting the tension roll out of my shoulders. Boy, I am competitive. "I have not seen that one. Double feature, it is."

It seems Jack is slightly competitive, too, because he's already shuffling the deck for another game. A bright flash surrounds our tent, followed by a distant rumble in the sky. Might as well play again.

"Perfect. Tell me the date and time, and I'll be there."

"I'll keep you posted." He splits up the deck, dealing the cards out evenly between us and setting up for the next round. We fall into a rhythm, the game starting out slow and building momentum. I can barely stand the quiet, and I want to attempt to break his concentration again.

"Favorite band."

"Too many to name." He quickly retorts, unfazed and throwing a seven of diamonds over my six of hearts before drawing from the stack again.

Grinning, I lay down three cards in one swoop, but shake my head at his answer. "You have to pick one."

He's silent for a moment, gracefully putting down five cards at once before smirking up at me, his eyes mischievous. He draws a few more from his stack to make up for the lack thereof in his hand. "All right, fine," he mutters, his concentration strong. "CCR."

"Shut up." I'm laughing, unable to help it—oh, man, he is so deliciously predictable it hurts. "I am not judging, I swear. That's a solid choice. It's just so on-brand for you."

His face is lowered, still quickly ridding himself of the cards, but I can see the upward curve of his mouth at my teasing. "But my favorite song is *One Headlight* by The Wallflowers."

"*One Headlight*? Really?" I laugh without taking my eyes off the game in front of me. "You mean like ..." I begin to sing the chorus, quite off-key, mind you.

It causes him to chuckle, the sound rumbling deep in his throat before turning into full-blown laughter when I continue the chorus.

Loudly.

I finish, holding the last note for a little too long because I like the way his laughter sounds. I laugh as well, watching him lean his head back and smile at the ceiling of the tent.

"Yes, that song." He's grinning when he looks back at me, shaking his head and wiping at the corner of his eye.

"Okay." I nod, catching my breath though the tears in his eyes are making that difficult. "Well, that was unexpected. Great song, though. I approve."

"All right, you have to answer now." Our game has stopped after taking another time-out since he couldn't hold it together.

I set my cards down with a smile. "That's easy." I shrug. "Train."

"Can't blame you there. I think I overplayed *Drops of Jupiter* when it first came out."

I'm beaming at that admission because, honestly, so did I. "Train is fantastic, but mainly their older stuff. I met Aaron at a Train concert in college. They were in the lineup for this spring festival. What's funny is he actually hated Train and was only there to casually run into a girl from his biology class that he had a crush on. But he met me."

"No one else stood a chance, I guarantee it," Jack teases, but it's genuine. It makes my heart flutter against my chest. It also feels nice to talk to someone about my memories of Aaron without getting a sympathetic smile. Even Simone is bad about *the look.*

"That's how he told the story, at least."

I feel Jack's eyes on me, but mine are focused on the abandoned cards between us. I pick up my hand and shuffle through it, putting it in a sort-of order.

"Can I ask you how he died?" The question is quiet, calculated, and gentle. He doesn't want to overstep, but he's curious. And I can't fault him for that. Curiosity is human.

That doesn't mean it's any easier to discuss.

"Of course." I feel as though I've exhaled all the breath in my lungs when I look up at him. "Sorry, it's always weird to talk about. Aaron being gone, I mean."

I'm making it uncomfortable, and the tent feels smaller. I feel suffocated.

"Pancreatic cancer." I'm quick with my words, swallowing the large lump in my throat. "It took him really fast. Within months of his diagnosis, actually."

Jack's face has twisted into a pained expression, his eyebrows drawn, and his mouth painted in a noticeable frown. *That look.* Dammit, that look has always crushed me. I can't explain it. It's like pity, but more than that. Like they're getting a taste of the pain I've felt, and I can see it in their eyes. And that look shows me what I looked like in the months after his death. I don't like seeing it.

"That's a really tough hand to be dealt, Eliza. I'm sorry."

I never know what I expect people to say after we discuss Aaron, but Jack's voice is so sincere that it calms the anxiety rising in my chest. I smile, pushing my ponytail behind my shoulder to get it off my sweat-dampened neck. "Thank you. It's been hard. I know I need to do counseling, and Simone has been really pushing me on it. I plan on making an appointment this week."

"Yeah? I think it's great that you're being proactive in that. Mental health is extremely important."

"I think it will open me up a little more and help me eventually move on. I just can't right now. And it's not that I don't think I could ever love someone again, because I know I could. I'm just not in the headspace for it."

My hands are resting on my knees that are still bent into a pretzel underneath me. He reaches forward and places his on top of mine. My stomach flips at the sudden contact—the sweet gesture shooting right into my soul.

"There's no timeline, okay? I know I've told you this before, but I need you to hear it again." He's saying what I already know, but it's comforting coming from his mouth. "Look, it's been seven months since my wedding, and I still haven't made it a point to date. I know I said I was just trying to stay away from the drama, but I really haven't wanted to put myself out there. I'm open to it, but it's not a priority."

We're quiet for a moment, but our gazes are locked. I break eye contact first and look down, taking a deep breath. I meet his eyes again. "I'm glad I met you."

"Me, too." Jack grins, squeezing my fingers. He removes his hand after that, so fast it's almost as if it were never there, and looks down at the card game that's messed up from our feet unintentionally kicking the stacks loose.

"My turn for a tough question?" I'm hesitant, but I don't know why. Jack has made it clear he's an open book.

He gives me a quick nod, reaching down to straighten what we messed up.

"Have you talked to Gwen since the wedding?"

"No." The answer is short and paired with a firm shake of his head. He glances up at me and sighs, his lips in a tight line. "You know, it's weird, but I sometimes forget you witnessed that. It's like you're two different people to me. The awkward make-up artist who got a front-row seat to my heartbreak, and then Eliza, my friend." He gives a mirthless chuckle and runs a hand through his hair before continuing. "So, anyway, Gwen wanted me to forgive her, and I do now. But, at the time, it seemed impossible. She didn't *want* to get married, and after you left the room and I pushed her a little more, it became apparent she wanted to be with Steven. He's my cousin, by the way. We haven't talked since. I don't feel it's necessary."

"Your cousin?" It comes out of my mouth before I can stop it, my eyes wide at this information. "Oh man, that's rough. Will you have to see her at family events?"

Jack laughs at, I'm sure, the look on my face and shakes his head. "We're not extremely close with that side of the family, so no."

A moment of silence hangs between us, and I have to break it.

"We're quite a pair, aren't we?"

He laughs again and leans back, stretching his arms above his head when he does. "Yeah, I think that's why we make good friends. Honestly, Gwen leaving me or, you know, admitting she cheated on me ..." He pauses and shrugs a shoulder. "It put me in a bad place for a couple of months. I felt bad about myself—like, I wasn't good enough. We had been together for years, and I had *no* clue."

It's my turn to feel that deep ache of sympathy. This beautiful man with the kindest eyes and patient soul, feeling less about himself because of someone else's actions?

"Well, that's not true. You're one of the best things this town brought us."

He lifts his head, looking back at me, the corners of his mouth barely turned, but it grabs me. It's sweet and honest and surprised. "Yeah?" He asks, his voice barely audible.

I nod, nudging his knee with mine to break up the potentially emotional moment between the two of us. "Of course, you goof."

Jack ducks his head down, but not before I catch a glimpse of the pink tint rising in his cheeks. He clears his throat and glances back up at me. "How about a game of Bullshit?"

"My specialty," I retort without missing a beat.

7

I think the raccoons are gone. Well, at least I can't hear them anymore. It's the first thing I checked upon getting back home. I sat on my bed for a solid fifteen minutes and listened. Silence.

Simone got back from her conference an hour ago and is insisting on a girls' night in to discuss my camping trip with Jack. She's going to be sorely disappointed to discover that we did *not* have sex in a tent. Her imagination runs wild when I don't rein her in.

I bring the large bowl of popcorn into the living room and place it between our two full wine glasses. She's already cozy beneath her favorite blanket, her feet tucked underneath her as she sits on her side of the couch. We have designated sides when Nova isn't here.

"When does the kiddo get back from your parents?" She asks this as she reaches forward and dives her hand into the bowl, grabbing a handful to pop in her mouth.

I take a large sip from my glass and lean back, pulling the knit blanket down from behind me and throwing it over my legs. "In two days. Mom is coming with her and staying for a few days as well."

"Oh, yay! Momma Mel!" Simone exclaims, grinning over at me. Yes, my mom is like another mother to her, especially after hers passed away when we were teens. However, my mom was never as hard on Simone as she was on me.

I narrow my eyes at my so-called best friend. "Every now and then, I would like you to note and appreciate the fact that four days with *Momma Mel* is not a walk in the park for me."

"She loves you."

"She's highly critical, and you know this."

Simone winces slightly because she does know this. She has a soft spot for my mom, and in all honesty, I do, too. She's not a bad person. She's just ... a lot. "Okay, you're right. I'm sorry. I will do everything I can to entertain her so you don't have to the entire time. I have a couple of scheduled days where I'm not on-call."

"I love you."

"I know." She smirks. "Now, tell me *everything*."

Instinctively, I roll my eyes, but I can't suppress my smile at her misplaced excitement. "Simone. Nothin—"

She cuts me off before I can finish. "I know you didn't have sex because you don't have the Eliza sex glow. But you can still fill me in on the other stuff."

I almost choke. I haven't heard her mention that ridiculous observation in *years*. Simone has always had this weird superpower where she can simply look at me and know I've recently been laid. Honestly, it's a gift.

I press my hand to my chest, trying to regain composure after almost dying by wine. "Okay, well, glad you still have your abilities. No, there was no sex. Or anything of that nature. We actually spent a lot of our time playing cards in my tent, though. The weather got bad. But, in all honesty, it was really fun, and I needed it."

I don't know why I'm keeping it to myself, that we fell asleep together after hours of talking about our families, funny college stories, and three rounds of twenty questions. Simone is my person. She's the one I would gush with about this stuff, but it feels weird. Jack isn't some hot guy I have a crush on. He's an actual friendship I cherish. I don't want to cheapen that.

"How you can spend hours in a small tent with him and nothing happen is beyond me, but I'm really glad you had a good time, E." Simone reaches forward and places her hand on mine, giving it a light squeeze. "You deserve it."

"Oh, he's also coming over next Friday. I discovered he's never seen *It Takes Two*, and that's a tragedy. We're going to have a movie night with Nova. You are more than welcome to join."

Simone raises an eyebrow before taking a sip of her wine. If I know her, and I do, that was to stifle the insinuating comment she had on the tip of her tongue. After a smooth sip and a smile, she shrugs a shoulder. "I'll have to check my calendar."

"Say what you want to say."

She's silent, staring right through me for the briefest moment. Then she shakes her head and places her wine glass back down on the table. "No. I love you, and I am very glad you've made a good friend. I am seriously only joking when I push you to sleep with Dr. Hottie."

I narrow my eyes at her, skeptical of this new perspective. But also relieved. "That's very big of you."

"I just like seeing you happy."

My heart swells. I turn on the couch so my back is facing her and then lie back, placing my head on her lap. I think about my conversation with Jack, about how grateful I am for this woman. "You're my favorite person. Well, besides my daughter. I hope you know that."

She looks down at me and laughs, nodding as she does. "Ditto, babe."

My mother has arrived in true Melonie Fitzgerald fashion—nitpicking every little thing she can. The cleanliness of my house (*Oh gosh, the dust is aggravating my sinuses.*), the blonde I put in my hair (*I wish you'd let your natural auburn hair grow out.*), and the breakfast I served to Nova (*Poptarts are not a proper breakfast food, Eliza.*).

I'm losing my mind.

Nova has decided she wants to attend the day camp three times a week at the local recreational center. Unfortunately, that means my Mondays off are not spent with her. That's already a bummer because I want more than Saturday and Sunday. But it's even worse this week because that's one day alone with Mom without a distraction. We spent the entire Monday planting flowers in my flower bed because *it looked tacky.*

Tuesday, I had to work. So, she spent the day with Simone.

Today, though, I'm taking half of the day off to entertain her.

Which is why I am currently sitting in my car after dropping Nova off and contemplating whether I want to go inside. This is ridiculous, I know. And I know I should appreciate a mom who wants to spend time with me and her granddaughter. I *know*. I just need a small breather.

I lean my seat back and close my eyes, exhaling a large breath to calm my nerves. Mom isn't awful. I had a happy childhood, and I didn't want for much. She paid for extracurricular activities, she kept me fed, and I always had new clothes. I should be grateful. And I am.

But she also watched my weight carefully, disapproved of almost every boyfriend I had, constantly asked me why I wasn't as ambitious as Simone, and questioned most of my life decisions—including how I raised Nova.

I take one more deep breath, tensing my entire body before relaxing one body part at a time. Ironically, this is something my mother taught me.

An unexpected tap on my window breaks my concentration, and I look up to see my mother peeking inside.

"What are you doing out here?" Her words are muffled by the window separating us, but I can still hear the irritation in her voice. Without answering, I position my seat upright and open the car door.

"Sorry. I had a headache. Just needed to lie back for a moment."

"Are you feeling better now? Do you need Tylenol?" Her tone is one of concern, and that makes me feel guilty for lying. But only slightly guilty. I never claimed to be a saint.

I place an arm around her shoulders as we walk toward the house. "I'm fine, Mom. I need to get dressed for work."

"You made a time slot for my hair appointment, right? I'm thinking of going a little drastic. Maybe cut off a few inches and put some layers in it."

I chuckle at her definition of "drastic."

"Yes, the appointment has been made. You're my first client of the day, so get dressed and follow me to the salon."

"Why don't I ride with you? You're off in four hours, anyway. I'm sure I can make myself busy after you do my hair."

Oh, boy.

"Sounds like a good plan." It's a miracle I held back a sigh.

The ride to the salon is filled with Mom chatting on the phone with my aunt, catching up on the last few days since they spoke. My aunt is notorious for not answering text messages, so they usually talk once a week to make up for that. We're almost to my shop when they say their goodbyes. I turn left onto Papaya Street, where my salon sits between a boutique and a locally owned sandwich shop.

"The shop needs a paint job, don't you think?" She's staring out the window as we pull into the back parking lot.

There it is.

I successfully suppress a pterodactyl screech.

I make a quick decision to let the comment roll off my back without reply, and I feel slightly powerful once I accomplish that.

As soon as we're inside, I grab a cape and lead her to my station to get to work on her roots. Luckily, she spots the ring on Claire's left hand and bombards her with questions about her engagement. So the attention is off of me.

I work in silence, smiling at Claire's gushing. She never gets tired of talking about her fiancé, Trevor. I can't blame her. He's an actual sweetheart—always bringing us lunch on Fridays. He wormed his way into my heart with a tuna melt from the competing deli across town.

I've got Mom at my station, dabbing the mixed dye to the top of her head and smoothing it down. Her drastic style consists of two inches off and added layers. Never one to be adventurous, she always wants a quick root touch-up to cover her grays. Nothing else.

My head habitually looks up to the door when our bell rings, letting us know of a new arrival.

My mood immediately lifts when I see Matthew, but falls slightly when I realize my inquisitive mother is in my chair. "Matthew, hi! What are you up to?"

"Hi, love." He walks straight over and places a kiss on my cheek. I love how affectionate he is—his husband and son are not open with their fondness. "I'm sorry I didn't call, but I am desperately needing a haircut. Apparently, some local nature magazine wants to interview me and David about our farm, and they're taking pictures! I have little to no notice."

"That's amazing! Of course. Let me get my mom to a stopping point." I glance at her through the mirror, and she has an expectant smile on her face.

Right. Manners and all.

"Mom?" Matthew exclaims, eyes wide and grin even wider. "I didn't know your mom was in town! She's got to join us for dinner. In fact, you should bring the whole family. I can make spaghetti. I know Miss Nova loves my spaghetti."

Oh, no. No, no, no. I keep my face as enthused as his, but my insides are dying at the thought of my mom intermingling with my life here. Is that awful? It is. I know.

"Mom, this is Matthew Peters. He's Jack's dad and a really good friend of ours."

The look she gives me warns of an upcoming intrusive conversation we will be having in the near future. "Well, I am so pleased to finally meet you, Matthew. I'm Melonie. Nova has spoken so much about you all and that beautiful farm. We would love to come for dinner!"

"How does tonight sound? I can have everything ready for 7:30. Don't bring a thing." He's so genuine, which makes everyone immediately adore him. David is more gruff, hard to get to know, but an absolute softy when you do. He and Matthew balance each other so well.

She briefly looks at me for confirmation and, without me even giving it, agrees. "We don't have any plans, so that sounds great. Will your son be there?"

"If I tell Jack that Eliza, Simone, and Nova are coming over, he will be there. I have no doubt." Matthew gives my mother a wink, and she smirks in response. It's aggravating—like when your mom and her best friend have a shared hope that you and their kid will get married and have babies. I feel like a lab rat thrown into a cage to mate.

He's pleased when his focus is back on me, and I'm trying my damndest to look as excited as they do. "Thanks for the invite, Matthew. We always love a good Peters' meal. Go on and sit in station five, and I'll come trim you up while mom's color sits."

"You're the best." He gives my mom's arm a friendly squeeze. "We just love your daughter so much."

Mom reaches behind her and places a hand on my wrist with a gentle pat. "I'm fond of her, too."

It's sweet. But as soon as I let my guard down even a little with her, I regret it. In small ways, but they stay with me. How many times do I have to say *she means well* before I stop making excuses? It's complex. I love her, but I know our limits.

In between getting her settled at the wash station and beginning Matthew's trim, I grab my phone and see a text.

Jack: *Spontaneous dinner plans?*

I need to send a text to Simone, too, and beg her to come.

Briefly, I reply: *Matthew met my mother. It was inevitable.*

Jack: *Not complaining. See you tonight.*

My face burns unexpectedly at his text, and I bite the inside of my cheek to stop myself from grinning at my phone.

"You should let them teach *you* how to milk a cow, Grams." Nova's rambling, her voice high and enthusiastic. She's all energy and hasn't stopped talking since we sat down for dinner. That tells me she's going to crash soon—and hard. "It's harder than it looks in the movies."

Don't get me wrong, I'm thankful for her abundance of conversation topics that help alleviate the tension between my mother and me. We left the house on a bit of a bad note when she decided to tell me she would do a better job choosing clothing that *fits me properly*.

At this point, we've been on the discussion of cows since Nova proudly informed my mom that the butter she was using to spread over her roll came from Delilah's family. That discussion started approximately fifteen minutes ago. No one else can get a word in, but the amused expressions on the men's faces tell me they don't mind a bit.

"Oh, goodness, sweet love, I think I'll leave the hard labor to you." I watch my mom as she grins adoringly at my daughter, rubbing her shoulder with an affection that was so rare to me. It would be easy for me to be envious of the relationship between her and Nova, but I'm not. I'm more thankful she's softened—well, at least to her.

"So, Melonie, I think Eliza has mentioned you own a few clothing stores, right?" The question came from Matthew after a long pause in the conversation due to my daughter shoving an entire overly buttered fresh roll into her mouth. Mom can be extremely particular about her line of work, but I am hoping she can answer gracefully, without that hoity-toity bite in her tone.

Her smile is genuine when she looks up from her plate and clasps her hands under her chin. "I own a chain of formal wear boutiques in three different locations. I don't specialize in suits or tuxes, but prom dresses, bridesmaid dresses, wedding gowns, etcetera. It's a fast-booming little business."

"How long have you had it?" The question comes from Jack after a long swig of his beer. He leans forward, impolitely bracing himself with his elbows on the table as he does. His forearms twitch, the movement of his muscle catching my eye. He looks like he'd be hard to the touch, and yet, a hug from him is as gentle as wrapping my arms around a Tempur-Pedic pillow.

My mother hums as she counts. "Eighteen years, I believe. You know, Eliza and Simone worked there through high school. They helped me keep the place afloat in my early years. Simone, my goodness, she had the best technique and attention to detail. She was steady and could sew a sequin or bead back on a bodice faster than anyone else. She had such an eye for it. It's no wonder she went in the medical field with that kind of precision—even if I would have given anything to have her be my full-time seamstress."

Simone snorts, the laughter sounding more like a choking inhale. I glance over to her with a smirk on my face, knowing her thoughts are close to mine: *No way in hell.*

"Eliza, however." My mother sighs, and I brace myself for the headache that will surface tonight due to clenching my jaw every time she begins a story with my name. "That girl was a handful and completely unpredictable. She was creative and energetic but kept my stress level to the damn roof."

"Oh, Mel," Simone cuts in, surprising us both. "If it weren't for Eliza, your business wouldn't have taken off as fast as it did. Sure, she was a little reckless, but she put your place on the map."

"Oh, yeah?" Jack perks up, his smile widening at this new information.

It makes my stomach twist.

David, who was previously too busy shoveling food in his mouth to speak, grins while wiping his lips. "A little reckless? Please, do tell."

"Okay, I mean, it wasn't *that* crazy or anything. So, at this time in our teenage life, Eliza had decided she wanted to pick up photography. She was always making me do silly photoshoots, and she honestly wasn't half bad. One time, we had a customer come in, whose wedding had been called off. She was a wreck and wanted to return her dress, but we had a policy where we could not refund money on a tailored dress. So, she loses it completely. I'm trying to console her, and Eliza is just standing there, looking deep in thought."

"Well, she's not great at consoling," Matthew adds, and I shoot him a playful glare.

A low rumble of laughter comes from all three women on my side of the table, and I feel betrayed.

"No, she's not. Anyway, she had this idea she got from some blog or magazine where women would have photoshoots of them destroying their wedding gowns for cathartic reasons." She glances over at me, her face warm, and takes a sip of wine. "She suggests this idea to the customer. Before the day ended, they had bought well over a dozen bottles of spray paint and had this entire photoshoot of her letting out all of her anger on the dress."

Jack is quiet, but his face is painted with amusement, the corner of his mouth quirked slightly.

Failed weddings.

Oh, man.

I hope this doesn't bother him.

"I think Myspace had just recently become a thing, and the girl posted pictures of her shoot on her little blog. Word got around, and all of a sudden, we had women coming in with wedding gowns from divorced marriages, wanting to pay for photoshoots. It's how Melonie's store became known in the surrounding areas." Simone finishes her story with a swig of wine. "So, Eliza's teenage antics paid off, did they not?"

"Of course!" Melonie grins, shaking her head. "I know my daughter was and is an asset, she also liked to make my blood pressure spike."

"Didn't we all do that to our parents?" Matthew laughs, his fork dropping onto his empty plate with a soft clank.

Jack locks eyes with me over the table, beaming and

shaking his head, the movement quick and almost unnoticed. "Do you do the same for wedding tuxes?"

The glint in his eye shows me he's joking, and I can't
help but laugh, the sound bursting through my nose in an
unexpected huff. I lean forward, narrowing my eyes
slightly. "Depends on how much you pay me. I've been
out of the business for quite some time."

"Does that mean you're cheaper or on the pricey
side?"

"Please," I quip. "My prices *only* go up."

"Worth every penny, I'm sure."

My neck flushes.

Our back and forth is interrupted by Matthew
bringing dessert to the table, bragging over the homemade raspberry filling in his dark-chocolate three-layer
cake. My mouth waters at the mere mention of dark
chocolate.

The table is distracted with refills, passing out plates,
and searching for the cake knife to divide the round treat
between the seven of us. I reach up to take a plate from
Matthew's hand as Jack moves forward to pour more wine
into my glass.

A tug on my shirt pulls my attention, and I look over at
my mother trying to pull it over my exposed skin. I sit
back and cock my head at her, an eyebrow raised. She's
already fussed over what I was wearing when I was
putting groceries up before we left the house, and I
thought I had shut it down.

She leans toward me to whisper. "I don't know why
you wear tops like this. It's not flattering to your body. It
keeps showing your love handles at the slightest
movement."

My entire body is pink. It has to be. I feel a hot flash

spread from the back of my thighs to the top of my scalp. I push her hand away, keeping my voice low. "Can you please drop it with the shirt?"

"I just don't know how you're comfortable in it." Her voice is still low, but her tone is exasperated. "You know I pay attention to the way clothing fits. It's my job."

"It fits *fine*, Mom." I pray she can detect the warning in my voice. "Stop."

Mom throws her hands up in defense, which is her signature sign for giving up. A smile replaces the grimace I caused, and she takes a plate of cake from Matthew's hands. He and Simone are in deep conversation and didn't even notice our side-stage spat.

But when I glance across the table, Jack's stare is on me. He quickly looks away when I notice and cuts into his slice before taking a bite.

My face is on fire. I hope he didn't witness that interaction.

"Grams, I bet they used milk from Delilah's family to make the cake, too!" Nova boasts, grinning from ear to ear with chocolate smudged at the corner of her lip. I feel lighter at her childlike excitement. If there was ever any doubt that kids were worth it, I can guarantee the ice-breaking quality they showcase during awkward moments will pacify it.

My car is running; Nova, distracted by her iPad, is in the backseat; and Mom is leaning against it with her cellphone to her ear. Dad always calls right before bed. It's actually really sweet. I step out onto the porch, followed by Jack.

"That was probably the best dessert I've had here yet." I lean back against the railing, smiling up at him.

Jack nods in agreement, but his face is far away, looking over my shoulder in the field of nothing behind us. I glance behind me to make sure there is, in fact, nothing there. When I look back at him, his chest expands under the loosely stretched material of his t-shirt.

"You okay?"

"I like your shirt," he blurts, averting his eyes to the wooden boards that are creaking underneath my feet. When he pulls his gaze back up to me, it's soft. "I think it looks great on you. In fact, I think you always look great."

I don't know what this moment is. But I know my feet want to pull me out of it. The air feels a little thick around us. "She's opinionated."

"I can tell, but she's wrong." He's nonchalant in this statement, but his lips are curving—less serious. "I just wanted you to know that. There is nothing unflattering about you."

"I—well—thanks, Jack." I bite my lip to contain the urge to beam at him. "I promise I never let her get to me. Well, not anymore. When I was younger, sure."

He nods once, his hands sliding into the pockets of his jeans. "Well, I'll try to wrap up Simone's conversation in there so you guys can get going. *I* will see *you* on Friday. Double feature. There better be popcorn and *Goobers*."

I choke on my laughter, looking up at him with wide eyes. *What?*

"Chocolate-covered peanuts, you perv."

"Oh my gosh, bye." My laugh echoes off the steps as I turn to walk down them.

I think you always look great. I don't dwell on it. I know what he was doing, and it was sweet, though unnecessary. Still, my body is buzzing from his compliment.

I reach the car just as Mom wraps up her call and slides into the backseat, next to Nova. I buckle my seatbelt, watching Simone exit the front door and walk toward us. In the rearview mirror, I see Mom going through her text messages, which buys me a few more minutes of silence. That wasn't as bad as expected. I count that a win.

As soon as Simone is in the car, my mom looks up and quirks an eyebrow.

"How long has Eliza been seeing Jack, Simmy?" The question is matter-of-fact, and I roll my eyes, not even bothering to suppress my groan.

Simone only laughs, leaving me to answer. Traitor. "We are not seeing each other, Mom. I have already said this. We're friends, and I am not dating right now."

Her sigh could power a windmill. "Well, you're a damn fool, then."

"Add it to my ever-growing list of disappointments," I grumble, pulling out of the Peters' driveway.

8

"*I* feel underdressed." Those are the first words out of Jack's mouth when I open the door to let him in. I give him a once-over, and my lips draw into a smirk at his navy gym shorts, alumni baseball t-shirt, and white sneakers stained with dirt at the edges. I'm only surprised to see black ankle socks peeking over his tennis shoes instead of the usual gold toe he wears. Like an old man.

Pulling my eyes back up to his face, I laugh, shaking myself out of my appraisal. "You're fine. I had errands to run today and haven't had time to change into my eating pants."

As he toes off his shoes at the door, he tilts his head to the side, his brow drawn at my remark.

"Pants with an elastic waist, Jack. Come on. Keep up."

"Jack!" Nova cheers, waving from the couch as we walk into the living room. "It is very important you know where to sit during movie night. Luckily, Aunt Simone is at the hospital, or you'd have to sit in the chair by yourself." She sits up on her knees, pointing to the empty spots on our couch. "Mom sits in the middle, so I have the choice either to rest my head on the arm of the couch or in her lap. You will sit on the left side of the couch because the right side is closest to the bathroom and I have to pee *a lot* during movies."

He's a mixture of overwhelmed and amused as she speaks without taking a breath. When his eyes fall on me, they've got a playful glint—he's excited. He directs his attention back to her. "Where would we be without your guidance, Nova?"

"Lost," she deadpans, her hands on her hips. That attitude, man. I don't even know—okay, I mean, yeah, she lives with Simone and me. I do kind of know.

"I see you have it under control. I'll be back."

I can hear their muted voices from the bedroom while I change, and it's surprisingly soothing. It fills me with a sense of home. Jack is pestering her, asking her if she's *sure* he can't have the seat closest to the bathroom. I should probably go back out there before she internally combusts at the suggestion.

"Oh, good, you're back." Her voice is relieved, exhaling a large breath as if seat-swapping was the most stressful thought she's ever had. "Can you please tell Jack he has the best seat?"

I look from Nova to Jack and smirk at his expression of faux-innocence. "Hands down. Simone usually gets it, and you know Simone only gets the best."

He's feigning contemplation, narrowing his eyes at both of us before slowly lowering himself onto the couch. "I feel like I'm being played. But I'll trust you for now."

Nova is overly pleased, her body relaxing as she settles into her spot and throws her favorite polka-dot blanket over her legs. I nudge Jack's arm once I sit between the two and playfully glare at him for his show of dramatics.

Being this close, I see a flash of dimples when he looks my way, his eyes light and teasing. He reaches forward and brings the large bowl of popcorn to us, tilting it toward me so I can get a handful.

Nova is asleep 45 minutes into the second movie, but I'm wide awake. It's weird—being this close to him, hearing the steady rise and fall of his breathing. It's not uncomfortable, but I think that's what is making it feel so strange. We watched *Camp Nowhere* first since Nova had never seen it, and I predicted (correctly) that she wouldn't be able to hang for both films.

I glance slyly toward Jack to make sure he's properly enjoying it. You know, giving adequate emotional responses when they are needed. He catches me and raises an eyebrow. He knows what I'm doing.

"You can't watch me watch the movie." His tone is matter-of-fact.

I shrug, looking back toward the screen. "I know that. I just wanted to make sure you weren't falling asleep."

"I'm not. The movie's cute." His arms are folded across his chest, and his posture is relaxed. He's sunk down into the sofa, with one leg sticking out straight in front of him and the other bent at the knee.

The Olsen twins are plotting over the phone when he leans over to me, his elbow brushing my arm. "We should do this more often."

I glance at him, adjusting in my seat so I can see him without making myself uncomfortable. "Hang out?"

"No. I mean, yes. But, more specifically, we should have movie nights. Make it a thing." He's saying it so casually, but his face is turning a light shade of pink. It's noticeable, but I don't think he wants it to be. He's also not looking at me, his eyes trained on the screen as he suggests this. I say nothing regarding either fact.

"If Nova is down, I'm down." I always need Nova to be comfortable, whether I want something to happen or not. "We can try to pick a movie one of us hasn't seen every time."

"And make it a nineties movie so we can culture your child."

I laugh at the thought of nineties movies being the cornerstone of culture for this generation, before agreeing with a hearty nod. "We can do every other Friday. That way, you can have some Fridays open to yourself."

"I don't care about that." He says it quickly before thinking, but shrugs after a second thought. "But that's fine. You're probably right. There will inevitably be some sort of plans made for one of us."

"I like this plan. I'll run it by my boss when she wakes."

Jack chuckles at my phrasing and nods, relaxing against the cushions again. "Oh, yeah. Of course."

Nova was thrilled at the idea of a bi-weekly movie night with Jack. Honestly, it's brought up in random conversation more days than not. However, while she saw it as nothing more than an extra friend, Simone was extremely inquisitive.

It's not until the third Friday of movies that Simone can join us. She doesn't have work, so she's excited to, in her words, *watch how we interact.* I could not have rolled my eyes any harder.

Tonight is *Homeward Bound II*, my personal favorite of the franchise, and *Space Jam*. It fills me with this unexplainable joy that Jack appreciates older kid movies as much as Simone and I do.

Jack arrives at the house on time with Oreo-flavored popcorn for Nova from a local business that specializes in hundreds of flavors—flavors you wouldn't even think of. He brought dill pickle for the adults to try but knew that small bag for Nova would brighten her day.

Since Simone is joining us, Jack opts for a pallet of pillows and blankets on the floor in front of us, but still looks relaxed as he leans against the bottom of the couch with Chief snuggled to his side. I try to see if his expression changes in the slightest while the girls and I sob at several parts of the movie.

He's a brick wall until *one* moment where he wipes at the corner of his eye. It's not a coincidence, I am sure of it.

After *Space Jam*, I put Nova to bed before joining Simone and Jack in the kitchen, where they are chatting and drinking the last remnants of wine from the bottle we opened before movie number two.

I walk in to the sound of Simone's voice, dreamy and wistful. "Oh man, that will be beautiful."

"I know." Jack's reply is almost giddy, his knee bouncing on the stool where he sits. "We've been planning it since Christmas."

"What's that?" I slip into the stool at the end of the counter and rest my elbows on top.

"Jack and Penny are going backpacking in Albania for a month."

"Oh! When? That sounds so cool." It does. Sound cool, I mean. But it also makes me sad. A whole month? What happens if Chief gets sick? Or I get more animals in my attic? I shake myself from those thoughts because they're bordering on dependent and anxious. I don't like being either.

He turns to me, catching my eyes as he speaks. "I'll fly out September 28th. We have a whole plan, so it's not completely spontaneous like Penny would rather it be. But we are doing the authentic experience of staying in hostels, so I think she's bending a little. You know I can't do without some sort of plan."

"I so wish I could go." Simone's statement is more like a whine as she finishes off the last drop of red in her glass. "I need a vacation, but I feel a month may be too long."

Jack leans forward, reaching for the bottle between them and eyeing the bottom for any leftover. He tilts it toward his glass and pours out the last of it. I take notice of the way his jaw ticks when he's concentrating. "You know the invitation is on the table for both of you. I didn't ask, because I know you guys have lives."

"You're right. Backpacking in Albania seems like such a burden from the lavish life I lead. Thank you for shielding me from that."

I snort at Simone's comment, standing from the counter to fix a glass of water. It sounds great, but a month away from Nova is impossible, and honestly, the thought is unbearable.

"Simone, you are more than welcome to come," Jack clarifies, a rumble of laughter falling out with his words.

She waves him off with a grin to show she's teasing. We all know Simone is too obsessed with her work to leave it for that long. Unless she needed to.

"Don't say I didn't ask."

"It's appalling you've never seen *Cool Runnings*." Jack walks through my door, DVD in hand, shaking his head in disappointment. He takes off his shoes, habitually kicking them to the side of the door, and scratches Chief's head as he walks past him.

I roll my eyes at his disapproval and gather the snacks in my arms to follow him into the living room where Nova is already waiting. "You haven't seen *A Simple Wish,* so we're even."

"Not even close. No one, and I mean no one, knows what the hell that movie even is." He stops in the living room and looks around before turning back to me. "Where's Simone?"

I attempt to finish chewing the piece of licorice in my mouth to answer his question when Simone flies through the living room, pulling her shoes on as she does. I simply point at her, still chewing the gummy candy.

"Hi, I have a date tonight." She shimmies her shoulders and bats her eyes, excited to finally be in something other than scrubs or a white coat. "I'm actually running a bit late. I tried to get Eliza to double with me because he has a twin brother. She refused."

Jack swings his gaze back to me then, curiosity in his eyes. I shrug in reply because she did offer. I didn't want to miss movie night.

I finally swallow the sticky candy. "I did refuse. I'm not dating right now. We all know that."

"And I am not pushing you! I'm stating a fact," Simone defends, holding her hands up as she walks backward to the foyer. "Okay, I really have to go now. I love you all."

When the door closes, Jack is silent for a moment before tossing the DVD in Nova's lap. "All right, let's get this party started."

I'm thankful he doesn't push the subject.

I'm tying the satin scarf over Nova's sleepy head as we watch the last twenty minutes of the second film. I'm surprised she's stayed up this long, but she's drifting. She's determined to make it all the way through one night.

I finish and smooth my hands over the top of her head, tilting it back to press a kiss to her forehead. "Sleepy, yet?" I whisper.

She doesn't reply, but shakes her head, her eyelids heavy. I can't help but smile at the lie. She crawls back onto the couch and gets cozy under her blanket, laying her head in my lap and reaching down to stroke Chief's ears.

I rub her back and look to the screen, glancing over at Jack as he watches the movie. Martin Short is one of my favorites, and I'm pleased to find Jack laughing *out loud* at his scenes. I usually only get a huff of amusement from him.

When the movie ends and Nova is out and tucked in her bed, Jack helps me with the dishes. It's silent but nice. I wash, he dries. His arm brushes against mine every so often, and it makes my pulse quicken. It's obvious I haven't had physical contact from a man in quite some time. Truly. It's pathetic.

"So, you leave in two weeks." I didn't mean for my voice to sound so sad, but I heard it, so I'm sure he did as well.

He sets down the dry plate, and the corner of his lip twitches slightly. "Don't sound so defeated. I'll email you. I'll send postcards for Nova." He pauses. "I didn't think you'd miss me this much, Davis."

"Oh please, I won't." I laugh at his tone, pushing him away with my hip. "You're so full of yourself."

"I mean, I'm glad to know my absence will make such an impact."

"It won't. I'll barely notice."

"Oh? Who is going to change out the lightbulb in your closet?"

I narrow my eyes. "I can find a step stool."

"Mhm and your gutters?"

"Excuse me, sir, I am very capable of doing these things on my own. You're merely a convenient option." I place my hands on my hips, facing him. He's enjoying this, nodding thoughtfully at my retorts.

He steps forward then, coming closer to me, and crossing his arms over his chest. "I guess I'm the only one, then."

I tilt my head upward. "Only one what?"

"That will miss this."

We lock eyes for a beat. It feels intense, and I am suffocating.

I look away first, turning back toward my task. "Nah, Nova will probably miss movie nights, too."

I'm almost afraid I've offended him, but his loud laugh assures me that's not the case. He picks up a wet plate I've already rinsed off from the sink and dries it. "Can I ask a favor of you?"

"Of course."

"Will you drive us to the airport that morning?"

Us? I look up at him, brow furrowed as I run the cup in my hand under the faucet. "Sure, but I thought you said you were meeting Penny there."

He nods, opening the cabinet above his head to stack the plates on top of each other. "No, I am. Callie is coming along with us. Didn't I tell you that?"

Callie. Or Dr. Morris. The new veterinarian at his

clinic. When I first met her, I was taking Chief in for a checkup, and she greeted me from behind the counter. Young. Perky. Adorable. Single. And apparently a friend of Jack's from vet school. A twinge of jealousy pulls at my chest. There's no denying it.

"You did not tell me that. Wow, that's great. Do you really think Dr. Carmichael can handle the clinic on his own for that long?"

Jack nods at my question, holding his hand out to grab the next dish from me. "I'm certain he can. I was the only vet there for a year before we went into business together."

"Well." I *honestly* don't know what to say. I feel a little nauseated at the thought of them spending a month back-packing together. There's no real reason. Well, other than me selfishly not wanting him to get into a relationship that will interfere with our time together. "That sounds great."

My voice is strained. I can hear it. *Fuck, I really hope he can't.*

If he does, he ignores it. "Oh, yeah. It'll be great. I can't wait to get away for a while."

The conversation fades shortly after, and he leaves, giving me a hug as usual.

Getting ready for bed, I feel uneasy. Like there's a heavy rock in my stomach that refuses to budge. I'm lying awake, praying to hear a tumble in the attic above me.

So I'll have a reason to call him.

Jack stayed over at my house last night after our last Friday night double feature—*Dr. Dolittle* and *Flubber*—

before leaving on his adventure. He drank too much wine and was wary of driving. Before Nova went to sleep, she hugged him tightly, crying because she was upset we'd have to miss two of our Fridays with him. It was sad. Cute and sweet, but *sad*.

I think it got to him, too, because his face was pinched with concern when I came back from putting her to bed.

We picked Callie up from her house at an ungodly hour, and Jack drove us to the airport. I insisted I would, but he felt guilty enough that I had to be awake before the sun. Simone stayed back with Nova, much to Nova's irritation the night before. She *really* wanted to watch his plane take off.

"You're a doll for doing this, Eliza." Callie's voice is even chipper before dawn. It makes me dislike her even more. Though, I have no reason to dislike her at all. At least I *know* it's irrational.

My eyelids are closed, but I smile anyway. "No problem. I owe Jack for all the shit I ask him to do around the house."

"You owe me nothing." I kind of love how rough his voice is in the mornings. It sends a shiver down my spine.

I catch him glancing back at Callie through the rearview mirror every few minutes. I briefly wonder if there is already a thing between them. He would tell me, right? Or maybe not. Maybe he thinks we're in the whole *not dating* thing together and doesn't want to betray me.

My mind is getting away from me.

When we get to the airport, Jack parks and I go inside with them. I feel weird just dropping him off. Callie is literally bouncing with excitement, but Jack is calm and stoic as usual. His easy presence is soothing.

I get as far as I can go and unfold my arms resting

right under my braless boobs. It was early when I got dressed. I forgot to put one on.

"Okay," I begin, getting his attention. "Don't forget to email me, tell Penny hi, and have the best time." I turn to Callie. "*Both* of you have the best time."

"We will. Thank you so much again." Callie's almost too happy that I'm about to leave her alone with Jack.

Okay, Eliza. Chill.

Jack steps forward before I do and pulls me into his chest, crushing me to him in a tight hug. "Take care of the girls. Oh, and Chief."

I step out of his embrace and squeeze his arms. "I will. Be safe."

"Bye, Liza." He waves to me before following Callie to their area. I stand still for a moment, watching them fall into step together, laughing at something the other said. Before I turn to leave, I see his hand hover over her lower back, guiding her in front of him.

My body tenses.

They look like the perfect pair.

I think I may want that.

9

It's been a week since I took Jack and Callie to the airport. I've been a nervous wreck all seven days. We haven't spoken, and I didn't expect us to, but there's a gnawing feeling in my chest.

At this point, I can't remember a time where I wasn't this way. Worry has become a personality trait for me, and I *miss* being carefree. The morning I found myself physically ill after googling backpacking accidents, I decided to finally call the number of the counselor Simone suggested. Cycles of irrational thoughts were becoming too common.

I see her in a few days, and I'm not looking forward to it. Talking about myself isn't something I enjoy doing. That's why I love my job so much. *They* talk to me and expect nothing of substance in return—usually. Two occupations get almost as much information as therapists: beautician and bartender.

"I got it!" Nova calls, running into the living room with a spray bottle in hand. I'm sitting on the edge of the couch, waiting for her to plop down in front of me so I can wash her hair.

She has the ability to bring me back to earth and make me more at ease. It's her superpower. Thoughts of my impending appointment are pushed to the back of my mind. "Perfect."

I take the bottle of anti-frizz shampoo and water from her and wait until she sits between my legs before I spray onto her part and rub it in with my fingers. I do this to each section as she watches the Disney channel in silence, holding a handful of her braids to keep track of where I've already washed.

This is such a routine part of our life that I'm basically on autopilot, watching my hands, but not really needing to. I've been doing Nova's hair longer than I've been a beautician. I find that hair days have become such an easy way for us to bond. When she was younger, she used the time to tell me stories, and now it's to share about everything she loves.

Today, she's more focused on the TV than me, but that's okay. I'm lost in my thoughts, methodically going through the motions. That makes me pause, my brain halting and backtracking over it.

Going through the motions.

I feel like my whole life is becoming like this. A routine. I'm living on autopilot, doing the same thing every day with little change. That's not me. I was always the type of person to jump headfirst into a project or an adventure that would turn my days or weeks unpredictable. Even when Nova was born, I tried to do something new with her, Aaron, or by myself. I never liked to know what the week held for me.

Now, the thought of any change to my routine brings me panic. I need to shake that and live a little more. Maybe I can plan some vacations with the girls and some weekend activities to break the mundane. Maybe ... dating will help.

We go to rinse out once I finish. After conditioning, rinsing, and wrapping her hair in a microfiber towel, we get back on the couch to put on a movie while her hair dries. I'll have to dry it more, but I try to get as much water soaked out beforehand so I don't apply heat to her hair for too long.

I'm a bit obsessed with hair care. Obviously.

My phone buzzes in my hand, and I see an email notification from Jack. My heart jumps to my throat.

You would love it here, Liza. It's beautiful. I've attached pictures so you can see it for yourself. Show Nova and Simone, and consider a girls' trip when Nova is old enough. Penny and Callie say hi. I miss you guys and am thinking of you.

Jack

He did attach pictures, and most of them are with Callie. My stomach churns. Their selfies are the ones that make me want to vomit. I click through those pretty quickly so I can get to the scenery, which is breathtaking. One of the pictures is of Jack standing at the edge of a waterfall with his hands on his hips. He's looking up and to the side, and I can see his back and profile.

He's stunning.

That's the only word you could ever use to describe him.

I nudge Nova to break her concentration from the movie and hand her my phone. "Jack sent us pictures."

"He did?" Her voice is shrill with excitement. She takes

the phone from me and expertly flips through the photos like she's had an iPhone since birth. She hasn't. "I want to go there."

"Me, too, kid." I laugh at her simple statement and peek over her shoulder to see which one she's looking at. The alarm signals the back door opening, telling me Simone is home.

"When is Jack coming back?"

"Not soon enough!" Simone's voice echoes as she walks into the living room. "Hi, girlies. We got an update from Jack?"

I hand her the phone over the back of the couch while Nova, quickly losing interest, unpauses her movie. "We did. He seems like he's having a great time."

"So, he does." Simone's tone is unreadable. "This girl is Callie, I take it?"

"Yep." I inhale the word, trying to take a deep breath. "That's her. She's cute, huh? They're cute."

She hums her response, handing my phone back to me with a tight smile. "We'll talk later. I need to go shower off my day."

It's late when I'm finished getting ready for bed. Nova went down pretty quickly after we dried her hair. She's very much like me in that it takes us all but two minutes to fall asleep when our heads hit the pillow. I'm in the living room, eating the last piece of pizza, when Simone plops down beside me.

"Is this why you wanted me to set you up? Because Jack and Callie are a thing?"

"They're not a thing." My tone is unreasonably defensive. I wince. She notices.

Her eyebrow is raised, and she leans back with her

arms folded across her chest. "Okay. So, me setting you up with Sam would have nothing to do with Jack taking a vacation with this woman?"

Absolutely not. I shake my head, pressing a napkin to my mouth as I swallow my recent bite. "No. Do you want me to go on a date or not? You've been begging me for months, I finally cave, and you question my intentions? I can't win."

Her hands go up in defense. "Okay. I'm just making sure you don't need to talk. Sam is very excited to meet you tomorrow. Do you know what you're going to wear?"

I'm pleased with the subject change, and I let out a breath I didn't realize I was holding. "No. God, I haven't even thought about it. I think I've forgotten how to date. Please help me."

"Let's go dig in your closet."

Who was I kidding? I'm a pro at first dates. I forgot how much nervous men enjoy rambling about themselves. I honestly don't mind it, and Sam has a knack for it. He can do it without being obnoxious—what a gift. Who knew I'd find college stories of a former baseball player so entertaining?

He is the Abercrombie definition of handsome. There isn't a single imperfection to his bizarrely symmetrical features. The fullness of his lips and the way they curve to display straight, blinding teeth, his brown doe-like eyes and long lashes, his broad shoulders but narrow waist. I doubt he's ever had to put forth any effort to pick up a woman before. Especially with charisma basically oozing out of his pores.

To top it off, he knows my soft spots. He asks about Nova and my friendship with Simone. He asks if I have any pets, and then acts engaged when I tell him all about Chief and his mischievous antics as a young'un. I'm pleasantly surprised that I'm actually having fun. I like him, and I didn't expect it to be that easy. I guess I should trust Simone's instinct more since she's known me for over two decades.

We've finished our meal, but neither of us has given the impression we're ready for the check. That's a good sign. I haven't bored him or seemed uninterested, which is something I feared would happen.

I take a long swig of the white wine in front of me, my mother's voice in my head. *White for dates, red for mates.* Basically, don't stain your teeth purple when you're trying to impress someone on a date. Wait until you have them locked down and drink all the red wine you want. It's a frivolous piece of advice, but unfortunately, it stuck.

"I know you have a babysitter for your daughter, so you tell me when we need to leave. Otherwise, I'll talk your head off for hours and not realize it."

I laugh at the same time as I swallow the alcohol. When the two sensations meet in the middle, I almost choke, an air bubble lodging itself uncomfortably in my chest. I wave a hand to him as I press my napkin to my mouth, trying to at least *look* like I have manners.

I'm finally able to speak. "We're good on time, but thank you for being considerate. Tell me more about this baseball tournament you have coming up."

"Oh God." He chuckles, shaking his head. "It's an old-timers' tournament where they get some high school alumni athletes to play all weekend for charity. It should be fun. You should come watch. I mean it's a couple of towns over, but not too far of a drive."

Sportsball. No. I smile and nod at his suggestion, anyway, because it's sweet. I don't have to break it to him that I *hate* sports. I'll save that for another date—if there is one. "That could be fun."

My phone is in my lap in case the babysitter needs me. I feel a buzz, so I look down and see an email notification from Jack. I'm excited to see his name.

I'm itching to open it.

I suppress the urge and look back up at Sam, who is, luckily, not even concerned with my distraction. He's still talking about how difficult it will be to play against teenagers who have full workout schedules. I'm barely keeping up.

Dammit. I hate that I saw the notification. Now, it's all I'm thinking about. I force my phone into my purse beside me, keeping an attentive smile on my lips. It probably looks awkward, let's be honest.

The rest of the conversation feels strained, and it's my fault. I feel guilty when he asks for the check. "I'm sure you're wanting to get home to your daughter. I know you don't date much. Well, Simone says you don't. I don't mean to assume."

"I *don't* date much." I affirm his statement with a tight nod. "I'm sorry. I hope I didn't come off like I wasn't having a good time."

"Oh, no. Not at all." If he's lying, he's damn good at it.

We fight over splitting the cost, but Simone warned me he would probably be old-fashioned. I let it slide, allowing his insistence to win. I'll get it next time. If he even wants a next time.

I wince.

We walk out of the restaurant, and he carefully reaches down to take my hand. I'm surprised. The skin to skin contact doesn't make me nervous, my stomach doesn't flip, and the only thing I can focus on is how clammy my hands probably are. It's nice, though.

"So, before I potentially make my life incredibly awkward by pissing off my current beautician and moving my business to you, do you think there could be a second date?"

The butterflies I've been missing all night appear low in my stomach, fluttering up a lost emotion. I laugh at his question and lean against my car. "Are you bribing me for a second date?"

"Is it working?"

Men in this town are charming. I cross my arms over my chest, pretending to mull it over for a moment. "I really don't like to turn away new customers."

"Next weekend, then?" Sam's smile grows, and he steps closer to me, causing my stomach to knot in anxiety.

Oh, shit. Is he going to want a kiss? Of course he is. Dammit.

I nod, pushing off my car and swallowing down the ball of unwanted feelings that has formed in my throat. "Next weekend sounds wonderful."

Why am I breathless all of a sudden? One step forward, and he leans down, brushing his lips against mine in a brief kiss. When he steps away from me, his perfect mouth pulled back in a smile, he nods. "I'll call you."

The kiss was nice and quick and nothing to write home about. It was pleasant. And he didn't try to shove his tongue down my throat. What a sad time for that to be the low bar men should meet. *Don't aggressively tongue a woman on the first date unless she seems open to it.*

I am almost positive I was not giving that vibe. Thankfully, Sam didn't read it that way, either.

My hands are shaking when I open my car door. Baby steps. I did dating. I did a kiss.

I slide into the driver's seat and let out a loaded exhale, pressing my head back against the headrest.

Next weekend. I have an entire week to prepare for another physical encounter. My heart is a jackhammer, angrily thudding in my body.

I didn't feel a spark with that kiss, but I was also close to passing out from nerves. Besides, sparks are overrated, right? Sparks are lines of bullshit from romantic comedies.

... I don't really believe that. I am a sucker for romance.

Once I start the car, I pull my phone from my purse, opening Jack's email before leaving the parking lot.

Hi. I was just thinking about you. Remember when we were watching Camp Nowhere *and you said you wondered what it would be like to share a cabin with ten other strangers as an adult? Like, it's normal to do that as a kid at summer camp. But, as an adult, it's less appealing. I don't know why I'm repeating your words to you. You know what you said.*

Anyway, my point is, I can attest that it is ... probably not your cup of tea. I know you. And I know you would hate the hostel life. Callie loves it, which is great, because if she didn't, it would be a miserable trip. I just decided to keep a mental note that if I ever did a backpacking trip with you, I'd have to make it to where you would have your own private space. It's a random thought, I know.

Here's a picture of my view right now. Tell the girls and Chief hi.

Jack

A picture of a pink skyline above the most beautiful mountains expands across my screen. It's incredible.

I try not to let it bother me that he's comparing me to Callie. I also try not to let it bother me that Callie *loves* hostels and I'm the prima donna who needs her own damn five-star hotel room. I mean, sort of accurate, but also I slept in a tent with this asshole.

I shake my head and read the email over again. I can't help the small smile that fights past my pursed lips this time.

Okay, he's right. I would not be able to share a space with strangers.

I laugh at the thought of him and his signature half-chuckle when he looked around the room and thought: *Eliza would fucking hate this.*

I reply.

Sounds miserable. You should probably come home now and save yourself. I'm glad you're having fun. That view is stunning. Don't love it too much. We need you here.

Eliza

―――――――――

My second date with Sam is in a couple of days, and I keep meaning to talk to Nova about it. I had my first session with Hannah, my therapist, and we talked about my apprehension of bringing up the subject of me dating with Nova. It was helpful. Being coached by someone, I mean. I'm sure she was easing into the session with me, but it was doable. I'd go back.

I stand at the door and look out at the treehouse where Nova is. It's getting late, the sun already setting and turning the sky a purplish-pink hue. I walk outside and pull my cardigan close. It's not cold, but when the sun goes down, the chilly breeze is a reminder that fall is on the horizon.

I climb the ladder and push the door up, peeking in before opening it completely. "Hi, Supernova."

She's curled up against her colorful throw pillows with her blanket wrapped over her knees. Her headphones are on, and her tablet is lighting up her face. Her eyes are pulled from the screen, and her lips form into a smile. I sit in the spot next to her, and she turns on her side and scoots closer to me.

She presses her head against me and places the tablet in my lap, but her eyes never leave it. I recognize the characters as a Disney show, but I can't recall the name. They all start to run together. And that, ladies and gentlemen, is how I know I am turning into my mother.

Placing my arm over her, we situate ourselves into a comfortable position. She unplugs the headphones so we can both hear, and it makes my insides warm.

We watch in comfortable silence for a moment before I look down and run my hand over her hair, pulling it over her shoulder. "Hey, Nova, you know we're a team, right?"

Her big brown eyes look upward, and she cranes her head to see me. "What do you mean?"

"You, me, and now Aunt Simone. We're a team. Like, we stick together, and we count on each other."

Nova turns, lying on her back with her head in my lap. She looks like she's thinking, her lips twisted to the side. "And Chief?"

"Oh, yes. How could I forget? Chief, too." Her heart is

so big. She'd never want to leave anyone out. She used to do that with her stuffed animals. *Well, if I sleep with Pinky tonight, then Gizmo will be sad.*

"And, Jack, too."

Oh, boy. I laugh at the finality in her tone and nod to appease her. "Sure. Jack can be a part of the team, too." Quiet satisfaction crosses her features. "So, as teammates, I wanted to run something past you."

"Are we moving?" The sound of her voice makes my heart sink to my stomach.

I rub her arm and squeeze it gently, shaking my head at the question. "No, no. Not at all." I inhale sharply. Why is this so difficult? "I went on a date. You know what a date is, right?"

"Yes." She says this simply, urging me to continue.

"Okay. Are you okay with that? I am thinking of going on another date with this guy, but I want you to be okay."

Nova's eyes light up. "Was it with Jack?"

I didn't expect this question. I hesitate for a moment, hoping the answer doesn't upset her. "No. It wasn't with Jack. I just had this date a few nights ago. When Miranda babysat you. His name is Sam, and he's very nice."

Her silence is deafening. Then: "Aunt Simone is on the team, too. Is she okay with it?"

"She is. She introduced me to him. You know she wouldn't do that if he weren't a good guy." I can't read her emotionless expression as she stares at the ceiling.

"Okay. I'm okay with it." She smiles then, her face softening into childlike innocence as her attention immediately focuses back on the show we were watching.

That was much easier than I anticipated. I don't think I'll push the subject unless I see Sam being something serious in our life. Which, at this point, is not likely.

I exhale my worries and snuggle down into the blanket with Nova to finish her show. When the next episode starts, I find myself struggling to keep my eyes open.

"We're learning about Ruby Bridges in school right now," she pipes up, jolting me awake after almost falling asleep during whatever this is.

I sit up slightly because I am simply *too* comfortable. How does she not fall asleep in this thing? "Yeah? Did you show them all how brilliant you are with your Ruby knowledge?"

When Nova was a baby, I made it a point to fill her bookshelves up with iconic females in history. There is nothing wrong with fairytales (we had our fair share), but I wanted Nova to grow up reading about the women who changed the world.

"No."

"No?" I'm surprised. Nova loves showing how much she knows about a particular subject.

She shrugs a shoulder, her eyes not leaving the screen in front of her. "Yeah. Thomas calls me a know-it-all or a show-off when I get stuff right in class."

Thomas. I know that little snot. He once put gum in one of Nova's friend's hair, and I had a time trying to make it presentable without cutting most of the length off. I keep my eyes on Nova, reaching forward to take her device from her hands. "That's because he's jealous of you."

"Maybe."

"Sweetheart." I need to use this moment to reiterate every lesson I try to teach her. "Never let *anyone* take your voice."

She looks up at me, her eyes big and full of innocence, but she knows. "I just don't want to be made fun of."

I smooth my hand over the top of her head with a sigh. "Nova, unfortunately, there will always be someone who tries to belittle your accomplishments because you're a girl *and* because you're a black girl. Until that changes, I want you to know your worth. Your worth is immeasurable. You are incredibly strong, and your brain is big and magnificent. You light up every room you walk into. The people who don't see that are the ones who are unintelligent, filled with hate, and *wrong*."

Nova leans her head into me, taking a large breath that moves her entire body.

"So, don't give up your voice. I hate it, but we still live in a time where you have to fight to be heard. And, as long as I'm alive, I will fight for you." I stop to watch her unreadable expression before continuing. "There is not a goal you can't reach. But there will always be a Thomas ready to try and take it away from you."

"Why?"

What a question. "Because they cannot stand to see you shine. Shine anyway."

She nods, careful and deliberate. When she looks at me, her eyes are heavy, and I want so badly to ease every worry she has. These conversations are hard for her—a kid who only sees the good in people doesn't want to know the bad that's out there. "So, it is okay if I tell the teacher everything I know about Ruby?"

"Of course it is." I smile. "You're so smart, babe. Show it off. Be yourself."

Her voice is soft. "Dad used to say I was going to rule the world one day."

I exhale an even breath, closing my eyes to try and hear his voice. "He did. And, I think he's right."

Nova reaches up, pressing a kiss to my cheek and grabbing her device back from me before snuggling down into her blanket again. I find myself watching her instead of the screen, wanting to keep her protected from every possible bad thing that comes her way.

10

———

I spot him almost immediately, towering over people on the escalator. His white t-shirt fits him as perfectly as every other t-shirt he owns. He looks tanner, and his hair is more golden than strawberry today. I don't know if it's my imagination, but he also looks leaner than usual. I'm taking a moment to watch him before flagging him over to me. I rarely get his serious expression—his face is usually lit up in some way. But his eyebrows are slightly pinched and his mouth is set in an emotionless frown as he watches the people around him.

When he reaches the bottom, his eyes scan the room until they fall on me.

There's that smile.

It's infectious.

My arms are outstretched, and I'm obnoxiously waving my hands to greet him, squealing in excitement. He's picked up the pace, and I swear he has me wrapped up in a one-armed hug in a matter of seconds, practically getting to me in four long strides. His other arm is holding his large camping backpack, but he's still able to lift me off the ground, burying his face into my hair. The contact affects me in a way it shouldn't—his hard torso pressed against my breasts. My stomach flips, my heart races, and then I remember he spent his backpacking adventure with Callie.

And then there's Sam.

"You're home!" I exclaim, holding him tightly, pushing those thoughts aside. He frees me from his grasp, dropping me back on my feet, so I have to look up at him. "I would have had Supernova with me, but you decided to land in the middle of her spelling test."

"Aw, man. I don't schedule the flights. I just book them." Jack laughs, throwing his arm over my shoulder and turning us toward the exit.

I lean into him as we walk, comfortably slipping my arm around his waist. I realize that, to any random bystander, we look like a couple who's just returned from a relaxing weekend. "I can't wait to hear all about your trip. The girls and I are coming to dinner tonight at your parents' place."

He nudges me with his hip. "I would hope so. You haven't seen me in almost a month."

"Drama queen," I tease, rolling my eyes. I glance at his hand, relaxed over my shoulder, and then back to his face. "You're so tan."

My remark incites a chuckle from him, and he squeezes me to him by hooking his arm around my neck playfully. "You're so awkward at small talk."

"*What*? I am not," I defend, my voice higher than expected. "And besides, we don't do small talk, Peters. I am merely noting an appearance change after a long absence."

"Oh." He's nodding with a smirk. "Okay. Cool. Well,

then, you changed your hair." His hand absentmindedly touches the ends of my blonde waves. "I like it."

Man, he knows how to win me over. Compliment me, and I am putty in your hand. That, I learned one night of wine-induced boredom, is my number one love language. *Words of affirmation.* I'm a vain bitch. "Thank you. I cut off four inches."

"Four? What a rebel," Jack teases with a faux gasp, laughing as he does. "What else is new? Did Nova get a tattoo?"

"Shut up." I laugh with him as we make it to my car. *What else is new?* Sam. Sam is new. And yet, the thought of telling him about Sam brings a hot-lava feeling in my throat. I don't think it's *telling* him about Sam that is bringing me this dread. I think it's him *meeting* and potentially not *liking* Sam that's making me nervous.

He leans the seat back in my car, closing his eyes and raking his fingers through his hair. "I am exhausted." He groans. "I can't wait to see CeCe and sleep in my own damn bed."

"I bet." I pull out of the parking lot. "So, you haven't dished on Callie. Pretty good bonding time, yeah?"

"There's nothing to dish." His casual shrug irritates me. "It was fun. We traveled well together. She got a flight to Minnesota to see her family before heading back here."

Must be nice to have so much free time. "That's cool." I'm aloof. Centered. Uncaring. Even though I want to crawl inside his brain, get cozy, and read all of his memories from the past month. "How was your Aunt Penny?"

"Wild as ever." Jack's voice sounds a little lazy now that he's gotten relaxed. "But you'll never believe it—she's engaged."

"What? How? Did she meet someone on the trip?"

He laughs, squirming in the seat to get settled. "Nope. She's been seeing him for a few months apparently. He proposed before the trip. She was so nonchalant in telling me, though. Like getting married was no big deal."

"Do your dads know?" I'm almost speechless, but mostly amused at the situation.

Jack turns slightly, looking at me with an expression that says *you know better than that*. "Of course not. She wants me to tell them."

"That'll go over well." I chuckle at the thought. David would roll his eyes at the delivery, and Matthew would call her in hysterics that she kept it to herself. Families, man.

"Right?"

I glance over at him and notice his eyes are closed and his hands are resting atop his head. "You know it won't offend me if you snooze on our drive over."

He exhales heavily, and I catch him shaking his head out of the corner of my eye. "No way. That's rude."

"It's not rude. Go to sleep." I turn the radio down. "Seriously. We have a twenty-minute drive. A nap won't hurt."

He grunts, attempting to put up a fight, but ultimately, his exhaustion wins. It's not even three minutes, and I hear a light snore from beside me. I glance over at his sleeping form and feel a tug at my heart that I can't quite place. That's interrupted by a loud buzz from my phone in its magnetic dash mount. I see a call coming through from Sam and quickly ignore it before it wakes Jack. Once again, why do I care?

I glance over once the snoring has stopped, but his eyes are still closed. Ten seconds later, another snore erupts from his body, and I exhale a breath I didn't realize I was holding.

———

Dinner at David and Matthew's is easily one of my favorite things to do. They're both the most adventurous, lively, and generous souls you would ever meet.

Matthew grilled steaks, because they're Jack's favorite, and paired them with a savory sweet potato hash. We spent dinner listening as Jack told us all about his adventure, and I had to push down the weird feeling in my chest every time he mentioned Callie.

It wasn't long after we finished eating that Nova fell asleep in my lap at the table. She's slowly becoming too big to do that, and it breaks my heart. I cover her with a blanket on the couch, and Chief curls up beside her on the floor. I grab another beer from the fridge and wander outside to where Simone and Jack are.

"What am I missing?" I ask the pair before leaning against the porch railing.

Simone throws an arm over my shoulder and kisses my temple. "Oh, nothing, just talking about how much we love you."

"Yeah, okay." I roll my eyes and throw my hip into her with a chuckle, causing her to laugh as well.

When I take a swig of my beer, she lets me out of her hold and steps away with a glint in her eye. "I'm going to look at the new bathroom remodel Matthew has been talking about all night." She winks before turning to Jack. "Jack," she says, leaning forward and resting her cheek against his arm. "I'm glad you're home. The gutters need to be cleaned."

"Go away." He laughs, looking down at her.

She bounces back inside with her wine glass in hand, and I watch her through the window as she follows Matthew and David down the hallway and disappears from sight. When I look back at Jack, I sigh heavily and pat my stomach. "I am so stuffed."

Jack chuckles and nods, leaning forward and resting on his elbows. "Tell me about it. I think I made myself sick. I really underestimated how much I missed Pop's cooking."

"And a win for David and that dessert. I didn't know he baked! I thought the kitchen was Matthew's expertise."

"He tries." His voice is light and happy. "Luckily for him, baking is a little more recipe-driven than cooking. He can follow directions."

I shrug at that explanation, still giving David credit in my head. "I'm really glad I'm included in these types of things. It makes me feel like I have a family here. I mean, I know I have Nova and Simone. They're plenty enough for me. I just mean—"

"I know what you mean." Jack cuts me off with knowing eyes, bumping me with his arm. "You guys complete our family, too."

It's silent between us, but it's comfortable. I look out at the pasture, and I am entirely content. Who am I kidding? If I like someone, of course Jack will too. He sees me as family. Family has each other's back.

"So," I begin, setting my beer down on top of the porch railing. I turn and lean my hip against it, beaming up at Jack as I do. "I finally gave in to one of Simone's blind dates."

His right eyebrow lifts slightly, a small smirk lighting up his features. He turns to face me, too, leaning back against the wooden post at the top of the porch stairs. "Oh, yeah? How big of a disaster was that?"

I laugh at the question, feeling less nervous now that we've dipped our toes into the first part of this conversation with no trouble. "Not a disaster at all, actually. We've gone out a few times since."

I watch his face as it falls slightly—or is that my imagination? He takes a moment, pressing the lip of his bottle to his mouth before taking a generous swig. He uses his wrist to wipe at the excess liquid at the corner of his mouth. "Oh, wow. Good for you," he replies, and then he smiles genuinely, and I feel relief.

"Yeah." I exhale. "We're going to go out again this week. I'm finally going to let him pick me up so he can meet Nova."

"He's meeting Nova?" Jack's brow is furrowed at the news. "Sounds serious."

"I mean, it's not serious, but who knows? It could be."

He nods, taking another long gulp of the bottle in his hand. I'm surprised he's not drowning as he finishes it off and tosses it into the bin below us. "Wow. That's ..." He takes a deep breath, bracing himself against the railing for a brief moment before facing me again. "I didn't know you were ready to date. I mean, what changed?"

Maybe this is a good time to remind him of where he's been for the past month. I clench my jaw slightly and lift my shoulders. "I don't know. When I dropped you and Callie off at the airport, I thought about the month ahead of you guys and felt myself wanting the same thing. I didn't realize it at that moment, but the more I thought about it, the more I felt like I was ready to emotionally connect with someone, too."

"Wait." He closes his eyes for a moment before

pinching the bridge of his nose. He opens them again, dropping his hand and tilting his head to the side. "You felt like you were ready to date again because Callie and I inspired you? Even though Callie and I are *just* friends?"

"Well, I know you were just friends *then*, but I mean, you spent a month together, I was sure something would build there."

Jack chuckles, but the humor is missing—not reaching his eyes. He shakes his head once and pushes off the banister. "All right, well, that's great. I'm happy for you. What's his name?"

Is he happy for me? That tone begs to differ. I glance down at the dark red paint on my toenails. "Sam. Sam Fletcher?"

"Sam Fletcher." He clicks his tongue with a tight-lipped smile. "Yep. I know Sam."

"I figured you did. Our town is only so big."

"Yeah." He practically cuts me off, turning away from me to face the pasture. He runs a hand down his face, letting the silence between us sit, making it harder to break. "Man, I'm really exhausted."

That serious expression I was so fond of in the airport isn't giving me the same feeling right now. I'd give anything for one of his genuine grins. I clear my throat and turn to face the pasture as well, leaning on the railing. "I'm sure you are."

"I should probably head on home. I'm back to seeing patients in the morning," he adds, his arms folded protectively over his chest.

I'm not one to bite my tongue, and I should have probably learned that sometimes it's needed. I raise an eyebrow and turn my head to him. "Yeah? That was quick. You were pretty animated a few minutes ago."

"Okay." Jack glances at me, his tone sharp. "I don't know what to tell you. It just hit me."

"What the hell, Jack?" I snap, shaking my head at this attitude he's giving me. I get jet lag, but shit. "Did something happen between you and Callie? Is that why she didn't fly home with you?"

His jaw clenches before he lets out an exasperated groan. "Fucking hell, Eliza. Nothing, and I mean *nothing*, happened between Callie and me. As in, we didn't screw, we didn't 'fall in love,' and there was no fall out, because there was nothing to fall out from. You conjured up this relationship between us in your head."

I have the urge to push him off the porch and watch him land in CeCe's shit, but I don't. I just stare at him, unblinking. I don't have time to acknowledge I jumped to conclusions with him and Callie. I want to focus on why he's being a huge asshole at this moment. "Look, I'm sorry things didn't pan out with her, but—"

"Are you kidding me?" Jack snaps. He closes his eyes again, his fists clenched at his side before relaxing. "Eliza, look. I'm tired. I really just need to get a good night's sleep. Thank you for picking me up, and thank you for coming to dinner tonight. I'll see you later."

"Jack, are you serious?" I raise my voice in surprise as he turns to walk towards the door. Is he really going to end the conversation like this?

"Eliza. Please," he says, stopping with his hand on the doorknob. "I'm just going to get crankier. I need to sleep off this trip." He doesn't give me time to answer. He walks through the back door and into the house, letting the door close loudly behind him.

What the fuck?

11

I don't want to go.

I tug on the top of my costume, which is basically a bra, and cringe. What on earth possessed me to buy this thing? I press my hands over my striking cleavage and groan, wanting to scrap the whole night already.

A mermaid.

This is the last time I let Nova pick my costume.

I lean forward in the mirror and check on the shimmery green scales I painted onto my face before I apply the glittery purple lipstick I purchased for the occasion. I opted for green spandex leggings instead of a tight skirt to act as my tail. I'm feeling self-conscious.

My stomach is exposed—which is something I normally don't do. Well, since college. I've always been curvy with wide-set hips, but I've noticed the extra weight I put on after Aaron died. I never bothered to do anything about it because I'm not the type to be obsessed with weight or being thin. I love my curves.

I'm happy with my appearance. I range anywhere from a size 12 to a size 14 in jeans, and I think I'm attractive.

However, I'm on my period. I'm bloated. And for that, my stomach is one of my insecurities. Luckily, the leggings I purchased are a little high-waisted with sheer fins that stick up at the waistline.

I sigh as I push my hair behind my shoulder and stick the seashell comb into my locks, right above my ear.

"Well, hello, sexy," I hear from behind me and laugh at Simone's seductive purr. I look over my shoulder and furrow my brow, shaking my head to show her I'm not feeling it.

"Can we not go?"

Simone frowns and walks over to me, placing her hands on my shoulders before resting her chin on one. "But you look amazing."

I don't feel amazing. Simone, on the other hand, is in a hot-pink genie costume with fake eyelashes, bright lipstick, and her hair in a long goddess braid, courtesy of yours truly. I look at her through the mirror and give a small smile. "Thank you." I breathe heavily through my nose. "It's really mythical how stunning you are."

"Oh, stop, you're going to make me steal you away from Sam." She winks, sliding her arms around my shoulders and clasping at my chest to squeeze me into a brief hug. "I promise tonight will be fun. He won't be able to keep his hands off of you."

I snort at that and glance at my bare feet, biting my lip slightly. I *know* why I don't want to go. When I look back up, Simone's eyebrow is raised.

"You still haven't talked to Jack?"

There it is. I feel my stomach sink at the question. *No, I haven't. He's a jackass.* I shake my head and go back to fixing my hair, not wanting to talk about it.

She drops her arms and steps back, sitting at the edge

of my bed as I check my makeup for the sixteenth time. "Look, something probably happened on his trip, and he took it out on you. It's not right, but people have their shitty moments. It's going to blow over."

I turn to look at her and sigh, my shoulders dropping. "Yeah, I know. But I'm pissed off at him. It's been over a week, and he hasn't texted or called or come by or anything. I picked him up from the damn airport, and he acts like this? He's being a dick."

Simone looks as if she wants to say something, but her expression warms instead, tilting her head with a sigh. "I'm sorry. But it's Jack. He will probably apologize as soon as he sees you tonight."

"Maybe." I walk to my closet to find my purple sequin flats. No, I did not buy them specifically for this. Yes, I do own purple sequin flats *just because*.

"Don't you dare let his bad attitude ruin our night! We never go to parties together," Simone whines, pouting up at me as she stands.

"I won't. Come on." I roll my eyes, grabbing my small purse before walking out of my bedroom with her. The clock reads 8:45 p.m. I lean down to kiss a sleepy Nova on the couch. "Hey, Supernova," I whisper. "Be good for Faith, okay? We won't be gone too long, but I expect you to be in bed when I get back."

Nova looks up at me with lowered lids and nods, sitting up to stretch. Halloween was technically last night, and we trick-or-treated for three hours. It's safe to say she's still exhausted. "You look like a real mermaid."

I laugh and glance down, giving a hip pop punctuated by a hair flip. "I mean, I do try." I grin when she giggles, and nod toward the bag of candy she collected the night before. "No more candy tonight. You've had enough, and you're going to end up with a stomachache."

"Okay." She drags it out, folding her arms across her chest in annoyance.

"Love you," I coo, grabbing the bag of candy to put elsewhere. I don't trust an eight-year-old with a sugar tooth. Not a chance.

She grumbles her response, plopping back down into a lying position on the couch. Simone emerges from the hall and looks down at Nova with her arms thrown over her face in an award-winning display of dramatics.

"See you later, kid." She reaches down to playfully pinch her cheek.

Our *Lyft* pulls down a gated driveway that opens as soon as we approach.

How safe.

I saw this house last year when we came for the party, but I forgot how overly massive it is. Dr. Combs, a surgeon at the hospital where Simone works, and his wife host this adult costume party annually. It's surprisingly fun. Last year, I didn't drink much, but Simone got hammered, and I basically had to carry her to bed.

It's weird to think that Jack was probably here last year with Gwen. I don't remember seeing them, but Jack talks like he goes every year. It's possible we didn't cross paths. Once again, the place is a damn mansion, and there are easily over a hundred people attending.

I thank the driver as we hop out of the car and look up at the insane decor. This year, they went for a shipwreck theme, equipped with an actual full-sized ship in the front yard. It's decayed and looks as though it's been haunted for several years, but it's incredible for decorations.

Hey, I'm in theme!

"Eliza!" I hear from my left and turn to see Sam approaching with a grin. He's in a baseball uniform with eyeblacks painted under each eye. "You're a hot mermaid."

"Thanks." I look down at my costume before looking back at him. "You're a pretty realistic baseball player. And, obviously, a cute one."

He swoops in for a brief kiss and slides his arm around my waist, pulling back to guide me into the house. "Come on, ladies." He nods to Simone. "The party is getting crazy already."

Sam wasn't lying.

We walk in, and it's a loud commotion of music mixed with laughter and yells from grown men having drinking contests. Charming. I glance at Simone, and we give each other a displeased look before she gestures to the game room.

"I need a drink!" she yells over the noise, and I nod enthusiastically.

Sam and I follow Simone through the crowd, getting to the less cramped area where a bartender is set up in the corner, his tip jar already overflowing. To the left of him, a group of people are playing an obviously intense game of darts.

My stomach tightens when I see Jack among those people. He's Indiana Jones tonight, and damn if he doesn't wear the costume well.

He's laughing at something someone else in his circle said, so I don't want to approach him yet—mid-conversation and all. I look up at Sam and grin, placing my hand on his arm. "Hey, I'm going to the restroom. You mind grabbing me a glass of white?"

"Not at all." He leans down to push his lips against mine again. It's not that he's a bad kisser; it just always comes when I'm least expecting it. I keep it short, leaning back as I pat his arm.

"Thank you." My eyes betray me and find Jack again.

He's looking at me.

Our gazes lock, and he gives me a tight smile, lifting his chin as a greeting before turning back to his friends.

I don't like the feeling it gives me.

I quickly walk toward the restrooms to put some space between us. I don't even know *what* happened between us. I just know it feels *wrong*.

The party is more fun this time, and I don't know if that's because I've met more people in the past year or because I'm allowing myself to let loose. Either way, I'm four glasses of wine in and dancing with Simone on the floor the Combs' have built in their backyard. My calves are starting to burn.

After *Footloose* ends, I jump off the platform to join Sam and let my feet take a break. Out of the tent and past the pool into the back of the house, I see he's still where I left him—talking football in the kitchen. It's been at least forty-five minutes, and he's still there.

I walk up beside him and playfully poke his side. "Right where I left you," I joke, and he acknowledges me briefly before getting back to the importance of player trading or ... something like that. Sports-talk is not my thing.

I try to stay for the conversation, but I'm dreadfully bored. Honestly, if I walked away, Sam wouldn't even notice.

I test that theory.

He doesn't.

Slipping away from his side, I walk to the next room, where an enthusiastic game of *Cards Against Humanity* is going on. I watch for a moment, taking the last sip of my drink and then head for the bar.

I take the back way there and avoid the waves of people as much as possible. Going through the foyer with the grand staircase is much quieter. As soon as I step through the doorway, I spot Jack coming from the bar, drink in hand.

"Hey, you," I try, though I know it sounds off. It *is* off. "Look at you. You pull off Indiana Jones better than Indiana Jones."

Jack smiles at that, and I think it's genuine. He leans against the wall once we meet in the middle, and carefully drags his eyes over my appearance in a way Jack Peters has never done. Not to my knowledge.

"You look," he begins, his Adam's apple dipping dramatically when he swallows, "Fucking incredible."

I feel like I've been dropped in lava. My body immediately heats to an unhealthy temperature at the slight growl in his voice. That was unexpected. I clear my throat and laugh, but I know my face is the color of the rum punch being served. "Well, thanks." I self-consciously push my hair over my shoulder.

"Much better than your date's original costume," he quickly adds. "I figured you'd make him match you or something."

"I'm not a couple's costume type of person." Though I

did make Aaron dress like Fred Flintstone once when I was Wilma.

Jack's eyes darken. "So, you're a couple now?"

Is that a serious question? I raise an eyebrow and place my hands on my hips, trying to keep my tone playful and not show him how annoyed I've been with him. "You would know if you'd have bothered to pick up the phone lately."

"What does it matter if I pick up the phone? You have Sam to pick up the phone."

Oh, okay. Cool. So he wants to act like an immature shit. "Oh, so because I'm seeing someone, we can't be friends?"

"Babe Ruth is not the only reason, just the biggest one," he bites out, his tone sharp and so unlike him. I've never seen him this way, even when he's aggravated at someone.

"Babe Ruth? How clever." It's not unnoticed that he said he wasn't the *only* reason. So there are other reasons we can't be friends. Callie, probably.

"What did he do? Dig his high school uniform out?" Jack's smirking, turning to press his back against the wall, his cup at his lips again to take a generous swig.

I lock my jaw at the insult and roll my eyes, tilting my head to the side to show him I'm not amused. "He played in college."

"Of course he did." He snorts, looking back down at the drink in his hand. "Halloween—the one day he can live out his glory days. Was that the peak of his life?"

"Wow." I glare up at him, crossing my arms over my midriff. *Where is this coming from?* "You're being a dick."

Jack looks back at me, his eyes glazed from the amount of alcohol he consumed. I can tell from the smell of it lingering on his breath as he speaks. He shakes his head, looking away from me and running a hand down his face. "I've got to get away from you."

His words stab like a knife in my gut. My throat tightens, and I drop my arms with what I hope reads as an angry expression. "Screw you." My voice is a growl, and I push past him.

"Eliza." I hear him groan behind me. "That didn't come out ..." He trails off as I make a beeline toward the exit. I knew it was a bad idea to come to this damn party.

I'm almost to the back door when I feel his warm hand gently grab my forearm and turn me to him, letting go almost immediately. I'm fuming as we stare at each other, and his face softens.

"I just meant," he starts, our eyes not daring to break contact. "I can't be around you right now, because you're ..." He stops, taking a deep breath, and gazes down at my costume before looking back at me. "You're—"

"Eliza, there you are."

I step away from Jack, my jaw still set in frustration. *I'm what?* I turn to see Sam beside me, and force a grin, though my heart is pounding so hard I can feel it in my toes. "Here I am." My voice cracks. "Are you ready to get out of here? I'm feeling pretty tired."

"Sure." Sam glances at Jack, who hasn't taken his eyes off of me—I can feel them burning a hole into my face. But I'm no longer looking at him. If I do, I may physically harm him for being *such* an asshole. "Hey, man."

"Hey," Jack replies, stepping away from us. "I'm going to go find some people I need to say hi to. Have a good night."

I don't reply. I refuse to. And I think Sam picks up on it.

"He's had a bit to drink," Sam mumbles, and I nod in agreement as we reach Simone, who's engaged in a conversation with a man by the front door. She looks up at us with wide *help me* eyes, subtly nodding to the door to show us she's ready to leave, too.

I glance behind me one last time and see Jack standing beside Callie, her head is resting on his arm. He looks up, our eyes like magnets, and slips an arm around her waist.

My insides twist into a new feeling of nausea and annoyance. I'm actually pretty angry at myself for having this type of reaction.

Maybe it's the wine.

———

I wake up with a slight headache and a blurry memory of a Jack I don't know. After we left last night, I came straight home and washed off the sticky film of the party from my body before passing out. Despite feeling like shit, I couldn't sleep past 6:30 a.m. With Simone and Nova still snoozing in their warm beds, I'm feeling even more alone, and I usually enjoy the peace.

I have an emptiness in my chest.

My feet are curled under me in the swing Simone's dad built for us. The mug of tea cupped in my palms spreads warmth through my body, calming the previous shivers when I first stepped outside.

Dreams of the night before plagued me throughout my restless sleep, and I'm trying to piece together what was said and what my substance-infused subconscious conjured up. It's still the same outcome: Jack was a jerk.

It's almost eight when I see his Bronco turn down my driveway. I tense up, clutching the mug tighter as I watch him come closer. I left my phone inside. Did he call? Is everything okay? My body is frozen to the swing, but I keep my eyes on the vehicle as it parks behind mine.

Jack's out in an instant, his fists clenched at his side as he makes his way up the steps. I hope he doesn't expect me to call out a warm greeting. I *want* him to feel uncomfortable.

He looks tired when he reaches the top. His normally vibrant eyes have dark circles, his face slightly pale. If I didn't hold grudges, I'd be concerned.

"I have been the biggest jackass, and I owe you an apology." His words come out in a rush, and his tone is marked with exhaustion, but the sincerity I know from Jack is there. I'm angry. But he's clearly sorry.

I brace myself by putting my foot down to stop the swing from its natural sway. "Want to tell me what the hell is going on?"

"First, I just want to tell you I'm sorry. I'm so, so sorry." He's coming closer to me, his arms hanging at his side. His hair is shorter than when I picked him up from the airport. His hat shielded that fact last night. That stings.

He's in front of me, and instead of taking a seat beside me, he squats down. His heels are holding his full weight, and he relaxes his arms on his thighs, his hands cradling his knees.

My hand has a mind of its own, and I'm reaching out, pulling my fingers through the short, amateur cut with a frown. Without saying a word, he casts his eyes down and hangs his head. He knows I'm pissed.

"Who?" I ask. Melodrama comes naturally to me.

Jack looks back up, his shoulders falling in defeat. "I went to see Benji a couple of days after I got home. Eliza, look—"

His old stylist? *Ouch.* "What the hell? What did I do to you that warranted *that*?"

"Nothing. You have done absolutely *nothing* wrong. It's me. I've been in a weird place, and that's not an excuse, but I'm so sorry." When I don't respond immediately, his eyes grow heavy, and he uses the heel of his palms to dig into them. "You were right the other night. Something happened on my trip, and I don't want to talk about it, but it put me in a bad headspace when I got home. Adding to that, I've got the stress of construction beginning on the house, and we're coming up on what would be my one-year wedding anniversary. I'm just feeling shitty."

Oh, shit. That *is* coming up. I relax into the swing, inhaling sharply before letting it out slowly. Does this excuse how he's acted toward me? Not even a little. Do I want to hug him and make it better? Absolutely.

"I should have never spoken to you the way I did. God, Eliza, I barely slept at all. I haven't been myself, and after being distant and stupid the night I got home from Albania, I just wanted to give you space. But then last night, I drank too much and took all of my shit out on you. I even missed trick-or-treating with Nova. I can't even explain to you how awful I feel."

"I'm not going to say *it's okay*, because it isn't, and I never want you to feel like it is ever okay to treat me like that again. But," I pause, our gazes locked, "I forgive you. Do you want to talk about what happened on your trip?"

His entire body relaxes as if I've physically lifted something heavy from him and gave him rest. He shakes his head, standing up and taking a seat next to me. The action makes the swing rock back, but he catches the post to stop us from moving any more. "Not at all, if that's okay. I just needed to make things right between us."

I stay silent for a brief period and glance at his fresh haircut once more. "Well," I begin, "we're not entirely okay, yet. You did let someone else ruin my carefully constructed masterpiece." His brow draws together, and I gingerly flick a wave with my index finger, causing him to break out into a grin.

"I am *such* an asshole, Liza. I'm sorry."

I wave him off, and we rock in silence, listening to the breeze cut through the bare trees and rustle the dead leaves collecting in my once lusciously green yard. It almost feels like we're already back to normal because this silence is far from tense.

"I need to apologize to Callie, too," he says, breaking the comfortable moment. "She's my next stop."

I take immature satisfaction in the fact I was the first person he wanted to see. And, oddly, I'm comforted that he didn't spend the night with her. But I'm also curious as to what happened after I left. "Messed up there, too?"

His nod is short, confirming my initial instinct that he didn't want to talk about that, either. Jack's hands are clasped in front of him, his thumbs wrestling each other as he fidgets. His knee bounces, and then he's rubbing his palms down the front of his light washed jeans. "Please say we're okay, Liza."

"We're okay. I promise. Just don't shut down on me like that again. Next time, I won't be so forgiving. You *really* hurt my feelings."

The pain in his eyes at that admission makes me feel guilty for no other reason than I hate seeing him hurt—even if it's his fault. "You know you're my best friend, don't you?"

My heart skips.

"I do now." My grin is unbearable. "Everyone has shitty moments, Jack. Yours wasn't irreparable."

His hand, large and warm, closes over my knee. With a gentle squeeze, he catches my gaze. "Let's catch up this week. Bring Nova, and we'll do something fun."

"Just tell me the time and place."

I feel better.

$\mathcal{M}$y bags feel ten times heavier than usual as I carry them into the house after mine and Nova's *long* trip home. Two layovers and a missed connection later, we finally made it. Nova has been an absolute crank since we landed. I even tried to play *I Spy* in the *Lyft* on the way home, but she was not having it.

I mean, I'll give her a break. It is two in the morning. She's exhausted.

We spent a couple of days visiting Aaron's parents in Colorado for the Thanksgiving holiday. They decided to move a few months after Nova's birthday party. I think it's been great for them.

Gail joined a craft club, and Henry joined the country club. They host dinner parties at their house. They've gotten their routine back, and I loved seeing it.

I'm quiet as I walk through the kitchen, but Chief is turning in circles at my feet, panting in excitement that his other two girls are home.

"Hi, man," I whisper in the dark, leaning down to

scratch his ears after quietly dropping my bags by the wall, careful not to wake Simone.

Nova is leaning against the doorway, her eyelids lowered. She's practically sleeping standing up. I so wish my phone weren't at the bottom of my monstrosity of a purse, because this moment is too cute.

"Nova." I lean down and place my hands on her arms. "Why don't you go on and get in bed? You can shower in the morning, and we'll wash your sheets tomorrow to get the airport funk off of them."

Her nod is barely visible, and she walks past me, patting Chief's head on her way through the kitchen and toward her bedroom. I briefly consider leaving the bags where they are.

But I don't. I carry them all to my bedroom, including Nova's, and place them at the foot of my bed.

I can't take my own advice and strip down to jump in the shower. I *cannot* sleep with this feeling on me. I've seen Nova climb into bed after crawling in the dirt outside —much to my dismay. I knew it wouldn't bother her.

I feel like it's almost daylight when I'm finally settled in my bed, but I'm wired. Tomorrow is going to be painful if I can't get to sleep *now*. Nova and I made it home just in time for *actual* Thanksgiving. We're going to the Peters' with Simone, but I will be in the worst mood if my mind doesn't turn off. I briefly think about texting Sam to tell him we made it, but it's way too early. He's somewhere far off for work and texting him just to say I made it home seems too serious.

I quietly scold myself for not remembering where he is. Montana? Nevada?

Staring at the neon numbers beside my bed, replaying our past conversations to jog my memory, I drift to sleep, barely feeling Chief jump up beside me, snuggling to my side.

I'm a zombie.

I'm barely able to form coherent sentences when I get to Matthew and David's house with my family in tow, Chief included. Nova is bouncing off the walls in excitement, and Simone is beaming with a well-rested glow.

I'm envious.

The house smells like heaven, and I follow the scent to the kitchen where I place my banana bread on the table next to the buffet of food.

"How many people are we feeding?" I'm amazed by the amount of dishes, but the tone of my voice is as flat as I feel.

"It's just us!" Matthew responds with a grin, dropping the stirring spoon in his hand to walk over and envelop me in a tight hug. He kisses my cheek and leans back to look at me. "You look worn out. Go prop your feet up until dinner."

"No way." I came prepared for this argument. I shake my head, pulling away from his concerned embrace. "I'm helping. It's why I came early. Put me to work, or I'll find something to do on my own and ruin the flow."

I can see the internal struggle. I smirk slightly when he exhales and rolls his eyes. "Fine, but don't pass out in my sweet potatoes."

Usually, I would laugh at that absurd request, but it's a fair evaluation. I don't know how Simone can go so long with minimal sleep. I've slept five and a half hours in the past forty-eight. I almost feel drunk—like I can't control what my hands are doing or what my mouth is saying.

I haven't seen Jack or David yet, but I hear their voices echoing from the living room. It's just ... too far for me to walk.

Standing is a hassle in itself.

Dinner prep and dinner go by in a blink, and yet, *I* feel as if I'm moving in slow motion. I catch Jack's eyes every so often, his brow furrowed in worry. Everyone's voices are clear, yet muffled, and I feel like I could pass out at any minute.

"Eliza." It's sharp, and I snap to attention, looking around the table to see where it came from—and why it's so urgent.

"Yeah?" My voice sounds rough. Have I not engaged in conversation this entire time? I look down at my plate, my fork in hand stabbed into an uneaten piece of turkey. What is *wrong* with me?

"You look really pale." The voice belongs to Jack, and I focus my attention on him, but my eyes want to drift close. "Maybe you should go lie down."

I wave my hand, but it takes so much energy to do so. A quick flick of the wrist makes me feel fatigued. Am I coming down with something? Surely, I can't be *this* tired.

A soreness begins in a slow thud behind my eyes, promising me a nasty headache in the coming hours. I nod to no one in particular and push myself from the dinner table. "Look, I don't want to miss the Black Friday sales. Please come wake me in an hour."

I made words. That was a feat.

Standing up, I turn to leave the room when I realize I'm not exactly sure if I remember where the guest bedroom is. I spin back toward the table, ready to ask, and

Jack is already standing up, rounding the edge to get to me.

"I'll show you where to go." He places a hand on my back, and the heat causes my steps to falter slightly—most definitely from exhaustion.

I slip off my boots and pull my sweater over my head when I reach the bed, not hesitating to pull the covers back.

"Are you good?" His voice is right behind me. My heart plummets to my stomach, my insides knotting at the closeness of him in this dark bedroom. I feel guilty.

I know Sam and I are not serious. I know we're casual and only seeing each other on the rare occasion he's in town. And yet, guilt.

"Yep." It's strained, high-pitched, and embarrassing. I quickly crawl into bed, the sheets soft against my skin, and pull the comforter to my chin. "Thanks for this."

With a simple nod, he backs out of the bedroom, shutting the door behind him.

I'm glad I trusted no one and set an alarm before slipping into the deepest nap I've ever taken. I sit up and realize I'm in a house with a bunch of traitors, not respecting my wishes to hit the after-Thanksgiving Day sales.

Simone has already left for a delivery when I march into the living room, glaring at Jack for not attempting to wake me. He fights me about going, arguing that I'm still too tired. But that ends with him agreeing to go with me to make sure I won't crash while shopping.

With David and Matthew watching Nova, Jack and I pull into the parking lot of our first stop. I squee in excitement, though my body is still fighting to stay alert. We got here as the end of the line of people was being ushered through the doors.

I take Nova's Christmas list out of my purse and blink my eyes a few times, widening them to force myself awake.

Come on, body. Just a few more hours.

"This is so stupid." Jack's voice is gruff beside me, and I glance over to see his arms folded over his chest. "You're tired. You're never going to catch up on sleep. You can't be everywhere all the time."

"What does that even mean?" I mumble my question while looking through the list in my hand, preparing my attack plan. Toys first, for *the* dollhouse she can't stop talking about. It's her only wish that's still childlike. The rest are DVDs, a laptop, a new skateboard, and some sort of gaming system. The only problem is, this dollhouse is the most sought-after toy this year.

Jack turns to me in his seat, his hand covering my handwriting so I have to look up at him. "It means you can ask people for help. I could have taken this list and come out here by myself while you slept."

"No. I'm not going to ask anyone to do that." I stifle a yawn. It wants to come out so badly, but I clench my jaw, holding it back. I'm unsuccessful. I press my hand to my mouth and let it out, groaning in aggravation at the timing.

"I know you're not. I'm just saying you *can*." He gets out of the truck and walks to my side, waiting on me to step out.

I can do it.

Just a few items to check off, and I can be back in bed.

The stores are crazy, as expected. Jack isn't bothered,

following me to every aisle in slow strides while I look through shelves of out-of-place items like a madwoman. I'm able to grab a few things from my list, but the dollhouse is nowhere to be found.

By the third store, I'm losing what little steam I had. And still, no dollhouse. I want to scream, but I keep cool, sighing in disappointment when I see an empty space where the boxes should be. I look up at Jack, and his head is tilted, sympathetic, but I read it as condescending.

"Don't give me that look."

He shakes his head, holding his hands up in surrender. "There is no look. I am here for as long as you need."

"Good because I want to look at clothes while I'm here," I challenge, crossing my arms over my chest. I do *not* want to look at clothes. I want to find this stupid house and go back to bed. Why do I have to be so stubborn?

"Then, by all means ..." Jack trails off, a knowing smile painted on his face. I narrow my eyes before turning away to head to the women's section of the department store. The rest of the mall is closed, waiting until tomorrow morning to open. But the larger department stores with sought-after items open on Thanksgiving night.

I kind of hate it. I miss the thrill of waking up at three in the morning to get in line for the doors to open at four or five. With the sales starting earlier, it takes the fun out of the experience.

I'm thumbing through the hangers of dresses, uninterested in every one I see. Jack leaves my side and takes a seat in the chair next to the nearest dressing room. He leans back and places his hands behind his head, grinning. "I like that color. You should try it on."

That sounds like a lot of work. I must do it. I pick a few

hangers off the rack and walk into the dressing room, shooting him a defiant look.

"You're insane!" he calls to me, leaning over the chair as I walk past him.

He's humoring me as I strut out in different outfits, twirling in front of him and posing in the mirror beside us. I make him give me a rating on a scale of ten for every half-assed choice I present to him. So far, I'm ranking high except on a crushed velvet turtleneck dress that he could not lie about, no matter how hard he tried.

Despite my only doing this to prove a point, I found a few cute outfits I plan on buying. The fun of modeling outfits gave me a burst of energy that's fading again. I glance down at my phone and notice it's pushing ten.

I also see a text.

Sam: *Hey, just checking in. I'll call tomorrow.*

Without thinking, my eyes find Jack to see if he can see the text. I don't know why. He doesn't care. *I* don't care. It just feels ... *weird.*

I type a fast reply: *Hope you're having a great time! Talk to you then. :)*

"All right." Jack's voice interrupts my thoughts. "One more store to find this house, and then you have got to go to sleep."

I walk with him to the checkout lines that are going surprisingly quickly and give in to his demand with a nod. "You're right."

"Oh. Please, say that again."

"I'll break your fingers."

The last stop is another bust. I'm so tired and so disappointed that I can feel a lump in my throat, pushing upward and causing my eyes to water.

Do not *cry over this, Eliza.*

It's a silent ride back to his parents'. I'm so close to sleep that anything I say will be a whine or possibly slurred. When I glance over at his easy expression, I can't help but smile. "Thank you for coming with me."

"I didn't want you to fall asleep at the wheel," he reasons before smirking ever so slightly. "You're welcome. I had fun. I'm sorry we didn't find the dollhouse."

"I'm not giving up." I let a yawn escape past my lips and lean my head against the window, closing my eyes for a brief moment. It feels so good to let them rest.

When I open them, I'm somewhere else. My feet aren't on solid ground, and I'm floating. How am I *floating*? I blink a few times and realize I'm being carried by Jack. I tense, and he looks down, the corner of his mouth lifting. "I'm just putting you to bed."

I relax against him, wondering how he could carry me so effortlessly. He sits me down on the edge of the bed in the guestroom where I napped a few hours ago. I sag slightly, lifting my head with all the energy I can muster to give him a grateful smile. "You're the best."

Jack squats in front of me and slips off my boots. When he looks up, he places a hand on my cheek. I lean into his warm palm, exhaling a sleepy sigh.

"Eliza." My name is a whispered breath, and he tries to catch my eyes in the dimly lit bedroom.

"Hm?" I hum the response because I'm too tired for words. His hand is like a pillow, and I could fall asleep like this.

I'm so close to dozing off that I can't tell if it's my imagination or if his thumb is lightly grazing my cheek. He shakes his head in response and stands up, guiding me to lie down under the covers. "Sleep tight," he mutters, shutting the lamp beside the bed off.

I'm certain I'm dreaming. I reach out and grasp his hand before he leaves the room, squeezing his fingers in between mine. "Don't leave."

Did I say those words out loud? This is still a dream, right?

Jack pulls my hand up to his lips and presses a soft kiss to my knuckles before placing it back on my stomach where my other hand rests. "Goodnight, Liza."

My insides flutter. Definitely a dream.

I awake with a jolt to Nova jumping on top of me with an excited grin. I reflexively catch her and smile, forcing my eyes open despite the sticky feeling of my lashes. I hate going to bed with makeup on.

"Matthew made brunch!" She cheers, her grin widening.

"Brunch?" I croak out the question, looking around the room for a clock. I reach beside me, blindly feeling for my phone.

10:12 a.m.

(2) Missed Calls.

Sam. Simone.

"Holy crap, it's ten?" I ask to no one in particular, but Nova nods anyway, sitting up on my legs. "How long have you been awake?"

She shrugs, but rolls her eyes upwards as if to try and pull the memory of when she woke up. Was it 6? 7? Did I make these men play babysitter and ruin their Friday plans? I sit up and pull my hair back, tying the knotted mess into a ponytail to look at least a little bit presentable.

"I think I've been awake since eight," she finally

replies, rolling off the bed and jumping down to the floor with a light thud. "I went out to the barn with David and Jack, got to see Delilah, and watched one episode of *Scooby-Doo*."

"Oh, okay. Man, I guess we were tired, huh?" I laugh, feeling much better and way more well-rested than I did the entirety of yesterday. "I'll come join you guys for brunch. I need to make a call first, okay?" I lean forward, dropping a kiss on her forehead before she runs out of the bedroom. I can't even remember falling asleep last night. I'm still in my clothes from yesterday. The night is a blur.

I try Simone first, but it rings for an eternity before I grow tired of waiting and hang up. So I call Sam.

"Hey, Eliza." Sam's voice is a chirp into the phone, and I can hear the smile in his greeting. "You've been incredibly hard to get a hold of."

I laugh at his statement because he's one to talk. I don't usually try too hard to get in touch with him, because I'm not at that level of dependency. But he's a healthcare consultant. His job is ninety-percent travel. I'm in the same spot from eight to five, five days a week. "Yeah, I had a very busy few days. I actually just woke up if you can believe it."

"Woah." Sam laughs as well, and I hear him rustling around with something in the background. "Did you party hard last night?"

"No. After the flight issues and then a full day of Thanksgiving festivities, Matthew and David watched Nova for me last night so me and Jack could go hit the Black Friday sales. I'm pretty sure I passed out as soon as I got back to their house." I stand up from the bed and walk to the adjoining bathroom, taking a look at my appearance. It's *rough*.

Sam is silent for a moment, the rustling stopped. "Just you and Jack?"

"Yeah. Simone had a delivery, and I couldn't take Nova. I was getting her Christmas list and all."

"And you stayed the night there?"

I pick up on the edge to his tone, and I do *not* appreciate it. His question does make me attempt to remember how I even got to bed. I have a vision of Jack carrying me and laying me down on the bed. I was talking to him, but I don't remember what I said. I also don't remember if that part was a dream or not. I was dead to the world. "Yeah, of course. Nova was already asleep by the time we got back. I was too tired to drive home. I've barely slept after our forty-eight-hour airport adventure."

It's silent for another brief second. And then: "Oh. That sounds awful. Are you well-rested now?"

Like he wasn't unreasonably irritated ten seconds ago. That's fine, though. I rather him let it go than deal with the jealous boyfriend act. For starters, he isn't my boyfriend. We have not had that conversation, and I *like* our casual dating. I let it go, too. "Yes, I feel much better. I'm not sure what my plans are for the rest of the day."

"It's Friday-night movie night, right?" There's that tone again.

I ignore it. "Yes, that's tonight. I'm not sure what we're watching, yet, though."

Don't leave.

The words, clearly spoken by me, form a recent memory as we talk. I hang onto them, trying to paint the picture. My stomach drops. Oh, no. Oh, *no*. I was weird, wasn't I? *Don't leave.* I asked Jack not to leave after he put me in bed last night. I don't remember him responding, but he certainly left. God, I hope I didn't make things awkward.

"I'm sure you guys will have fun. I need to get going, but I will talk to you later?"

I nod, but remember he can't see that. "Yes, of course. I'll call you later. Have a fun trip."

We hang up, and I splash water on my face a couple of times before walking out to join the others in the kitchen. Nova is already seated with a full plate, waiting to dig in.

"Morning, sleepyhead." David grins at me, handing me a dish before guiding me to the table. "I'm glad you got some rest."

"Me too. This smells delicious, but I need to feed Chief. I'm so sorry I've just thrown all of my responsibilities on you guys."

"Already fed him." I hear Jack's voice as he walks through the kitchen, the corner of his eyes crinkled in a pleased expression. "Don't apologize. You needed rest."

Okay. He's acting normal.

Shaking my head, I sit next to Nova and look up at him. My eyes are swollen and rimmed with black makeup, and my hot-pink lipstick is slightly smeared, stained on my skin. I saw exactly what I looked like before I came to the kitchen. I could do nothing about it. "Thank you. We will be out of your hair soon, I swear."

Jack rolls his eyes, not even the slightest hint of concern at my appearance. He grabs a plate from David and walks to sit across from me. "You are never *in our hair*. Stop being a brat. Also, we're watching *Rookie of the Year* tonight. Is Simone in?"

"As far as I know, we will have a full house."

"Just how I like it." He grins before shoveling a large piece of waffle into his mouth.

13

My hands are numb even though my newly purchased leather gloves are covering them. They're stuffed into the pockets of my coat, and a scarf is snug around my neck. Obviously, I still haven't gotten used to the winter weather of Connecticut. Nova, high on adrenaline, isn't even shivering as she runs in and out of the rows of trees at Peters' tree farm.

"You okay?" Sam tugs my arm. I snap out of my daze, turning my head slightly to him with a smile, but still keeping Nova in my line of sight.

I squeeze his hand as reassurance and laugh at the question. "Of course I am. Just trying not to lose Nova. The place is a little crowded tonight, isn't it?"

"She'll be fine. I pretty much know every face I see." His laughter is carefree, and it makes my stomach knot. The nonchalant air of a guy who's never taken care of anyone but himself. I try to shake that feeling because I know I'm trying to self-sabotage. I nod at his attempt at calming my nerves, but my eyes find Nova again.

I clear my throat before raising my voice slightly to get

her attention. "Nova Claire," I call, causing her to whip around with an excited grin. I tilt my head, matching her smile, because how can I not? "Can you stay close, please?"

She sighs and nods, walking closer to me as I stand in front of a row of seven-foot to eight-foot trees. She's quiet when Sam is around, and quiet is definitely not one of her traits. She's not a shy kid, even if it takes her a bit to warm up to someone. But, Sam's been around for a couple of months now. She warmed up to Jack quicker than that.

Sam's voice brings me back to reality, and I feel guilty for being so distracted on our first outing with Nova.

"Sorry, what did you say?" I hear a slight sigh as he replies.

"I said, why don't you get a bigger tree?" he repeats, his voice even, but to my trained ear, I hear annoyance. "Your ceilings are really high." I feel like I'm in a classroom, getting scolded by my teacher for doodling during the lecture.

I wave a hand at that and look down at Nova, placing my hands on her shoulders. "Oh, well, I know they are, but you know, I'm short. Nova's short. Simone's short ..." I trail off with a laugh. "Trying to steer clear of ladders this year, so I need something I can reach on the step stool."

"Oh, I can help with that," he says, genuinely, stepping closer and placing his hand on my lower back affectionately.

I feel Nova tense under my hands, and she speaks before I have time to reply myself. "You're decorating our tree with us?" Her tone isn't rude, but it's not filled with Christmas joy. I gently squeeze her shoulders and give Sam an apologetic smile as he looks from her to me, his brow furrowed as if he's unable to figure out how to answer the unreadable question.

"That's really sweet of you, Sam," I reply, trying to diffuse the potentially uncomfortable situation. "But we've kind of made the decorating of the tree a family tradition with us three girls. I'm sorry."

I'm not *really* sorry, seeing as we're not super serious, but I feel like I need to tiptoe around his feelings right now.

His smile falters, but not entirely; it's just not reaching his eyes. "Sure," he says, stepping back with his hands up. "I would never try to interrupt a tradition. It's totally okay."

It's quiet for a moment, all three of us unsure of what to say. My eyes are watering, my hands still numb, my nose basically ice, threatening to break off at any moment. I break the silence when I see a woman in a red apron walk past us.

"Excuse me." She turns with a warm smile. "We'll take this one." I point to a random tree I haven't even examined. I have an overwhelming feeling of discomfort, and I want to get out of here.

We have a lighthearted argument over who is going to pay for the tree, which is utterly ridiculous, seeing as it's going in my house. So, not exactly lighthearted? I win, anyway, and I'm pretty sure it's because my smile looked more like a clenched jaw and gritted teeth after the fourth time I insisted.

When the man whose name tag reads "Marvin" hands me my change, I turn my head to see if Sam and Nova are still behind me. Sam is, but Nova is out of sight. Before becoming irrational, I look around us to see if she's near.

She's not, and the crowd has thinned since we first got here. I should be able to see her.

"Where is Nova?" I ask Sam, trying hard not to snap at him for not watching her for the five minutes it took me to pay for the tree. He was probably too busy pouting that I paid for my own. Damn. Tree.

Sam looks down at the now-vacant spot beside him and then up at me, shaking his head slightly. "I don't know. She was just here." He turns in a complete circle, looking around while I walk away from him. No time to bitch. I need to find her.

My heart rate spikes, and I can feel my pulse in my throat. I feel hot and cold all at once, my neck damp with a nervous sweat.

"Nova?" I desperately call out, the rapid pace of my heartbeat making me lightheaded.

It's no more than thirty seconds before I hear her cheerful voice, and I take a calming breath. I exhale and press my hand to my chest, seeing her come closer, beaming and riding on Jack's shoulders. He's wearing a matching smile.

"Jesus, Nova," I breathe out. "Do *not* do that again. Do you know how terrified you just made me?"

"But I saw Jack, and I wanted to go tell him we were here!" she calls back, unfazed by my concern. Jack is here. All is well in Novaland. To be honest, all is well in Eliza-land, too. One look at his boyish grin, and I feel calmer, the tenseness between Sam and I no longer on my radar.

Jack's eyes roll upward, and he tugs Nova's leg, which is thrown over his shoulder. "Hey, don't run off from your mom. That's not safe," he states, which earns a slight nod from Nova.

She looks down at me and delivers a sheepish smile,

her hands clasped on Jack's head. "I'm sorry," she says, as sincere as I'm going to get from her at this point.

I sigh a little and look down at Jack as he maneuvers her to where she's clinging to his back now, instead of being perched on his shoulders.

"What are you doing here?" I'm pleasantly surprised to see him once I can catch my breath.

"Hunting buffalo," he replies, seriously, before rolling his eyes. "I'm getting a tree, crazy. What do you think I'm doing?" I watch as his smile fades noticeably, and he nods to something behind me. "Hey, man."

"Jack." I hear as Sam comes to stand beside me. His arm is around my waist as soon as he stills, tugging me into his side. It doesn't feel right. None of it feels right. My face flushes, no longer cold from the night chill. I think I see Jack's jaw tic, his nostrils flaring slightly, but it could be in my head. It's in my head, right? "Funny running into you here."

"Is it? It's my parents' farm," Jack deadpans, hoisting my daughter higher on his back after she slid down a bit. Nope, definitely not in my head. I briefly wonder if Nova has confided in Jack things she hasn't told me. Like ... why she's not Sam's biggest fan. "Didn't mean to interrupt your date, Liza."

"Oh no, you didn't," I reply, quickly. Oh, look, it's tense again. I can't help noticing the common denominator here. "Are you here alone?"

He shakes his head, smiling again as he looks back at me. "No, uh." He pauses and gestures back towards the entrance with his head. "Callie is here, too."

"Callie," I repeat, nodding way too enthusiastically, which I notice, but cannot stop. "Right."

"Yeah. She needed a tree, and who best to help her pick one out, right?"

"Cool, cool," I reply. Boy, it's difficult to swallow at this particular moment. I hear my name over the noise of the crowd around us, signaling that our tree is ready. "That's us," I say, moving away from Sam as Nova's feet hit the ground. She hugs Jack tightly before taking my outstretched hand.

"I'll see you soon," he says with a wave. Nova and Sam are both quiet on our walk to the entrance, and when I glance back, Jack's eyes are still on us. He glances away when I catch him and turns to head in the other direction.

I walk into the living room from the backyard and peel my gloves off my hand. I love walking in to a lit Christmas tree overloaded with shared ornaments Simone and I have collected, separately, over the years. Decorating it three nights ago was the therapy I needed. Simone loudly singing carols while Nova carefully chose which ornament should be the first to go on. We finished up with hot cocoa by our fireplace, and *Home Alone*. Yes, we did the tree thing a little later than normal—only a week before Christmas. But this season was busier than expected, with weddings almost every weekend. I'll do better next year.

This evening, it was building snowmen in the backyard after Simone got back from a delivery at the hospital. She's Wonder Woman, I swear. I unravel the scarf from Nova's neck and help her get her puffy jacket that's zipped to her chin off. Once she's free of the winter clothes, she runs to the couch and gets under the blanket, teeth still chattering.

Sam walks in with a coffee mug in hand, coming up behind me and pressing a kiss to my cheek. "You're cute when your cheeks are all rosy." He grins. He steps up behind the couch and looks down at Nova. "What are we watching?"

"*Jack Frost*," she replies, simply, smiling politely at him. She turns her attention back to the television.

My focus switches to Chief, who has been mopey all day. He even groaned when I tried to play with him earlier, which concerns me. But, other than a sad attitude, he hasn't shown any other signs of being sick. I walk over to him and get on the floor, running my hand through his gold locks. "Hiya, Chief. Not feeling so hot?"

His eyes roll up to look at me, and he gives me a quick lick on my cheek as a response.

"He was like that this morning, too," Simone pipes up from the kitchen, putting away the leftovers from dinner. "He wouldn't eat."

"So he hasn't eaten all day?" I furrow my brow in concern, running my hand over his side to bring him a sense of comfort.

Sam walks over and kneels down beside me. "My sister's dog used to not eat when she was angry about something. Maybe he doesn't like sharing you with other men."

I inwardly roll my eyes at that response. Chief is probably petty, but he's not hunger-strike petty. The boy loves his food. "I'll keep an eye on him, I guess."

"You could call Jack," Simone replies, walking over to inspect him as well.

I shake my head in response, remembering his not-a-date with Callie. In case it turned into a date, I don't want to contact him. That would be awkward. Well, for me. "I'll call him if something else happens."

"Yeah, I'm sure he's fine," Sam adds, but deep down, I know that's because he's jealous of Jack and the relationship he has with us.

After Nova has been put to bed and Simone is in the shower, Sam and I are standing on the back patio, watching Chief as he shuffles around the yard to look for a place to pee. He's not bouncing around in the snow, like he usually does, so I watch him closely.

I step off the patio and make my way to him as he lifts his leg against a tree. When he finishes, he walks past me and to the back door. I glance down to where he peed and notice the slight red tint. Is that blood? What could that mean? I can hear my pulse—there are at least a hundred different horrible scenarios in my head because I'm an irrational overthinker.

"Sam, does this look like blood to you?" I ask, and he quickly walks over to see what I'm pointing to.

"I really can't tell, but if you think that's what it is, maybe you should watch him closely tonight."

I nod, but walk past him and back into the house to grab my phone. Callie be damned, I'm calling Jack. I feel a pressure in my throat—a lump I can't swallow. *Please, be okay.*

Jack picks up after the first ring. "Hey, I was just about to text you."

"Hey," I reply, swallowing thickly. "Uh, so, something is wrong with Chief. He won't eat, he's mopey, and I think I saw blood in his pee." As I say the words, I feel tears spring into my eyes.

"Okay," he says, calmly. "It's okay. How about I meet you at the office, and I can take a look at him?"

"Okay," I reply, not trusting my voice any longer. "We'll head over now."

After quickly giving Simone the rundown, Chief, Sam, and I are all in my car and headed to town. I'm quiet on the ride, sitting in the backseat with Chief's head in my lap as Sam drives. He looks so pitiful, I can't help but let the dam break. I'm trying to keep my cries silent, not wanting to alarm Chief. Absurd or not, I feel like he can tell when I'm worried or upset.

When we get to the clinic, I help Chief out and walk him inside. Sam is catching a phone call as he gets out of the car, and I don't have time to wait. As soon as I'm in the lobby, Jack walks over and pulls me into an embrace. This is what I needed. His hugs have a sense of safety that I crave.

"He's going to be okay, all right? I'm almost positive you're describing bladder stones." He pulls back and looks down at me, giving me a sympathetic smile as he wipes a tear from my cheek. "Do you want to come back with us?"

I nod just as I hear the door chime behind me, signaling Sam's arrival. I glance at him with a small smile. "I'm going to go back with them."

"I'll wait out here," Sam suggests, and I feel bad for treating him like a chauffeur.

I smile and reach back to squeeze his hand softly. "Thank you."

I follow Jack to the back with Chief's leash tight in my hand. When he's on the exam table, Jack calms his shaking with a few good ear rubs. I'm leaning against the wall with my arms crossed over my chest, ready to hear the worst. I feel like that's been my life for the past couple of years—just waiting for the worst.

"Yep," he says, his hands feeling low on Chief's stomach. "I'm pretty sure I can feel bladder stones, which means they're pretty big. I'm going to give him an X-ray. Stay here, and we'll be right back."

I nod with a small smile, still nervous as I don't know what bladder stones entail. I pace the exam room as I wait for them, trying to think of how to tell Nova if anything bad happens to him. She's already been through too much. I focus on anything else to stop myself from over-thinking and almost sending myself into an anxiety attack. It isn't working. It's a matter of minutes, and Jack is back in the exam room, Chief slowly following him.

"It's bladder stones," he confirms, walking over to me with a soothing expression to, no doubt, combat my frantic one. "Look," he says, placing his hands on my arms. "To get rid of them, we need to schedule a surgery. I think the sooner, the better, so he's no longer feeling discomfort."

"A surgery?" I exclaim, my heart beating out of my chest. "Is it usually successful? Have you ever lost a dog during one of these surgeries?"

He holds my gaze, rubbing my arms with his warm palms that I can feel through my jacket. His eyes are kind and greener than usual. "Eliza, you have to trust me. It's a really simple surgery. What about tomorrow?"

I stare back at him, more at ease. Something about Jack comforts me. I wipe my nose, still stopped up from crying. "Okay." I nod, looking down at Chief, who is lying down by my feet. "Thank you so much."

"It's literally my job." He grins, laughing as he does.

"Yeah, but I made you come down here after hours, and I'm acting like a basket case."

"He's your family, Eliza. I think nothing of it. You needed me—I'm here. It's how this thing works between you and me. Now, get here at seven in the morning. I want to keep him calm the few days after surgery. If you need me to, I can keep him at my house so Nova doesn't excite him."

This thing between you and me. My stomach flips at his words, and I feel selfish that my focus has momentarily shifted from Chief. I shake my head and take a deep breath. "Yes, that would be great."

"Go home and get some rest. He is going to be just fine, I promise." His smile is kind and reassuring, his hands still secure on my forearms. He leans down, pressing an unexpected kiss to my forehead. "I really hate seeing you cry," he mutters against my hair.

Oh, *man.* The feeling that rushes through me when I'm around him is sometimes too much to handle. I feel more in those brief moments than I do with Sam at any time, and that is not okay.

I really need to end things.

"I'm sorry." I wipe my eyes. "Thank you again. Even if this is your job."

"Seriously, Eliza. Anytime." He leans down to scratch Chief's side before we leave.

ecause you're in love with Jack.

That's what Sam said to me when I broke up with him. And I haven't been able to shake it. Not because I believe it, but because *he* does. It was the night after Chief's surgery. The procedure went well, but I was a wreck all day, concerned about any little thing that could go wrong. It wasn't that I didn't trust Jack. I did. But I had this knot in my stomach and the worst scenarios invading my thoughts.

I had a plan to manage this overwhelming feeling of panic—focus on my clients, pick Nova up from school, and get back to Chief as soon as possible. That's why I ignored most of my texts for the majority of the day.

Okay. That *and* the fact that I was avoiding Sam. I knew it had to be done. I knew I was stringing him along and waiting until after Christmas was cruel.

That night, after Nova had gone to bed and I was already emotionally spent from a taxing day of anxiety, I did it. I broke it off.

"Six days before Christmas?" he asked me with a bitter

laugh, leaning against his truck with his arms crossed over his chest.

That made me wince, but I stood my ground, telling him all of my carefully constructed reasons. *We aren't compatible. We don't have a future. I need to focus on Nova. You want more kids.*

It was a great speech, and yet, it was like he was staring straight through me. When I was done, breathless from the cold, he slowly nodded and glanced down at his feet for a long moment.

Then he said it.

"You don't have to give me these fabricated reasons, Eliza. It's because you're in love with Jack."

It was like he had punched me in the stomach. All of that oxygen around me, and I couldn't seem to take one solid breath, leaving me nauseated and lightheaded. I vocally disagreed after I was able to properly swallow, but that didn't change his stance.

I would have rather the alternative. Yell at me. Call me names. Tell me I'm heartless. Don't tell me I'm in love with my best friend, laugh off my firm disagreement, and then leave with the last word. That's fucking torture.

I stood frozen in our driveway long after his taillights disappeared.

When Simone asked how the breakup went, I told her he took it well. I did *not* tell her his misguided opinion on my relationship with Jack. I didn't want her to overanalyze it. I tried to forget it, and let it roll off my back. But that hasn't worked.

It's safe to say it's still on my mind.

My feelings are all over the place.

And Jack is plaguing my brain more than usual.

I'm in the middle of brushing today's hairspray out of

my waves when my phone lights up beside me. I glance down, one hand full of hair, the other holding the handle of my brush. Speak of the damn devil.

Jack: *Are you up?*

I raise an eyebrow at the message before glancing at the time, which is 10:27 p.m. Letting my hair loose, I quickly type out a reply. Something must be up. This kind of text is out of the norm for him. In fact, he's usually in bed by now.

I want to comment on how his text reads like a booty call, but I'm worried. Instead, I text: *Yes. Everything ok?*

Jack: *Come outside.*

This is so unlike him.

I look at myself in the mirror and notice my thin pajama top. It's the day before Christmas Eve and snowing. Not the best outside attire. I throw on a heavy cardigan and slip my fleece-lined boots on before walking through the living room to get outside.

Meet Me in St. Louis is still illuminating the screen, and I groan at myself for forgetting to pause it when I went to get ready for bed. I can get so distracted. I slowly pull the front door open, not wanting to wake Nova. I don't have to worry about Simone since she's at the hospital tonight.

Jack's at the back of his Bronco with the tailgate open, but I can only see his work boots and denim-clad legs—the upper half of his body bent into the back of his truck.

"It's freezing out here." I'm great at stating the obvious. I move from one leg to the other, trying to warm myself up.

My voice gets his attention, and he looks up over the open tailgate with a grin. His strawberry waves are dusted with snowflakes, and a few specks have fallen onto his beard. "This won't take long," he assures me.

My porch light isn't doing a great job at shedding light on him, so I squint to make out the large box he's pulled out of the truck. I have no earthly idea what it could be. My previous apprehension turns into excitement.

In all honesty, there's no being nervous when you're around Jack. His mere presence creates a calming atmosphere. He's a safety blanket with reassuring words and the ability to fix any problem. I can't help but be drawn to him—no one can.

The box is covered with a black trash bag, and he's carrying it over his shoulder with ease. That means nothing in regard to the weight, because I'm pretty sure I've seen him lift a pig the same way. And those little bastards are heavy.

"This is very dramatic. It better be good."

He chuckles at my teasing and rolls his eyes. Once he reaches the top step, he drops the box gently, but it still makes a thud. With one quick swipe, he removes the bag and looks up at me, his eyes lighting up.

It's *the* dollhouse.

I feel a lump in my throat.

I look up at him, smiling in bewilderment, but my lips are quivering. "But we checked. It's sold out everywhere."

"Not everywhere," Jack corrects, his grin growing. The lines around his eyes make my heart flutter against my chest. They're so genuine—like he's only ever lived to bring joy to other people. "Don't ask me my sources. Just know it was purchased legally."

"Jack." I don't even know where I'm going with that sentence, because I'm so damn happy. Nova is going to be thrilled. And the fact that this man loves her enough to go who knows where and get her the dollhouse she's been talking about for months ...

Without another word, I practically leap forward and wrap my arms around him, hugging him tightly to me. He laughs in my ear, and his large arms envelop me, squeezing me into him. He smells like linen and cold sweat, and my insides tighten at the sensation.

"You're welcome."

I lean back and look up at him, shaking my head in disbelief. "Thank you. Thank you so, so much. Nova is going to be so happy. Let me get some cash for you—"

"No." It's simple, but punctuated with a firm shake of his head.

"Okay." I nod. "So, put your name on the tag? Do you want to come over and watch her open it?"

"Nope. It's from ... Santa." He winks at me then, his enthusiastic grin turning into a kind smile.

I'm still in his arms—a fact I am very aware of. My breath hitches. I can't even make a joke about how Nova doesn't believe in Santa anymore. I'm, surprisingly, at a total loss for words.

I've never noticed the faint dusting of freckles across his nose—nothing like the clusters on my cheeks and nose, but enough to be visible. He is as attractive up close as he is from afar. And, truthfully, this feels nice.

Standing there with him, on my porch, with Nova's Christmas wish at my feet, I unwillingly hear Sam's voice. *It's because you're in love with Jack.*

Oh, no.

Oh, fuck.

I gracefully slip out of his embrace and keep my hand on his arm, squeezing it lightly. My heart is a brick in my stomach. Does my smile look as unsteady as it feels?

"I'm going to have to come up with something better than Santa." I laugh, but it doesn't feel like my own. It's like I'm watching these two people on my porch, stumbling through an awkward moment after a minute-too-long hug.

His face falls slightly. "No. Really?" he asks, visibly disappointed. "Nova's at the *Santa doesn't exist* age, already?"

"She'll grow out of it," I tease, smirking when he rolls his eyes. My gaze falls back on the dollhouse, and I touch the edge of the box. "You know, my gift for you is now pathetic compared to this gesture."

"You think this is your Christmas gift from me?"

My shoulders drop, and I exhale a laugh, pressing my hands to my face. "It is your prerogative to make me the inadequate half of this friendship."

"There's no possible way." His voice is smooth—as was his line. But, in all honesty, it's not a line. It's never a line from him, because he's too honest in his approach to concoct something insincere. I know this because it was downright impossible for him to fake his approval of an outfit I tried on during the Black Friday madness. His smile was so forced, it looked like a caricature of him.

Yep. My stomach is my heart's new permanent home.

I inhale as much as I can, shrugging a shoulder with a smile that I want to seem calm and collected. "I guess now would be the best time for me to give you your present."

"Yours is in the truck. Let's make it happen."

I laugh at his preparedness and tilt my head to the side with narrowed eyes. "Were you going to keep it in there if I didn't mention buying you something?"

"No. I was going to come deliver it on Christmas night," he replies, rolling his eyes at my insinuation.

I stay playfully skeptical, my gaze still narrowed with a smile on my face as I turn inside to retrieve the carefully wrapped box in leftover *Frozen* wrapping paper. As soon as I walk back onto the porch, he's holding a tall but skinny box also wrapped—but much more decoratively. Shiny gold paper held together with a white ribbon making an X where a bundle of pinecones and holly sits in the center.

"Matthew wrapped that, didn't he?" I accuse, earning another laugh from him. He can't deny it.

"Would you just take your present?" he asks through laughter, holding it out to me with one hand. I place the small box into his free hand and brace for the heavy one in his arms, but it's surprisingly light.

I nod to him, grinning. "You first."

The box looks smaller in his hands, and he's mindful with it, unwrapping each corner with care. It wouldn't surprise me if Matthew taught him to be gentle with the wrapping paper when he was a kid. And probably still.

He pulls the item out of the box and unwraps the tightly packed bubble wrap. Laughter immediately erupts from him, his grin almost cracking the dimples perfectly placed on either side of his mouth. Even through the closely trimmed facial hair, you can see them. "Eliza." He pauses, holding the personalized Jack and CeCe bobble-head in his hands. "This is incredible. It looks just like me! And CeCe with that tiny black spot on her nose. This is the coolest thing."

"Do you really like it, or are you just being nice?"

"We both know I'm bad at faking emotions." His eyes don't leave the mini-him in his hand. He inspects it from top to bottom, and his excited expression never softens. Little Jack is in black scrubs—*my favorite*—with his arms across his chest and a pencil behind his ear. CeCe is looking up at him adoringly, her purple collar sparkling slightly. "I would have never thought of something like this. Oh my God, I'm like Dwight!"

Duh. That's his favorite television character. How does he think I got this idea?

"I'm so glad you love it!" I'm practically squealing internally, excited that I did well. I'm not good at giving gifts, so I was nervous I entirely missed the mark with him.

He looks up at me, gesturing to the slim package in my hands. "All right, Davis. Your turn."

"Can I make guesses?" I ask, trying to ease the awkwardness I feel for no good reason as I rip into the back flap of the paper.

"You could try. Or you could just open it."

"So touchy." Grinning, I let the rest of the paper slide off. I rotate the large rectangle in my hands, looking for the opening to the box. When I finally pry it apart, I reach my hand inside and pull out a smaller rectangle covered by protective wrapping. When I finally get it off, my body relaxes with a large exhale at what's in my hands.

An original Penny painting from the photo of Nova, Simone, and me that sits on my station at the salon. The picture he asked about the first time I cut his hair. I'm telling you, my emotions are way more inconsistent the older I get. I feel hot tears spring behind my eyes, and I smile at him, laughing at the absurdity of my gift compared to this thoughtful, heartfelt one.

"I told you you're trying to outdo me." My voice cracks, and I blink a few times to make the tears back off. "What the hell, Jack." I laugh more, feeling the wetness spill over my lids despite my attempt to stop them. I brush the drops away before they can be seen—I hope. "It's absolutely beautiful."

"I was hoping you wouldn't find it creepy that I snapped a picture of the picture at the salon and sent it to Penny." He looks sheepish, his smile bordering on discomfort. "So, those are good tears?"

Well, shit. "Yes." I roll my eyes, staring at the incredible brushstrokes against the canvas. "A seemingly unattainable dollhouse and a beautiful painting of my family, and I give you a bobblehead."

"Stop. This bobblehead is one of the most *me* gifts I've ever received from someone other than my parents." He takes a deep breath, glancing down at it again before looking up at me. "No one has tried to know me like you have. Not even Gwen. It means a lot to me. So stop comparing."

It's silent for a moment—both of us looking at our present from the other. With a sigh, I look up at him, unable to stop the corners of my mouth from turning upward at the mere sight of his expression.

It's because you're in love with Jack.

I shake my head, ridding myself of the thought that causes sweat to break out on my otherwise-freezing body. "Merry Christmas, Jack," I say after a moment.

His breath is coming out in visible huffs, his nose and cheeks are pink from the harsh cold. He's completely lit up. The lights from my Christmas tree in the window cast a glow onto his face, making his eyes shine when he looks up at me.

It makes my heart hurt.

"Merry Christmas, Eliza."

Jack: *I didn't think about it when I was there last night, but you're welcome to come over to my parents' tonight for a Christmas Eve dinner. I don't know what you and the girls have planned.*

I'm taking ingredients out of my cabinet for my famous pound cake when I finally see the text that was sent earlier this morning. A warmth spreads through my body like heat from a campfire on a chilly night. Christmas Eve dinner is at my house tonight with my parents, Aaron's parents, and Simone's dad, so I know I can't. But I love that he wants us there.

I type out a quick reply: *The whole family is in, and we're doing dinner at my place. But you know I love you for—*

Nope. Deleting that.

Try again: *The whole family is in, and we're doing dinner at my place. But you know we would have loved to. Thanks for the invite. :)*

Maybe I can sneak over there after dessert and deliver a pound cake. I think that's a solid idea. I'll double my recipe. Easy. Not at all an inconvenience.

Simone's voice breaks me from my measurement calculations. "Dad has decided to bring his new girlfriend tonight. Do we have enough?"

"Of course!" I turn to Simone to read her expression, wondering if she's as okay with this as she sounds. Her dad hasn't openly dated or brought anyone home to meet Simone since her mother died. But this most recent girl-friend has been around for over two years. Bringing her to family holidays is new but, I guess, not entirely unexpected.

If it were anyone else, I'd find it odd that he lives two

hours away and Simone's never met the person he's dating. But their dynamic has always been a little different than most. Both dedicated to their work, both science nerds, and both used to the on-the-surface relationship they've built. They adore each other. But their personal life is never discussed.

Surprisingly, Simone's face reads neutral and maybe a smidge exhausted from her night on-call. She's not looking at me as I study her, staring down at her phone with her thumbs flying over the keyboard. When she does finally glance up, her eyebrow lifts.

"What's with your face?"

"Excuse me?" I sputter.

Her head falls to one side, and she softens. "I'm completely okay with this, you know? I'm actually excited, but also nervous because what if she doesn't like me?"

"Okay, I think *she* is supposed to be concerned *you* won't like *her*."

"Fair."

I turn back to my task at hand. "Besides, no one has ever *not* liked you."

Simone leans against the counter with a grin. She loves being complimented. We're one and the same.

"Anyway, back to your initial concern. I love how my dad has been since he started seeing Yvonne. If anything, I'm grateful for her. So, please don't watch me all weirdly tonight to see if I'm uncomfortable. Okay?"

I promise nothing, but I hold my hands up in surrender, and my expression pacifies her for now. Simone isn't the only one in this house with a protective nature. She turns to the oven and opens the door, peeking in at the turkey my dad has been prepping all day. I inhale a large whiff of rosemary and salivate.

"Oh my, this is what heaven smells like." I love her dramatics. "Where are your parents, anyway?"

"They went with Nova and the Davises to look at Christmas lights so I could have the kitchen to myself for desserts. Want to give me a hand?" I pull open the cabinets above the sink before moving on to the ones closer to the fridge, searching for an extra pan. "Also, do we have another Bundt pan?"

"Why do you need two?"

There is no pan in this cabinet, but I refuse to tear my eyes away from it to answer her question. I clear my throat before turning back to Simone, cheerful as I shrug my shoulders. "I figured I'd bring a cake to Jack and his parents."

Her interest is piqued, turning slowly from where she is presently looking. "Yeah? That's nice."

"Yep." My attention is on anything else but her at this moment. "He came by last night. He, uh, well ... he found that dollhouse Nova was wanting and brought it to me."

"What? We couldn't find that damn thing anywhere!" she exclaims, but her face is radiant as she continues. "He hunted it down?"

My laugh is nervous as it falls out. "Yeah, he went completely out of his way and, somehow, pulled some strings to get it for her. Isn't that great?"

"Nova is going to flip."

"That's what I'm hoping for." Ah! Another Bundt pan! I triumphantly pull it from the back of the bottom cabinet and set it on the counter, next to the other. "And you should go look at his gift to me. It's on the dining room table, and it's stunning."

Her lips have curled into a smirk, obnoxiously so, and she leaves me for the next room over. It's quiet for a moment before I hear her voice echo through the foyer. "This is incredible!"

She's back in the kitchen, painting in hand, and awestruck. I can't be sure, but I'm almost positive she's mirroring my exact reaction—minus the tears. I stop what I'm doing, nodding in agreement without saying a word.

"This is some gift, E," she breathes out, running her hand over it. "God, Penny is extremely talented. We need to hang this over the fireplace."

"That was my exact thought."

"Did you show Nova?"

"She is obsessed with it." It's true. When she came down for breakfast this morning, she audibly gasped and kept saying how much she loved it. Then again, she's at the age where she loves literally *everything*.

Simone looks up at me then, her face scrunched up as realization dawns on her. Dammit, she knows me so well. "You know the bobblehead is just as good as this gift," she assures me, aware of how embarrassed I was by it compared to this. "It's actually kind of the same thing. And perfect for him."

"He loved it, but yeah, I felt like a doofus."

"No!" The painting is tucked protectively in her arms. "It was so incredibly thoughtful. Please tell me you aren't making him a cake because you feel like he outdid you. Eliza, I swear if that's the reason ..."

I pour sugar into my measuring cup and simultaneously shake my head. "No." I laugh. "I'm not *that* insecure about my gift. He invited us over for Christmas Eve dinner at David and Matthew's house tonight, but since we're having our own thing, I want to bring them something."

"Interesting." She doesn't miss a beat. "Are you bringing it to them before or after dinner?"

"After dinner. I'll let it bake while we're eating. Now, make yourself useful."

She's amused, but she doesn't voice it as she sits on the stool across from me and measures out a tablespoon of vanilla extract. I know she wants to pry, but she's holding back. I'm proud.

———

I texted Jack before I began my drive out to the farm. Simone stayed back and helped clean up after dinner, wanting to spend more time getting to know Yvonne—who is honestly a doll. I have Nova in the backseat with the cake in her lap, singing along to the Christmas station I refuse to change during the holidays.

We pull up to the house as the last notes of Mariah Carey's *O Holy Night* fade into the radio DJ's jingle.

"Okay, kiddo, we can't stay long." I get out first and open the back door, getting the cake out of her lap so she can exit without dropping it. The driveway is slippery from the ice, so I hold her hand and help her up the porch steps.

I don't even have the chance to knock before the door swings open and Jack appears with joy beaming from his face. His green long-sleeve shirt is form-fitting and highlights the muscles on his shoulders. They mimic rolling hills, and I have the sudden urge to run my fingers over them.

If I had a free hand, I would slap myself to rid my mind of those thoughts.

"Well, Merry Christmas. What a lucky man I am to be visited by the Davis girls. And with cake? What did I ever do to deserve it?"

"Merry Christmas!" Nova exclaims in a sing-song voice, practically bouncing in place. He opens the door wider, allowing us to step in.

I wipe my shoes on the mat after Nova has already bounded in, and glance up at him. "Who says you deserve it?" My voice is playful, causing him to chuckle.

I can't see the living room from where we're standing, but I can hear Matthew ask Nova if she wants to open her gift from them. I narrow my eyes at Jack as he leads me to the kitchen. "Your dads got her a gift, too? That girl is spoiled."

"That girl is loved," he corrects.

As soon as I step through the doorway, my stomach drops. The rug has been pulled out from under me. I hope my face isn't betraying me.

Callie.

"Eliza, hey," she says, her voice cheerful, but her face neutral. She's squeezing icing onto a gingerbread cookie.

I hate it.

The cake has gotten heavier. Or is that my arms? I place it on the counter next to me anyway, pressing my lips together in an attempt to look excited to see her. "Callie! I didn't expect you here. Merry Christmas. What you got there? Cookies? They smell delicious."

I ramble when I'm nervous.

This is making me uncomfortable.

Fuck this. Why is Callie here? I look at Jack like he owes me some sort of explanation, but he doesn't. Of course he doesn't. He also doesn't look the slightest bit fazed by my shock.

"Yeah, gingerbread," she answers, looking up at me with her eyebrows raised.

Oh. *Oh.* She doesn't want *me* here, either. My gaze is

back on Jack, who is at the sink, leaning against it and drying a plate he must have washed before answering the door.

"Gingerbread," I repeat. "Delicious."

"You should stay for some." Jack's clueless. Honestly. And it's not even endearing.

Luckily, Nova runs in at that moment with a large toy horse in her hand and a toothy grin. "Mom, meet Agatha," she says, thrusting it upward so I can see it. Even in the tensest of situations, she can ease my nerves and put a smile on my face.

"Agatha? What a majestic name." I reach down and run my hand through its soft mane. It is honestly a beautifully made toy and a welcome distraction from the growing discomfort. "Did you tell them thank you?"

Her face is so animated, her nod fervent as she cradles the plastic animal to her chest. "I did. They told me to come get some cookies for the road."

"Oh, they did, huh?" I laugh, smoothing my hand over her hair carefully. I nod to the counter where a fresh plate of cookies is stacked. "Grab a couple. I'll be right back."

I can take a solid breath when I'm out of the kitchen and back in the foyer. I let Sam get to me, and that's why this was such a blow. I would have never been this affected if it weren't for him getting in my head.

"There's my girl!" Matthew bellows, walking over to me with his wine glass in hand. He leans forward and hugs me with his free arm, kissing my cheek in the process. "Thank you for the cake. Nova said it's basically the best thing she's ever eaten, so I'm offended and excited."

"She likes to build me up." I hug him tightly—almost

too tightly—before leaning back. "So don't take her too seriously. But it is a damn good cake."

David gives me a brief hug next, patting my shoulder as he pulls away with an affectionate, "Merry Christmas, girly."

"Merry Christmas to you guys. I'm sorry we can't stay long, but I've got to get her in bed so Santa can get his job done. We need to do dinner soon." The words feel weighted as they leave me, almost as if I'm slurring. I feel so out of sync. It's selfish of me, really, to think I'm the only person invited to their holiday dinner.

"You know, I'm not far from bed myself." David is always early to bed, early to rise. I like that about him because it's so much like my dad.

"Promise to make time for us soon?" Matthew's face is pinched, like he's trying to read me. He won't have to try too hard. Exhaustion is making my face an open book.

I hear footsteps behind me and see Jack with Nova on his heels. "I promise," I say, slightly distracted. "You ready, Nova?"

"No! We just got here." Her pouts are cute and can usually move mountains. Not tonight, though. I feel … weird.

It's because you're in love with Jack.

A boulder is on my chest. I shake my head at Nova and nod toward the door. "Come on. We have a big day tomorrow. We'll see them all soon, okay?"

She's reluctant in her nod of agreement and drags her feet to the door. The goodbyes are quick, but Jack seems thrown by how fast I am getting out. His face isn't quite as jovial as when we first arrived.

"Have a wonderful day tomorrow, guys," I say before closing the door behind me and walking with my chatterbox back to the car. I let her distract me by telling me all about the adventures she is planning with Agatha and her doll, Lucy. She's eating a gingerbread cookie, red icing smeared on her chin.

My mind drifts back to Callie standing so comfortably in the kitchen. I'm sure I was rude. I couldn't help it. Envy isn't green; it's red icing, piped on a gingerbread man.

I grip the steering wheel in aggravation but mostly directed at myself. Jack is not mine. I have no claim. I guess I'm just tired of him pretending that nothing is between him and Callie when she's *always* around.

I shake those thoughts, feeling guilty for not fully focusing on Agatha's stories. With a sigh, I look back at Nova in the rearview mirror, my entire mood shifting at her bright face. "Where are Agatha's parents?" I ask her, and she lights up even more before beginning her next story.

15

*I*t's 12:32 p.m. I have exactly six and a half hours to get everything together before our guests arrive. This may seem like a lot of time, but with everything I need to get done, it might as well be thirty minutes. It's been a rough couple of weeks already with Chief's procedure and him staying at Jack's place. On top of that, breaking it off with Sam was more difficult than I expected it to be. Not because I was second-guessing myself, but because he made me second-guess my feelings in a way that has made me incredibly uncomfortable. Then there was the whole Callie thing on Christmas Eve.

I shake it off.

I have two pies in the oven, I'm rolling out the dough for Nova's favorite oatmeal cookies, and Simone is running late to pick up the sandwich trays we ordered from a deli that's closing early for the holiday. I hear the faint noise of celebration coming from whatever movie is playing in the living room. I glance up to see Nova in front of the TV, sitting with her legs crossed, putting together the paper photo-booth props she begged me to buy for tonight.

The front door opens, and heavy footsteps come down the foyer before Jack appears in my doorway with four plastic trays in his arms. My stomach clenches and my blood goes hot. "Hey, you." He smiles. "Simone called and asked me to grab these. There's a wreck stalling traffic on her route."

"You've got wings, baby." I quote the always-relevant Lorelai Gilmore. This earns me a laugh from him as he sets the trays on the countertop and peeks in the oven at the golden-crusted desserts. "How's my pup?"

Popping a pretzel in his mouth, Jack leans against the island beside me, watching as I press a cookie-cutter into the dough to make star-shaped treats. "He's doing okay. The drugs are keeping him calm even when I pick up his leash to take him out."

"Thank you so much for watching him." I shift and face him. The corners of his eyes crinkle in response, and he reaches forward, brushing his fingers against my nose. I scrunch up my face and lean away from him.

"You had flour on you." He chuckles. "And you're welcome."

"Oh." I rub my nose to get any leftover powder he may have missed. Things are awkward between us, but Jack has no idea of that. So, I guess things are just awkward for me. We've only briefly chatted a few times since Christmas Eve, and most of that was in regard to Chief messing up his stitches and his longer-than-expected recovery.

One pie comes out, and the sheet of cookies goes in. I start the timer and grab a rag from under the sink to clean as I cook. Jack is casually scrolling through his phone beside me, and I can't help but stare at him for a moment. He's wearing a navy v-neck underneath his worn bomber jacket that he's yet to take off. His hair needs another trim soon, but his beard is groomed nicely for the party, cut close to show off his jawline. He glances over and catches me mid-stare then narrows his eyes. "What?"

"Nothing." My eyes cast downward as I wash the powdered rag. "Are you bringing Callie to the party tonight?"

He's amused. I can tell because one eyebrow is raised slightly, mischievously. "Now, why would I bring Callie?"

"Why would you spend Christmas Eve with Callie?"

His amusement grows, and he shakes his head, tilting it slightly, but not taking his eyes off my now-flushed face. "Do you not like her?"

"I have no problem with her." My voice is shrill. I clear my throat. "I barely know her at all. She seems nice. She's pretty, too. Tiny. Like a little pixie." Jesus, I can't stop, and that stupid smile won't leave his face. He's onto me.

"Uh-huh," he hums, but doesn't dig any deeper into the meaning of my sudden inability to form sentences. "Well, no. Callie is not my date tonight. Look, she was only at my dads' for Christmas because she couldn't make it home to see her parents. So she was going to be alone."

I nod, my head basically bobbing off my neck. "I mean, no need to explain yourself to me."

"Mom," I hear, and if I didn't already love my child more than all the stars in the sky, I would at this moment. I look up to see her watching the end of one of my favorite Hallmark holiday films. Yes, I have favorites. No, I'm not ashamed of that. "Why do people make a big deal about who they kiss when the ball drops on New Year's Eve?"

It's a sweet question because I remember asking the same one to my mom years ago. I smile, leaning against the counter and glancing at Jack, who is also smiling in adoration of my daughter. Okay, so *this* is why I keep him around. "There's this belief, stemming from an old myth, that whoever you kiss when the clock strikes twelve is who you'll spend the next year with. It's superstitious. Remember that word?"

"Yeah, like broken mirrors and black cats." She grins, pulling herself up on the stool across from me.

"Exactly, but instead of bringing you bad luck, this brings you a companion for the whole year."

She looks at Jack and squints at him as if she's trying to read his mind. "What do *you* think about that superstition?"

He's silent for a moment, feigning contemplation, before looking at her with a shrug of his shoulder. "I think there are worse superstitions."

"But do you believe in it?"

This is what I love about Jack. He understands the magic of being a child, of believing in things that don't make sense or have no logical explanation. He doesn't want Nova to grow up too fast, but he also doesn't treat her like a kid when the situation calls for it. In this instance, he sees the opportunity for a little magic and nods his head. "Absolutely."

The corners of her mouth turn upward, and she looks bashful. She's at the age where she finds romantic movies to be dreamy but is also embarrassed of loving the idea of love. Give her a few years, and she won't feel so weird about having crushes or seeing adults kiss in movies.

I look up to give Jack a thankful smile, pleased that he

doesn't try to make Nova a realist like my dad does. When I do, I find him already looking at me.

I'm feeling a little bashful, too.

Poor Nova fell asleep at 10:45 p.m., unable to hang and wait around for the New Year. The house is full—thirty-seven people in feather boas or New Year's Eve crowns. It's 11:57 p.m., and I'm doing my best to run around and make sure all the guests have a full glass of champagne to ring in the new year. I hand out unopened bottles, throw away empty plates, and turn the music down so we're able to hear Ryan Seacrest countdown.

In the midst of my frantic scurry, I feel a touch on my elbow, and I look back to see Jack holding two glasses in one hand. "Stop playing hostess and enjoy the party. I'll help you clean up when everyone leaves. I promise."

He wants to spend this moment *with me*. I can handle not being in control for the next few minutes. "Okay." I take the glass from him, causing his smile to widen. "I'll hold you to that."

I scan the room and see Simone hitting it off with Nova's soccer coach, whom I invited. We lock eyes, and she grins, holding her glass up to me. I do the same, and we both take a sip. I hear someone *shush* the room, signaling the last minute before midnight.

I close my eyes briefly and think about the past year. Beginning it so determined to let go of a lot of anger and resentment and ending it better than I could have imagined. I take a deep breath and open my lids again as the crowd around my television joins in when the host hits "ten." I glance at Jack, who's counting along with a carefree grin on his face. I'm positive he's ready to start this new year better than his past one began.

It's crazy how in such a short time, I've met people and formed relationships I can't imagine ever losing.

"Three, two, one ..."

The ball drops.

The room erupts in cheers and claps, kisses and hugs. Champagne bottles pop and fizz over the side, confetti from the poppers Nova insisted on purchasing, fly in the air, littering my recently waxed floors.

It's corny to say, but it's an almost magical feeling— standing in a storm of little shiny squares of paper in the exact minute a brand new year is beginning.

I look at Jack, laughing at the chaos around us and holding my drink up to him. "Happy New Year."

He looks down at me, his smile never faltering, and tilts his head ever so slightly. The way he's looking at me —the intensity ... I suddenly feel nervous. Is this in my head? Am I imagining this moment between us? Is it the alcohol or the excitement of shaking off the year? Is it the party and the overwhelming displays of affection around us? Is it this feeling of magic? I don't know what it is, but *I am nervous.* And I can't be nervous because it's Jack.

It's just Jack.

It's because you're in love with Jack.

And then he leans down and gently presses his lips against mine. It's brief. The contact gone before I can even react. I feel like the wind has been knocked out of me. My reality shattered when my body reacts to his touch in a way I didn't expect. Warm and cold. Calmed and elec- trified.

Sparks. Holy New Year, there are definite sparks.

I'm not exactly sure how my expression reads to him at this moment, but he doesn't seem alarmed.

He shrugs a shoulder, the corners of his mouth turned slightly upward. When he leans forward, I catch my breath and close my eyes, expecting him to kiss me again (wanting him to kiss me again?). Instead, I feel his breath on my ear, his cheek pressed to my temple as he whispers, "Just wanted to ensure I'd spend the next year with you and the girls."

I almost melt at the gesture, and my heart is attempting to leap out of my chest. When he leans back, I clutch my champagne flute and bring it to my lips, taking a large gulp as a buffer. It burns my esophagus and creates a bulge behind my breastbone that feels like a ball of fire. I clear my throat, pressing my palm to my boobs as the sensation subsides. With a shake of my head, I muster up a smile and convince my eyes to lock with his again.

"Yeah. You have us for another year," I say, trying to play off the fact that I choked on cheap champagne because our lips touched for half a second. I'm pathetic.

"You *kissed*?" Simone asks me for, honestly, the third time in a total of five minutes. "I knew it. I knew this would happen." She's excited, her smile wide. "What does this mean?"

"Nothing." I shake my head. "It means nothing. It was in the heat of the moment. He didn't act different around me for the rest of the night, and he even clarified later that the kiss was friendly. Just friendly."

Simone groans, rolling her eyes. *Same, sister.* "Men are the worst."

"I don't know how to act around him, now. It was just a stupid kiss that I barely felt, and it's got me all turned inside out."

"Was there tongue?"

I give her a look. "No. Because, like I said, it was an innocent, in the moment, playful kiss."

She's annoyed with both of us, and I can tell from the look on her face. "So, what? You both ignore this even happened and go on with your anything-but-platonic friendship? No."

"Simone, I can't ruin our friendship. I know that's such an annoying cliché excuse, but I'm serious. Nova thinks the world of him. What happens if we don't work out?"

"What happens if you get married and live an obnoxiously adorable happily-ever-after?"

Do I want that? It's not like I haven't thought about Jack in that way before; I just never thought he was an option. I felt like we smacked the "friend" label on us in the beginning. "I don't want to be the one to bring this up. He'll think I'm overthinking things, and it'll get weirder."

"Eliza. Honey. All right, look, why do you think you broke up with Sam?"

"Because I felt nothing for him and felt guilty for stringing him along."

"Okay, sure," she agrees, but raises her eyebrow. "But what made you realize that?"

"Several things. I just couldn't find the courage to end it." That's an honest answer.

"Ugh." She groans again, but *much* louder. "Eliza Danielle Fitzgerald Davis, what moment solidified your decision to dump Sam? Stop lying."

"God! Fine. The way Jack made me feel when Chief

was sick," I confess—my whole body on fire like I've told the deepest, darkest secret of my life.

She exhales, at peace. She's internally gloating. "You're never going to be platonic."

She's right. Deep in my soul, I know she's right. But I'm too chicken to do anything about it.

16

*M*y eyes shoot open and adjust to the darkness of my bedroom. My heart is hammering against my chest, and a cold sweat has dampened my forehead and neck. Another intrusive anxiety invaded my dreams.

I compulsively get up and tip-toe down the hallway to see if Nova is safely in her bed.

She is.

I release a breath I didn't know I was holding and walk to the kitchen for a glass of water—my mouth incredibly dry.

The neon lights on the oven let me know I should still be in bed for at least another two hours, but I'm up now. I might as well get things done around the house before going into work.

I'm shoving clothes in the washing machine when I hear soft thuds enter the kitchen and flip on the light. When I peek my head around the door of the laundry room, I see Simone staring quizzically at the already-made pot of coffee, her hand pressed against the silk scarf tied around her head.

"Morning." I say it quietly so I won't startle her, and leave the room with a basket of towels I took from the dryer. "I had a restless night, so I woke up earlier than usual."

Simone jumps at the sound of my voice, her hand flying to her chest. She huffs out a laugh and nods at my explanation. "Got it. I'm sorry. Anything in particular?"

"Just another unsettling dream." I'm being vague in hopes she won't push, because she knows. I have dreams about losing her, losing Nova, losing Chief, losing Jack, and sometimes, I still have dreams about losing Aaron—those are often the worst because I can't immediately put myself at ease when I wake up.

I'm folding the towels at the kitchen counter as she sips her coffee. It takes a moment for her to come to her senses. Neither of us is really a morning person. It's more of an issue for her than it is for me since her work hours can be unpredictable.

"When's the last time you saw your therapist?"

"I love interrogations in the morning."

"Don't be a drama queen." She rolls her eyes and brings the mug back to her lips, blowing before taking another sip. "You gave me permission to ask you about this stuff."

My focus is on the striped towel in front of me and the makeup stain that refuses to come out of it. She's right. I gave her permission. "It's been a bit," I answer, honestly. "I just haven't found the time. Please don't lecture me. It gives me more anxiety."

"I won't. But—"

"I know. I'll make an appointment."

We're silent for a moment, and I take it as Simone being pleased with my submission.

"So, Penny's engagement party is tonight. Are you heading over soon to beautify her before?"

"Yep." I exhale the word, exhausted at the thought of working today and pretending that I'm *not* emotionally fried. "I told her it was on the house. She's Jack's family and all."

Simone's eyes are narrowed, but her face is soft as she stares at me. "You're not as hard as you pretend to be, Davis."

I agree. I'm pretty weak most of the time. Especially lately with the whole Jack-kissed-me-and-the-universe-has-tilted thing. I'm still holding the basket of clothes when I lean my hip against the barstool next to me. "Do I pretend?" I snort a laugh. "I'm not. I feel weird seeing Jack now."

"Hmm." She hums, picking her mug back up to take a large gulp. "I don't see why. *Platonic* pecks and all."

"You're not pretty when you're bitchy." That's a lie. She's always pretty.

Her laugh is contagious, causing me to join her despite my nerves. Yes, nerves. I'm getting nervous pretty regularly about things I'd never think twice about. Like talking to a boy who kissed me. What am I? Thirteen?

"Just," Simone pauses, looking over my shoulder as she tries to find the best words to use, "trust your gut."

"Sound advice."

"And don't be a twit."

I always wanted Nova to be into hair and makeup, but she's my little adventurer instead. Not that you can't be both. She just has no interest in the former. If I had it my way, she'd be like me, dreamily watching as I use Penny's face as a blank canvas. She's not like me, though. She thinks doing her hair is a waste of time, she's rough, and when I once tried to put lip gloss on her, she immediately used the back of her hand and wiped it clean.

That's why it was no shock that she begged me to let her go with Jack and David to feed the cattle instead of staying with me. I guess it *could* be boring for an overactive eight-year-old to sit still for as long as this is taking me. But Penny's red hair falls in the middle of her back, and she wanted dramatic eyes. This takes time.

"You have the prettiest skin, Penny." I'm not only complimenting her because she's a client. She doesn't have a single wrinkle, and her complexion is free of rough patches and dark circles. She's sixty-two and looks every bit of forty. It's incredible.

She rolls her blue eyes upward and waves off my compliment. "I look like an old hag."

"Not even a little bit. Kyle is going to eat you up when he sees you." I turn back to her with mascara in hand, ready to coat her orange lashes. My steady hand paints it on, occasionally telling her to blink. When I finish and step back, she's beaming up at me. My heart skips.

Her happiness is contagious.

"What was right about it this time? Getting married, I mean."

The question came out before I could think about it.

"Getting married? Well, I don't know. Jack keeps saying he can't believe I'm finally settling down, but you know, I'm not. Kyle is like me. He's a traveler, and he's retired, so we can go wherever, whenever. It was always such a weird thought to my parents, to David, and basically everyone in my life that I didn't want *their* life. I didn't want marriage or children. I wanted to fall in love a lot—with people, with places, with ideas."

I lean in, carefully dusting specks of eyeshadow from the corner of her eye. "And did you? Fall in love a lot?"

Her eyes are closed, but her features relax at the question. "I did. You know, Eliza, I *was* in a long relationship once before—twenty years ago. I was stubborn and wouldn't marry him, because I knew he'd eventually resent me for everything I couldn't be for him. I didn't want to hurt or hurt him, so I broke it off. After meeting Kyle and falling so unexpectedly fast, I realized I just need to jump into that fear so I can be happy *now* and worry about the rest later."

Her words stir something inside of me. I don't push it away like I normally would. I let it ruminate. Be happy now. Worry later. A tight band squeezes my chest at the thought.

I'm in a daze, staring down at the eyeshadow pallet in my hand, but not really looking at it.

It takes extra effort to swallow.

"Eliza?"

"Lipstick." It comes out as a squeak, and I clear my throat. My face burns. She doesn't say anything else. She only nods and lets me go back to my task, but I can tell she's watching me.

Nova walking around in boots and a cowgirl hat is the highlight of my night. She mimics Aaron's dad and sticks her thumbs through her belt loops, tipping her hat in greeting to every person who walks by.

The barn is decorated in fairy lights and picnic tables. They set up a bar and added stools. They even have a DJ. It's not that I didn't expect David and Matthew to pull it off, but I didn't expect the barn to transform quite like this.

There's already a crowd of people twirling on the dance floor when we arrive. Simone leaves our side to go find Gabe. I *knew* they'd connect. Nova, on the other hand, spots David and tugs my hand to quickly lead me to him. She loves Jack, but he's got nothing on his dad.

I laugh and follow her over, giving David a hug before looking around the room to see if I can spot Jack. "The place is amazing, Dave."

"You think?" He's looking around with a smile, and it hits me right in the heart. "All Matthew has to do is tell me what he wants, and I deliver."

"As you should," I tease. "And where is the happy couple?"

"Oh, Penny and her rodeo cowboy are around here, somewhere."

I chuckle, but my attention isn't on him. He notices.

"Looking for anyone in particular?" He has a certain tone that tells me the question is rhetorical, and I'm caught red-handed. He's giving me a knowing smile, an eyebrow raised.

"Nope, just taking it in." It's a lie, but I hide that behind a beaming grin.

David shakes his head and looks down at Nova, who is preoccupied by CeCe and the red handkerchief tied around her neck.

"CeCe, girl! I didn't see you." I lean down to pet her,

avoiding the inevitable conversation David is trying to have. "Penny let you crash her engagement party?"

"It's not a party without CeCe." The raspy voice comes from behind me, and I turn to find a grinning red-head with arms outstretched to pull me into a hug. She's absolutely glowing. "I'm so glad you girls could make it! Kyle is around here, somewhere. You're going to love him."

"I have no doubt." I lean back from the hug, my hands on either side of Penny's arms. "I like that you're embracing this western cowboy vibe."

"Oh, sweetie," she begins, eyebrows raised. "Only for this party. My wedding won't have a lick of hay or twine. This was my compromise."

I'm stepping aside to let Nova hug Penny when Jack's smooth, honey-like voice rumbles near me.

"All my favorite girls in one place." Charmer. Nova leaves Penny rather quickly and tackles his legs in a bear hug. "Look at you! I dig the hat, kiddo."

Oh, *boy*. I thought Jack in scrubs was enough to kill me, but this getup. Sheesh. Who knew I had a thing for western wear? His red-and-white plaid button-up is tucked into his dark-wash jeans. His boots are brown, and his cowboy hat is jet black. And his smile steals my ability to take a breath.

"Where's your hat, Liza?" His eyes narrow. "Too cool for dress up?"

I exhale, shaking myself free of the tragic-schoolgirl-crush train of thought.

"Hey, I'm wearing the boots and belt buckle," I defend, my breathlessness disguised as a laugh. "My hair was just dirty, so I opted for a ponytail."

"At least you're honest. Where's Simone?"

I nod in her direction. She's got her head back, a wild

laugh escaping her lips while her hand's on Gabe's arm. Damn, it's good to see her happy. Jack looks back at me with a playful smirk after catching sight of the same scene.

"You're a matchmaker, Davis." His praises please me. He looks past me to the bar. "Want a drink? Or are you driving?"

I shake my head at his question. "Simone is on-call, so she's our driver tonight. But I think I'll stick to a beer or two."

"Come on. We'll get a strawberry milkshake for Super-nova and a beer for us." He looks down at Nova and tilts his head to the side. "Sound good?"

Nova grins and takes my hand to go with us, nodding her head enthusiastically. "Yes!"

"I think your dads are mad I'm not an authentic cowgirl from Tennessee." I laugh at the thought, taking a swig of my drink as I sit knee to knee with Jack on the barstools.

He chuckles and shakes his head before swallowing the liquid he had in his mouth. "Oh, for sure. You're lucky Penny's fiancé gave them a reason to throw a party in the barn."

I feign shock, gasping with my hand over my chest. "You mean they just made friends with me so they could, one day, throw an elaborate hoedown?"

"Yep. They're users," he teases, grinning as he does. We both know that's far from what he thinks about his parents. I take that moment to look for Simone in the crowd and smile when I see her follow Gabe to the dance floor as the music changes from an upbeat tempo to a slow song.

"I have felt so selfish for so long," I blurt as I look back to Jack. "I feel like I'm keeping Simone from living her life. It's really good to see her doing something that doesn't revolve around Nova and me."

"Hey," Jack begins, shaking his head as he leans forward to look me in the eyes. Those magnetic eyes. "Simone and I talk. She would not have her life any other way. She told me she was lonely and miserable before you three moved to town. Please don't feel like you've hindered her. That's not fair to you or her."

My heart aches at the thought of Simone ever being lonely or miserable. She kept that from me—probably so I wouldn't uproot Aaron and Nova and make them move to Connecticut with me. "I hear you." I shrug my shoulders. "I think I'm just happier when Simone and Nova are happy."

He gives me a genuine smile, leaning forward and squeezing my knee under his palm. "That's what I love about you."

My heart leaps into my throat, and I grasp the bottle in my hand again, taking a long swig so I don't look alarmed or say anything stupid. *It's a figure of speech, Eliza. Cool it.*

"What do you say? Dance with me?" The request is so calm, his tone low but confident. It momentarily catches me off guard.

I glance down at the beer in my hand and set it on the bar next to us. His face lights up, and he grabs my extended hand, dragging me to the dance floor. He's smart in our positioning, keeping me close enough to watch Nova. But she's playing checkers with David, so I'm less worried.

Jack slides a heavy arm around my waist and takes my hand in his, curling his fingers into mine. We fall into a comfortable rhythm immediately, like we do with everything else.

"Penny looks happy." The thought makes me giddy, and I look up at him as we step to the slow beat.

"She does," he affirms, tugging me closer, the movement almost habitual.

"Where's Callie?"

Jack rolls his eyes, squeezing my hand lightly in his. "Why do you always ask me about her?"

Laughing is my defense mechanism. I use it like a shield when moments become uncomfortable. "Because every time I've come around recently, she has popped up. I figured she'd be close by."

"That's—" he exhales, shaking his head, "not true."

"Oh, yeah?" It's the universe's joke that I spot her over his shoulder at that exact moment. She turns away when I lock eyes with her, but I know she was watching with the same longing in her eyes that I have when I see Jack with anyone else but me. My chest burns. "Then, how come she was just staring at us like I stole you away?"

Jack clenches his jaw, closing his eyes briefly. "I don't do workplace romances."

So *that's* the only thing stopping him. Noted. I watch our feet because I need to focus my attention on something other than the irrational lump that has formed in my throat. "If you like her, and you're both consenting adults, then, I don't see the problem. So is that the case? Because she's really pretty, and she's nice. It's obvious she has a thing for you. Why won't you just let yourself be happy and go on a date?"

He looks uncomfortable, gazing over my shoulder to

avoid my eyes. "I don't want to talk about Callie. Or this subject at all, really."

"Fine," I relent, giving him my best *you're exhausting* look. I have a knot deep in my stomach, the thought of him and Callie *actually* being together making me sick. My mind is in overdrive. *She's too pretty. She's too great. They have so much in common. They definitely have a spark.*

"What's the rest of your weekend look like?" He interrupts my mental spiral, and I'm thankful. It needed to be interrupted.

But I find myself not wanting to answer the question. That *damn* kiss. I smile when I look up at him. Maybe my smile will help the tension. Or maybe he knows me well enough to know it's forced. "I have a date tomorrow night."

A thick silence hangs between us for a brief second, Jack looking at me with an expressionless face. He loosens his grip on my waist. I don't like it, but I obviously can't tell him to keep holding me. "Oh."

Oh.

"Yeah. It's a guy I was set up with. I haven't even met him." I'm frantic, trying to save whatever shift just happened between us. "He's a loan officer or something like that."

I needed to move on from something that will never happen.

Jack nods slowly, a smile forming, no longer unreadable. "Sounds great. Maybe you'll hit it off."

It was genuine, but it stung. Part of me feels like these feelings I have aren't one-sided. It's in the way he touches me or the way he smiles when I walk into his office.

Then this other huge part of me remembers how adamant he was about our kiss being nothing. And maybe he doesn't want to talk about Callie, because he thinks I am holding on to that brief moment. I can't read him, and it's driving me crazy. And, ironically, the only thing that can soothe this uncertainty is *him*.

The music is loud, pulsing through me. The slow melody of Sturgill Simpson's *The Promise* makes my heart swell, and I lean my head against Jack's chest, my arms coming around his waist and hugging him close to me.

He adjusts to the new position by encircling my body and resting his chin on top of my head.

I fit him. Neither of us ever says it, but it's impossible for him not to think the same when we're touching in any way.

His smell sends my head spinning. Is it possible that a childhood of working with Christmas trees can make you permanently smell of pine?

We don't speak, lost in our thoughts. I feel like the silent moments between us are always the loudest. At least, on my part.

Why can't he read my mind?

Why can't I *speak* my mind?

When the song fades to an end, I step back and give him a light-hearted smile. "I'm going to see if Nova wants to hit up the dessert table." I run my nails over my scalp. "Do you want anything?"

A barely visible twitch of his lips crosses his face, and he shakes his head, looking back over his shoulder before turning his attention back to me. "No. Thank you, though. I need to say hello to a couple of people. I'll catch up with you later."

"Sure, sure." I give him an awkward wave before walking toward David and Nova with my heart bleeding in my hand.

"Did you have a good night?" I ask Simone on our drive back to our house. Nova has fallen asleep in the backseat, her head resting against a jacket of mine that's balled up into a makeshift pillow.

Simone's grinning, her eyes sparkling but staying on the road, so she doesn't give too much away. "It was ..." She pauses, biting her lip. "You were right. Gabe is such a catch. I'm glad I invited him."

I've never been more excited for someone else's love life. "I knew it!" I exclaim in a whisper, careful not to wake Nova. "So, are you going to go on a more official date?"

"I don't know. He hasn't asked me, and for the first time in my life, I'm scared to ask again and ruin this fun flirtation," she says with a shrug. "I won't wait too long. I just want to give him time to make the move."

I laugh and shake my head, but bite my tongue because, once I comment on her fears, she'll turn the conversation to me. At the thought of that, I get a knot in my stomach. I didn't see Jack again after we shared a dance. I also didn't see Callie. That did nothing for my nerves. I feel my chest tighten.

"What's with the face? I saw you and Jack dancing. You looked cozy."

No, no, no. Please, don't let my emotions run wild again. I nod and glance out the window with a deep breath. "Yeah, it was nice getting some time with him." My voice cracks, and I wince, hoping she didn't catch it.

She doesn't comment as we pull into our long drive-way. Once she parks in the garage, she turns her body to face me, glancing back at Nova to, I'm sure, make certain she is still asleep. "E." She's gentle. "What's going on?"

"I don't know. I'm going crazy because I have all these feelings and I don't know where to put them."

"Is this about Jack?"

I don't answer her; I just suck in a breath that's becoming increasingly difficult to catch. "I am *such* a selfish bitch. You're here, trying to talk about Gabe, and I start whining like a brat."

"Eliza, you are anything but selfish." Simone rolls her eyes, taking my hands in hers. "*You* introduced me to Gabe. You have literally gone above and beyond every time I have needed you in my life. You have had a shitty few years, and you haven't fully dealt with it. You're allowed to break down even if I'm happy."

I lean my head back against the seat and pinch the bridge of my nose, my eyes closed. "You're a saint, Simone. Seriously. What did I do to deserve you?"

Simone laughs, leaning the right side of her head against the headrest as she watches me. "So, what happened?"

"Sometimes I think Jack feels about me the way I feel about him. But then, sometimes, I feel like he just *really* cares about me. He likes Callie. I can tell. He said he doesn't do workplace romances, but never denied any feelings towards her."

"If that were true, there would already be something there. They went backpacking together, for crying out loud." Simone glances to Nova then back to me. "Look, Jack doesn't talk to me about this stuff. But we all see the way he looks at you."

"Then, why won't he do anything about it?"

"Why won't *you*?"

I hate when she makes a point. She knows my reasons. I've told her my apprehensions. But I think I could get past it. I think I could risk losing our friendship for what we could potentially have.

Be happy now. Worry later.

I don't want to make that leap without knowing he's in. I shake my head and unbuckle my seatbelt. I don't want to continue this conversation. I want to have a self-pity cry in my bed. "It's too late now."

"Eliza."

"It is, Simone. I told him I had a date tomorrow, and he didn't even care. He said he hopes we hit it off."

She's fed up with me. Again. Jack and I are exhausting her. Believe me, honey, I get it. She always wears a patient face, though. Even when she wants to snap me in half. "Well, what are you going to do?"

"Just go on my date with that guy tomorrow and ignore this feeling," I respond, honestly. "That's my plan."

She's quiet for a moment but squeezes my hand with a nod. "If that's what you think you need."

I shrug and attempt to give her a smile. "I don't know what I need. Other than some clarity that I'm not getting."

17

*M*y head is not in the game. I know I'm disconnected from this date, and at this point, I'm not even concerned with whether he can tell. I have felt myself tune out of this conversation several times, and the guilt has distracted me.

Ugh. I'm usually so good at dates.

I wait until he finishes his story, and I show the right amount of enthusiasm at the end, but then I put my napkin on the table and clear my throat. "Can you excuse me for just a moment? I need to use the restroom."

"Of course." He nods, standing up as I stand up to leave. It feels awkward. I smooth my dress down and walk towards the ladies' room.

Once the door shuts behind me, I take a deep breath and lean against it, trying to shake myself out of this fog. I walk to the sink and turn on the water, running my wrist under it to cool myself off. I don't know if it works, but my mom always told me to run cool water on my wrist if I was feeling flushed. Well, Melonie, my pits are sweating, and this isn't working.

I hear a stall open, and when I look up, I want to laugh at the irony of seeing Callie. *Cool, cool, Universe.* I needed this tonight. I give her a polite nod. "Hey, girl."

Does it sound as forced as it is?

"Eliza, hi," she replies, walking over to the sink next to me. "Date night?" She raises an eyebrow at her question.

I look down in my purse for anything to distract me from this conversation. Jack would have told me if he had a date. She has to be here with someone else, right? Girls' night? Hopefully. God, I can't see him right now. "Yeah," I answer, later than I mean to. "Uh, another Simone set-up."

She turns to face me and crosses her arms over her chest. "What?" Her brow is furrowed, confusion crossing her perfectly symmetrical features. "Not Jack?"

So, she's *not* here with Jack. Good to know. "Uh, no. Not Jack. Why?"

She's silent as she looks me over. I fight the urge to squirm as she turns back to the sink. She leans forward into the mirror and checks her lipstick before wiping the black smudge under her left eye. After a moment, she speaks again. "I don't get it."

"Don't get what?"

"You have *the* most perfect man falling at your feet, and you're blind to it."

I'm startled by her comment. My cheeks are burning, and I can feel them turn pink as I speak. "Excuse me?"

"Jack. You know I'm here with someone else tonight, right? Not Jack. Trust me, there were plenty of times on our trip where something could have happened, and it just ... didn't work out that way. Instead, he talked about *you*."

I'm sorry. Was she reading my mind? My throat is tight. Why can't I swallow? I'm lightheaded. "He what?"

"Every single day, Eliza. He worked you into every conversation. Look, it's none of my business. I just." She shrugs, leaning against the sink. "I just need you to know that if your hesitance is because you think he has feelings for me, there's not a chance."

My heart is beating faster at this revelation, but I'm still so unsure. He's had so many opportunities to say something. Anything. I look back at Callie and try to read her face. "Do you have feelings for him?"

"I did. I don't now, but that's irrelevant. He doesn't see anyone but you." Her tone isn't bitter, but it's also not friendly. She sounds like Simone after I forget to buy toilet paper—exasperated. Callie crumples the paper towel in her hand and tosses it in the trash can beside me. "Tell me you see that."

I'm a complete asshole. This poor guy has tried all night. But I was somewhere else—my house on New Year's Eve, in a tent staring at Jack's face over my deck of cards, in his embrace in the lobby of his clinic. I tried to keep up with the conversation, laugh at his jokes, talk about my daughter and the crazy antics in a house of all females plus Chief. I felt guilty the entire time—knowing I wanted someone else to be across this table. Callie's words echoed in my head for the rest of the night. *He doesn't see anyone but you.*

And then Sam's: *It's because you're in love with Jack.*

What are we *doing*? How do we keep missing this?

Walking to the car with Peter, I can't tell if he noticed

something was missing from our date. He's smiling, going on and on about this amazing charity he volunteers for. In another life, at another time, this could probably have gone somewhere.

He's nice. He's handsome. He's successful. He likes kids. Despite all these positive attributes, I take a tentative step back when I realize we're close enough for a good-night kiss. He doesn't attempt it. I'm thankful.

I glance up at him with a small smile and reach forward to take his hand in mine, giving it an awkward shake. "Thank you for tonight." I glance over at his car. "But I, uh ... Look, I'm so sorry. I really need to be somewhere."

"I—" He stops and shakes his head with a confused half-smile on his lips. I'm awful. "Is everything okay? Do you need me to take you?"

That would be tacky and rude, so I shake my head and squeeze his hand lightly. "No, I think I'm going to catch a *Lyft*. The date was really lovely, and I feel terrible for ending it this way, but ..." I trail off and look away from him, feeling an unnecessary urge to cry. There's a lump lodging itself in my throat, making it difficult to choke back any tears.

"I've been there." His voice is gentle, surprising me. When I look back at him, he's still giving me a warm smile. His eyes are knowing and kind. He deserves all good things. "Good luck. It was nice to get to know you, Eliza."

"You, too." He retreats to his black sedan, and I take a shaky breath before ordering a ride.

Jack's lights are off except for a glowing lamp from the window to the right of his door. Knowing him, he's probably fallen asleep on the couch with *The Office* reruns playing in the background. I thank the middle-aged man who drove me in silence—no great, eye-opening advice-giving guru like in the movies—and exit the vehicle. He also almost runs over my foot by gassing it as soon as I shut the passenger door.

I stand on the sidewalk, trying to talk myself into walking up Jack's porch steps. I don't know what I'm doing, to be honest. I regret this decision as soon as I shut the car door, but I'm here now. What's the worst-case scenario, right?

Oh, I know.

He looks at me like I'm an idiot and reaffirms the fact that we're *just friends*. That. *That* is the worst-case scenario and would be absolutely humiliating. Who cares what Callie said? Maybe she's trying to sabotage me.

I twist my hands together as I stare at the door my feet magically carried me to. With another nervous exhale, I knock twice before recoiling my hands like the door is on fire. I pull my coat tighter and wait, wanting to give up after about thirty seconds of nothing. As I debate on whether or not to knock again, Jack opens the door with a furrowed brow and tilts his head to the side, looking me over.

"Didn't you have a date?" he asks me, stepping out and craning his neck to look at either end of his porch.

He's in a gray t-shirt that's stretched over his muscled shoulders, black sweatpants that I want to curl up in, and gold-toe socks that *almost* make me smile—I *love* his predictability.

But I can't. I can't smile or reply to his question or

breathe, because I'm staring at him, and holy shit, he's marvelous.

"Earth to Eliza." He steps back to lean against the door he's still holding behind him. "I said, didn't you have a date tonight?"

Shit. What do I say? I've prepared nothing. It's not like I can tell him I think about him all the time. Or that I get cranky if a day goes by without us talking. Or that I can't eat popcorn without remembering that brief, buttery-salted kiss he surprised me with on New Year's. I can't tell him my heart swells every time he and Nova are together or that I get excited to bring Chief to the vet because I get to see him in scrubs. And I certainly can't tell him I am ninety-seven percent sure I could potentially fall in love with him. So I stare at him and decide to tell him the date was shitty and I needed a beer.

"We're idiots for not being together." I immediately want to shove the words back in my mouth, chew them up, and swallow them. That's not the route I was planning to venture down.

"What?" His expression turns serious.

I press my hands to my face, covering my eyes for a moment, to gather what dignity I have left after that bold admission. I laugh, to both of our surprise, and move my hands to press against my chest, shaking my head.

*Okay, Eliza, this is easy. It was a slip of the tongue. Tell him you meant to say you wanted a beer. Tell him you're drunk and stumble down the steps a little as you tuck your tail between your legs and run. You can do thi*s.

"You and me. We've been complete idiots," I continue because, apparently, I have something to say, and I'm not turning back. "You, because you have never once told me how you felt. You keep hiding under our friendship. And me? I'm doing the same damn thing. But I have had a reason. Callie. Callie is my reason. What was yours? *Before* Sam."

His mouth is slightly agape, his brow furrowed at my outburst. He steps out onto the porch. "That wasn't your reason. It was your safety net. I told you plenty of times that Callie and I were nothing, but you didn't believe me."

"What did you expect, Jack? You went on this romantic backpacking adventure in Albania and expected me to *not* think you two would hook up?"

Damn, it feels good to be honest.

I've cracked his shell. I've poked the bear and awakened the intensity burning inside him.

I love it.

"Yeah, you're right. I went on a trip with her, and you know what? She kissed me. Once. And after that kiss, I thought about *you*. All I did that entire trip was count down the days until I saw *you* again."

I practically swallow my tongue. It's a lot different, hearing those words come out of his mouth. I want to melt into a puddle. "Why didn't you ever say anything?"

"Do you know how much I care about you? All I ever heard from you was how not ready you were to date. You said it to me several times. I would be in the room when Simone would offer out a guy's number, and you'd shut her down with the same excuse. Why would I push you into something you're not ready for?" His breathing is slightly uneven, his cheeks pinker than usual. He's flustered, and he's usually so calm and collected. "What is this, Eliza?"

I hesitate, unsure of how to answer that question. "I *did* have a date tonight."

"Okay?" he replies, his tone annoyed and questioning.

"He was a great catch."

"Great," he deadpans, his jaw clenching.

"And he didn't cringe when I told him I had a daughter," I continue, my heart crawling into my throat.

"Fantastic, Liza. Sounds like a winner." His tone is so bitter, I can almost taste it.

"But." I stop and gesture to him. "Dammit, Jack. He's not you. You know, when you kissed me on New Year's Eve, I believed you. I believed that it was just an impulsive, friendly kiss. But that didn't stop it from ruining me. *You* kissed me, and now the only thing *I* can think about is doing it again."

He sharply inhales, placing a hand on the doorframe. "Liza, please tell me what you want." He's pleading, and it comes out hoarse. He looks pained, like he knows what he wants to do, but he can't step over that line.

"I want you." I can hear my heartbeat, and I'm surprised I haven't passed out. I still may.

His face is intimidating, but it's also a comfort. He moves toward me, his hand reaching out to rest on my waist. I stop him by throwing both my palms up as if I were using a spell to freeze him. He looks wounded, confused, frustrated, and concerned all in one expression. "I don't understand," he says, quietly.

I don't, either. Terror, possibly? Reflex to push away something I want? I shake my head at my actions and drop my arms, gazing at his tense form. I've scared him, and he won't make a move out of fear that I'll bolt.

Good going, Eliza.

Oh, to hell with it.

I step forward and place a hand on his hip, tugging him closer by his t-shirt before pressing my lips against his. The pressure of his mouth against mine sends a wildfire loose in my veins, spreading from my now-flushed face to the tips of my toes crushed into my pointed heels.

His left hand catches my cheek as soon as our lips touch, and his right is warm against my lower back, pulling me into him.

Our kiss quickly turns from a hesitant display of affection to a desire that's been burning since the first time our hands brushed. I need to taste more of him. I'm starved for him. My teeth lightly capture his bottom lip, and I hear a rumble in his throat before his mouth parts mine again, allowing his tongue to slip inside, and he kisses me with a fierce urgency. His hands run down my face and farther down my body until his arms are wrapped around me. I am, by no means, a tiny woman, but I feel like fucking Thumbelina when his arms envelop me and pull me against his body.

I'm drunk off his kiss—high off his touch. I need to get control of myself. I push against him and move my feet, walking him backwards into his house. Once inside, I kick the door shut behind us and lean back to push my coat off, letting it fall on the floor as I step out of my heels. I watch his eyes roam, taking in the rare sight of me in anything other than dye-stained t-shirts and Chuck Taylors.

His hands are on my waist again, but he's at arm's length, making me squirm under his dark stare. His jaw clenches, he swallows slowly, and his thumbs rub my hips. I'm melting. "This dress." He exhales, pressing his palms flat against me and running them up my sides and down my back, stopping just above my ass. Everywhere he touches catches my skin ablaze.

"Kiss me," I whisper, practically begging. I'm on fire, and yet I'm covered in goosebumps.

One step closer, pulling his eyes from my body to my gaze. He presses me into him—torturing me as he pushes my hair from my face. So close, our mouths could be—should be—touching. "Please, let me look at you." His voice is low, his heart racing under my hands. "I've wanted you for so long. I *need* to look at you."

I catch my breath. My heart is pounding so hard it's like it's trying to escape my chest. I feel weak. I follow his lead and look at him, our eyes locked for a long moment before I scan his face, finally allowed to stare at him. It's incredibly intimate—breathing each other's air, learning the lines of each other's face, dying for our lips to connect.

And when they do, it's every longing look, every missed chance, every late night, every stolen touch. It's every time, in the last year, either of us has wanted to do what we are doing right now. It's slow and sweet. It's finally tasting each other. We're savoring it.

Our tongues touch, and our kiss becomes more aggressive, more impatient. It's a back and forth of wanting to take our time, but not being able to. His hands slide lower, over the curves of my backside, before cupping underneath. Jack pulls back for a moment, and my lips already miss his.

"Put your arms around my shoulders," he mumbles, his breath warm against my mouth. I follow his lead, and he lifts me, my dress sliding up my thighs as my legs lock around his waist, my damp panties pressed to the seam of his pants. I lean forward and kiss him again.

He holds me against him and walks to his couch, sitting down and placing me on his lap. I moan into his mouth when I feel his erection through his sweatpants and against the thin material of my underwear. "Oh." I'm aching to thrust my hips. I hold his face in my hands, learning his kiss, letting him guide the moment before I lose control. I can barely contain myself, his tongue coaxing me. I clutch his shoulders and rock against him, causing a growl deep in his throat.

Jack pulls his mouth from mine, and his fingertips dig into my side as he grips me, guiding me. "Eliza," he breathes against my neck, grazing his teeth against my sensitive skin. My lips brush his, then his chin, his jaw, any skin my mouth can reach. His muscles are tightening under my hold. His head falls back against the cushion, his neck strained and his eyes closed. He hisses at the friction our bodies are making every time my hips roll forward.

His hands move from my hips to my ass. He squeezes before lifting me again and placing me on my back, hovering over me. "You're killing me."

He's groaning, claiming my mouth once more as his. We're devouring each other, teeth scraping, tongues sliding. When he sits up, he pulls his shirt over his head and looks down at me, pulling his fingers through my hair as he does.

I am almost sure I have died. He's between my legs, gazing down at me, his chest bare, his eyes a little wild. My eyes are drawn to the tattoo on the right side of his body, covering his ribs right under his chest. My fingers brush over the inked lines, following the design. "I seriously need a picture of this moment for when I'm ... you know ... alone." I breathlessly laugh. "What kind of tree is this?"

"My favorite," he replies, watching my hands trace the diamond framing the image of a singular tree standing in front of a skyline of mountains with a large moon above them. "Shasta fir."

I want to ask him why he chose that tattoo—why that tree? But I can't form sentences any longer. I run my hands down his body to the unfair v-cut that leads to the bulge in his sweatpants.

It's almost as if he's wincing when I touch him, but when he opens his eyes, there's an intense look of need. He leans back down and takes my mouth captive once more. The taste of him is so intoxicating, I almost forget to breathe. He presses his length against my arousal and thrusts his hips in a slow rhythm, a deep pressure building. I'm going to lose my mind.

He pushes my dress up around my waist with a growl, his hands grasping my thighs. His mouth moves to my chin, my neck, the exposed skin between my breasts. He takes his time, driving me to the brink of ecstasy then slowing back down.

Jack's kisses make a path down my stomach, the warmth of his mouth seeping through the fabric. His rough hands push my dress up even higher, and he nips at my pelvic bone before his tongue grazes the inside of my thigh. "Please, Jack," I breathe, pushing my hips forward. "Please touch me."

"Fuck, Eliza." Jack's chuckle is breathless as he peppers kisses against me through my panties. His fingers hook the elastic band, and he slowly begins dragging them down my legs.

At that same moment, his phone lights up on the coffee table, the ringtone interrupting the sounds of heavy breathing and lust. "Oh God, ignore that damn phone," I exclaim, my fingers locked in his hair.

He smirks up at me and leans over, ignoring the call before throwing my underwear to the side and kissing from my calf to the inside of my knee. The phone lights up again, and I am so close to grabbing it and throwing it across the room.

Jack groans and sits up, grabbing the phone from the table and fumbling with it before answering. "This is Jack Peters." His tone instantly goes from a husky rasp to a professional boom.

I watch as he listens, his jaw clenching and unclenching, his chest heaving. I am seconds from touching myself to soothe the aching need.

"How much did she eat? What kind of chocolate?" He runs a hand through his already tousled hair. "Hey, it's okay. Just take a deep breath. How long ago did she eat it?" He's moving to stand beside the couch. No, no, no. He looks at me with a pained expression and apologies in his eyes. I slap my hand over my face and feel like I could cry from the lack of release.

Then he says the dreaded words: "I'll be right over." He throws his phone onto the couch cushions and groans so loud the house practically vibrates. "I'm so sorry, Liza. Trust me, no one wants this more than I do."

"Is the animal okay?" I ask, attempting to get my mind off the orgasm I will not be getting from Jack.

"She ate Baker's chocolate about ten minutes ago. I've got to go take care of this." There's remorse in his voice. I reluctantly slide my panties back up my legs and watch his retreating back disappear into the laundry room. When he comes back out, I'm sitting upright, smoothing down my hair and he's now in jeans and tennis shoes.

I smile up at him, trying my best to hide the obvious torture and longing. He runs a hand down his face before kneeling in front of me, his fingers clasped over my knees. It feels like minutes pass while we stare at each other with a look of *what just happened?* But it's only seconds.

He takes a deep breath, shaking his head. "You are so damn beautiful," he admits, his fingertips stroking my knee. He leans up and presses a kiss against my lips. "Stay here. I won't be long."

God, that sounds so good. But I know I need to take time and think, and I probably should go home anyway. My sympathetic smile causes him to frown as I take his hand in mine. "I need to go home, but I'll call you," I promise.

"Please don't change your mind," he replies, leaning forward to kiss the top of my exposed thigh. "I have to go."

Change my mind? Not a chance. I plan on wrecking his bed before the end of the week. I can't show my hand, so I simply nod, and he stands and walks to the door. "I'm going to get a *Lyft*, but I'll lock up."

"You don't have your car?" he asks, standing in the open doorway. "No. Ride with me. I'll drop you off at your house. Or you can wait for me."

"Jack. That dog is going to die if you don't leave. I'm fine," I say, smiling softly to show him I'm serious. "Go."

He sighs heavily and shuts the door behind him, leaving me there to overanalyze the entire interaction.

18

Two days ago, I was on Jack's couch with my panties on the floor. And yet, we haven't spoken since. In all fairness, only one full day has gone by without us communicating. I was on a field trip with Nova, and he does have a demanding job. Maybe he's waiting for *me* to reach out to *him*. Come on, Jack. You know me better than that. When I have moments to myself, or moments when I am easily lost in a distraction, my mind is on him. His hands. His mouth. The actual fire burning in his eyes. I almost lose my breath at the memory.

I rid myself of those thoughts and focus on towel-drying Minnie Cecil's short hair. She's been one of my weekly wash-and-style clients for over a year. With permanently rosy cheeks and mischievous eyes, Miss Cecil is the person to go to for anything that's going on in the town. I love her standing appointments.

She's grilling me for information on Simone and Gabe when I reach forward and grab the mousse on my station.

I hear the door chime as I shake the bottle in my hand and go to apply it to Minnie's scalp.

"Well, there's Dr. Peters." Minnie grins, causing my heart to leap and my finger to clamp down on the nozzle, creating way more mousse than I intended. I quickly turn to my right and try to swallow at the sight of him.

His scrubs are black today.

I'm in trouble.

"Hi." I sound more breathy than I intended to. *What am I doing?*

"Hey." He flashes a grin, walking toward me. "I'm sorry I haven't called. Do you have a chance to talk after this appointment?" He looks down at my client and smiles, giving her a wave. "Hi, Minnie."

"Dr. Peters." She nods and gives a saucy grin.

"Yeah, of course. Just wait in my office, and I'll come find you when I'm done." I earn a nod from him as he walks to the back. I look back at Minnie in the mirror and cringe at the large white glob on her head. "I'm sorry, Ms. Cecil."

"Honey, I'd lose a little control if that man was coming to see me, too." She winks. I want to disappear. I give her a faint smile and discard half of the mousse in my hand into the wastebasket beside me.

She's rambling about one of her past "lovers" as I work the mousse into her hair and style it to her satisfaction. I'm usually such an attentive listener, but I have a man in my office, waiting for me. Not any man, but Jack. Jack, whose lips were all over my body less than forty-eight hours ago. Forgive me, Minnie, I can't focus. After a quick blow-dry and the magic I can perform with my straightener (no, I'm not modest), I unclip her cape and free her from my chair.

"Eliza," she begins, putting her payment on my station like she does every week. "We've all been rooting for you two."

My usual instinct is to quickly change the subject or deny that anything is going on at all. But I can't this time. I glance down at the cape folded over my arm and try to suppress the grin bursting through. "Same," I reply with a wink, causing her smile to grow. "See you next week."

When she's gone, I let Claire know I'm taking a quick break, and try my best not to break out into a sprint to get to my office. I walk through the open doorway leading down a hall containing one restroom, one break room, and my office. When I enter, Jack's looking at a painting hanging on the wall beside the doorframe. I close the door behind me and bite my lip—nerves are getting the best of me.

I'm not naive.

I lock the door behind me. My pulse is hammering in my ears. I walk past him and lean against the front of my desk, crossing my arms over my chest. "I'm glad you stopped by."

"Yeah?" He turns toward me with one of his charming smirks and a raised eyebrow. Then he walks toward me until our toes are touching. I crane my neck to look up at him, and feel a rush of excitement course through my veins. "Have you changed your mind?"

I take a deep breath and let my arms fall to my side, shaking my head in reply. "No. Have you?"

"What do you think?" His voice is lower—a little huskier. He reaches forward and pushes a strand of hair behind my ear, letting his hand trail down my neck. "Can I kiss you again?"

I let a sigh escape, my eyes drifting shut at the electric

feeling his skin gives me. I nod, lifting my chin slightly. He takes that opportunity to lean down and press a kiss against my mouth.

He's keeping it light, our lips playing tag. I stand up straighter and move my hand to the back of his neck, my nails running through his freshly trimmed waves at the base. He shivers under my touch and tentatively tastes me with his tongue, causing my mouth to open in a low moan.

His tongue is caressing mine, coaxing me. He steps closer, pressing me back against my desk once more, his hands firm on my sides. I pull myself up to sit on the edge, and he's between my legs, our torsos pressed together as our mouths explore each other.

My fingertips love to wander, learning every hard line and curve of his body. I slip them under his scrub top, his back warm against my palms. When I lightly dig my nails into his skin, he growls and gives my lower lip a soft bite. Why haven't I been kissing him from the moment we met?

His right hand has made its way under my shirt, sliding up my side. Heat is pooling between my legs. I can't form coherent thoughts. I need him.

When I run my hand over his waistband and graze the front of his pants, he pulls his mouth from mine and our eyes lock. Mine feel heavy; his are glazed over. He leans forward and presses his lips to my shoulder as the door alarm in my office signals my next appointment.

"No." He groans, his voice hoarse.

I'm unable to speak for a second before clearing my throat and removing my hands from him with an agonizing smile. "We can't do this here, anyway."

Jack presses his lips to mine again, a slow, lingering kiss before leaning away from me. He exhales and runs a hand through his strawberry blonde waves I love so much. "When can I see you?"

"I'll call you tonight, and we can come up with something." I slide off the desk. My limbs feel like jelly when I try to walk. I can only imagine what one full night with him is going to do to me.

After properly adjusting ourselves, we both head for the door. I glance in the mirror on the wall and make sure I look presentable, running my hands through my hair to brush it in place.

"You look perfect." I catch his eyes in the reflection.

I feel my cheeks flush at the comment. "You're going to ruin me."

I'm smiling as I say it, and it causes him to as well. He leans down and kisses my neck before we leave the office.

"You've emptied your closet, E."

I'm standing in front of my mirror, staring helplessly at the dress hugging my wide hips. I love it. It's a great dress. I've had many flirtatious comments and free drinks sent my way on girls' nights because of this dress. It doesn't feel right, though. My first official date with Jack, and nothing in my closet feels *right*.

Too casual. Too dressy. Too dark. Too bright.

I'm overthinking it. I know I am.

"Hand me the green dress again." I ignore my friend's comment, turning to her while I unzip the dark purple garment that barely covers my thighs. I need us to at least make it through dinner.

Simone shakes her head, standing up and walking to the other side of my bed, where clothes are haphazardly thrown on top of each other. She digs for a moment while I kick my dress across the fabric-littered floor.

"This." She pulls out my faux-leather skirt and an off-the-shoulder maroon long-sleeve. I stare at the outfit in her hands and tilt my head to the side. I didn't think of those two together. She tosses them to me before walking to my dresser.

I successfully catch the top, but the skirt falls heavily by my feet. She quickly pulls out a pair of black stockings and balls them up to throw at me.

"With your black ankle booties. Now, stop obsessing. You're going on a date with Jack. He is the last person to care about what you're wearing."

I'm pulling the new outfit on in a hurry even though my date is hours from now. I feel like I'll be less nervous when I know what I'm wearing. I'd already have my order planned if I knew where he was taking me.

"You're right. I'm just—" I stop, taking a deep breath after I tuck my shirt into the skirt at my waist. I'm adjusting my top with a flustered sigh before giving Simone a pointed look, a smile threatening to break through my nerves. "It's Jack."

An easy grin crosses her features, and she sits on the edge of my bed. "It *is* Jack. And, honey, he's already crazy about you."

My chest glows from the inside, the heat crawling up my neck and flushing my cheeks. *Crazy about me.* I bite my lip, turning back to the mirror. Damn it, Simone.

"Now." She gets up and comes to stand behind me. "You look hot as hell, you *know* this guy, and you have nothing to be nervous about."

"Thank you." I exhale in a *whoosh*, looking at her in our reflection.

I almost think Simone is more excited than I am. When I told her about us, she squealed so loudly that it caused Chief to howl in solidarity.

"I need to head to the hospital." She kisses my cheek, giving my ass a tap as she turns away from me. "I want to hear all about it tomorrow!"

When she leaves me, I stare at myself a little longer, running my hands over the lines in my outfit to obsessively smooth them. I gather my hair in my hand, pulling it up on top of my head and briefly wondering what hairstyle would make him crazier.

I'm feverish at the thought.

How am I going to make it through dinner when I already know how his mouth feels against my skin?

His eyes have inadvertently dropped to my bare shoulder several times, and it makes my stomach pinch. Jack has never been anything but a gentleman in my presence. Well, minus a couple of welcome moments in the past few weeks. So his mind must be where mine is—*not* at this restaurant.

"So, you know, the winter carnival is coming up soon." This is his attempt at small talk, and it's adorable. He's twisting the spaghetti noodles around the tines of his fork, his plate suddenly of interest to him.

I nod, pressing my napkin to my lips to swallow the huge bite of eggplant. "Yeah, Nova is very excited to go. You know she'll hound you to join us."

"She won't have to try too hard, I assure you." Jack's half-smirk is a showstopper. Honestly, what divine creature made his face? The more I get to unashamedly stare at him, the more in awe I am. His light freckles, peppered across his nose. His beard. His bright eyes and perfect lips. His jaw, so sharp. His grin, so lively.

"We should talk about us." I blurt it unintentionally. Ah, *damn* his pretty face. My stomach drops almost immediately. Is normalcy too much to ask of myself?

Jack sets his fork down and takes a quick gulp of water before clenching his fists on the table. "I agree. Let's talk."

Is he bracing himself? Does he think I'm second-guessing? Is he?

I place my napkin back in my lap and push my hair back before clearing my throat. "It's obvious we have *really* good chemistry."

"No doubt."

"Yeah. It's also obvious we've both been waiting to release this tension between us. And we *also* really care about one another." Jack nods in agreement, and I continue the best way I can. "So, I guess I'm just being pathetic and asking for there to be some kind of label here. I don't want to get confused or hurt in this. With ... this. With us."

That was tragic.

Jack is quiet for a moment. He lifts his eyes to mine and inhales, his entire body moving with that one breath. "Liza, I'm all in."

"All ... in?"

He leans forward, purposeful. "I don't want to scare you away. I don't want you to be afraid that I'm *here* if you're not there yet. But I'm in this. Long term. Anything you want me to be, I'm it."

I'm breathless, to be quite honest. *Anything you want me to be.*

"Look," Jack starts again, his face softening from his

earlier weariness. "I've loved before. I've been in relation-ships that meant something. Hell, I was about to marry someone the day you awkwardly stumbled into my life. But, God, I'm so glad I didn't. I never knew what was missing from my life until you and Nova came into it."

My throat is on fire. Like fire ants have decided to move in and set up camp. My vision is blurred. My heart has soared out of my chest and to the frickin' moon. *Oh, man.*

When I don't speak, he continues.

"So, yeah. I'm all in."

I reach across the table and place my hand over his, squeezing it before intertwining our fingers. My body hums at the way his eyes roam my face, like he's studying every line. The curve of his lips renders me weak.

All in. What the hell have we been doing? He should have been mine the second our eyes met. I guess, in a way, he has been. I wet my lips that have gone dry from the heavy breath that occurred when he spoke. "I'm not scared. I'm—I'm in, too. I'm *all* in."

"Yeah?" He tightens his hold on my hand, our eyes locked. "Glad we established that."

That eases the tension, and I relax, laughing at his generic statement. "I should probably let go of your hand because if I don't, we'll never be able to get out of here."

"Are you being suggestive, Ms. Davis?" He feigns being aghast, lowering his voice to a scandalized whisper.

The corner of my lip pulls, and I lean forward, running my thumb over his. "If you're asking if I am hinting at finishing the night at your place, the answer is yes."

I see his Adam's apple dip after I speak, a low growl rumbling in his throat, that I'm not imagining, as he reaches for his glass of water, my hand forgotten. I am satisfied. I raise an eyebrow and lean back in my seat, accomplished. Without missing a beat, I pick up the fork and take another bite of my dish.

I can't let him know his reaction has caused my mind to fog.

"Please stop apologizing. It makes me feel icky." His eyebrows are drawn together as if he's wincing, and he places a hand on my knee while the other clutches his steering wheel. "It's like you feel bad because you think I'm mad. I'm not mad. Nova comes first."

Of course I know he isn't mad. But I teased him with the promise of a nightcap, only to have my babysitter call and say she thinks she has a stomach virus. Jack immediately got the check, insisting to pay since *he* asked *me* to dinner, and drove me home. "No, no." I shake my head, placing my hand on top of his. "I just know it's probably difficult, dating a single mom. I don't want you to feel—"

"Liza." Jack's tone is exasperated when he comes to a stop in my driveway. "I told you. This is everything I want. You being the caring, compassionate, superhero mom that you are, is the sexiest quality about you. If anything, you're just making me that much more into you."

I'm not going to lie; I'm probably more bummed than he is that my night got cut short. Especially since it's past Nova's bedtime and she's probably asleep already, anyway. I squeeze his hand under mine and shake my head, exhaling into the warm cab of the truck. "You're smooth. Walk me to the door?"

"Planned on it." He winks, opening his door to meet

me on the sidewalk. My arm immediately loops through his, like it was meant to. Like our arms were made to intertwine and our steps were made to always fall perfectly in sync. Someone, please punch me for being so gooey.

I turn to him once we make it to the door, and he pulls me close by my jacket. One look at his sea-green eyes, and my legs turn into sand and blow away in the wind. He has a superpower—making *me* feel like I'm constantly floating.

"Rain check?" I'm hopeful, head tilted back as I gaze up at him. His hands fall to my waist, firmly gripping my sides and pulling me so close that our torsos touch.

His nod is brief, locked in on me as he leans down and captures my lips. I expected it, and yet it still causes me to suck in a sharp breath. He tastes like happiness, and I'm needy for it. It's soft—our lips teasing each other before our tongues deepen the kiss. He has my back against the front door, one arm wrapped around my waist, the other braced against the doorframe.

I can feel *every inch* of him pressing into me.

I think this kiss is causing more harm than good. I could honestly finish this in the cab of his truck.

I pull back, breathless and burning with want. Jack's forehead rests against mine while I work to slow my breathing.

He drops another sweet kiss to my lips and leans back. "Definitely rain check."

19

I saw Hannah this morning for the first time in a while. I made the appointment a week ago after another dream caused me to lose sleep, and I woke up with a throbbing headache in my left temple. So, at three in the morning, I was googling symptoms of brain aneurysms and trying to talk myself out of self-diagnosing. They're becoming somewhat less frequent, but every now and then, I'll wake in a panic with a new concern to plague my mind.

Canceling the appointment after a week of serenity and peaceful rest seemed like a fair call. Unfortunately, the guilt of not going, ate at me enough to follow through. Thinking back to this morning, I'm pretty sure I never even mentioned my spiral into WebMD madness and spent my entire fifty minutes gushing over my relationship with Jack.

Once I was done, she was smiling. She said being excited about something can sometimes distract from anxious thoughts trying to slip through. I made a joke along the lines of: "Great! Guess I'm healed!" Which we both know is comically untrue.

And yet, once again, I didn't commit to making another appointment at the end of our session. We did our usual song and dance. She attempts, and I tell her I'll call her after I look at my calendar.

It's got to be frustrating as hell, having me as a patient.

Simone, Nova, and I picked Jack up at his new house that's still under construction. He was dying to show it off, and though a lot of the Sheetrock has been hung, it's still hard to picture what he's describing. The view was incredible, though. There was no need of imagination for that.

It filled me with a sense of ease—seeing Jack's entire being light up as he excitedly described his plans for each room. In every one he guided us to, he would somehow find a way to touch me. His palm on the small of my back, his hand bumping against mine, our shoulders brushing as we walked down the hallway. I found myself looking for ways to come in contact with him like it was a game. Occasionally, we'd catch each other's eye and share a *look*.

Now, walking closely through the crowds of people at the carnival, my heart flutters every time Jack so much as glances in my direction.

Seriously, who *am* I?

Ever since that night I showed up on his doorstep and practically mauled him, we've shared some intensely hot make outs—including the slightly unprofessional one against my office desk over two weeks ago. But we haven't had the alone time necessary for what we *really* want to do to each other. Our busy schedules have made going on a second date impossible. It's obviously driving me to the brink of utter insanity. And yet, despite the way he currently looks in the jeans and bomber jacket he's wearing, I try to put a lid on that desire for the night. We are at a family function, after all.

Nova is trailing beside me, her hand clasped in mine and a big stuffed animal under her arm. Jack is a champ at literally every game we've come across, and he's always patient in teaching Nova how to play. She looks at him like he's a superhero. There's a small ache in my chest when she gets that look. I've missed it. Not that she doesn't adore me or think I can take on any closet monster. It's just a different admiration when she watches me.

"Mom! Can I ride that?" Nova exclaims, her hand pointing to *The Sizzler*.

I reach in my pocket to grab another handful of tickets for her and come up empty-handed. "Oh, shoot, Super-nova, we're out. I'm sorry, babe."

She gives an understanding nod, but I can tell she's plotting in her head. "Can we get just a few more tickets? I can skip the cotton candy."

Bargaining. She's my child.

"Yeah, we can, but you know the line is a little longer now. You're going to get bored standing there." I try to reason with her, not wanting to stand in another line myself.

Simone is quick to pipe in. "Why don't I take her to the petting zoo and you and Jack can go get more tickets?"

I look up to her, and she gives me a wink. Sneaky. *I see what you're doing, Locke.*

Jack shrugs beside me and nudges my shoulder with his forearm. "Come on, let her ride a little longer."

"You're both enablers." I laugh before looking down at Nova and scrunching my nose playfully. "All right, kid. I'll go get more tickets."

"Thank you!" she exclaims, dropping my hand for

Simone's and practically dragging her away. "You're the best!"

"Yeah, yeah." I chuckle as I watch them pick up the pace to see the animals. When I turn to Jack, I step closer, looping my arm through his. His hands are in his pockets, and he pulls his arm gently to his side to squeeze mine against him. "Let's go."

We stop at the back of the ticket line, and Jack pulls me to him, turning me to face his broad chest. He's a large man. I like it. I smile up at him as he slips his arms around my frame, sliding his hands into the back pockets of my jeans. Our affection is so exposed—satisfying the animalistic craving I have.

"Hi." He grins at me then, leaning down and faintly brushing his lips against mine. I need more.

"Hi," I mimic, my cheeks burning in excitement at our bodies being close. I reach up and kiss him again, taking his bottom lip between mine. We're exhaling an impatient, yearning breath into each other.

His eyelids are heavy when he breaks the kiss. He presses one to my forehead, and my eyes drift shut while my heart works overtime to keep up with the wild butterflies in my stomach. "Your hair smells good," he warmly mutters against my scalp. "It's a bit intoxicating."

"I could say the same." I lean back to look at him again. "Except you're too tall for me to get a good whiff of your hair. I'm mainly talking about your natural scent."

Jack laughs at that, his eyes bright and more lively than I ever remember them. We take a few side steps forward, moving with the line in what could look like an awkward embrace but feels so right. "It has been torture not having you, yet."

I need to remember to breathe when he talks like that.

I bite my lip, clutching his shirt in my hands. "You have to be careful with your words, Peters."

"But I *really* like the effect it has on you," he quickly replies, grinning as he leans back down to kiss me. How is it possible that my lips ache for his?

He likes to tease me, nudging my nose with his, his breath hot against my mouth. He keeps the kisses light, featherlike caresses, with each press to my lips. When he pulls back, his soft smile and intense stare are earth-shattering.

"What?" I whisper, running my hands up his chest and over his shoulders underneath his warm jacket.

"I didn't think I'd get this lucky." He doesn't miss a beat.

I'm seconds away from making everyone around us uncomfortable with the searing kiss I want to plant on him when a voice saves me from that loss of control.

"Jack?" I hear, and he looks over my shoulder, a polite smile washing away the longing he had moments ago. I turn around in his arms, and he keeps one around my waist.

Suddenly, I'm back in that bridal suite, soothing her cries.

"Gwen." His voice is light and friendly. Oh, *that* comforts me. "I didn't know you were back."

Her eyes haven't even swept over me, yet. I can't blame her. Jack is someone who holds the attention of everyone around him. His presence is commanding.

"Oh, not permanently. I'm visiting my parents. I moved to New Jersey." She pulls her cardigan closer to her frame and looks at me, narrowing her eyes slightly, trying to place me, I'm sure.

Jack's arm has not moved from me, and I get an immature delight from that. *Mine*. "Yeah," he replies. "I know. Your mom brought Pepper for a checkup a couple of months ago, and she told me."

"Eliza." Gwen finally blurts my name in an uncomfortable laugh. "Wow. Small world. I didn't know you two ..." She trails off, crossing her arms over her chest. "This is kind of weird."

I mean, sure. It's probably weird *for her*. She skipped town and left Jack to deal with the aftermath of a very public breakup. I give her a smile, anyway, even though my protective nature is kicking in. "Hi, Gwen." I step out of Jack's way and nod at the shortening line. "I can leave you two to chat. I really need to get Nova her tickets."

Jack furrows his brow at my abandoning him and shakes his head. "No, you can stay."

"Really." I give him a pleading look. *Please don't make me be here.* He picks up on my discomfort and nods, watching me as I turn to catch up with the back of the line. I want to snap at Gwen for ruining our perfect little snowglobe moment. I can hear their voices from behind me, but barely. The line is about a foot from where they stand.

"What did you do? Take her home from the wedding?" I hear from Gwen, her tone is teasing, but I can tell there's a smidge of anger or jealousy underneath. Boy, she's gutsy.

Jack laughs, and I feel a shiver down my spine. It's not the genuine laugh I get from him when I'm doing the choreography to B*Witched's *C'est la Vie* in the passenger seat of his Bronco. No, this laugh is sour. Like taking a whiff of out-of-date milk and discovering it's gone bad. "You're kidding. Gwen, I am not having this conversation with you. My relationship is none of your business."

"So that's a yes?"

They are delusional if they think I can't hear this entire exchange.

"No," he replies, and I don't blame him for defending his character, though he's right—none of this is her business. "I don't want it to be like this when I see you, Gwen. I have no hard feelings. I am genuinely happy to see you, and glad you're doing so well. But I don't owe you anything."

She's silent, or at least, I can no longer hear her for a brief moment before she speaks again. "You're right. I think that just threw me. It's really good to see you, too. I'm glad you're happy." A beat. "Are you happy?"

I hold my breath for an unknown reason because I know Jack, and I *know* he's happy. It's still a rush of joy when I hear him reply.

"Very." I can hear the smile in his voice. I feel like such a creep for listening in. I move up in the line, and their voices become more distant. That's okay. I got what my needy little heart desired.

Several minutes pass, and I'm nearing the ticket booth when I feel Jack's arms wrap low around my waist, his cheek against the side of my head. I melt at the way his torso feels against my back. "Hi again," he says. "I'm sorry about that."

"Oh gosh, no." I lean my head back against his chest and look up at him with a smile. "Don't be at all. Her parents live here. It was bound to happen sooner or later." I'm playing it cool as a cucumber, like I'm not possessive in the least—though, I am.

"Still unfortunate timing."

"For sure," I agree with a nod. "She's kind of known for that, though, isn't she?"

I want to take it back as soon as I say it, but he

surprises me with a loud laugh. He squeezes me briefly and tilts his head to the side to get a good look at me. "That's one of my favorite things about you."

"What?"

"Your lack of a filter." He grins and kisses my temple. "It's cute to watch you squirm after you say something you didn't mean to say."

My elbow lightly connects with his abdomen playfully. "Jerk."

We reach the window, and I purchase another book of tickets. I'm thankful Jack didn't try to pay for them like he's done before. He's catching on to my independence. With the book in hand, we walk back to the petting zoo, our hands clasped.

"I can still buy Nova some cotton candy, though, right?" Jack asks, nudging me gently as we walk.

"Fine." I grin over to him. "She thinks you're Superman, you know?"

He's quick to disagree, shaking his head as he tugs on my hand. "No, you've got it all wrong, Liza. You're her hero. You hung the damn moon in her eyes." He looks over at me, and I catch his gaze. "In my eyes, too."

The stuffed jaguar Jack won for Nova is bigger than she is, but that isn't stopping her from making room for it in her bed.

I sit on the edge, looking down at her. "You're crashing. I told you that sugar high wouldn't last."

"Worth it." Her tiny voice cracks, sleep attempting to take over as her eyelids lower.

Her serene expression makes me happy—like I'm

doing something right. "Did you have fun?" I whisper it into her quiet bedroom as if I'll wake the jaguar.

Her eyes open, bright and excited. "Yes. Can we go again tomorrow?"

"Uh, I'm a little carnival'd out. But we'll find something fun to do this weekend, I promise."

Nova nods, falling asleep again, so I take it as my cue to kiss her cheek and leave her be.

"Hey, Mom," she says as I'm standing to leave. I look down at her and tilt my head to the side, letting her know she has my attention. "Is Jack your boyfriend now?"

I think of the secret smile he gave me when we dropped him back off at his place, and my stomach flips like a pancake. "Uh—I—well ... what would you think if he were?"

There's no hesitation. No pause. Just, "I'd be really happy."

"Yeah?" Relief. A held breath flows out of me, and I'm lighter. "Good. Because I think he is."

20

*N*ova is at a sleepover with a friend. Usually, I'm cautious about letting her stay the night at other places, but I've known Monica's parents for a while. I trust them. My worry isn't completely gone, but at least it's under control with the promise of a couple of check-ins.

I've decided an adult sleepover of my own would be the perfect distraction.

I called Jack as soon as I agreed to let Nova go, and he made plans to cook dinner at his place. I was bouncing in anticipation all day.

As soon as I got to his house after dropping Nova off, a craving for ice cream took over. Jack, ever the yes-man, grabbed his keys and went for a pre-dinner treat.

My appetite will probably be ruined, but sitting in his truck, watching his mouth slide over the frozen custard on his spoon, I have the fleeting thought we may not make it through dinner.

Or maybe we will. Jack has been pretty neutral since I

first showed up. Maybe it's just *me* who can't keep my hands to myself.

"I'm excited to see you lose a little control." Oh. Okay. I said that out loud.

It surprises him as much as it does me. "What was that?"

With a guarded chuckle, I shake my head, bashful. "You know, you're always pretty chill around me. I'd like to see you lose a little bit of that."

"Me? Chill?" Jack snorts, obviously disagreeing. The quick swipe of his hand is a dismissal of that thought.

"I'm serious. I've been dying, not getting alone time with you, and you've seemed unfazed. Nothing bothers you." I roll my eyes, cleaning chocolate off my spoon.

Jack laughs, putting his truck in park before grabbing his ice cream from between his legs. "I promise I'm just very good at hiding it."

"Give me an example, then, Mr. Cool-calm-and-collected."

"Okay." He complies, shoveling a scoop of cherry-vanilla ice cream into his mouth as he ponders. A moment passes before he turns in the driver's seat to face me. He reaches his hand to touch the end of my ponytail resting over my shoulder. "It drives me crazy when you wear your hair up," he admits, pushing my hair behind my shoulder before placing his warm palm against my neck, his thumb grazing my jawline. "It makes it incredibly difficult to not taste you."

Our eyes meet, and an involuntary shiver travels through my body. How do I follow that up? "What's stopping you?" I exhale, leaning into his touch. I'm like a cat in heat, my skin aching for his.

And he's enjoying it. He smiles, moving closer to me

on the bench seat of his truck, but stays far enough away for me to meet him halfway. Not a chance, Peters. This is your move. "Well," he begins, holding the decorative cup up for me to see. "I have to finish my ice cream."

What a *tease*. I nod in understanding before reaching up and sliding my finger along the edge of the cup, gathering the cold custard that's spilling over. I don't tear my eyes from his as I slowly smear the dab across my collarbone. I raise an eyebrow and suck the remnants from my fingertip. "Whoops," I whisper, watching his eyes darken at the action.

Jack's smile lights up the dark cab. He places his ice cream cup in the cupholder near his knees and moves closer to me, our lips only a second from touching before he dips his head down and licks the dessert from my skin.

That movement ignites the match.

I audibly gasp at the feeling of his cold tongue against the heat of my flushed skin. Fire builds inside me, settling between my legs. His mouth moves up my neck, stopping at my ear, where he gently nips my lobe before brushing sweet kisses against my cheek and landing on my lips. The moan that escapes me is unexpected, but the soft pressure of his mouth on mine is quenching my thirst for him.

He immediately takes control of the kiss. His cherry-flavored tongue mixing with the chocolate taste of mine. His hand, once secure on my neck, cups the back of my head. His fingers tangle themselves in my hair that's held in place by an elastic band.

When he tugs at the strands, I moan again—the sound muffled by his mouth. He slows his kisses, his lips caressing mine in a tantalizing manner. I pull away from him, breathless, with eyes half-open. "I can't do what I want to do to you in the cab of your truck."

"Agreed." His voice is strained. Not even a second goes by, and he's moved away from me and out of the vehicle.

If I weren't so ready to rip his clothes off, I would have found the speed at which he escaped to be quite comical. But I'm out and following him up his porch steps just as quickly.

Once we're inside, he doesn't even flip on a light. His hands fall to my waist, and his lips find mine in the dark. Magnets. We have always been magnets. Our kiss isn't urgent here. We're in no rush. You'd think with kissing being the only thing we've done, we'd grow tired of it. I haven't. His mouth is magic.

I feel his slightly calloused hand brush against my cheek, moving my hair behind my ear. Every single touch makes my skin ache for more.

After a moment, he slowly pulls away from me and takes my hand, locking his eyes with mine as he guides me down the hall. It's not a hurried scurry of scattered clothes and clumsy hands, but that's not what I expect from Jack.

Jack, who is confident, sexy, and experienced.

Jack, who knows what he wants and knows how to do it.

That thought alone makes me walk faster, pushing him in the process.

"Liza." He chuckles my name, stepping through his doorway before turning to me. "Eager?" he teases, my mouth meeting his almost before he can get the word out.

I swallow his playful taunt, and he reciprocates, sliding his hands under my thin t-shirt. Oh, hell, his skin against mine is a feeling I didn't know I was missing. Blood rushes to the most sensitive areas of my body, my nipples tightening as if they weren't already hard enough.

He tosses his shirt over his head before ridding me of mine, and his hands are sprawled against my back, inching toward the clasp of my bra as he leaves a warm trail of open-mouth kisses down my neck and across my shoulder.

I can only explore him with my hands while his lips are on me. I run my fingers over the ridges of his torso, my fingertips tracing his sexy tattoo that frequents my dreams. I move them lower, tightening my grip on the bulge in his jeans. His teeth sink into the curve of my neck, and I let out a sharp gasp. His tongue immediately soothes the bite, only making me hungrier for him.

Our caresses are more animalistic with every piece of clothing we shed. I want to mark him. I want him to mark *me*. Where this possessive urge is coming from is a mystery to me.

I press my hands to his bare chest and push him to a sitting position at the end of his bed. I enjoy the way he follows my lead, letting me take control of the moment.

He leans back slightly, his hands on either side of his body, a lazy smirk on his lips. *Fuck me*, I think I actually have a fever from this sight. His arms are extended and tense from holding himself up in this position. His thighs are an actual work of art, bulging below the seam of his briefs. The lines of his muscles are sharp—like he's made of stone.

"You okay?" His voice is quiet, his chest heaving. He leans up and places his palm on the back of my thigh, grazing my skin with his thumb.

I shake myself from my long appraisal. "Yes."

I nail the sexy-librarian move with a quick pull to the elastic band holding my hair up and straddle his legs, lowering myself onto his erection straining behind the material of his underwear. A low groan rumbles in his throat, and he grips my waist, his mouth brushing against the swell of my breast. Every feeling is intensified, my skin like an exposed wire. Jack pulls my bra straps down my arms and reaches behind me to expertly unclasp it and get it out of his way.

He's gentle when his mouth covers my breast, his tongue swirling against my taut nipple. I lean my head back, inhaling sharply and thrusting my hips into him. He's slow in his movements. It's an agonizing pleasure of *needing* him to take his time, but also wanting to feel everything all at once.

Like I said, he *knows* how to do it.

Jack's arms encircle my waist before lifting me from his lap and turning in one quick motion, laying me on my back.

He crawls up my body.

He's hovering over me.

I'm not sure how I became so confident—having my naked body on display to this objectively perfect human. But I like it.

"Eliza." His breath is hot against my ear. "You're so incredibly stunning."

I melt into the bed and close my eyes as our lips touch again. He lightly sucks my bottom lip, which incites a spontaneous whimper, and hooks a finger into the side of my panties, pulling them down.

My pulse is between my legs.

My teeth graze his tongue, tempted to bite when I feel his finger caress my swollen clit. He gives it special attention, causing my legs to tremble at the contact.

"Please." I hiss the word into his mouth, bucking

against his hand. His lazy kisses trail down my body, his tongue outlining the curve of my breast.

He looks up at me, tracing my entrance with the tip of his finger. I squirm under his touch, wanting so desperately to feel the pressure of him inside me.

When I do, I can't suppress the sharp moan that escapes my lips. I push my hips upward to meet him, but he steadies them with his free hand, looking at me with dark eyes and a deliciously hot, wicked smile. Oh, *he* wants control here.

I can't catch my breath when he slides two fingers inside me, hitting the right spot over and over until I'm close to coming undone.

The thought of being exposed, without any type of fabric covering my body, has always horrified me, but at this moment, I don't have the time or brain capacity to be modest. I push the padding of my feet against the mattress, my toes curling at the sensation swirling inside me. My eyes are screwed shut, my teeth are sunk into my bottom lip, my breathing is unsteady, and my heart is pounding in my throat. I am so close to the edge I can barely stand it.

"That's it, babe," Jack whispers against my skin, his mouth below my breast as he moves his fingers in a perfected rhythm.

I hum in response, his movements getting faster to match the thrusts of my hips he can no longer contain. With a quick kiss to my side, he moves lower and flicks his tongue against me, his fingers continuing to curl into me.

It's all too much.

Pressure mounts deep inside.

All it takes is for me to look down and lock eyes with him, his mouth still on me, and I lose myself.

My entire body trembles, my stomach clenching and unclenching as I ride the wave with a guttural purr.

I'm in a fog.

My eyes have to adjust to the room when I open them again.

I can barely feel it when he presses kisses against my sensitive skin, watching me as I work to calm my erratic breathing. I smile, and he presses a kiss against my lips. He leans back, staring at me with intensity, tilting his head.

"What?" I exhale, running my hand through his wavy hair.

Jack grins and shakes his head, kissing me again, but keeping it short. "Are you okay?"

"Oh, I'm perfect. In the time it will take you to grab a condom, I'll be ready for you to be inside me."

He chokes on his reply. I'm sure he didn't expect me to be so blunt. I enjoy the look he gets in his eyes when he's turned on.

I chuckle and raise an eyebrow, reaching up to pat his ass. "Get to it, big guy."

He smirks and rolls over to the other side of his bed, digging in his nightstand drawer for protection. I close my eyes, take a deep breath, and listen as my heart slows to a normal pace. I feel him move beside me, and open my eyes to see him pushing his underwear down, the condom package between his teeth.

Oof, he's gorgeous.

Grinning, I sit up and crawl over to him, taking the packet from his mouth and ripping it open. He pushes himself up a little higher, his back against the headboard.

I straddle him and roll the condom down his hard length. I hear a small grunt from him and look up to find him staring at my hand as I stroke him. His jaw is tense, and his hands reach for my body, roughly grabbing my hips to position me over him. He leans forward, covering my nipple with his mouth. I'm breathless. I can't wait any longer. I lift his head to me and capture his lips with mine before sinking down onto him. I can feel the vibration of his approving groan against my tongue.

I end our kiss with a light bite to his lip and take my time, digging my nails into his shoulders as we move. His hands tightly grip my hips, his eyes locked on mine. I fight the urge to close my own as he fills me. Looking into Jack Peters' eyes while he's inside me could quite possibly make me come on the spot.

"Damn, Liza." His voice is like sandpaper—hoarse and raw. His hips jolt upwards, and I gasp, using my legs to guide myself up and back down at a slow pace.

The buildup is incredible. His dick twitches inside me, urging me to go faster. I press myself tight against him, feeling another climax building.

We're moving in sync, his arm around my waist, my head buried into his neck. I run my tongue along a strained vein under his jaw and nip at his skin, earning a hard jerk. I bite harder at his loss of control and hear a growl deep in his throat.

That does it. My movements are a lot more frantic now, and I'm craving that second release.

I'm almost—almost—oh, *fuck*.

I sigh as I come around him, causing him to curse under his breath. Shuddering against his body, I fall onto his chest and press my head further into the space where his shoulder and neck connect. I can't breathe. I don't even think I can feel my toes.

It takes a moment before I can move. I lean back and

squeeze his shoulders, clenching around him. My hand slides through his hair, and I touch my forehead to his.

"I'm going to come." He's barely audible, pushing his hips upward and thrusting into me again.

At that movement, I fall onto his chest again, trying to catch my breath against him when he tucks his hands under my ass and swiftly flips us over. He leans down, running his tongue across my bottom lip before capturing it between his. It's a savory kiss, like his mouth is memorizing mine.

Once I'm completely drunk from his slow kisses, he moves them down my neck and over my breast before licking a trail down the valley between my breasts. My throat burns with need, and he lightly sucks at my sensitive skin. I grip the sheets, enjoying the warmth of his lips. When he stops, his knee is between my legs, spreading them. I feel my heart pound against my ribcage when I feel the tip of his head push against my entrance. "This okay?"

"Yes. Please, yes."

He looks up at me with a lazy smile, kissing my lips again before he pushes into me.

I'm already on fire, ready to release this desire for him again and again. His hands find mine, and he slides them up my body and clasps them above my head. He's in a trance, his movements rhythmic, his face buried into my neck. Explosive want is building again. My abdomen tightens as he rocks into me. When he finally lets go, I feel him come undone inside me. His hands squeeze mine, and his forehead falls against my shoulder—his body rigid before relaxing.

After a moment, he holds himself up and rakes his eyes over my disheveled appearance. With a smile, he leans down and peppers kisses across the swell of my breast.

"Totally worth the wait," he mumbles, nuzzling the goosebumps covering my skin.

"Speak for yourself." I look up at him with a contented sigh. "I should have been doing this from the second I met you."

"Oh, yeah?" He chuckles. "At my failed wedding?"

"Yep. I should have led you to a coatroom and mounted you immediately." I can't help but laugh at my words.

Jack leans down and silences me with a sweet brush of our lips before looking into my eyes. "I'm glad it worked out this way."

"Me too. But now I need to pee."

He laughs. "Yeah, I need to clean up."

"Hot," I deadpan as I run from his bed into the attached bathroom. I know if I let myself get too comfortable, I won't get up to pee. I would eventually have to, and I'd probably hold it until I either dreamed about toilets or felt so much discomfort, it would be unbearable *not* to go.

I wash my hands and hurry back to the bed, freezing and naked. His giant body tangled in his comforter looks inviting and toasty. I slide up to him, pulling the covers to my chin and pressing my cold nose into his ribs.

"Shit!" He hisses, followed by a chuckle as he pulls away from me. "It's like a little ice cube on your face."

"Warm it up." I scoot closer again and throw my leg over his to trap him. "You know what I just realized?"

His chest rises and falls as he hums. "Hmm. That you forgot to say hi to CeCe when we walked in?"

"No, but crap, we need to go get her." I lift up, and he

pulls me back down into him, wrapping both arms around me.

"Not yet." His voice is muffled in my hair.

"What I realized," I begin again, my cheeks hurting from my inability to stop grinning, "is that we skipped dinner."

"Oh, yeah." He rolls back onto his back and runs a hand down his face. "I promised you a homemade meal. I should probably get started on that so we can eat before nine."

"Or ..." My tone is playful, and he glances down at me after he sits up. "You could make me breakfast instead. Save dinner for another night. We can order pizza and watch tv."

"Breakfast, hm?"

I grab his arm and pull him back down, finding his lips with mine in the darkness of his bedroom. "Breakfast," I affirm in a quiet mumble.

His lips quirk upwards against mine, and he breaks first, shaking his head as he pulls back from me. "Then, I need to go order our dinner before we get trapped in here."

"Trapped? You make it sound like it's a bad thing."

Jack's eyes narrow into a glare, yet it's anything but menacing. "Don't twist my meaning, woman. I'm going to order our food and crawl right back in here with you."

"We're nauseating." It falls out of my mouth in a giggle. I could literally choke on the sap. He throws me a grin and leaves me to check my phone for a text or call from Monica's mom. She texted me ten minutes ago to let me know they were back at her house and eating dinner. I appreciate that she listens when I request updates, because I know it can be a pain in the ass when trying to wrangle three eight-year-olds.

I get lost in my phone for longer than I intended after clicking a link Simone sent me of a clip from our favorite talk show. I get stuck watching the video that played after and the one after that, and suddenly, Jack is back in the room with dinner and two glasses of water. Hero.

Eating in bed goes against everything I believe in, and yet I also feel like I've been missing out on one of life's greatest treasures. Once he slips in behind me and flips the lid to reveal the gooey goodness of extra cheese on my half, I'm sold.

The pizza box is warm on my legs that are shielded by Jack's worn quilt.

I would probably have put up more of a fight when Jack suggested we eat in bed if he were wearing more than just his briefs. But, alas, I was blinded by his almost naked form delivering a box of pizza to the bedroom. What sane woman would say no?

I'm snug between his legs, my bare back pressed against his torso. When I lean my head back, it rests on his chest so comfortably it confirms, again, our bodies were *meant* to fit like puzzle pieces.

When I look down into the box to pick up a second slice, I cringe at the chunks of fruit on Jack's half. "You know, if I would have known you put *pineapple* on your pizza, I would have steered clear of this whole thing."

Jack pauses to swallow his bite, but I feel a chuckle rumble deep in his chest. "Have you ever tried it?"

"No. Pineapple doesn't belong on pizza."

"Wait, you're being this harsh, and yet, you've never tried it?"

"I know what I like." I shrug, taking a bite of my own deliciousness.

"Unacceptable." The word is firm, and he pushes his half-eaten piece in my face. "You must try it."

"Get that abomination away from me." I laugh and shove his hand out of my vision, turning my head for extra protection. "I don't even want to kiss you in fear that I'll taste it." *Well, that's a lie.* "CeCe!" I desperately call for backup. She doesn't budge.

I can't see his face, but I can sense the eye roll behind me. "You're absurd." He laughs but attempts to put the pizza back in my line of vision. "One bite."

"Ugh." I groan, giving in way too easily. The pull he has on me is unreal. I'm about to eat *pineapple pizza*. I lean up to his hand and take a small bite, chewing with a wince. "This offends me. It goes against what pizza should be," I review as I munch. Yes, I'm talking with my mouth full. I'm an animal. I swallow after a moment and immediately take a bite of my pizza.

"Well? Final verdict?"

I lean my head back against him and look up at his face. Even upside down, he's absolutely beautiful. "I will never eat a bite of your disgusting pizza again."

"Uncultured." He leans down to press a kiss against my hair.

"But it's not bad enough to deter me from kissing your pineapple mouth," I finish with a grin. I focus my attention back on the *Boy Meets World* re-run I chose. I could do this forever. I could do *Boy Meets World* and pizza forever, but I mean *this*. I could do Jack and Eliza forever.

21

I'm addicted.

This addiction probably has everything to do with me not being able to see him as often as my needy little soul would like to. That's okay. I like not losing my identity to a man. I like that I still have my girls' nights with Simone and alone time with Nova.

But when I do have those moments where I can steal a phone call or grab an unplanned lunch, I'm easily consumed by him. Four months of being with him, and I still don't think that's wearing off any time soon.

I pull into the parking lot of Jack's vet clinic and reach into the passenger seat for the styrofoam container holding his favorite muffuletta from the Italian deli near my salon.

Walking past the reception desk, I head straight down the hallway to his office. The door is open, and when I peek my head in, his brow is furrowed in concentration, his hand over his mouth, as he stares at the computer monitor in front of him.

"Delivery."

Jack's eyes lift to mine, and his face softens. My. Heart. "Delivery, huh? Smells like a muffuletta. Are you trying to butter me up for something?"

He rounds the corner of his desk, coming to stand in front of me, his hand resting on the open door. I hold the plate between us with a smile. "No. This is a celebration muffuletta. It's move-in weekend!"

"I know. I have so much shit to do, and I'm fighting with the moving company I already secured. I think they messed up the dates or something." I'm tugged closer to him, and he shuts the door behind me with a smirk, glancing down at his lunch. Taking it from my hands, he places it on his desk behind him and slides his arms around my waist. I don't even care that he's covered in dog hair. "Thank you."

"Moving company? Why the hell would you waste your money on that? You have me, Simone, Nova, your dads, your friend Charlie. You have an entire team of movers. Cancel that, get a refund, and use the money to take me to dinner." I'm grinning as I finish my thought, and he leans down to press a kiss against my cheek.

"What an expensive dinner."

"I think I'm worth it," I tease while his lips trail across my jawline and down my neck. My eyelids lower, and I grasp his scrub top in my hand, sucking in a satisfied breath.

The only other guy I've ever dated that had facial hair was Tyler Agnes during my senior year of high school. I remember hating the way it felt on my neck—the rough texture would pull me right out of the moment. And yet, I *crave* the feel of Jack's scratchy beard against my skin. It means he's touching me. And I don't ever want Jack to stop touching me.

"I promise this isn't what I came in for." Even as I say it, I'm sighing at the way his mouth caresses the sensitive skin beneath my ear.

Then his lips are gone, and I regret my words. With a smile, he touches them to mine. "I apologize. I told you what it does to me when you wear your hair up."

"Oh, no. Never apologize." I pull myself even closer, playing with the hair at the base of his neck. "I took the day off to help you pack. When do you get out of here?"

"I can head out now." He says it with a shrug but glances over his shoulder. "Or after I eat my lunch. Don't you have an appointment today?"

Therapy. He remembered. "I did, but I rescheduled so I could help. It's no big deal."

His eyes study me. Mine say: *Please don't*. But then he stops and nods, stepping away to grab his lunch. "Well, all right, then. I'll put you to work."

I glance at the clock after taping up the last box in his kitchen and listen for him. I need to pick Nova up soon. We've been working in silence, trying to get the last remaining items boxed up before moving everything to his new place tomorrow.

A sense of déjà vu floods me and causes an icky feeling in the pit of my stomach.

Some memories are better left buried, and the memory of Aaron passing out in our living room days before moving into a new house is one of them. It's vivid, and I want so desperately to shake it. I was surrounded by boxes in the hallway, calling out to Aaron that I needed more packing tape. I didn't get an answer, but I heard a crash. When I ran into the kitchen, the floor was covered in pots that fell from the counter when he tried to catch himself.

He had a gash in his forehead from the corner of the dining room table. But that was the least of our concerns after we left the hospital late that night.

I'm flushed and take a swig of the water next to me, trying to calm the unnecessary whispers of worry. The human brain can be a total bitch when she wants to be.

"All right, my closet and drawers are done. How's the kitchen?" Jack's voice echoes down the hall before I see him. When he turns into the doorway, he tilts his head, his brows pinched in concern.

I really need to work on my poker face.

He quietly approaches me, placing his hands on my upper arms. "Are you okay? You look pale. Do you need to sit? I told you to stay hydrated."

"I'm fine." I cut him off, before his rambling continues, and give him a smile. "I stood up too quickly and got lightheaded."

Reaching behind me, he pulls the stool up closer and playfully lifts me on top of it. "You sit here, then. I don't need you fainting on my watch."

Fainting. I get a cold sweat. My hands feel clammy and like they're not mine. Swallowing is difficult. Maybe I do need to sit. I try to take a deep breath, but I can't satisfy the need. I grasp for my water bottle again, but Jack grabs it before I can, quickly taking off the top and putting it to my lips. *Do I look that bad?*

I take a generous sip and look up at him, his eyes focused and not leaving my face. "I'm good," I assure him, but it feels disingenuous as it leaves my mouth. "I haven't eaten much today, so my blood sugar is probably low or something."

Jack nods, unconvinced. I can read it on his face. He stays close as if he's afraid I'll fall over any minute. A knot forms in my stomach when my mind goes in overdrive.

What if Jack gets sick? What if he spends so much time taking care of everyone else he never takes care of himself? How can I ensure he's okay? When was my last workup? When was Nova's last appointment? Last month. Okay. Simone? Have I checked in on Simone's health lately?

"Liza." His voice is soft, pulling my focus back on him. I had locked eyes on the refrigerator behind him when my thoughts slipped away from me. "Do you need to lie down? Do I need to go get Nova? I don't know if you should drive."

"Do you get checkups regularly?" I blurt the question unintentionally. I catch him off guard. He steps back from me like the question was in physical form and thrown at his head.

Jack folds his arms across his chest, but he remains neutral. "Are you asking if I've recently been tested?"

"Oh God, no." I shake my head, pressing my hands to my face. The question is dangling out there, unanswered, and causing my heart to race at the turn of the conversation. "I mean, I hope you have. I feel irresponsible that I'm just now asking you. But I meant regular yearly checkups. You know, blood work and all."

At this question, he grabs the other stool, placing it in front of me. When he sits, he leans forward, taking one of my hands in his. "I go every February to get a full workup. I have a perfect bill of health. I could probably lay off the sugar, but I have a sweet tooth, and I'm an imperfect person. As for the other, I got tested after Gwen and didn't sleep with anyone else until you. To be safe, I got tested when I had my annual exam in February. I'm good."

It eases my nerves that he so casually answered without hesitation. I take a deep breath, finally, and smile, squeezing his hand. "Good to know. I am, as well, by the way. Tested and clear." I'm so awkward. "I'm sorry. That was kind of out of left field. I just—sometimes, I have thoughts that come out before I can process them."

"Is everything okay?"

I could tell him. I could tell him I will always be this way, even though I wasn't always this way. I could tell him to beware of the fact I will rush him to the nearest clinic the second he coughs funny or runs the slightest bit of fever. Or that I've looked up more symptoms on the internet in the past year than I ever have and I don't know how to stop. I could even tell him that his answer didn't satisfy me, because I want to know his entire family history.

I *could* tell him. I just *can't* tell him. I can't, because I don't want to accept I am forever plagued by the fear of a gash on the forehead leading to a cancer diagnosis. I need him to not have to take care of me.

"Yes." I place my other hand on his cheek and lean forward, my lips finding his. "I just had a weird moment. I'm fine."

His jaw clenches and unclenches, ticking like he's concentrating. He wants so badly to pry more, and I'm not ready for that. But his eyes tell me he doesn't want to push me. I take advantage of that by not offering any more explanations. "Can I drive you to get Nova? It will make me feel better."

"Of course. She would love that."

Jack presses his lips together, still studying my face,

before leaning forward and placing a kiss on my forehead. "Come on."

He's fine. I'm fine. I stand up to leave with him and internally repeat that over and over until I've somehow convinced myself it's true. We *are* fine. I need to get better at discerning my irrational fears from my rational ones. Which, I know, would be better done in therapy.

Jack loads CeCe up in the backseat because she loves a good car ride, and we head out. It's silent for the first few minutes until he finally breaks it by turning on the radio. At a red light in town, he pulls up his phone and scrolls through his music before New Radicals blares from his speakers.

My favorite.

It immediately makes me grin.

Thirty seconds in, and I can't help it; I'm singing at the top of my lungs with Jack joining me on the chorus. I'm not fully over the feeling—my chest still feels tight—but belting out questionable yet incredible nineties hits with Jack is medicine in itself. Or, at least, it's a good temporary distraction.

I went to bed last night in a weird headspace. After an afternoon with Jack and Nova, my heart was floating. We went for burgers and milkshakes, watched a movie of Nova's choosing, and after she went to bed, I relaxed on the couch with my head in Jack's lap and a *Sister, Sister* re-run playing.

And yet ...

My body felt out of place for most of the day.

This morning, nothing was wrong. I slept well, I didn't

have any nightmares, and I was excited to spend the day with my favorite people. I even had the fleeting thought of how my worries from yesterday were silly and overdramatic. Though I haven't gotten too deep with Hannah in therapy, I have picked up some helpful tools.

For instance: *Identify the problem.* I got worked up over my loved ones having fatal ailments. *Identify the trigger.* Easy. I had a raw memory of a moment that has caused immense pain in my life. *Was it rational?* In the moment, it felt like it was, but no. It was irrational.

That's pretty much where I stop. I don't know the entire work-through, because she's only said it once, and my brain identifies with rationality. Therefore, as soon as I tell myself something is irrational, I can usually let it go. *Usually.*

Okay, so it's not a perfect process.

Today, however, I've had no time to let myself get lost in unwelcome thoughts. We've been up and moving since six this morning. Every box, piece of furniture, and appliance has been cleared out of Jack's old house and brought to his new one.

There is still work to be done to it. He wanted his doors and shutters to be custom-made by him and David, so they're on the hinges, but not stained and ready. The landscaping is also incomplete because he enjoys yard work and didn't want to hire anyone for that. Other than that, it's incredible.

Chief and CeCe are running in and out of the house, tracking dirt in, which would normally drive me crazy. However, we're all dirtying up the floors as we unpack Jack's belongings.

"Aren't you glad you didn't hire movers?" I ask, on the verge of being breathless. I stand up and feel a tight pull in my lower back, my calves burning from the all-day event of carrying everything from the U-Haul into the house. He's leaning against the counter in a sweat-stained t-shirt, effortlessly chugging an entire bottle of water as I speak. How is everything he does so damn sexy? He's drinking water, and I'm salivating like he's performing a striptease.

He finishes with a sigh of satisfaction and wipes his glistening forehead with his arm before giving me a smile. "Yes, thank you." He walks toward me and quickly tugs me into him with a playful grin, enveloping me in his arms that are slick with perspiration.

"Ew," I whine, fighting against his hold and wrinkling my nose at the cold dampness of his shirt. It's only a second before I give way to laughter and sink into his gross hug. I lean up and press a brief kiss to his lips. "You stink."

"So do you, cupcake," he quips then presses his face into my neck, taking a dramatic whiff. "Who am I kidding? I love your scent."

My laughter doesn't subside, and I shake my head when he leans back again. "You're such a weirdo." Even so, I pull myself even closer. "Hey, I was thinking you need an egg hammock."

"I don't know what that is."

With a good-natured roll of my eyes, I sigh, exasperated. "Just *Google* it. Or we'll go shopping, and I'll show you. It would be perfect on your front porch."

"Jack!" we hear from outside, and he releases me from his hold, looking down at me with a sigh.

"You're being summoned." I smile, nodding toward the door. "Go. Simone may have broken something important."

"Shit." He groans before heading for the front door. I look around the cluttered room. Even with piles of boxes, the living room is still spacious. I absolutely love the wall of windows that looks out to his deck. The house sits on top of a shallow hill. From this angle, I can see the dock, directly behind the fenced yard that leads to the lake. The place is a dream. I have to stop myself from imagining my life here.

Echoing footsteps vibrate off the empty walls, and I turn in the direction of the hallway to see Nova's grinning face appear in the doorway. "I organized the bathroom! Come look."

"Jeez, kid, you're making the rest of us look bad." I laugh before taking my hair out of my loose ponytail so I can throw it back up a little tighter.

I follow her into the empty master bedroom that leads to the biggest master bath I have ever seen, equipped with a fancy clawfoot tub in front of a huge window. What could Jack Peters possibly do with a bathroom of this size? Mr. Modest Means is getting too big for his britches. I must tease him later.

"I hung that picture." Nova points to a portrait of CeCe that Penny painted. I must say, it fits well in the area she chose to put it. "And I also put all of his stuff in cabinets."

"He's probably going to reward you with a sundae." I grin, looking down at her pleased expression. "Want to help me in the living room?"

Her eyes light up in excitement, and she takes off full speed to beat me. This kid loves to clean and organize.

I take my time following her, looking into each room that I've seen dozens of times since their completion. Four bedrooms, three baths, a loft upstairs, a fireplace, and a huge backyard. One thing is for sure—a man doesn't build a house like this unless he wants a family to fill it.

Butterflies fill my stomach, but not the good kind.

Nova is already unwrapping picture frames from a box labeled *living room* when I walk in to help. Simone has started unloading dishes into cabinets, and Jack is coming through the front door with his phone in hand after unloading the headboard and placing it against the empty wall of the foyer.

"All right, team." I snort at how ridiculous he sounds. But, dammit, he's a cute lame. "Everything is officially out of the U-Hauls. Dad is picking up dinner, and I have a chest full of drinks in the kitchen. I can't thank you enough for your help. Let's call it a day." He looks from Simone to Nova, both mid-task. "Or finish your current project, and then we call it a day."

"Aye aye, cap'n," Simone teases from the kitchen, earning a smirk from Jack.

He follows me into the kitchen, where I help Simone put up plates and glasses from the plastic containers on the counter, and begins unpacking the easy stuff. Mindless chitchat helps the time go by until we're finished.

We eat dinner on the back porch, enjoying the cafe lights Matthew hung earlier in the day. It feels amazing, with only a light breeze and a space heater. I see many future evenings spent on this porch.

After two servings, I'm stuffed and worn out, wanting nothing more than a shower and a full night's sleep. Well, almost nothing more. The urge to cuddle with Jack takes precedence over my need for sleep.

Simone cut out first and took Nova with her since she had already fallen asleep on the couch. We exhausted my poor girl. David and Matthew left soon after, followed by Jack's friend Charlie.

"We should try out that shower," Jack suggests casually once we're alone. "Maybe it'll wake you up. We don't need you falling asleep on your way home later."

"Oh? How late do you plan on keeping me?" I smirk, already walking backwards toward his bedroom. I boldly pull my t-shirt over my head as I do, and he picks up the pace, ridding himself of his own. Once in his room, he pulls protection out of his bedside drawer before wrapping his arms around me from behind and joining me in his bathroom.

We're tangled limbs and locked lips, shedding our remaining clothing and climbing into the shower together. He tastes like Tennessee—barbecue and beer. It's unexpected but intoxicating. I find myself pulling his mouth back to mine every time he tries to move it to another part of me.

I love that he's strong. I love that he can pin me against the shower wall, holding me up when I lock one leg around his waist and try to steady myself with the other, my foot planted on the ledge. Our hips connect at this angle, and I'm careful not to slip off the edge when he slides into me. His grip tightens on my waist, and our teeth almost clash in an aggressive kiss.

There are times when Jack goes slow, savoring every inch of me like I'm the last piece of birthday cake until the next year. Then, at times like now, he's so needy for me that his caresses are just the right amount of rough and greedy.

His fingers pull through my hair, cupping my scalp before he gently tugs. My head falls back, a strangled gasp escaping as he lowers his mouth to my collarbone, licking the water droplets that have pooled there.

I shudder against him as I come, my knees weak. Jack immediately grabs my thigh, lifting my other leg to keep me from falling. He slides deeper, in this new position, and my nails dig into his shoulders. Once, twice, three times more, and he joins me, his neck tense, letting go and pressing himself against me with a deep exhale.

My feet finally touch the floor, and I push my forehead to his wet chest, my head buzzing and my body tingling. Our labored breathing slows, and I look up with lowered lids. "I should actually wash my hair now."

The corner of his mouth lifts, and he nods, smoothing his palms over my head. "Yeah, we're pretty filthy."

He wiggles his eyebrows, and I try to contain the laugh that sputters from my lips as I push past him to grab the shampoo bottle. "You're so dumb." I giggle, running my hand over my face to wipe the water away.

———

I could fall asleep right here. Head against his chest, blanket draped over our legs, and his fingers gingerly brushing through my damp hair. It's my catnip.

"Tell me about your tattoo. You don't seem like a tattoo guy."

The hum of a low groan fills my ears, but his caresses through my hair never cease. "I wouldn't say I'm *not* a tattoo guy. It was a college decision. My freshman year, a few of my friends and I said we'd get a tattoo after finals. We made some sort of deal. I don't know why. I think we were drunk when we did it." He laughs and loops a strand of my hair around his finger. "Anyway, I couldn't think of anything I wanted on my body permanently. That same year, I wasn't able to make it home for the holidays and it really upset me. I *missed* Christmas trees. I cursed those damn trees all year long when I was living there, but the second I realized I would go a year without working on the farm ... I don't know, it just made me sad. And it made me miss my parents. So I decided to get a Shasta fir as my tattoo. It's silly, but it reminded me of home when I was away."

How is it that the sexiest quality about him is his longing for home? I'm such a weirdo. He mentions being homesick, and I immediately want to straddle him. "I don't think that's silly at all." My words come out in a forced rasp.

He leans down, kissing my hair before resting his chin on top of my head. I could not possibly be more content.

"How are you feeling?" he asks, breaking that comfort.

My stomach tenses at the question, knowing exactly what he means. I was hoping he'd let that go, but I guess I worried him more than I thought. I play dumb anyway. "I mean, my legs are aching from being a boss today."

His chuckle vibrates in his chest. "That's not what I meant. Do you feel lightheaded or anything?"

"I'm okay." I smile, assuring him as best as I can with my head tilted back to catch his gaze.

With our eyes locked, I feel his chest rise and fall dramatically against my back, exhaling through his nose. I lean forward and turn toward him, tilting my head to the side. "What's up?"

Jack's thumb grazes my cheek, stopping at my chin. "I love you."

I feel hot.

And cold.

I'm sweating, and I can't focus on his face, my eyes jumping to different pieces of furniture around us. I need something to *focus* on. It would also be smart to breathe. Why can't I swallow?

"Liza, I don't want you to say it."

What?

"I don't want you to feel any obligation or guilt. I just want you to feel loved. I just needed to tell you because I felt like I was going to explode. And I've never felt like that. That's how I *know*."

He's genuine. He means everything he's saying, and it's everything I want.

But I can't find my voice, so I lean closer and kiss him instead. He returns it immediately, pulling me into him and wrapping an arm low around my waist.

He loves me.

22

————

S ometimes I think I live in two universes. In one, I hold hands with Jack and take Nova and our dogs to the park. I share a kitchen with him and Simone, cooking a fun meal for Friday night movies. I kiss him whenever I want and call him just to hear his voice. He's a magnetic force, and I'm, without a doubt, electrically charged.

Then when Aaron's parents are in town and we're chatting around the kitchen counter, it's like nothing has changed in the past four years. It doesn't even feel like there's an emptiness. The energy they bring, somehow manifests Aaron's presence, and his warmth surrounds me like the bear hugs he always gave.

The only difference in those moments is my mind drifting away to another man. A tall, unapologetic personality that shifts both realities, pulling them together to create one. That's how it's been all week. It doesn't take away the love that swells inside me during those fleeting seconds of warmth. It simply reminds me my heart is healing and learning to be in love with someone else.

It's like breathing again after not being able to catch my breath for so long.

My phone buzzes on my lap, and I glance down, tearing my mind away from my thoughts and my eyes from the crappy movie I landed on while flipping channels. I grin as soon as I see Jack's name. It's been a long week with scarce time for him since my family is visiting for Nova's ninth birthday.

Her party was today and a success. Now, she's tucked away in a sleeping bag on the living room floor with three of her friends.

Because I'm a sucker.

Jack:*What I would give to have you in bed with me right now.*

I practically melt into my sheets, sliding down under my comforter as if I'm hiding my late-night texting from my mother.

My cheeks are pink as I reply: *Have you missed me?*

Jack:*I barely saw you today and you were still a huge distraction. You tell me.*

There's an actual pitter-patter happening inside me. I'm fucking *giddy*. Honestly, with the way the week has gone and how busy I was today, I thought he would think I was avoiding him. I'm not, but I half-expected him to act differently after he told me he loved me and I ... said nothing.

He hasn't. He was sincere when he said he didn't want me to say it. There has not been a single difference in the way he's been towards me.

I love him. I *really* love him. I just can't tell him that over text, and I can't say it in passing at my daughter's birthday party.

Impatient without the sound of his whiskey voice, I call him.

"Oh, now you're just teasing me," he answers, and I hear his grin. "Hearing you before bed *and* not being able to touch you?"

I bite my lip, suppressing the goofy expression he elicits from me. "I'm wicked, what can I say?" After a warm chuckle from his throat, I continue. "What are you doing tomorrow?"

"I don't have much planned. Dad and Pop want to see me before they go on their European adventure next week. Would you be interested in dinner at their place?"

I quickly do a mental calendar check. I don't *think* we have anything going on. "We can probably make that work."

"Good." His contented sigh is long and deep, and I can practically hear him stretch against his ridiculously comfortable pillow-top mattress. "Call me tomorrow?"

His voice is drifting. It's insane how quickly he can fall asleep once his body hits his bed. I like that about him. I also like how early he goes to sleep and how early he wakes. Even when I'm grumpy and silent, waiting at least thirty minutes before I speak, I like that he's already smiling and ready to start the day.

"Yep. Sweet dreams."

I swear he's asleep before I even hang up the phone.

My hands are underwater, scrubbing the residue from the pot that held spaghetti sauce. There isn't a meal Matthew can't cook, but his spaghetti takes the cake. I'm practically bursting out of my jeans as I lean over the sink to help with the dishes. There's no such thing as one serving in this house.

A dramatically out-of-breath Nova runs into the kitchen, leaning against the cabinets to my right. "Matthew and Jack are about to go check on the crops. Can I go, too?"

I catch David's smile out of the corner of my eye as he packs away the leftovers to store in the fridge. They're simply charmed by my daughter, and who can blame them? She's basically me in miniature form.

"All right." I nod, looking over her head and through the foyer to see if I can get a glimpse of Jack in the living room. "Be careful and listen to them."

Without another word, she's bouncing out of the room, calling out for them to wait on her. It's silent after the door closes behind them, her chatter fading, turning into a quiet clank of dishes as David and I maneuver around the kitchen.

Whenever it's Matthew and me, there's no use in anyone else trying to get a word in. And with Jack, it's flirtation and stolen glances. However, when I'm alone with David, it's a comforting silence I relate to home. He's warmer than my dad, but they both exude a strong safety.

Jack gets that from him.

"I'm really happy he found you."

David's rough and unexpected voice pulls me from my thoughts, and I glance up with an eyebrow raised and a smile on my face. "Yeah? I'm happy we found him."

"I saw him get really hurt, and I just—" David stops, but I turn to him to give him my full attention. I didn't realize this was going to get deep.

I am not prepared for this, sir. I liked your comforting silence.

"I have never been this dad, and I never planned on being this dad, but Jack is gone. You've completely done him in." David's dimples are on display as he speaks, the light red scruff on his face not heavy enough to hide them. "That boy has never been tongue-tied since the day he learned to talk, but the second you walk through any door, he can't form a sentence to save his life."

Does the entire family know my love language? I look down at my pruned hands before meeting his gaze and matching his smile. "I didn't know if I would get this again. I didn't know I would get a Jack. He knocked me completely off my feet."

"It's safe to say you've done the same. We love it. He's excited about life and the future and you."

The way the sun warms your skin when you're lying on the beach, content, the wind blowing slightly, swirling the scent of sea salt around you—that's how I feel right now. "Yeah, me too. He's brought a lot to my life. Well, our life."

David nods, his smile wavering, but not completely— just enough to let me know he's about to get serious. "Good, because he asked me about my mother's ring."

That sentence hangs in the air for a moment. His words clutch my lungs and squeeze so tightly that any breath that could escape is too terrified to. *Ring.*

"Pardon?"

David winces at my reaction, or at his admission, I can't tell. He pulls the kitchen stool out and sits on it. "Don't freak out, because he wasn't asking *for* it. He just asked me if I still had it. When he wanted to propose to Gwen, I offered him my mom's ring. She wanted that for him. But he said he was too nervous about something happening to it. It was too much pressure. That was odd to me."

I'm a satisfied little brat right now, but my hands are shaking as I mindlessly reach for the towel to dry the rest of the dishes stacked in the sink. I need to do something with my hands.

"Then the other night, out of the blue, he asked me if I still had it. It was casual, and neither of us went *there*. But Jack has never asked me about it before."

I've never been scared of commitment. I've never been the type of girl to shy away from long-term relationships and dreams about forever. But something about this makes my blood rush to my head, and I struggle to catch a breath.

It has nothing to do with Jack or where I want our relationship to go. I just suddenly can't feel my feet.

He asked about a ring. Are we at that point? I'm probably overthinking it. Honestly. He's planning, but not *now*. Right?

"I didn't mean to scare you."

No, please don't think I'm scared. *Am I scared?* I shake my head, turning my attention to David once more. "No. I'm not. A future with Jack—the *thought* of a future with Jack has always been on my mind. I've been having some shortness of breath lately. That's all. I—you surprised me."

The protective glint in his eyes warms my entire body. "Are you sure?"

"Yeah. He's the life I want."

Even as I say it, even as I believe it, I still feel unsteady.

My body is doing that thing. That feels-like-I'm-vibrating thing—and not in a good way. My chest is humming, and my eyes won't focus on one thing for too long. Loud noises, like Chief's bark or Nova's squeal, have me on edge.

Anxiety. There you are.

David changed the subject pretty quickly after a thick stillness fell over us. I think he was afraid he stepped over some invisible line. It's his son. He's protecting what he loves. It makes me love the entire family even more. After the kitchen was picked up and we indulged in the most awkward small talk, I made my way outside.

Now, I'm sitting on the front steps as Matthew's truck slowly parks. Nova and Jack climb out of the bed, and she immediately runs off to play with the dogs, waving at me as she passes. This is her strategy to stay longer—look busy. Avoid.

"How are the crops?" I ask, confident in a positive answer because Matthew's brow isn't furrowed in a tense frown.

Jack's light blue t-shirt is stained with sweat that I would normally find gross, but I don't. He leans down and brushes his lips against mine before plopping beside me with a grunt. "Right on schedule."

"There are a few I need to monitor, but it's a good crop." Matthew wipes his hands together after taking off his gloves and walks past us on his way inside. "I'm getting water. I'll bring you two some."

"Thanks, Pop." When Jack turns back to me, he pushes a rebellious strand of hair behind my ear without even thinking about it. His movements are much more effortless than they've ever been, and part of me wonders if it was because he was trying so hard *not* to touch me for so long. "I'll probably be house-sitting out here with CeCe while they're gone."

"Perfect. I love an excuse to come to the farm." I lean my head against his shoulder and look out at the field in front of us. The seclusion could seem lonely, but I find it romantic. You and yours, and a huge open sky. My damn heart couldn't be sappier if it tried. "Nova and I are going out of town tomorrow for a girls' day. I have tickets to a small-town theater production of *Hairspray*."

His far-off gaze becomes more focused, turning his head to me to study my face. "Tomorrow? You know it's the twenty-fifth, huh?"

Ugh, Jack. I *need* to stop telling him when my therapy appointments are. I play dumb. "Yep. Nova is out of school, and it's a Monday, so the salon is closed. It's the perfect day."

I almost feel guilty at the quick mental gymnastics I see behind his eyes as he's searching for the best way to bring it up.

I have to jump in, or he will explode of internal politeness. "Hannah had to reschedule with me."

The lie came out before I could stop it. I hate it. I want to take it back, but the twisted knot in my stomach tells me that if I do, he'll be angry at my quick lie. Or he'll be upset I canceled counseling once again. I'd rather let it fester inside me.

He nods carefully but doesn't reply immediately. Finally, he says, "Well, then a day with Supernova is a great choice for self-care."

"I thought so."

My hand is clammy when he takes it in his, interlocking our fingers without a word. My bare ring finger draws my attention. I suck in a breath, squeezing his hand in mine for the briefest of moments.

I could say it right now. I could say: *I love you.* It's right there on the tip of my tongue. *I love you so much the feeling suffocates every other emotion or thought in my head when you're around.*

But I'm almost positive an anxiety attack is building, and I don't want that to overshadow how perfect he is for me. I don't want my surprising sudden fear of commitment to take over the indescribable joy he brings me.

The contradicting feelings make my head pound.

I am a clusterfuck.

23

He just got held up at the farm.

That's what I've been telling myself for the past thirty minutes. When we talked two hours earlier, he said he had to secure the animals before the storm hit, and then he'd be on his way. I expected him already. Especially since we're in the middle of said storm.

Luckily, my worries didn't surface until after I put Nova to bed, because she can usually read my face even if I am doing my best to mask it. She knows me better than anyone—even Simone. You don't go through the loss of the most important person in your life together and not build an even deeper bond than just mother and daughter. We fought the same war. We lost the same soldier. Thoughts of Aaron aren't helping calm me down.

Jack's phone has gone straight to voicemail the past three times I've called, and that anxious bubble in my stomach is rising to my chest, lodging itself there and making it difficult to catch a breath. I know that feeling, so I try to shove it down—ignore it and hope it's irrational.

I pace in front of the French doors in the living room,

periodically looking out to see if headlights are turning in the driveway. I try not to look at the clock again, because it will reiterate that too much time has passed since Jack was supposed to be here. I attempt another deep breath, but I can't satisfy that tight feeling in my chest. The thought of not being able to get enough oxygen makes me lightheaded.

I dial Jack's number again.

Hi, you've reached Jack Peters. I can't get to my phone right now, but if you leave a message, I will get back to you as soon as possible. If this is an animal emergency, please call our veterinarian emergency line at 860-555-3448. Have a good one.

When I hear the tone, I clear my throat and give a breathless laugh into the phone. "Hey, you, I'm just really worried. Can you call me back and let me know you're safe? I hope you're not trying to drive in this. Okay. Bye."

I hear the tremble in my voice.

I inhale again, breathing in deeply, but still feel unsteady. It's a difficult feeling to explain, the need to feel that little catch before you exhale. Not feeling it, makes you panic more. I know this, and yet, it still consumes me.

I sit down on the edge of my couch and stare out the window, watching the wind bend the trees backwards. My mind slips away from me, and I start going through all the scenarios that would explain Jack's inability to answer my phone calls. As rational as *his phone died* sounds, my mind isn't satisfied with that.

Okay, so his phone died, but how does that explain the fact he's an hour later than I expected him to be?

Every scenario leads me back to the worst outcome —*something happened to him*. I rock back and forth, rubbing my palms against my jeans to calm my nerves. Not being able to pinpoint exactly where he is, not being able to hear his voice, or know he's okay ... I shake my head at those thoughts, though tears are already gathering in the corner of my eyes as I dial his number again.

Hi, you've reached Jack Pete— I end the call and clench my jaw, closing my eyes to calm my breathing. He's okay. He has to be okay.

Please, let him be okay.

I can't feel this again.

I stand up when I can no longer endure the waiting, and I pace again. Back and forth. Over and over.

Then I catch sight of headlights at the end of my driveway. They're most definitely not his Bronco. I would recognize those. It's a sedan of some sort, but I can't tell what at this time of night. My heart leaps into my throat but doesn't slow. My head is pounding from the rapid pace, my palms are sweating, and I feel a chill down my spine as it slows to a stop behind the garage door.

A sedan. It couldn't be—no. Cops don't actually come to your house in *those* circumstances, right? That's just in the movies. Even telling myself this, doesn't help my growing nausea.

I can't stand this.

I open the front door and step out onto the porch to see Jack running down my sidewalk and up my porch steps in long strides. *Oh, thank God.*

Relief washes over me at the sight of him—even though he is covered in mud and completely soaked.

"Hey," he calls, winded by the time he reaches the top step, but he's out of focus. "God, I'm so sorry. My truck got stuck out in the field, then my phone fell in a puddle, and it stopped working—" He stops and takes a step toward me. "Eliza? Are you okay?"

It's only then I realize I am clutching the side of the

door, unable to calm my erratic breathing or stop the flood of tears that spilled over as soon as I laid my eyes on him. I try to open my mouth to speak, but it comes out in hiccups. "I can—I can't catch my breath," I manage to get out, pressing my hand to my chest. But I can't form a coherent thought or calm myself down. I take short gasps because one deep inhale is impossible to obtain.

Everything is a blur, my body is trembling, and I feel like I could pass out at any moment. His body heat is radiating through his cold and muddy shirt when he envelops me and holds me tightly to him. I can hear the hum of his voice before I make out any words. But I can only cry into his chest and try to regulate my breathing.

"It's okay, Liza. I'm okay," he whispers into my hair as he slides his hand up and down my back. "Take a deep breath with me."

He says that several times before I can even attempt to. It's shaky, but I successfully follow his lead. It's too much, though. This feeling. This lack of control I have in the universe. I can't handle it—the unknown.

I push myself out of his arms and step back, shaking my head as a new batch of warm tears form. "I can't do this." It feels like someone else speaking. "I ... can't handle *this* again. Losing someone too soon and having to heal all over again? I can't."

"Hey." He steps toward me with his brow furrowed in confusion. "I'm here. I'm okay. Nothing happened."

"But I thought it did, and it could!" I rub my palm against my nose as I sniffle, my eyes are jumping from the rain to his car and back to him. "It could, and I cannot go through it again. I can't feel this hard for someone again just to have some uncontrollable circumstances take them from me. I can't. *I can't.*"

Breathe.

Why can't I breathe?

Jack stands in front of me, silent, his face painted in worry. I know he doesn't know what to say, and I don't know how to *not* feel this way.

My cries are hard to rein in, so I let them flow without holding back. I lean over and put my face in my hands, allowing this sob to rack my entire body. "I can't."

He's so quiet, but I feel the tension from him—wrapping around us like a life jacket that's not doing its job, shoving us farther down instead of bringing us to the surface.

He's letting me have my moment.

He's not crowding me.

But I can *feel* it.

Focus, Eliza. Focus on something.

My eyes find a spot on the banister, and I stare at it, unflinching. It needs a paint job.

Breathe.

We're on the porch, with hard winds and steady rain interrupting the silence between us. It seems like an hour, though it's merely minutes, before he finally reaches for me. I'm leaning back against the house, my eyes closed, my emotions steadier. His hand is on my arm, and I open my eyes, looking up into his, which I notice are swollen. *I* did that to him.

"Please talk to me," he whispers, taking another step closer, but his eyes never leave mine. "What can I do?"

I open my mouth to respond, but I feel breathless.

This is going to hurt like hell.

But I am saving myself from a worse pain of losing him unexpectedly. "Nothing," I answer, looking away again. "I just—" I pause, shaking my head as I run my fingers through my hair. "I never thought I could feel for anyone as strongly as I felt for Aaron. I just didn't think that kind of all-consuming affection came around more than once for someone." I pause, wiping at my nose again. "I was obviously wrong. And the thought of having to go through losing someone like that again ..." I shake my head. "I can't do it."

I'm staring out into the night as I speak, and he's not replying, which makes me turn my attention to him. I can see he's trying so hard to find the right words. I don't know what those words could be.

"I'm not going anywhere." Jack finally finds his voice. "You're not going to lose me."

"How can you even assure me of that, Jack? *How*?" I'm angry at his blind promise. My nails are digging into my palm. "I'm trying to protect myself. Don't you see that? I was shattered when Aaron died, and I can't make Nova go through that again. And *I* can't do it again, either. I'm not that tough. I'm *not*. My reaction to not hearing from you for a mere two hours proves that."

"You are tough," he assures me, confident in his words. "This is something that can be worked through."

"I don't see how."

He presses both hands to the top of his head, inhaling deeply with his eyes screwed shut. When he opens them, he drops his arms and shrugs. "So, what are you going to do, Liza? Push away every new relationship in fear?"

"Maybe." I know how irrational it sounds, but it's the only way I can think of to get a handle on my emotions. "I don't know."

He steps in front of me, placing his hands on my fore-arms, urging me to look at him. "I'm about to cross a line I have been very careful about not crossing, but I'm doing this because I care. I think it would be a good idea if you saw your counselor regularly."

"Wow, Jack." I shrug his hands off of my arms. I've been verbally slapped. "How long have you been holding that one in? Just waiting for the perfect moment to tell me I need more therapy?"

"Stop, Eliza," Jack warns, but his voice is anything but angry or cold. "You know you haven't been seeing her like you should."

"I haven't needed to!"

"Yes, you have!" he barks back, but immediately steps back and takes a deep breath. "Look, if I thought you were trying to break us up because you just didn't want to be with me, then I'd step aside. But this is more than that. You *admit* it's more than that. You've been using our relationship to feel better, and that's not going to heal you. *I* can't heal you."

I clench my jaw at his accusation. "How dare you imply I'm using you as some sort of band-aid. Is that what you really think? That I'm just trying to heal myself with you?"

"That is not what I'm trying to say," he argues, his tone exhausted. "You said you didn't need counseling. Why? Because you've been happy? I'm not saying that's a false happiness, Eliza. I'm just saying that no matter how happy our relationship is, it can't help your grief. It can't help your anxiety. It's masking it, but you need more than a mask."

I won't even let his words sink in. I'm angry that this has turned into another situation where the people I love expose a weakness and try to fix it. I'm exhausted. My body is tired. I feel weak from my meltdown. "I'm so glad you're able to finally get this off your chest. It feels like it's been festering there for a while. So I'll make it easy. You don't have to be my *mask* anymore."

"Don't do this, Liza. Please don't push me away," he begs, and I feel my chest tighten at the desperation in his voice. "I want to help you. I want to be there for you through all of it."

"I told you," I reply, wiping under my eyes before the next batch of tears can roll down my cheeks. "I can't be in this relationship. It's too much."

This isn't how tonight was supposed to go.

I'm losing control.

I look away from him, unable to bear the look on his face. When he turns away from me, I watch his shoulders rise and fall as he exhales.

My ears are ringing at the sudden stillness.

I need to escape.

"Stay here until the storm dies down," I mutter before walking back into my house.

"Eli—" I hear behind me before shutting the door. As soon as I step inside, my chest feels like it has burst wide open. My throat is raw. The selfish part of me wants to run back outside and wrap my arms around him. But I can't. I just can't. For my sake. For Nova's. For his.

I glance behind me to see him lowering himself onto the porch steps, staring out at the rain.

This town is small. That's been proven before. It's impossible for this to be the last time I see him, but something about this moment makes me think it will be.

I haven't so much as seen a glimpse of a red Bronco in a week. My phone has been lonely without his good-morning texts, and Friday passed without him barreling through the house, ranting about whatever his choice of movie was for the night. I feel achy, tired, and like there's a constant lump in my throat.

I can tell Nova's maturing, because she hasn't even asked me where he is. Can she sense it? Did Simone get to her before I could?

That would make the most sense. The morning after I obliterated *us* on my front porch, I couldn't move from the bed. If I sat up, I was sure I would have a panic attack. I'm ashamed I lied to my kid, telling her I was coming down with a bug. In reality, I was heartsick. When Simone came in to check on me, I lost it, and she crawled into bed beside me until I could calm down.

And now, I just have guilt. An overwhelming sense of guilt is strangling me. The one thing I didn't want to do when we started our relationship, and I did it. I took Jack Peters out of our life.

That thought breaks me.

I force a smile when Nova barrels through the kitchen with her camp t-shirt tucked away under a pair of denim overalls.

"First day of art camp!" I cheer, getting back to the task at hand—spreading mayonnaise on a slice of bread for her turkey sandwich. I nod to the counter where the rest of her unpacked lunch lies. "Cheddar or sour cream?"

She reaches for a bag of chips to throw into her lunchbox. "Cheddar. Is Monica's mom picking me up?"

"Yep." My tone is cheerful. I'm a fraud. "I'll get you after, though. We can take Chief to the park, or we can come back here and talk about painting your bedroom."

Nova's eyes light up. She's been wanting to paint her bedroom for months, and I'm using it as a distraction? I'm shit. I'm desperate for Nova not to feel a void without Jack around, but I'm also shit.

"Purple?"

"We'll see." Despite the crater in the center of my being, I smile at her excitement. With all the struggles of babies and toddlers, after they hit a certain age, they're basically tiny life coaches that make you warm when your soul is cold.

A white SUV catches my eye, and I look up through the window to see Monica's mom pull behind my car. I grab a bottle of water from the fridge and pack Nova's food into her thermal lunch box.

"Okay, kiddo. I'll see you at three."

"Bye! Think about purple!" She grabs her things and jumps off the stool, hugging me briefly before running out the front door and to the car. I wave from the doorway and watch until I can no longer see them.

I'm cleaning up the kitchen when Simone comes in,

wrapping her braids into a bun on top of her head with sleepy eyes. Her smile is muted as she slides past me to the coffee maker.

"Hey." I close the door to the fridge and lean back against it, watching her pour rich brown liquid into a bright mug Nova painted for her when she was four. It's my favorite. "I need you to do me a favor today if you can."

She glances at me over her shoulder, grabbing for the honey as she does. "What's up?"

Rip the band-aid off, Eliza. "Can you take Chief to the vet for his appointment at two?"

Simone turns to me, her face pinched in either aggravation or concern. She sighs, shaking her head as she does. "E ..."

"Please. I just—I can't, okay? Please." That lump that's made a home in my throat is growing, and my eyes are stinging, threatening me with the possibility of tears. I blink rapidly to push them away.

"Okay, but—"

"Yeah." I stop her, already knowing what she's going to say. "I have an appointment with Hannah this afternoon. I promise."

"Good." Simone takes a long sip of her coffee, staring at the ground before bumping my hip with hers. "Why don't we paint the whole house? Give us a project and a little change around here."

The tight band around my ribs loosens. I'm grateful for the relief. "Yes," I breathe out. "That sounds great."

Two consecutive sessions. Even Hannah was surprised when I showed up without attempting to cancel. She's been keeping it light, and I appreciate her for it, but I think I'm at the point where I need her to dig deep. I need to fix the constant storm of breathlessness and palpitations. I need to be able to smile and mean it. I need to be able to *think*.

Our house has smelled of paint fumes for over a week. It hits me as soon as I open the door even though we try to sleep with every window open to air it out. A sheet is spilling out into the foyer from the living room, where the furniture is shoved into the middle of the room, plastic draped over it as a form of protection. Cyndi Lauper is blaring from the soundbar on the fireplace mantle, and Simone is shimmying on a step stool with a brush in hand.

"Hi!" I call over the music, causing her to turn over her shoulder with a flash of white teeth.

She steps down and grabs the sound remote, turning the music down a few notches before using the back of her hand to wipe the sweat from her brow. "Hi. I was just getting the edges. Want to jump in?"

"Sure, I just need to change." I love the way the house is looking, transforming into something new and causing a distraction for all of us. I even gave in to Nova and her pleas for Plum-tart—the deep shade of purple coating her walls.

Once I'm in a worn t-shirt and shorts, I grab a brush to begin the bottom edges on the opposite side of the room. The music is still at a low volume, but I'm humming along, focusing on making the strokes look even.

We work without words for the longest time. After fifty minutes of word-vomiting to a perfect stranger, I don't feel the need to fill the room with casual conversation. Luckily,

Simone is one of the rare people I can peacefully ignore without guilt.

I stand up after the wall I am working on is complete and let out a satisfied sigh, feeling lighter even with the heavy feeling of an anchor weighing my heart down.

"I do believe our work in this room is complete." Simone comes to stand beside me, placing an arm over my shoulders as she does. "I'm too tired to cook. Pizza tonight?"

"God, please."

I briefly rest my head on her shoulder before gathering the brushes in the paint tray to wash out in the sink. She follows me, and though I can't see her, I know she's holding something back.

My fingers slide through the bristles, the hot water basically melting the paint off—or that's what it looks like. I hear Simone's muffled voice order pizza in the hallway, and then she appears next to me, placing her phone on the counter.

"Twenty minutes," she confirms before hoisting herself on the countertop. "I can go get it."

My eyes find the clock, and I shake my head. "No, I'll get it on my way to pick Nova up from camp."

"We can ride together." Her voice is hopeful as she suggests this, and I'm suddenly concerned. It's not that we aren't obsessed with each other, because we are. But there's an urgency about her that's not the norm.

I turn to face her, my eyes narrowed in suspicion. "Okay, Locke. Spill."

"What?"

"Why are you being clingy? Or whatever this is. What's going on?" That rubber-band wraps around my ribs again, my mind immediately going to the worst scenarios. *Who's sick? Who died? What bad news are you about to give me?*

Simone's hands immediately fly in front of her, physically stopping any more words from coming out of my mouth. "Okay, stop. I can see it in your face, and I didn't mean to freak you out. It's really nothing. I just ran into Jack today at Lila's Pie Shop, and we ate lunch together. I felt immensely guilty afterward because I'm Team Eliza. So if we are supposed to not like Jack, I can do that."

I immediately ease the tension in my shoulders and sigh, shaking my head with a soft smile. Sure, hearing his name cracks the fragile shell holding my heart together, but if that's all she was worried about, then I can breathe easy. "Simone, really. I would *never* ask you to cut Jack out of your life, and I don't think there's a universe in which anyone could not like Jack Peters. Please, keep being his friend."

Her smile is warm, but her eyes are worn. Her brows are slightly pulled together as she watches me. "He asked about you. I didn't know what I was allowed to say."

I've opened the door and given her an opportunity to speak freely about him. Hopefully, this won't last long. I'm breaking. "I have no secrets from him. I want him to know I'm doing the work on myself. I never want him to worry about me. So, please, tell him I am seeing a counselor and I'm okay."

She nods, but she's mulling over something in that beautifully complex brain of hers. I don't know if I want to hear it. I take the opportunity of silence to steal another glance at the clock. I wipe my hands on the dry towel next to me and nod toward the door.

"Are you still going with me?"

Simone jumps down, her feet hitting the tile in a loud thud. "Absolutely."

The drive home from my weekly sessions is always my most peaceful. I will never admit to Simone how much therapy has been helping me. She's not the type to say *I told you so*, but I am the type to not give her the chance to. Hannah has been able to put so many of my fears and doubts into words I couldn't find. And, by doing that, she's been able to pick them apart and show me how to get a better grasp on my anxiety. Of course, I still have a long way to go, but I leave her office feeling lighter every time.

I pull down our gravel driveway and feel my chest tighten when I see Jack's truck parked in front of our porch. There goes that easy-breezy cloud I was riding in on.

Five weeks.

It's been five weeks since I've seen that cherry-red vehicle.

What is he doing here? Is everything okay?

I get out of the car and reach for my phone that was shoved in my purse. I glance down and quickly read the text from Simone that came fifteen minutes earlier.

Hey, Jack came over to install those ceiling fans on the back porch for us. Just giving you a heads-up. I'll let you know when he's gone. Hope therapy went well. *kiss emoji*

Oh, well. Okay. I walk up the steps of my porch and let myself in the front door, reaching down to scratch Chief's ears when he greets me. I don't know why I am moving through my house like a spy on a mission, but I'm slowly peeking my head into every room before entering. My feet carry me to the kitchen, where the window above the sink is pushed open, making it easy for me to hear the conversation going on outside.

"They look so great!" I hear Simone shriek, and then my heart leaps in my throat at the sound of Jack's friendly chuckle.

"Well, I didn't design them," he teases. "But, yeah, they're really nice. Glad I could help you out."

"No, but it would have been a disaster if me or Eliza tried to do it. We're pretty self-sufficient, but wiring is not our thing."

Truth.

I pull a glass down from the cabinet to keep myself busy because I can't leave this room. I hear him throw his tools in the toolbox that must be right under the window, and then the low squeak of our porch swing.

His voice is faint, and I can barely make out a, "Can I ask you about her?"

"Of course. She's doing okay. I can tell she's struggling, but she's doing ... better." My heart tugs at the love in her voice. "She told me to tell you that she's seeing her counselor more."

"She wanted me to know that?" Jack quickly asks, a hint of hope in his tone. Without waiting for a reply, unless there was a nonverbal one, he continues. "How is that going for her? I mean, I don't want to pry. I just—"

"Jack, you love her. It's okay. Eliza *wanted* me to tell you she's seeing Hannah again. I'm sure she knew you'd ask if it was going well." I hold my breath, awaiting her answer to his question. "She's doing what she needs to do. You know Eliza. She is one of the strongest people I have ever met. And I think a small part of her thought going to therapy would make her weak. She's always been a huge proponent of it, especially when Aaron was diagnosed. She pushed him to go to every session. She was his biggest support, but ... I don't know. I guess she thought she could handle her own problems with as much grace as she handles everyone else's."

God, she *knows* me so well. It's quiet for a moment, and I know this is the part where I should make my presence known, but then I hear his voice, and I can't tear myself away. I hate myself for this intrusion of privacy, but my feet will not move.

"I'm so worried about her. And not because she ended things," Jack clarifies. "But because I hate seeing her hurt. I hate that she has to deal with this. I—" He stops, and I turn to leave the kitchen, forcing my feet to walk away.

I shouldn't be eavesdropping.

I'm almost to the doorway leading to the hall when his voice finds me again.

"I would give anything to take it away from her. I would *do* anything to bring him back for her if it meant Nova could have her dad and Liza wouldn't suffer anymore. I just want them to be happy. I just want *her* to be happy."

Every organ drops to the pit of my stomach at his words, and I feel a lump lodge itself in my already aching throat. I shouldn't have heard that. I feel so guilty to have listened. I slowly walk upstairs, their voices now mere hums in the distance.

I can't tell you what's going on in this episode of whatever show I'm staring at. I'm sitting on the edge of my bed, my eyes zeroed in, but my mind everywhere and in the same place all at once. When I walked in my room, it was second nature to pick up the remote and create background noise to quash the lump burning in my chest.

He's precious.

Jack, I mean.

Not in the normal Tennessee way the word is used, cooing over a newborn baby with the cliché: *Oh, how precious.* But in the way that something is so valuable and unique and one-of-a-kind that you want to hold it somewhere safe and not let the world have it. Or you give it away because you're too scared to break it.

My bedroom door creaks open, and Simone slips in, her eyes dim with concern. She sighs when she sees me and shakes her head. "I am so sorry. I didn't know if you were going to pick Nova up after therapy, and I tried to warn you. Are you okay?"

"Simone, it's fi—"

"I called David first to ask him if he could help me with the fans, but he said he was—I don't know, buying cattle or something? So before I could say anything, he said, 'Oh! Jack isn't busy. I'll call him.' I didn't even have time to object when he hung up, and in like five minutes, Jack was texting me to offer to do it, and I thought I could—"

"Simone." My voice is gentle, but firm. I need to stop her rambling before she implodes. "I'm fine. It's really fine."

My throat is so tight I can't even swallow.

"This is all so silly. I hate it. I hate feeling like I can't be with Jack, because I'm scared he's going to die? Or I'm scared I'll break him? Who has those thoughts? I just want to burst in anger at myself and my broken brain." Despite being on the verge of tears, I produce an absurd laugh. The sound is disingenuous and foreign to me.

She's by my side in an instant, her hand over mine. "Your brain is *not* broken. Eliza, you went through hell. You lost your husband, and you have dealt with that so gracefully for years. It was bound to catch up with you. You're doing what you need to do, and you're doing *so* well. I'm just sorry I've caused a setback by having him here."

"You didn't," I'm quick to assure her, using both hands to wipe at my cheeks. "I promise. I'm fine."

I want this conversation to be over and this bubble in my chest to go away.

Deep breath.

I reach down and squeeze her hand. "You know, since you're in here, we should talk about that girls' trip you keep bringing up."

"Yeah?" Her smile is infecting me, causing my lips to curl, too. "Let's do it."

The distraction is welcome, but I can still hear his voice: *I just want her to be happy.*

25

*W*eddings are a great way to keep myself busy. I've had several in the past weeks that needed my professional touch. After every wedding, I get an excited woman running up to me, asking for a card. So, not only is it fun for me to treat them like my personal dolls, but it's good for my business.

This wedding is in a quaint chapel in the mountains where there's little phone reception and the wireless internet connection drops so often it's not worth having. The place literally has dial-up. I knew it would be like this because we came out here to prep the bride for her bridal portraits a couple of months ago. However, I was only out here for an hour and a half last time. Today was *all* day.

As suspected, my phone didn't have signal the entire time, and that would usually be enough to make me incredibly anxious, but I didn't stop working long enough to think about it. I took the necessary precautions before I left for this random Friday ceremony: Nova is at her day camp. She will go to Monica's after. I should be home around five to pick her up.

I've repeated the routine in my head when I felt myself get worked up about everything that could go wrong in my absence. It's calmed me down and gave me something to focus on while I drove here this morning. But five bridesmaids and one picky bride kept me distracted enough to not need to, once I arrived.

My beauty tools and cosmetics are packed into my car, waiting for me to jump in and drive off before the guests start arriving. The bride was overly emotional and hugging me like we were long-lost best friends as I went to leave. With check in hand, music turned up, and the windows rolled down, I set off for home.

It was thirty minutes on the road before my phone began catching up, vibrating in the cupholder and signaling dozens of unanswered text messages. At the red light, I glance down and see I had a missed voicemail and ten texts from Simone.

Cold sweat. Tense shoulders. Tight chest.

"Call Simone," I command to my car and listen to it ring a couple of times before she picks up.

"Please don't be mad. I didn't know what else to do." She doesn't sound panicked. She doesn't sound like someone died (*Jesus, Eliza. Your brain.*). She just sounds worried.

"About what? I just got to where I have a signal, and I don't even know what's going on. Is everything okay?"

"You didn't get my texts?"

I roll my eyes at the obvious question because I'm *literally* on the edge of my seat. "No. I'm driving. Simone, what is going on?"

Simone exhales into the phone before she speaks. "Nova has some sort of stomach bug. She got sick at camp and threw up. When they called me, I was about to go into a delivery. I asked them who else was on the contact list, and they said Jack. So, I called him to see if he could pick her up."

Jack? That makes no—*oh.* I filled out the paperwork when we were still together.

A stomach bug. Of course that would happen. I sigh and squeeze the steering wheel. "Have you talked to him? Is Nova okay? Is she running a fever?"

"She has a low-grade fever. She's fine. Jack is at our house with her now." Simone's voice is calm, and her words sound almost rehearsed. "Are you mad?"

"No, of course not. Thank you for taking care of this. I'm so sorry I was out of reach. I knew—"

"I'm going to stop you there." She cuts me off, rather harshly. "I knew you were going to freak out about not being reachable, but don't. It's a stomach bug. You are lucky enough to have a community of people who will step in when you are taking care of other responsibilities."

She's right. It would do no one any good for me to harp on this with her.

... I'll just do it with myself once we're off the phone.

"Yeah," I breathe out. "Thank you. I'm about to be home, and I'll let you know how she is."

"Okay. Love you."

The call ends, and I'm trying my damndest not to speed to my house. I feel guilty. It's a feeling I can't help. Guilty for not being there for Nova, guilty for making Simone worry, and guilty for making my ex-boyfriend take care of my kid.

Ex-boyfriend.

Oh, I do *not* like referring to Jack as that. It sounds harsh. It doesn't feel right in my brain.

When I pull into my driveway, I see his truck with every door open, his toolbox on my porch steps, and *him*.

His back is to me, and he has Chief's favorite rope in his hand, rearing back before throwing it toward the backyard for Chief to chase after.

He's wearing my favorite black scrubs that form over his back muscles, showcasing every line.

I'm weak.

I don't take my time, jumping out of my car as soon as I put it in park. I'm an impatient person. He turns to face me after taking the rope from Chief's eager mouth and smiles.

But it's not a full-blown Jack Peters smile, and that makes my heart ache.

Jack saunters over to the porch steps to meet me because my goal is to see Nova. And, yes, avoid him.

"Hey." Well, that was lame. "Thank you so much. I'm sorry for putting you out. Is she okay?"

He looks deflated at my words, and he shakes his head, glancing down at the rope in his hands. The one Chief is staring up at with perked ears. "Don't apologize, please. She's asleep right now. She threw up in the truck," *that explains the open doors,* "and then fell asleep against the window. I put her on the couch when we got here, and she only woke up once, wanting water."

Because that's her favorite place to be when she's sick. He remembers.

"She has a low fever. It's not even one hundred right now. Simone told me where some medicine would be, and I gave it to her."

I'm overwhelmed with a thousand different emotions. Grateful, sad, regretful, anxious, tired, concerned ... loved.

God, I love him so much. "Thank you. She's lucky to have you."

"You probably want to change her clothes and bathe her. There's no throw-up on them, but you know, germs."

My lips curve into a smile, and I nod, chuckling at his words unintentionally. "Yes, of course. Thanks for the tip."

Jack's eyes light up at my normal sarcasm, and he smiles, too. "Also, your banister was loose." He gestures to his toolbox. "I was bored, so I just fixed it. No big deal."

"You didn't have to do that." My hand automatically touches the top of it, attempting to wiggle it, but it's sturdy.

"I wanted to."

Hug me. Kiss me. Make me better. Fix me. Something.

I clear my throat, nodding to the house. "I'm going to go take care of Nova. You're welcome to stay around, but you don't have to."

"No, it's okay. I have things to get to." This is the first time we've faced each other since that horrible night, and I'm craving to reach out to him. "I'm really glad to see your smile. I've missed it."

I miss everything about you.

The front door opens before I can reply, and Nova peeks her head out, her eyes weak and her face in a frown. "Can I have some crackers?"

"Hey, kiddo." I move away from Jack and walk up the remaining steps to pull her into a hug. "I'll give you one to see if you can hold it down, but we also need to get you in the tub."

She groans, annoyed and exhausted, and turns around to go back inside. She's clearly out of it.

When I turn back to Jack, he's loading his tools into his truck a few feet away. I cross my arms like they're a shield and lean against the railing on my porch steps. "Thank you again. I'm really happy to see you."

"Anytime." Jack nods, turning to face me. "I'm happy to see you, too."

There's an invisible vortex between us, sucking every word we want to say to each other and spinning it around so it's lost in the air forever.

My heart is hammering against my ribs so hard I'm almost sure they're going to break.

But there's nothing else said. And in a matter of minutes, his Bronco is already halfway down my driveway, getting smaller and smaller as it literally leaves me in the dust.

Nova is back on the couch when I walk inside. Despite her illness and the fact that I could be the one throwing up tomorrow, I sit beside her and pull her close. Her skin is warm like she still has a fever.

"Is Jack still here?" Her voice is scratchy and weak, like she's falling back asleep.

I rub her back and shake my head. "No," I whisper, my hand going in circular motions, which always puts her to sleep. "He had to go."

"Oh." Her voice is even lower. "That's sad. I liked him being here again."

"Mhm." I hum in response, hoping she will fall asleep soon and not ask any questions. Luckily, she doesn't, and even though I need to get her bathed and changed into pajamas, she begins a light snore, and I can't make myself wake her.

A weekend getaway with Simone was something I desperately needed. We went to a spa that my mother offered to pay for because she was worried—that's a new emotion for my mother. It was in a secluded area surrounded by woods, and I spent a lot of time sitting outside, on a huge rock, and thinking. That was the most relaxing part. Not my shoulders being rubbed, not the wonderful mud bath or the cozy robes, but being able to *think*.

As soon as I got home, I made an appointment with Hannah. I found it odd at the time, and I still do, that it was my first instinct. Call my therapist.

Hannah's office is calming. I'm sure it's supposed to be. Her walls are white, but not stark, and the lighting is soft. Her furniture is light blue and tan and reminds me of a condo on the beach.

She's young, a little bohemian, and has platinum hair twisted in a braid and pinned into a bun. She is not at all what I expected when I first started seeing her, and I love Simone for knowing exactly who I needed.

As I sit on her tan couch and lean back into the comforting embrace of the cushions, I feel more at ease. Even so, I'm, frankly, all over the fucking place.

"I mean, I'm glad we're talking about this. I felt you avoiding it for quite some time now." She's gentle with her words, but I like that she doesn't *feel* like a doctor or counselor. She feels like a concerned friend.

I shrug in reply, but shake my head, running my hands through my hair in aggravation. "I miss Jack. I want him in my life. And on my trip, I realized I can't be myself again if a part of me is missing. I had closure with Aaron. He died and left this earth, and when he left, there was no doubt about who we were to each other. With Jack, he's still out there. There is doubt. There is no closure. And *that* is why there's a missing piece."

"Do you want closure? Or do you want to make it work?"

What an easy answer, for once. "Oh, I want to make it work. I don't want to be without him. But I will say, I'm still scared of being together and having something happen that takes him away from me."

Hannah crosses her legs, leaning forward and placing her elbow on her knee, her hand underneath her chin. "But, do you think you cutting your relationship short makes it better than an uncontrollable circumstance? Isn't it still the same outcome?"

Keep up, Hannah. "Yes, it is. I know that. And, on my trip, when that realization finally hit me, I immediately wanted to call him. But then I thought ... he doesn't deserve this."

"Doesn't deserve what?"

It's simple. There's a man who loves me and my daughter so purely. A man who would carry the weight of my problems on his back until it crushed him into nothing. I just *can't* let him.

I feel guilty enough having panic attacks in my bedroom when I should be making Nova dinner, or waking Simone up in the wee hours of the morning because I had a dream she was hurt. I want to fix myself before I bring someone else into my mess.

"*This.* Me, like this. I'm broken, and he's ready for this amazing, huge adventure with someone. He built a house with bedrooms and a yard. He wants a life *with* someone, and he wants that now."

She has a good poker face. She never lets me know she

wants to shake me even when I feel like she does. "You're not ready for that?"

"I—On paper, yes. In reality, I'm a mess. Forever was cut short for me once already."

Hannah leans back again and takes a deep breath, nodding as if she is mulling over my words. It makes me nervous, but I'm also used to it. "For starters, you are not broken. You are not here to be fixed, because you don't need to be fixed. You are here to learn and to take those lessons and apply them to how you handle those moments of uncertainty and anxiety."

"I know." I'm a scolded child. "I know."

"But." She begins again with a soft smile. "I also know your feelings are valid. So if you *feel* like you need to be fixed, I cannot tell you you're wrong. You view therapy however you need to view it if that is what will help you get the most out of it. Now, let's talk about what you said about forever."

Oh, *that*. Can we not? I run my hands down my face and nod, shrugging a shoulder. "Okay. I was supposed to have forever with someone, and I don't have them forever now. That is terrifying to me. I couldn't control Aaron's illness. It doesn't take a rocket scientist to realize why I have so much anxiety revolving around death. It's because I like to have control, and that is something I cannot control."

"But you can control your relationships with people that are still here. Right?"

Maybe. I look out the window to my right and exhale a satisfying breath that seems like it's been locked away inside me forever. "Not if I've already ruined them."

"You made a rash decision in a moment of uncertainty. It doesn't make it a permanent decision. But I feel like you think it does." Hannah stares at me, and I don't know how to answer her.

I finally nod because she's right. I feel like that door is closed.

"Okay. Rapid-fire questions. Do you feel like therapy has been helping you?"

"Yes."

"Do you feel like you could be better?"

"Well, yes. Yes."

"Do you think having Jack would make you happier?"

"Yes."

"Would you rather have him than not have him, even if you fear him being taken away from you?"

"I think so. Yes."

"Then, why don't you try? Just try. Talk to him because you're right. You won't be able to concentrate on your healing without closure of some sort. If you can do it, you just need to put it out there."

My stomach is twisted into a knot of fear. She makes it sound so easy, but she knows it's not. It's never easy, no matter the circumstances. I broke his heart. I don't have the right to beg him to heal mine.

But maybe a conversation would help him, too. Maybe he needs this as badly as I do. I'm going to have to tell myself that in order to work up the nerve to do it.

"I'll try."

26

I stare at the clinic in front of me, a balloon expanding in my chest with every passing second. The potted plants on either side of the entrance make me smile—they were my idea.

It'll brighten up the building; it's too plain as it is.

We spent that evening planting purple coneflowers in large ceramic pots and then utilized his office for a little afternoon delight. You know, before I decided to hit the flashing self-destruct button on my life.

The balloon grows another inch—it's bound to burst and leave me with an excruciating ache I can't soothe.

I take a deep breath, gripping the steering wheel one last time before turning off the ignition and stepping out. It's late in the afternoon, and the clinic looks busy through the windows, but maybe I can catch him in between patients.

I know it's cowardly.

Try to have this talk in a small ten-minute interval and then run. Hannah would not be proud. But then again, I'm here, dammit.

I'm like a ninja—slipping through the waiting room without having to greet the many familiar faces. If I get sucked into a conversation or even light pleasantries, I'll lose my nerve. It's fickle like that.

Jack's office door is slightly ajar, but I push it open to find it empty. When my eyes do a quick scan, they fall on a framed picture next to the lamp in the top-right corner of his desk.

My heart flutters.

I'm laughing beside Barney, David's horse, with my arm wrapped around my stomach. Nova is perched on top of the horse, her hand over her mouth, her eyes squinted from her fit of giggles. I remember this day. The balloon expands a little more. It's in a simple black frame, and I can't help but smile when I imagine him trying to choose one. Printing this picture. Bringing it to his office. The butterflies in my stomach are over the top. I need to see him *now*.

"Eliza?" I hear from behind me and turn to see Callie in the doorway, a hesitant smile on her face. "What's up? Everything okay?"

"Hey." I smile, turning around with my hands behind my back. I feel like I've been caught doing something I'm not supposed to. Which, I guess, I am. I'm snooping in Jack's office. "Is Jack here? I just wanted to talk to him."

She stares at me, and it makes me uncomfortable. I mean, sure, she works here, too. I'm sure she knows we aren't together anymore.

With a tilt of her head, she gives a small smile. "He's off for a few days, working on some things at his new place."

"Oh. Okay." I do my best to smile back and give a nod of my head. "I'll give him a call, then. Thanks, Callie."

She returns my nod but doesn't say another word as I duck out. I use the back exit so I'm not caught in the waiting room. Once I'm in my car, I give Jack a call, my hands shaking as I find his name in my contacts.

No answer.

Oh well, Peters. I've worked up the nerve, so I'm not going to give up.

His gravel driveway is longer than ours, and the house is not visible until you're basically twenty yards away. His Bronco is parked in front of the porch steps, and the back hatch is open. I spot him immediately, carrying paint cans up the porch steps. He looks over his shoulder at the sound of my car turning in to pull up behind him.

Jack's slow in his movements, turning slightly to watch me, but his brow is furrowed and his mouth is set in a frown—or, at least, not a smile.

I practically jump out of the car, the anticipation of this conversation fueling my sudden adrenaline.

He sets the paint cans by his feet, but only walks down one step. "Is everything all right?" He asks, hesitantly, taking another cautious step down.

"Hi," I say, my smile forced. "Everything's fine. I just needed to talk to you. Is that okay?" I walk up the first few porch steps until there are four separating us. He's looking down at me, his face hard, but his eyes soft. Always so soft.

"Of course," he replies with a shrug, gesturing behind him with his chin. "I was just about to stain the front door. Nothing urgent."

It gives me a moment to take in the appearance of the

house since I last saw it. It's not that it's been that long, but Jack works fast. It's beautiful.

My eyes fall on the hammock swinging on the edge of the porch. Is he trying to make my chest explode?

"You hung an egg hammock," I state, my voice almost breathless. When I look back at him, he's staring at it as well, a faint smile on his face.

"It was a good idea." He turns his attention back to me. "You were right. It makes it look more like a home. I'm holding off on the tire swing for now, though."

I chuckle, pushing my hair behind my ear before glancing down at my shoes. I'm trying to think of how to start this conversation, and I know he's waiting on me, because he's said so much already.

It's my turn.

When I look back up at him, his eyes are on me, but they're not expectant. They're *kind*.

"I handled everything really poorly," I begin, deciding to speak without carefully planning out what to say. "But, at the time, it seemed like the best option for me and Nova and, honestly, you." I pause for a long moment, noticing his expression has not yet changed. "I was wrong."

I walk up the next few steps, and only one is between us. He uncrosses his arms, as if letting his defenses down. But he's staying silent—urging me to continue. Fair enough.

I take a shaky breath, running my palms over my jeans because I'm sweating. "You didn't deserve how I shut you out or the things I said to you." I'm lighter now that I can get this off my chest. "You know, my whole life, I've been super reckless and fearless. I have always been the protector, the caregiver, and I never worried about anything. I had this blind trust that nothing could touch me."

His lips curl ever so slightly at that—just the faintest hint of a knowing smile.

"When Aaron died, that illusion was shattered. I just didn't know it until I found myself worrying over the smallest things. But those small things started becoming big problems. I would overreact and get so worked up that I couldn't catch my breath. I knew it was something I needed to figure out, but I just felt like I would fall apart if I did."

The urge to reach out and touch him is stronger than it has ever been. Having Jack the way I've had him, loving him the way I do, makes distance—physical and emotional—indescribably painful.

His brow is drawn in concern, and a breeze picks up, surrounding me with his scent. This has to be what it's like to inhale regret.

"That night we broke up—" My throat is tight, so I try to clear it. "It was like my anxiety cracked wide open. And I thought removing you from the equation would somehow lessen it."

Jack's silence is appreciated while I'm trying to stumble through this, but I also desperately want him to say *something*. Instead, he steps closer to me, his hand hesitantly grabbing onto mine as I speak, lacing our fingers together. My body practically purrs at the touch, as if our hands have missed each other.

"It didn't," I add, running my thumb over his. "I kept thinking I needed to 'fix' myself before I could ever be in love again. But that was stupid. Because I don't know how I will heal if other parts of my life feel empty. And, my God, there is such an emptiness inside me."

His eyes, so concentrated on my words, turn sad. I can visibly see the change.

I continue before he can speak. "I know now that being with you and working on myself don't have to be mutually exclusive. But, even so, how can I put *this* on you?"

Jack's jaw tenses at my words, and he slowly shakes his head, bringing my hand up and pressing it to his lips before cradling it to his chest. This familiar gesture brings a burning sensation behind my eyes. "You're not putting anything on me that I don't *want*. Eliza, I meant what I said to you. I want to work through this *with* you."

His words are everything I want to hear, but I'm still so scared this will all be too much.

"I'm still a mess, you know?" My voice cracks slightly. "The anxiety will always be present. I'm still working on it, and I'm not even close to learning how to fully manage it. I need you to know that."

His face is so solemn, his expression serious as he listens to me frantically ramble without taking a breath. I stop and look up at him, our eyes locking. I think I used to take advantage of the fact I could look into his eyes whenever I wanted.

Without a word, he pulls me into him and wraps his arms around me, pressing me against the solid comfort of his chest. I greedily accept his embrace, my arms snaking around his waist as I breathe him in. I feel the warmth of his lips above my forehead as one of his hands cups the back of my head, holding me against his large frame.

My body relaxes. I press my cheek to his chest, closing my eyes to soak in his touch. We stay like this for a long moment. I'm scared this is closure. Is this what closure is like? Is this how mature adults say goodbye?

"I'm so sorry that you are struggling with this." His voice is low, soothing my previous nerves. The lump in my throat grows. "I will be here for all of it. Whatever you need from me—whatever you want. Please, don't ever think you are too much for me. You are *everything* for me."

That balloon stuck in my chest, suffocating me with the worst possible outcomes, deflates at his words, calming the hurricane of emotions relentlessly swirling inside of me. I don't trust my voice at the moment, but I tighten my grip on him, letting him know that this is exactly what I want *and* need.

The other shoe is going to drop. It has to. It was too easy to get back into his arms and too easy to hear him say the words I needed to hear. I pull back from him to look up, a new batch of tears stinging the corners of my eyes. "I was so afraid you weren't going to want to talk to me."

A smirk tugs at Jack's lips, and he shakes his head as if my fear was unreasonable. "I don't do games. Our relationship is way more serious than that kind of pettiness. I don't do hard to get. I don't do silent treatments." He pauses, using the pad of his thumb to wipe a tear from underneath my eyelid. "Liza, I am completely in love with you. I gave you your space because you wanted it. But I *love* you. You can always come back to me."

I press my hands to his chest because, to be quite honest, my knees feel weak and I need to steady myself. Being swept off your feet is *real.* My heart is pounding in my ears, and all the blood in my body has rushed to my face. I'm lightheaded. But it's not a bad feeling—not at all. It's like I bungee jumped and the cord did its job, catching my body before I crashed into the ground. I've never done that before, but I can imagine the relief and the love for life that you get at that moment. I feel it right now. "Just like that?"

"Always. I mean," a hesitant smile forms on his lips as

he cups my cheeks with his calloused palms, "I would prefer to not have to go without you for this long ever again, but I can't see myself ever closing the door on you. Just no more running. Talk to me. Don't just leave again."

"Yes. Yes, yes, yes. I promise." I close my eyes, a contented exhale calming the tremble in my voice. "I love you," I whisper, opening my eyes into his green ones.

Jack's thumbs brush the apples of my cheeks, his face lit up, causing my heart to swell. "Good," he mutters, his eyes dropping to my lips briefly. "Because I'm all in."

Those are the last words spoken before I reach up and press my mouth to his.

Our lips were made to touch.

He moves his hands down either side of my neck and kisses me carefully, his mouth pressing promises of forever against mine. It's not like our first kiss, or our second, or even the last kiss we shared before this. It's an assurance of safety and love that isn't going anywhere. It's perfect.

When he pulls away from me, he's slightly breathless, but the lips that make me melt are curved upward.

EPILOGUE

TWO YEARS LATER

*N*o matter how many times I drive down this driveway, the skeleton sitting on the tree branch never fails to make me jump. Jack loves Halloween way too much.

I round the sharp curve at the beginning of the drive, and my new home comes into view.

My new home.

I can't help but laugh at the newest decorations that have appeared since I left for my once-a-month therapy session this morning. I'm sure Jack suckered David into helping—probably Nova, too.

He hung orange and purple lights from the roof. He lives out in the middle of nowhere, and it is rare we get more than thirty trick-or-treaters, but that doesn't stop him.

Christmas, though, we're both on board to turn the yard into a winter wonderland.

I park behind Simone's SUV, excited to see she's already here.

She's in my bedroom when I finally find her, measuring my window. I clear my throat to make my presence known, and she throws a smile my way.

"Hi. I want to buy you curtains for a wedding gift, so I needed exact measurements. Jack and Nova went to pick up paint for her bedroom and are bringing home tacos." Simone is walking toward me with the measuring tape in hand as she updates me. "How was Hannah?"

"Good." I nod, taking a deep breath. "Honestly, I talked to her about feeling guilty for leaving you."

Simone raises an eyebrow, placing her hands on her hips. "I'm sorry. What? No. No, ma'am. We talked about this. You are getting married soon. This needed to happen."

Her instinct to go into explanation mode brings a warm smile to my face, and I step forward, wrapping my arms around her in a tight hug. "I know. I just love you and can never thank you enough for taking me and my little family in when we needed you."

She relaxes into my arms and tugs me closer with hers, resting her chin on my shoulder. "I needed you guys just as much as you needed me. I assure you."

I lean back first, and both of our eyes are shining from unshed tears. "So, maybe now we can talk about if a certain someone will be moving in with you."

"Nope." Her face glows red, and she shakes her head, untangling herself from my embrace. "It's still too new. He hasn't mentioned it, so I don't want to be the first to."

"Okay, okay." I don't want to make her uncomfortable or push her limits, because this guy is different from any other man she's dated. He's her polar opposite, and yet they fit better than I would have ever guessed. She lets her guard down around him, and it's something to see. "But I bet he's thinking about it."

A beat. Then a hopeful, "You think?"

I laugh and nod, looking around the room at my unpacked boxes. "Oh, I definitely think." With an overwhelmed sigh, I go after the nearest one and lift it, setting it on the edge of the bed. "Shall we start the unpacking process?"

"If we must. And while doing so, you can tell me your observations that led you to this conclusion."

"Hi, beautiful."

Heart eyes.

I grin and lower myself onto Jack's lap in the rocking chair on our front porch, wrapping my arms around his neck as I do. "Hi."

The porch lights haven't cut on yet, but the sun is halfway down, casting an orange glow. He places an arm around my waist to hold me, but the other is gripped onto his beer that he was enjoying after a long day of unpacking.

I lean into him, capturing his bottom lip between mine. I slip my tongue into his mouth, and he reciprocates with a sigh, moving his hands up my back and to my cheek, cradling my face.

When we come up for air, he presses his forehead to mine. "Well, that's a hell of a greeting. How's the bedroom looking?"

"It's all done and waiting for us," I tease with a smirk, eliciting a groan from him. "But first, we have been summoned to the living room to watch *Hocus Pocus* with Nova."

"Cruel woman."

"What?" I mock offense, shrugging my shoulders at his slight. "I can't come kiss my fiancé?"

"Always. But *that* kind of kiss is one you can't start unless we can finish." He tilts the glass bottle to his lips, pouring the rest down his throat before patting my ass.

I place a kiss to his neck and smile against his skin. "Oh, we can finish. Tonight. In our bedroom."

"*Our* bedroom," Jack repeats my words, nuzzling into my neck when I pull back. "I really love the sound of that."

My lips find his once more, but we keep it brief. He follows me inside, where Nova has set up the living room for the perfect movie night. Candy, popcorn, soda, and a bottle of water for Jack because he hates carbonation. Weirdo.

Jack goes to the hall closet to pull out our movie blankets, and I walk to Nova's bedroom to see where she ran off to. Chief and CeCe are both asleep at the edge of her bed when I slip in, and she's dusting off her dresser, where she's already unpacked most of her pictures and knick-knacks.

"Movie time?"

She turns with an excited nod, her round, childlike eyes starting to mature. Eleven years old. I hate it. I want to put her in a bubble so she never grows and stays my little Supernova forever. But then I also love it. She's independent, the youngest member on her middle school debate team, and one of the coolest people I know. She's so inquisitive about real-world problems and wants to help everyone she meets. It's amazing *and* sad to watch her grow.

"Yes! What do you think about my bedroom? Jack and I picked out a light shade of gray for three walls and then this patterned wallpaper for my accent wall. He said we could do it Sunday."

"I think that'll be super pretty. I'll help." I cross my arms and look around her bedroom. "I like where you put everything."

My eyes fall on the pictures framed on her nightstand. She has my favorite one of her, Simone, and me at the beach, one of her and her dad when she was two, and one of her, Jack, me, and the dogs outside of the Peters' home last Thanksgiving.

I feel teary.

I'm such a mess.

She follows my gaze and grins, rolling her eyes at my emotional state. "I wanted everyone I love close to me when I go to sleep at night."

"That's a very sweet gesture." I blink a few times to rid myself of those annoying happy tears. "Ugh, I don't know what's wrong with me. I'm a basket case lately. Come on, let's go watch the Sanderson sisters."

Her laugh is a loud giggle that sounds so much like mine. I follow her out of the bedroom to the couch, where we both plop down, immediately getting under the blanket.

"Are we ready?" Jack asks, placing the popcorn in my lap and grabbing the remote.

I place an arm around Nova's shoulders and lean my head against Jack with a contented sigh. Part of me feels like that's a loaded question. Ready for what? The movie? The wedding? What comes after?

Whatever meaning that question holds, I nod my head. Because the answer to all the above is: "Yep, I'm ready."

———————————

Keep reading for an excerpt from *Elevator Love Letter*, Blair's second novel! And be sure to sign up for her newsletter so you'll know the instant it's available: https://blairleighauthor.com/

ELEVATOR LOVE LETTER

COMING SOON FROM BLAIR LEIGH

VALERIE

Sweat. Cosmetics. Hairspray. Leather. The scents linger—so strong they jolt me awake in the middle of the night. My heart is pounding, the force brutal; my chest feels as though it's rattling. I reach for the hot pink stiletto-shaped lamp next to me before remembering that I no longer own one. Instead, I feel behind me and run my fingers along the edge of my headboard until I find the button flush against the side. My room lights up and above me is a dark, cherry wood headboard with bright lights shining down into my eyes.

"Jesus," I hiss, turning my head to protect my retinas from potential blindness. *I really regret buying this bed.* When it was advertised, the convenience of being able to turn on lights that were built into your bed, without having to physically move, seemed appealing. They forgot to mention it's equivalent to stadium lights coming on in the dead of night and illuminating an entire town.

Distracted, it takes me a moment to notice the scent

that woke me is gone, replaced with lavender detergent and rose scented lotion I put on before bed. I throw my head back into my pillow with a dramatic huff and inhale sharply, trying to find that particular and familiar smell again.

It's useless.

This happens at least once a month.

It's better than the alternative—the smell of blood and burned rubber coupled with a shooting ache in my hip and the sound of metal crunching on pavement. Unfortunately, those occurrences are rather common, too.

Now that my eyes have adjusted, I catch sight of the digital numbers beside me and groan. I hate waking up just minutes before my alarm. I take the remaining moments I have before my feet need to hit the ground and use them to gather myself.

I am no longer Valerie Greene the dancer.

I'm Valerie Greene, career recruiter.

A bitter taste invades my senses at that morning reminder.

I'm good at what I do. I enjoy it for the most part. It's a stable job with benefits and a healthy salary. I'm well respected, I'm liked, and I have job security, because half of our company's clients were acquired by me.

This has become some sort of mantra for myself.

I press my hands to my forehead, roughly rubbing my skin before sliding my palms to my eyes. There they will stay until I have convinced myself to drag my ass out of bed and fix the knotted mess on my head that I created in my sleep.

It's donut day in the office.

Davin is out for vacation this week.

I told Ian I'd bring him the stack of CDs I unwillingly inherited from my mother's ex-boyfriend.

That'll do it. Interaction with my work crush is enough to make my desperate little heart eager to start the day.

Tragic.

Even though I expect my alarm to go off, I still jump at the sound, and quickly slap the top of it to stop the obnoxious buzzing.

Morning routines are the worst, because if you're anything like me—i.e. organized in every single aspect of your life except getting ready—you procrastinate and give yourself a solid ten minutes to pull yourself together for the day.

My signature perky ponytail does the trick, and I throw on my favorite emerald blazer just to give myself extra confidence before talking to Ian.

Ian is another recruiter, but, unlike me, the job comes naturally to him. He has that Prom King personality that immediately eases the nerves of applicants, and our clients adore him. Our clients aren't the only ones, I guess. My boss thinks he's the universe's greatest gift to earth, and though it aggravates me, I'd be lying if I said I didn't agree to at least some extent.

Our company started just two years ago, but we've grown substantially due to Davin's reputation in the community. We came from a bigger career recruitment firm where Davin was the top recruiter, and the CEO, Michael Chambers, was a total slimeball. I started out as an assistant to Davin with absolutely no office experience, and after a year, he was encouraging me to spread my wings and take on clients of my own. At the time, I didn't know his plans to jump ship. I wasn't privy to the workplace drama and growing distance between Davin and Michael.

One mundane Thursday afternoon, I came back from lunch to all hell breaking loose. I could hear Michael yelling behind his closed office door and not even ten minutes later, Davin emerged with white knuckles and a forced calm expression.

He told me to pack my things, and the next thing I knew, I was on the ground floor of a new business owned by him. In two years, we've grown into four recruiters, six staff, thirty-seven clients, and over two-hundred successful placements. A little over a month ago, we rented a new office in the O'Connell building, which is one of the biggest buildings in the city, and though we aren't a threat to my former employment just yet, we're getting there.

Before I'm even out the door, my phone begins vibrating in my purse, and I suppress an eyeroll. I haven't had coffee, yet, and already, I'm one hundred percent sure that's a nervous applicant needing assurance before an eight o'clock interview.

I take a deep breath, and then: "This is Valerie Greene with Davin Porter Career Services."

"Just remember to ask them the questions we went over. Employers love applicants that show an interest in the job they are being hired to do. If they ask you if you have any questions about your position, ask them what they value in an employee. That is the most important one if you blank and forget the rest." It's like I'm reciting lines at this point, which is monotonous.

I do genuinely care about the applicants, I swear. I also

genuinely care about my job, but is it my passion? No. Maybe that's why Davin worships the ground Ian walks on. Ian acts like this is the job of his dreams.

"And if they try to talk about my salary?" The hesitant voice on the other end of the line tries to sound confident, but I can hear right through it.

I nod to myself as I approach my building, phone settled between my shoulder and ear, and CDs for Ian stacked in my hand. "You tell them that you are under the impression that salary negotiations are between them and the recruiters. Okay?"

"Got it. Thanks, Val."

My tone is chipper as I enter the building, but in all reality, I need a cup of coffee and three more hours of sleep. "Yep. Call me after and let me know how it went, alright? Good luck!"

I grab my usual at the counter and resituate my belongings, sliding my phone into my purse as I hold my fresh cup of coffee in my free hand and tuck the stack under my arm. Standing by the elevator doors, I let my mind drift back to my sleepy state this morning, when I was desperately trying to hold onto the thick scents that woke me.

Just four years ago, I would have laughed if you told me I'd be working in an office setting, wearing skirt suits, and drinking black coffee like my hydration depended on it. I used to be water only with the nightly glass of red wine after a long day in the studio. A leg-warmer, tights, and crop-top girl that spent every waking moment practicing routines in front of the mirror with 5, 6, 7, 8 on mental repeat. I was energetic and flirtatious, and I had the world at my fingertips.

With a heavy heart, I erased that part of me. It was

easier to just let go than to pine for a time that I couldn't get back. Healthy, right? It's the only way I hold on to my sanity. I come from a less than supportive family, and most of my friends were other dancers that I just can't bear being around anymore. Now, I have Daphne, the office manager we hired one week after starting the new company, Gabe, Davin's assistant, and Eloise, my college roommate who I talk to at least once a day.

I lean against the wall beside the elevator and wait for it to stop on the bottom floor. Distracted in my own thoughts, I didn't notice Crossword had been behind me until the elevator doors opened and we stepped in. That's his name in my head—Crossword. He's taller than me, usually in slacks and a button-up shirt, and almost always has some sort of puzzle tucked under his arm. Crossword puzzles seem to be his favorite, but lately he's carrying around a book of Sudokus. Sometimes, he leans against the back wall of the elevator, pencil in hand, and concentrates so intently on whatever one he's doing that his jaw clenches and his brow deeply furrows. His almost-black hair is cut short, but slightly mussed, and his eyes are an intense shade of blue-grey. He's not a muscle-y guy, but he's lean with strong shoulders.

I find myself staring at him often. His total lack of care for the world around him is refreshing. Once, there was a couple in the elevator with us, and they were not-so-discreetly arguing. Their tones were clipped and their volume was rising. Crossword never looked up. I liked that. So, I watched him, just to see if he was purposefully ignoring them or if he was so enthralled that he truly didn't notice.

His teeth were sunk into his bottom lip, which was kind of sexy, and his pencil was scribbling letters into tiny boxes. At that exact moment, the female of the pair let out a: "You wouldn't know a clit if it introduced itself to you!"

I was stunned, momentarily glancing in her direction before looking back at Crossword to get some sort of camaraderie from him. He didn't look up, but his lips pulled into a smile that he tried to suppress by sinking his teeth into his bottom lip. That quick flash of perfect white teeth made my stomach drop. He was *more* than handsome.

Today, however, nothing else has his attention. We are the only ones in the elevator, and though my back is to him, I feel his eyes on me. I should say something. Introduce myself, maybe?

We're basically friends at this point, no? It wouldn't be too devastatingly awkward if I just turned and said: *Hi, I'm Valerie.*

Before I can talk myself into it, his phone rings, and he's once again, in his own world.

NATHAN

My phone buzzes to life in my hand, jarring me out of my morning pre-coffee haze. The drive from my house to the office and the walk from my car into the lobby of my building is fuzzy—which is kind of scary since I was operating heavy machinery.

I can't even remember what I was thinking about on the drive over or what was on my mind moments before my phone started going off. Is that the sign of a dull, boring life? Doing the same thing over and over until it becomes as routine as breathing and you can't even remember doing it?

That's depressing.

My feet bring me to the end of the coffee line. My phone hasn't stopped it's incessant buzzing so I glance down to see the family group message ten messages deep. Not only does my family rarely use this thread, it's extremely out of character for it to be this lively at seven in the morning.

I open to the latest message.

Naveen: *A congratulations would have sufficed, Delia.*

I narrow my eyes and scroll up until I get to the first message of the morning, which is a picture of a sonogram from my younger brother, Naveen. I immediately feel my stomach tighten.

Naveen: *Jessica and I are expecting! She's due January 5th!*

Allison: *What??? Are you kidding?*

Allison: *Not that I'm not excited! Just surprised! Congratulations!*

Dad: *So glad you're finally announcing. Can't wait to have the family over to celebrate.*

Mom: *We're over the moon, sweetheart! Give Jessica our love!*

Delia: *Hold on. What? I thought you and Jessica were broken up.*

Delia: *Are you moving back in with her? How long have you known? Mom? Dad? You both knew?*

Delia: *??? Hello??? Nathan, are you going to chime in?*

I've been summoned. I could take the same route as my younger sister, Delia. Or, I could go the route of my twin, Allison. It's no secret that no one in the family is a fan of Jessica. Jessica and Naveen have been on and off since college and their relationship is far from healthy.

Hell, she even hit on me last Christmas after one too many eggnogs. Now, she's going to be the mother of his child. *Great planning, Naveen.*

My thumbs hover over the keyboard as I contemplate what to type. I've never navigated these situations well. Luckily, this was not done in person. I've been told my expressive face can be insulting.

I respond: *Woah! This is big! Congratulations, kid. Let me buy you a drink this week.*

Delia: *Well, that was no fucking help.*

Mom: *Delia. Enough.*

Naveen: *Thanks, you guys, we're excited. Nathan, drinks sound great. Delia, you're not invited.*

Delia: *Whatever. We'll talk later. Congrats, I guess.*

Before I can get sucked into the verbal war that is bound to happen between my siblings, I silence my phone and shove it back in my pocket. I grab my usual tall coffee from the barista behind the counter and nod with a polite smile, dropping my change into the tip jar.

When I turn the corner to get on the elevator, I see her.

Ponytail.

It's not the best nickname—I know. I don't know what else to call her. I've seen her almost every day for five weeks since her company moved into the office space on the third floor, and every single time, she's wearing her red hair in a high ponytail.

The first several times she'd get on the elevator with me, she'd have her phone glued to her ear, a smooth professional tone exuding confidence as she spoke. It only took a couple of unintentional eavesdropped phone conversations to realize she was a career recruiter.

However, she has never mentioned her name. No one

has ever gotten on the elevator and greeted her by name. I've even attempted to see the scribbled chicken scratch on her coffee cup, but can never make it out. So, as shallow as it may seem, her name has remained Ponytail.

And, to be honest, I'm into her.

She's sharp. I mean this in terms of the way she carries herself and her appearance. I've overheard her give countless pep talks and advice to clients, always framing her words around their own strengths, and *always* sounding like she could interview in their place and get the job over them. It's impressive.

And when I say her appearance is sharp, I'm not taking away from how stunning she is. Her cheekbones are high, she has a pointed nose, and her jaw cuts in a strong angle. Her skin is pale, but her cheeks are covered in freckles that highlight her bright green eyes. She doesn't exactly give off a warm and welcoming vibe, but she doesn't seem cold, either.

Unapproachable is probably a good word to describe her—which is why I've never *asked* for her name. The first few encounters I had with her, she was busy. Other times, she would have the world blocked out in her headphones. Then, too much time had passed as her elevator companion and popping that comfortable bubble of silence now just seems awkward.

Today, though, as I step onto the elevator after her and lean against the back wall, I notice she's carrying an arm full of CDs. Elton John and the *Against All Odds* soundtrack are the only two I can see. She's also undistracted. This is possibly the perfect opportunity to strike up a conversation.

Favorite Elton John song. Go.

Getting rid of your collection?

Throwback day at work?

All of these seem better than: *What's your name?* But, should I? Do I bother her when she's just trying to go about her normal day?

Before I can open my mouth, my phone starts vibrating. I thought I had silenced it. I reach in my pocket and hit the side button to ignore it.

It begins again.

My jaw is clenched as I close my eyes, briefly, ignoring the call once more. By the third attempt, I pull my phone out and mentally curse Delia for her persistence.

"Hi, I'm at work." My voice is lower than usual, but Delia is too focused to notice. Without a second thought to my greeting, she dives in headfirst.

"Woah this is big? Congratulations? Let's get a drink? Thanks for leaving me hanging there. Am I the only one pissed off at him for being so careless?" Her voice is shrill and getting louder with every angry word.

My elevator partner glances back at me, and my lips draw into a tight apologetic line. It's a quick look, and I'm sure it's because of the erratic volume bleeding from the speaker of my phone. "Delia, you need to take a breath."

The doors open onto the third floor and Ponytail steps out, disappearing from my sight as they close once more and take me to the next floor. *Fucking Delia.*

"We need to have family dinner on Sunday and discuss this. What is he going to do, Nate? Marry her?"

Delia is the youngest of the family, but easily the most level-headed and put together. Which, apparently, makes her the most judgmental. I sigh at her question as the doors open to my floor.

Wilcox Graves Paper Company: pain in my ass.

"I don't know. I don't see him doing that, exactly, but

he will probably try to make their relationship work. And, like it or not, a baby is involved. We need to be supportive."

She's silent. Maybe I got to her.

"I'm going to call Allison. Be free for dinner on Sunday."

Or, maybe I didn't. She hangs up before I can put up any sort of fight. I can only hope that Allison will rein her in because I didn't stand a chance. I'm already frequently accused of playing devil's advocate.

Walking into my office, a stack of papers greets me, reminding me that the new sales director is starting next Monday. Unfortunately, I have no time to tend to it which means I'll be here in non-working hours this weekend to pick up that slack. We really need someone else in my department.

I'm overwhelmed before I can even sit down.

Elevator Love Letter **is coming soon from Blair Leigh. Subscribe to her mailing list for sneak peeks and buy links when it's available!** https://blairleighauthor.com/

ACKNOWLEDGMENTS

This section may be a little lengthy, because there are so many people who helped me crank out my debut novel.

First and foremost, my husband, Jacob. Without even knowing it, you give me so much inspiration for the characters I write. Your complexity, romanticism, and wit consumes me. You are, without sounding incredibly cheesy, my muse. You are also the most encouraging human being. I don't need anyone else in my corner if I have you. Thank you for always holding me accountable, and for putting all other swoon-worthy heroes to shame.

I also want to give a general thank you to the following people who started my love for reading and writing, or who molded me in some way:

My mom, who, for as long as I have been alive, has always had a book in her hands. Thank you for raising me to always have one in mine.

My dad, though he has, as far as I know, never written fiction, he has written poems and lyrics. My writing ability comes from you.

My siblings, especially my two sisters, Erin and Hailey,

thank you for always encouraging me in every aspect of life.

My step-parents and in-laws, thank you for the never-ending support.

My granny, who will never read this book—every good part of me came from you.

My friends that have never made me feel like I was anything less than capable of ruling the world. There are so many, but these people have never made me doubt myself and are *my* safe place to land: Lacey, Bryan, Ivy P., Lauren M., Courtnie, Endya, Shelby, LaKeisha, Koty, Tori, Brooklee, Haley J., Lauren F., Heather, James, Joshery, Hillary, and Ivy W.

As for the book itself, these people inspired and lifted me up throughout my entire process. I need to thank every one of them personally and publicly.

My editor, Trusted Accomplice, you helped me shape this novel into something worthy, something to be cherished and loved forever.

Rebel, thank you for your honest feedback, your cheerleading, and your ability to make me see a new perspective that always enlightens me. You are a fire that continuously glows. I am in awe of you.

Sara, thank you for guiding me in every direction I needed to go for the process of self-publishing. I cannot thank you enough for your invaluable expertise and selfless devotion of your time. You are a genuine soul.

Tori, who was always eager to read whatever I sent her. She gave me critiques, compliments, and edits that formed this book into something I am immensely proud of. She was also one of my first draft editors.

Ivy, my other first draft editor. It started with red ink hearts all over small sections I'd send you and ended with ... this. Your constant uplifting encouragement pushed me through my most difficult writer's block. Your love for my characters helped me in times when I could barely look at my laptop.

LaKeisha—thank you for helping me bring Simone and Nova to life in the most amazing way. Your helpful feedback helped me create my two favorite characters. Their beauty and uniqueness could NOT have happened without you guiding me. You have inspired them and you inspire me.

Becci, you are a true gem. You are a beam of light; a ray of optimism and hope. You are a nurturer, a lover, and an advocate. You believed in me and this book more than I did. I thank you so much for talking me out of so many spirals. Your love and adoration for Eliza and Jack helped me continue to create them.

Erin, my sister, who has made it her mission to make sure I am on every bestseller list possible. Good luck. I do love the effort, though. Thank you for your unwavering support and constant marketing of my novel.

AJ Parca (Ali and Justin)—is it weird to thank your website designers/marketing team? No. I don't think so. Especially when you are more than that. You have my back. You're loyal. You guide me when I am lost, and I would not have half of the following I have if it were not for you.

The Hating Game by Sally Thorne gave me the push I needed to get back into my writing. That novel is a breathtaking beauty. To quote a dear friend: "My heart lives within that book." Sally, your words and characters reawakened my passion and for that, I am eternally grateful. You also unknowingly led me to the next group I need to thank.

Erin and Melody, from Heaving Bosoms Podcast, and my beloved HBs. The first episode I listened to was their episode on *The Hating Game*. But, I have since listened to most of them and fell in love with the group of followers I talk to every day. The friends I have made through that group gave me courage and the beautiful support I needed to continue writing even when I didn't think I could.

Which leads me to the amazing women I became close with through that group: Our everyday chats and your everyday support has been a bright light even on my toughest days. You know who you are. You are a part of my heart.

Finally, thank you to every beta reader that took the time to read my book and provide me excellent feedback. I've named a few already, but the others: Marianna, Lauren, Ashley, Kimberly, and Lauren.

MEET BLAIR LEIGH

Blair lives in the South (U.S.) with her husband, who is her own romance hero, and their two dogs, Doug and Birdie. Blair describes herself as an attorney by day and a writer by heart. Having always been a sucker for happily ever afters and sweeping love stories, it was only natural that her own work mirrored that.

Website: https://blairleighauthor.com
Instagram: @blairleighb
Facebook: https://facebook.com/blairleighauthor
Twitter: @blairleighb